BY GARY SHTEYNGART

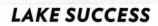
LAKE SUCCESS

LAKE SUCCESS

A Novel **Gary Shteyngart**

 RANDOM HOUSE NEW YORK

Copyright © 2018 by Gary Shteyngart

All rights reserved.

Published in the United States by Random House, an imprint and division of Penguin Random House LLC, New York.

RANDOM HOUSE and the HOUSE colophon are registered trademarks of Penguin Random House LLC.

LIBRARY OF CONGRESS CATALOGING-IN-PUBLICATION DATA
Names: Shteyngart, Gary, author.
Title: Lake Success : a novel / Gary Shteyngart.
Description: New York : Random House, 2018.
Identifiers: LCCN 2017043962 | ISBN 9780812997415 (hardcover) |
ISBN 9780812997422 (ebook)
Subjects: LCSH: Marital conflict—Fiction. | Midlife crisis—Fiction. |
BISAC: FICTION / Literary. | FICTION / Satire. | FICTION / General. |
GSAFD: Satire.
Classification: LCC PS3619.H79 L35 2018 | DDC 813/.6—dc23
LC record available at https://lccn.loc.gov/2017043962

International edition ISBN 978-0-525-51172-4

Printed in the United States of America on acid-free paper

randomhousebooks.com

9 8 7 6 5 4 3 2 1

FIRST EDITION

Book design by Simon M. Sullivan

LAKE SUCCESS

DESTINATION AMERICA

Barry Cohen, a man with 2.4 billion dollars of assets under management, staggered into the Port Authority Bus Terminal. He was visibly drunk and bleeding. There was a clean slice above his left brow where the nanny's fingernail had gouged him and, from his wife, a teardrop scratch below his eye. It was 3:20 A.M.

The last time he had been to the Port Authority was twenty-four years ago. He had gone on a bus trip to Richmond, Virginia, to see his college girlfriend. That youthful bus ride unspooled in his mind whenever the S&P was crushing him or whenever he would discover a new and terrible fact about his son's condition. When Barry closed his eyes, he could picture the sweep of the highway, his country calling out to him from both sides of the road. He could feel himself sitting on a hard wooden bench at some roadside shack. A thick woman with a crablike walk and many stories to tell would bring him a plate of vinegary beans and pulled pork. They would talk as equals about where their lives went wrong, and she would waive the price of the meal, and he would pay for it anyway. And she would say, *Thank you, Barry,* because despite the vast difference in their assets under management, they would already be on a first-name basis.

He stumbled over to the line of policemen and policewomen guarding the nighttime barricades meant to shepherd travelers from the streets to the gates. "Where are the buses?" he said. "I want to get out of here."

To the cops he looked like just another New Yorker. A bleeding man; roughed-up, sweat-clumped nighttime hair; a Patagonia vest over his Vineyard Vines shirt with the single word CITI. He was tall and had a wide swimmer's build, his thick shoulders tapering to two feminine wrists, a liability at any point in history, but never more so than during the year 2016, at the start of the First Summer of Trump. He was breathing heavily after having dragged a carry-on rollerboard from his apartment on Madison Square Park, a total of twenty blocks. The night was warm and windy, a perfect Manhattan I-don't-want-to-die kind of night, and with each block he walked he had felt more assured of what he was about to do to his marriage.

"Downstairs," one of the cops said.

Barry did as he was told, the little rollerboard twisting behind him. The air here was different. He could say with certainty that he had not in recent memory, or any memory, really, breathed air of this quality. The easy way to describe it would be to say that it smelled like a foot. But whose foot? The man was not in the habit of smelling feet, except perhaps in the locker room at Equinox where his own feet smelled of chlorine, because he swam. His wife's feet, he was sure, smelled of honeysuckle like the rest of her, but he was not going to think of her now.

There was a Greyhound counter, but its gate was shuttered and there was no note about when it would reopen. "Socialism," Barry said aloud, even though he knew that Greyhound Lines was a Dallas-based subsidiary of the Scottish company FirstGroup, and not a service offered by our government. He had drunk twenty thousand dollars' worth of Karuizawa whiskey that night. He could make mistakes.

There was a Hudson newsstand and Barry headed for the old South Asian man behind the counter. "Where are the buses?" he said.

"Downstairs," the old man answered.

"I *am* downstairs."

The old Indian shrugged. He was watching Barry and his bleeding face with his hooded eyes as if he wanted in on his ruination. Barry hated him. He could hate him because his wife was Indian.

"Do you have *WatchTime* magazine?"

"No."

"*Watch Journal?*"

"No."

"Anything about watches?"

"No."

There were no further interactions to be had here. He took another look around. The socialist Greyhound counter was still shuttered. *Un-fucking*-believable. There was a sign that read TO GATES 1–78. So maybe that's where the buses were. The escalator leading downstairs was broken and yet another Indian wearing a Hudson News vest sat on the top steps holding his head in his hands. He appeared to be weeping. One of Barry's top traders was a guy named Akash Singh, but he was a *killer* on the floor.

He dragged his rollerboard down the broken escalator, worried about the watches inside. The automatic ones were safe within their Swiss Kubik watch winders, but the manually wound ones should not be exposed to such shocks, especially the Universal Genève Tri-Compax, which was from the early 1940s and in frail health. Barry normally couldn't go on a trip without at least three watches to keep him company, each was an old and rare friend, but he would need no fewer than half-a-dozen timepieces to complete this journey. He picked up his luggage, but lifting it made him want to throw up. He sat down on one of the escalator steps and considered the crying Indian man sitting above him. He would get through this. He could get through anything after what he had been through this year. His wife didn't love him. Didn't desire him. And although he wanted her, he wasn't sure he loved her either. He thought of that long-ago trip to Richmond, Virginia, to see his college girlfriend, Layla, and the wind in his hair as the bus whipped into the Lincoln Tunnel and then into New Jersey. Was the wind really in his hair? Did bus windows open back then? Yes, they must have. Would they open now?

Probably not. But he could imagine the wind in his hair, the little that was left, because unlike what his wife had said, *he had an imagination*. He got up and holding his rollerboard with the watches tight to his chest walked down the remaining steps.

It was not good here. It was not good at all. It smelled like someone had eaten a fish sandwich. There were people sitting on benches, sitting on their luggage, sitting on the brown linoleum floor. There were gates with numbers and destinations, like at an airport, and outside the gates the buses all waited in the stink and gloom. That was the thing. You could go anywhere within our country. The open road! Barry had taken an Acela to Boston once on a dare with Joey Goldblatt of Icarus Capital Management, the train was faster and nicer, but this was the open road, and once you got on the open road the whole country would rush out to say hello and refill your ice tea. You would become a traveler and no one could tell you you had no imagination or no soul or whatever his wife had said to insult him in front of the Guatemalan writer and his Hong Kong doctor wife whose apartment he had left in ignominy just a few hours ago in the whiskey-heat of the night. To be demeaned in front of others, to be cut down in front of one's *lessers,* he had seen this before with his hedgie friends' wives, and it had always been the first step to divorce. In his field, pride was nonnegotiable.

Barry looked at the destinations. Washington Express. Cleveland Express. Casino Express. Everything was an express. Then he found what he was looking for. A gate that read RICHMOND, VA. It was the only bus that was not an express. Fine. He would go to Richmond. In the last two months, since his son's diagnosis, he had done some very hot and heavy Facebook snooping and it turned out that Layla was in El Paso, Texas, of all places. But Richmond was a start. Richmond was about memories. Her parents might still be there. Wouldn't that be something, if he just showed up. Not on his NetJets account, but on a Greyhound?

There was something he remembered from that long-ago bus trip to see Layla. The way the departing Greyhound had turned and turned again through the mysterious dark passages of the Port Authority, but then had emerged onto this golden overpass, beneath which the city glowed in all its art deco metalwork, enticing and beckoning. Barry had thought of that leave-taking, that exit ramp into the sky, with increasing frequency over the last three years, whenever the soul-dismembering red numbers crept onto his Bloomberg terminal, next to which he kept a large framed photo of his son, Shiva, in all his dark-eyed beauty; Shiva, sullenly holding a baby doll named Maurice but never looking at it. Beneath the frame Barry had the words I LOVE YOU, RABBIT put in in gaudy gilded letters, just to remind himself that he did, more than anything.

A young black man in a green vest stood before the Richmond gate. It was hard to tell what he was doing there, but he had a green vest on. "I want to buy a ticket," Barry said to him.

"Damn," the man said. "What happened to your face?"

This was the first time all night anyone had noticed his pain. "My wife hit me," Barry said. "And my son's nanny."

"Uh-*huh*." The man had a string of pimples across his face.

"I want to go to Richmond."

"Uh-*huh*," the man in the green vest said.

"I don't have a ticket."

"You go *up*stairs to the ticket counter."

"It's closed."

"Yeah, but they open it eventually."

"Where's the restroom?"

"It's busted."

"Busted?"

"There's one on the third floor, but I gotta key in the elevator to let you up."

"I better go get my ticket first."

"Bus ain't going nowhere. I might as well key in the elevator and let you up. Face all busted."

It was time to close the deal just as if this man were a potential investor. "I'm Barry Cohen. It's really nice to meet you."

"I'm Wayne. You sure you don't want the bathroom?"

"I'm going to get my ticket first, Wayne. You're a real stand-up guy. Wish I had someone like you working on my team."

"You work at Citibank?" Wayne had noticed his Citi vest.

"No."

"Then I got to question your taste in apparel there," Wayne said. He smiled and Barry smiled back at him. His first smile of the night.

Barry walked back up the escalator with his rollerboard. The man in the Hudson News vest had stopped crying and was now looking blankly down the broken escalator steps with puffy eyes. The Richmond bus was leaving in twenty minutes, but the shutter was still drawn against the ticket booths. A woman wearing purple mesh bunny ears and a wifebeater that had PARIS rhinestoned across the front of it was holding on to the links of the shutter, looking at the empty ticket counters the way a navy wife might look at a ship pulling out to sea.

"I got to get out of here," Barry said to her.

The woman appraised his face. She was thirty or fifty, it was hard to tell, and Barry imagined every second of her life had been painful. "No shit," she said.

"Why won't they open it?"

"There's a ticket counter upstairs, but the guy said it was closed because of some technics difficulty."

"*Technics* difficulty?"

"That's what he said."

"This isn't right. My bus leaves in twenty minutes."

"Tell me about it."

"This isn't right," Barry repeated.

"What you want *me* to do?" the woman said. One of her mesh bunny ears drooped over her face. Her bottom teeth seemed to be where her top teeth should be and she had no bottom teeth. She was white. Just an hour into his journey, Barry was starting to get something about the Trump phenomenon. Like an idiot, he had thrown 1.7 million, almost two bucks, after Marco Rubio. What choice did he have? He had sat through a five-hour dinner with Ted Cruz in a private room at the Gramercy Tavern after which Joey Goldblatt had turned to him and whispered, *"He's a psychopath."* So they all bet their millions on Rubio. They should have met this woman first. There was nothing Rubio could do for her.

He couldn't get on the bus without a ticket. But the ticket counter was not open. He fingered his phone.

No.

Stop.

The point of this trip was that it would just be him out in the world solving his own problems, just like the woman with the bunny ears, just like his nineteen-year-old Princeton sophomore self. Where did he lose that nineteen-year-old? The one who had been so ready for love and so ready for heartbreak, not the kind of heartbreak his son, Shiva, had brought him, but the kind that healed.

The woman in the mesh ears was talking to a trans woman eating a bag of Lay's with a lot of emphasis. Barry was standing a foot away from them, but he was being completely ignored.

He called Sandy on her emergency number. It was three-thirty in the morning, but of course she would answer, and it would take no more than two seconds for her to get the sleep out of her voice. Sandy had worked for Pataki in the same capacity when he was governor, that's how good she was. He pictured her lying next to her big-boned Dominican partner ass to ass. Barry was a Republican, but he had been long gay marriage since third quarter 2014. He couldn't shut up about gay marriage. He had actually once given Sandy this huge spiel about how she and whatever-her-name-was should get married, because the problem with our country was—

"What's wrong?" Sandy said.

"I need you to book a Greyhound bus to Richmond, Virginia, *now.*"

"Observation," Sandy said. "You don't sound so hot." She said a bunch of other things in quick succession. She wanted to know if there was anything *up* from a legal perspective, which they shouldn't talk about on the phone, but she would Uber over right away, just hold tight. Whatever this was about, the morning would bring "resolution." She mentioned "optics." *Did he know what it was like on a Greyhound?* If he absolutely had to go, there was NetJets out of Teterboro. He could be "wheels up" in two hours. There were direct JetBlue, Delta, and United flights to Richmond. There was Acela plus a regional train. Why was he doing this? Her competency was beautiful. Sandy was the only woman at his firm, other than the hotties in investor relations. They had employed a tart-tongued Oxford ex-biologist who ran risk management, another lesbian who had once actually called him "retarded" to his face, but after three disaster-filled years, their assets down by more than half, plus *that other thing,* she had pivoted to a start-up in the Valley.

As Sandy's competence grew in scope and pitch across the line, Barry looked at the woman in the mesh rabbit ears and the trans woman with the Lay's chips who kept ignoring him. The anger that may have just cost him his family was still in his veins. Men and women, women and men. His anger couldn't be stopped. "When you hired me as chief of staff, I told you I needed to trust my principal," Sandy was saying. "And this is what I need to know. Can I trust you now?"

"Just do your fucking job!" he screamed.

The trans woman next to him stopped eating her chips. She and her companion surveyed his broken face. Instinctively, they looked around for protection, but despite the Port Authority's name, there *was* no authority this far beneath the organized precincts of the imperial city. So this was who he was now—a man who screamed at women. Who bullied disabled children. He saw Seema's and Shiva's frightened faces. He had to run away before he caused more damage. "Okay, okay," Sandy said. "Just stay there." By this point her partner was probably all awake and glossy lipped behind her, scared by the commotion ringing through their nine-hundred-square-foot 1.3-million-dollar Downtown Brooklyn glass box, thinking what every New Yorker always thought in times of trouble: *Will I have to leave this place?*

And so, after destroying his wife and the Filipina nanny, he had ruined the night of two other women.

The transgender Lay's woman and Bunny Ears had moved across the hall and took turns watching him. They were muttering something, probably about him being crazy, about knowing guys like him, possibly dating guys like him, although not in the stupid Patagonia Citi vest. He had to calm down. The violence was still there, pulsing red at his fingertips. Whenever he felt this out of control, when the world lurched around him and his own body felt counterfeit, he remembered what his shrink had told him: "Look at your watch."

He looked at his watch. It was a Nomos Minimatik with a champagne-colored dial. Nomos was his new thing. They were not expensive watches, they topped out at 20K, but they were made in the tiny German town of Glashütte, far from all that overpriced Swiss razzle-dazzle, and they stuck to a strict but playful Bauhaus aesthetic. The watch did its work. It calmed him. The creaminess of the dial, the great rushes of open space between the arabic numerals, and, most important, the tiny orange second hand, a child's hand, really, elegantly, sweeping around its little subsidiary dial, as if life were easy and bright. The watch sucked up the inhuman glow of the space around him and substituted beauty and hope. He remembered three-week-old Shiva asleep in his arms, this sweet brown rabbit, and even then he whispered through all his agnostic lapsed-Jew bullshit, "Please, God, just don't do anything to him, okay? My sins are my own."

He breathed. And smiled. This was the crazy thing. A good watch made him smile in the way his son used to make him smile back when he was just a helpless, perfect little thing. The way Seema made him smile before they got married, when she argued with everything he said about life and politics and aesthetics. He thought it was cool for people of his stature to marry someone who disagreed with them across the board. The loyal opposition. "She's the most *beautiful* and *smart* woman I've ever met," he liked to tell his friends after they had stopped loving each other.

He could pinpoint the moment exactly. They had been at a birthday party at Eleven Madison, ten hedge-fund and private-equity couples, and she was talking to Joey Goldblatt and his new barely postadolescent wife of the moment. Seema had been spending all her waking hours since the diagnosis finding services for Shiva and hardly acknowledging Barry. Already he felt alone. But now he also heard her voice for the first time in weeks and it was too loud, too drunk for its own good, as she said to Joey's young new wife: "Our only *real* indulgence is a personal chef." That typical hedgie humble-brag. It sounded so false. So not Seema. Like an open confession to all of his friends: *All we have left between us is our money.*

But *what* friends? He had so few left. She had been his best friend. She used to read him Paul Krugman over breakfast and he would read her Hemingway's Nick Adams stories under the covers, feeling virile and masculine all the while. She had been his best friend, and two hours ago she had announced that he had no imagination (or was it no soul?). An hour ago she had grabbed his face, impounded her fingers deep into the skin below his left eye, and thrown him off their screaming son. How do you come back from something like that?

"Are you Barry Cohen?" A middle-aged Latino man approached. He was wearing a thick mauve vest with some kind of pin that maybe denoted his high status in the Greyhound Lines priesthood. Even in the scorching nuclear afterglow of the Port Authority's orange tile walls, he had managed to retain a perfect pompadour.

The man began to open the shutters to the ticket counters, he beckoned Barry to follow, then shuttered down again.

"Wait up!" Bunny Ears shouted as the gate crashed down in front of her and the Lay's woman. "We need tickets, too! That ain't fair!" The man walked up to a kind of monitor with a printer attached. The setup reminded Barry of the Commodore 64 he had loved to program in his youth.

"Do you know Wayne from downstairs?" Barry asked the Latino man. "He's in the green vest."

A ticket for Richmond came out of the printer. Barry looked at his watch. It had taken Sandy three minutes to rearrange the world for him. Bunny Ears and Lay's were shaking the chains of the shutter, demanding respect, but the ticket man in the mauve vest had no respect to give them.

Once more, Barry dragged his suitcase down the broken escalator toward the gates. The Indian man on the escalator had fallen asleep, his head in his lap, a day's sorrow behind him. Barry walked over to Wayne in the green vest by the Richmond gate. "I got my ticket!" Barry said.

"I knew it'd work out for you," Wayne said.

"Can I use the bathroom?"

"Yeah, but it's busted. So—"

"I know you gotta key me in to the third floor."

"You catch on fast, Barry," Wayne said.

By the third floor, another landscape of orange walls and yellow barricades, Barry's anger had given way to sadness. *He shouldn't have called Sandy!* He couldn't rely on Sandy for this trip. He had to assume full responsibility. No Sandy, no Seema, no Filipina nannies, no Estonian cooks, no Bangladeshi drivers. No one but Barry Cohen in charge of his fate. He took out his phone and shut it down. He looked around. The bathroom was empty. He opened the trash can and threw the phone in and stuffed in a bunch of paper towels after it.

He thought of throwing his wallet out as well, but then how would he pay for things? He walked over to a broken toilet and threw up instead.

BARRY'S BUS settled pneumatically outside the gate, a happy sound he distinctly remembered from his college trip to Richmond. Hanging near the gate was a black-and-white photograph of the Greyhound company in brighter times, a ribbon-cutting ceremony presided over by a real greyhound with the words LADY GREYHOUND written on her sash. The destination on the bus read AMERICA.

Many passengers were still asleep on the dirty benches, their ski caps pulled over their eyes against the glare of the Port Authority, their mouths open. Why were they wearing ski caps in the summer? Was it because of drugs? Did the drugs make them cold? There was something tender about poor people sleeping. The old woman ahead of him, with her heavy breathing and pink, unwell eyes, had a luggage tag that read CLARKSDALE, MS. That must be a journey of days. Looking around, Barry began to envision the Greyhound as a form of transport for African Americans, a way to stitch their families together across an inhospitable land. There were also a few ex-military Latinos in fatigues and people of all races wearing wristbands probably denoting discharge or escape from some facility, their shirtfronts damp with effluvia. He could still turn back. He could still feel the warmth of his wife's granite-smooth back against his chest. But he couldn't do that to Shiva, whose face, convulsing with terror, was the last thing he saw as the women tore him away. He reached instinctively for his pocket, but his phone was gone.

He was free.

Wayne was helping the woman bound for Clarksdale, Mississippi, with her considerable luggage. Before Princeton, Barry felt like he could understand more of what was being said out on the streets, but now he needed subtitles. Maybe Seema was right. More than twenty years in finance and his imagination was shot. He had to re-learn the way people spoke in his country. Wayne was carrying the old woman's bags clear across the hall to the bus. What if the rest of our country were as kindly as Wayne? "I just want to thank you for everything you've done for me," Barry told him in passing, reaching out to shake his hand.

"What I do?"

"Just noticed me."

"You be good to yourself, Barry," Wayne said.

Barry pictured a down-lit urban bar where he and Wayne could get seriously hammered and, against the backdrop of a neon palm tree and a curvy barkeep in a Coors T-shirt, he could tell him about Shiva. *I had a cousin like that,* Wayne might say, stroking the fine mesh of his green vest. *Wouldn't say a word. Spun in circles. Now he works for the VA. Three kids. Don't believe what they tell you. Nobody knows nothing. These doctors.*

Outside the gate they had to give their tickets to the bus driver, a short black man in sunglasses and a leather jacket that read MARINES. Barry showed him the printout, expecting him to scan it, but the bus driver wanted the actual copy. *"Sir!"* he said. "I need to give the ticket to Greyhound."

"I thought I could keep this copy for my files," Barry said. "As a memento."

"*Sir!* You need to relinquish me this ticket or you will not get on this bus."

Barry hesitated. His drunkenness was fading, but the anger remained. What the hell had happened to courteous people like Wayne? "Look, I don't want to get into an argument over a piece of paper—"

"*Sir!* Are you gonna stand there wasting everyone's time or are you gonna relinquish me the ticket? You gotta make up your mind."

Barry looked down at the bus driver. He could do so because he had at least half a foot on him. But he no longer had his phone and he no longer had Sandy, so there was nothing to be done. He had to submit to this small, gnarled Vietnam veteran with a New York State commercial bus driver's license. He had to give him the ticket, the only proof he had that he was allowed on this bus, that he could complete his journey to Richmond. He had to trust his counterparty, the bus driver, not to throw him off the bus at some point, the way his guys had to trust Barry at bonus season after a big year. Not that he was really having any more big years.

He gave him the ticket. *"Thank* you!" the bus driver said, his eyes rolling visibly behind his sunglasses, in a way that was supposed to remind the other people in line to behave or face humiliation. He hadn't even noticed that Barry was *hurt,* that he was bleeding.

Inside, the bus was dim and neon lit like a secret nightclub. It also stank of urine. It stank of urine and also disinfectant, which, in its own cloying way, made the urine smell worse. Barry didn't want to ask if this was standard operating procedure or if something was wrong, but he noticed most of the passengers clustering away from the bathroom. He was learning another rule of Greyhound. *You sat up front.*

He also realized that the overhead compartments such as they were would never accommodate his rollerboard and the six precious watches inside. He could check the rollerboard in to the bus's hold as others were doing, but the idea of the watches down there, being jostled by the rude luggage of others, was too much to bear. He could surrender, he could submit, he could open up his nostrils to the Greyhound Empire of Smells, but he would let no harm come to his watches. He squeezed his luggage into the seat next to him.

The bus driver had climbed on board. "My name is [something unintelligible] and I'll be your motor-coach operator to Richmond. Are the outlets working? A simple yes or no."

There were a few sleepy yeses as people plugged in their electronics. The driver turned on the woman sitting in the front row.

"*Ma'am,* that seat is reserved for the handicapped."

A gentle Latino croak: "I handicapped."

"You're handicapped? What's wrong with you?"

"I *alllways* sit up fron'."

"*Ma'am,* if you talk back to me, you won't travel on this bus. That's a fact. Now I asked a question and you're going to answer me. How are you handicapped? What's wrong with you?"

"My knee, it hurt."

"Well, my knee hurts, too. Now what's *really* wrong with you? How are you handicapped? Ma'am. Don't talk back now. *Ma'am!* Answer the question: How are you handicapped?"

Barry followed the conversation to its logical conclusion, as the weak-kneed woman shuffled back to the more urinary part of the bus still muttering about her knees. It was amazing to witness. In Barry's world you could not exercise complete control over your wife or child or even many of your employees without repercussion. There were safeguards built in. Lawyers. Social workers. The media. But the bus driver's authority was complete. Barry began to suspect something about our country. That we were, at heart, heavily regimented and militaristic. Despite our cowboy ethos, we were really all under orders, and anything we said or did in protest could be construed as "talking back," and we could all be thrown off the bus. The Greyhound was like a branch of our armed forces. And Barry was a buck private.

The engine ground to life. Barry looked at his Nomos, its creamy Bauhaus dial lost to the darkness, but the gentle feminine shape of its lugs unmistakable. He knew something. Unlike his friend Joey Goldblatt's many tabloid divorces, he would end his marriage with unusual grace. Even in failure, he would set an example, and one day, many years hence, Seema would say to him: "I'm glad you had the courage to end it. I'm glad you knew when it was time to run away."

And now the great thing was going to happen, the great thing that he had dreamed of all those days looking out the window of his Astor Place office building at the lively young NYU late-afternoon girls in purple sweatshirts milling about the felaferies of St. Mark's Place. The bus was going to twist around some dark, dangerous corners and then, full speed ahead, shoot out into the light and glimmer of a steep Manhattan overpass, the city beneath him, fading, then gone.

But it didn't happen this way. They passed a dispatcher booth with a sign that said SAFETY FIRST, and then they were immediately outside on lifeless Forty-first Street, past a Yotel, whatever that was, and a sign that read SUNSPIRE. ADDICTION TREATMENT YOU CAN TRUST. Right away, they were zooming through the empty fluorescent tube of the Lincoln Tunnel.

On the other side of the Hudson, at 4:00 A.M., Manhattan was mostly dark, like a pre-Dutch version of itself. For once, it looked powerless. Awaiting some unknown fate. He glanced over his shoulder, trying, in vain, to catch the transparent dark glass of his residential skyscraper, of Shiva, who would have been screaming through the night, unspooling his sequence of tortured gasps, Seema and the nanny patiently by his side, taking turns squeezing his son's little body to give him the sensory stimuli he needed to know he was still afloat in the world.

• • •

THE DINNER had been his wife's idea. Hers and the Hong Kong doctor's. The elevators in their building were all keyed in to the residents' individual floors, so you rarely met your neighbors, but Seema and the Hong Kong doctor had met in the lobby and started chatting, as women tend to do. Now, that wasn't precisely a dig at women on Barry's part. Chatting was *his* primary activity. The office was overrun by quants and other assorted math geniuses, half their staff now seemed to flow from MIT or its less-endowed counterparts from around the world, while wide-shouldered, charming Princetonians like Barry were left to handle the big picture of yearly separating guys named Ahmed of the Qatar Investment Authority from 2 percent of the assets Barry managed. He did that by talking to them in the broadest, most backslapping former-athlete way possible. All of those hours practicing his "friend moves" in front of the mirror back when he was at Louis Pasteur Middle School had finally paid off. "Friendliest dude on the Street," some young bro had once called him. No one else could lose money three years in a row and still have the Ahmeds of the world come calling. He was very proud.

The dinner. It was Seema's way of forgetting Shiva's diagnosis for a while and going back to doing what hedge-fund wives did best, building a carefully curated life for the family. As it turned out, the Hong Kong doctor was married to a writer whom Seema had read and admired. A *writer*? In *their* building? Where even the one-bedrooms with a view of the back side of a taco joint started at three million? Something about that didn't sit right with Barry, but he let it go.

Seema was a reader, which was one of the artsy things about her that had always attracted him to her. She read the kinds of books most people in their right mind had long abandoned. The writer, a favorite of hers, was a Guatemalan, who wrote in a kind of fantastical way about the political situation there, which wasn't good. Barry looked up the writer's Amazon ranking—1,123,340—and after reading one page of his novel, Barry could see how the ranking came to be. The prose was impenetrable. There were dozens of acronyms of local political parties and organized gangs and tons of Spanish terms and words that had been left untranslated for no good reason other than to taunt Barry's whiteness. It wasn't that Barry was a philistine. He had a minor in writing from Princeton's excellent writing program. His hedge fund, This Side of Capital, was named after Fitzgerald's first novel, set among the Gothic quads of his alma mater. He had rented his offices in a new Astor Place monolith overlooking storied, once-bohemian St. Mark's Place as a way of acknowledging his own brief creative spark. Even his dreams of crossing our country by bus were supplemented with the possibility of one day setting his journeys down on paper. *On the Road* but in thoughtful middle-aged prose.

"You told me this wasn't going to be formal," he said when he saw Seema putting on a dress that he knew was reserved for occasions when she had to impress. One of the many things on his marriage checklist was to marry a woman too ambitious to ever become fat. Seema, barely a year out of Yale Law when he met her and clerking her way to the pinnacle of whatever was left of the legal profession, certainly satisfied that requirement. Still, the dress brought out every inch of her body and clung with great emphasis to her large, magnificent bottom. This bothered Barry further. Why was she dressing up for this writer and his wife?

Across their bedroom's private sitting room, across the hallway with its sparkling herringbone floors, over the three linked living areas separated by double-sided fireplaces, and across the nanny's snug bedroom, Shiva's shrill little cries were drilling through the air, puncturing the timeless scene of two well-bred people, one powerful, the other beautiful, preparing for an evening of culture and wit.

"You can't put on something better?" Seema said. "Vineyard Vines is fine for a pool party in Westport. It looks like you're still selling bonds to old ladies at Morgan."

Since the diagnosis, Seema had said things like this. A little fountain pen, its nib soaked in cruelty, always seemed to be at her disposal. She was exhausted, he knew. Exhausted because he had contributed nothing to Shiva's care, and while she loved their nanny, having a child with the diagnosis meant in essence being the CEO of your own small business. *Not like she has a real job*, he thought with his own brand of cruelty. Not that it was entirely her fault. Marrying an accomplished woman and taking her off the job market was a way to telegraph success among Barry's peers.

"Fuck Morgan," Barry said, "check *this* out!" He came out of his closet wearing a Citi vest he had gotten at some golf thing.

Seema was sitting at her vanity with her red lips and her sharp gaze. Unlike white wives, she could wear many grams of gold around her neck, the miraculous hue of her skin catching its glow. She was, Barry sometimes noted in disbelief, a twenty-nine-year-old beauty with whom only one person in the universe had failed to fall desperately in love, that person being himself. And did Shiva love her? Would he ever be capable of love? The extracts Seema had messengered to his office seemed to suggest so, that his diagnosis was just another way of being. "This is not a tragedy," she had written in her full-bodied handwriting across a memo sticking to the latest scientific study Barry couldn't bring himself to read.

"So tonight is going to be a joke to you?" Seema said. Her angry voice lived in a deep whiskey register all its own. "You keep complaining about how we don't know our neighbors. Well, here's the chance to meet some really interesting ones. I, for one, want to make a good impression."

He shrugged, took off the Citi vest, and threw it on the bed. "I'm going to pick out a watch," he said, heading toward his watch safe where the implements of his true desire rotated smoothly in their winders.

Luis and Julianna Goodman lived in a much smaller unit on the third floor. Like a long-haul jet, their building was divided into economy, business, and first. The first eleven floors held several apartments, each of no more than three bedrooms apiece, and accommodated middling millionaires on the "sell" side of finance,

Goldman managing directors and the like, the wives on their first or second child. The next eleven floors held a single apartment per floor and belonged to the principals of hedge funds and private equity firms and one Argentine model and her soccer player boyfriend who spent no more than a week out of the year in New York. The top three floors belonged to Rupert Murdoch.

The elevator zipped down from the twenty-first to the third floor, Seema in her finery staring straight ahead, Barry checking his Nomos Minimatik, a clever choice given that the product copy suggested it was a perfect watch for creative souls like architects and writers. The watch sat around his wrist like something from a gilded, well-engineered universe, and it telegraphed just what kind of man Barry Cohen was.

The Goodmans both greeted them at the door of their apartment. Luis Goodman was tall and as pretty as his book jacket suggested and he spoke mid-Atlantic English suspiciously well, perfectly in fact. He was wearing a big IWC Pilot's Watch, nonvintage but vintage looking, the kind of thing that Barry could never pull off. He had on a white Brooks Brothers shirt opened at the neck. His wife was nearly as gorgeous, tall and compact. She had a vintage Jaeger-LeCoultre Reverso on her wrist, a watch British colonials used to wear while playing polo. The women hugged each other with delight. Seeing them made Barry realize how cooped up his wife was in their four-thousand-square-foot apartment with Shiva's diagnosis and her emotionally vacated husband. Perhaps out of spite, Seema's wrist was bare of the many timepieces he had bought her, including the 70K Cartier Crash, a watch that, on purpose, looked as if it had been mangled in a car accident. He noticed that the Hong Kong doctor was wearing jeans and a decent summer blouse, probably A.P.C. or something (that's where Seema bought his sneakers), but her informality made a joke of Seema's sinuous dress, her curved perfumed body.

The apartment was minimalist and strategically unlit, but the basics were there, all the Liebherr and KitchenAid stuff that denoted some measure of one-percenter stability. A small distressed-wood dining table was laid out with Pan-Asian and Pan-Latin foods to which Seema added her mother's prized *sambar,* a lentil-based vegetable stew heavy on the tamarind that even an acknowledged carnivore like Barry could not resist. This was a caring move on her part, since bringing down a two-thousand-dollar bottle of wine would only accentuate the distance between the twenty-first and third floors. "Oh my God," the Hong Kong doctor said (in the five hours they would spend together, Barry would never remember her name; he never remembered women's names), "I made Hakka cuisine, salt-baked chicken. Seema, you're not a vegetarian, are you?"

"I get the Brahman meat sweats, but I still eat the bird," Seema said. The women and Luis laughed knowingly, and Barry felt like the only white guy in the room. He noted that Luis Goodman the supposed Guatemalan was far paler than he was and, given his last name, probably just as Jewish.

"So I started reading your book," Barry said. "It's extremely interesting."

"I'd ask which of my books, but they're all basically the same," Luis said. "American colonialism, crimes against the indigenous, yada yada yada."

"Barry's reading *The Sympathetic Butcher,*" Seema put in, "a personal favorite of mine."

They were seated around the cramped table coating their plates with a mixture of *sambar* and rice and slapping on mounds of yucca and fragrant chunks of the salt-baked chicken, which Barry knew immediately would be the star of the show. Julianna was a full-time doctor, but she still had time to celebrate her heritage in the kitchen. Barry looked sadly at his wife's naked wrist. The doctor was at least a decade older, but her looks had kept. If she got tired of the writer, she could probably marry a short, heavyset man on the middle rungs of private equity.

They ate happily and talked about Trump for a bit, the men dividing the discussion between them, then ceding small portions of the conversation to the women who added their own worry about their nation's future, framing it in terms of their children and the world they would inherit. The Goodmans had one boy, too, and he was the same age as Shiva. "Is the little guy asleep?" Seema asked. (That's what Barry sometimes called his son too, "the little guy.")

Barry looked at her cautiously. "Well, no need to wake him up," he said.

As if on cue the Goodmans' Filipina, a much older and clearly less-well-paid version of the Cohens' own, trooped out a sweet Eurasian kid who appraised the guests for a second with his sly pale-green eyes and then hid behind his nanny's skirts. He peeked out, smiling with every megawatt of toddler charm at his disposal, and then stuck out his tongue. "Arturo's a real comedian," Julianna said. "Today he saw a pigeon on a wire, and he said to him, 'Pigeon, don't fall!'"

"Sounds like I should replace my head of risk with Arturo," Barry said. They all laughed, but Barry knew that the presence of this normal boy, this *talking* boy, would hurt Seema terribly. Arturo ran up to the radiator, hoisted his tall, stringy frame atop the cover, and, pointing at the moon, sang, "I love you, moon!" His nanny ran to pull him down, apologizing, but they all knew no apologies were necessary, everything had been scripted in advance, as it always was with perfect Manhattan children.

"Shiva loves the moon, too," Barry said. Which was true, Shiva also climbed up on the radiator when the moon was full and looked at it openmouthed, his eyes blinking in rhythm as if he were an alien from *Close Encounters of the Third Kind* trying to make contact with an inferior civilization. But he never *declared* his love of the moon, like the three-year-old Arturo did. He had never said a word in his life.

The nightmare continued. The nanny got out a bumblebee hat and affixed it upon the little child's head, his hair as light as his father's, the supposed Latino. He ran up to the dining table and established eye contact with each diner. Once he knew they were his, he drew a deep breath, the kind of preparation that would last him through Collegiate and Yale and HBS and see him through the ranks of a fund like Barry's until he had the track record to start his own fund and move up the seventeen flights to Barry's apartment beneath Rupert Murdoch's mansion in the sky.

"Okay, Arturo, maybe we don't do the song tonight," Julianna said. "We're still eating, porcupine."

But Arturo was taught that every drawn breath was precious and must end in song.

IIIIIIIIIII'mmmmmmmmmmmmm . . . bringing home my baby bumble-
  bee
Won't my mommy be so proud of me?
I'm bringing home my baby bumblebee.
OUCH! It stung me!

"That's good, Arturo, thank you!" the doctor said as her breathless boy was about to launch into the second stanza. Perhaps she sensed something was not landing right with their guests.

"No, no, let him sing," Seema said, her body clenched. "Let him sing. He's so good."

Arturo beamed his dimpled, chinless smile and, with a wild fleck of tender childhood drool popping out from between his gapped front teeth, launched into the second stanza. Barry looked at his wife. At her steely lawyer's composure. At the uneaten Hakka chicken beneath her brown Brahman fingers. *I want to love you,* he thought.

"Won't my mommy be so proud of me?" Arturo was wailing. Why did that lyric hurt Barry the most? They wanted to be *proud* of Shiva the way their own parents were never proud of them. The way the Hong Kong doctor and the faux–Central American writer were hopelessly proud of every stupid hammy thing Arturo would ever do. Shiva wouldn't have to accomplish as much as Arturo. He was a rich man's son. He could go to Skidmore or launch a clothing line made out of hemp, but his parents needed a sign that he knew he was a part of their tight, illustrious family. This could be acknowledged with hugs

and kisses and words, but the moon seemed to mean more to him than his closely orbiting mother and Barry, the falling star occasionally streaking across his nighttime sky on its way to Teterboro and "wheels up" to beg some client in Baton Rouge not to ask for an early withdrawal from This Side of Capital.

"This is going to bring us closer together," Seema had said when they got the diagnosis. They held each other close in the crowded Weill Cornell hospital elevator, and he had said, half in jest, "Us against the world!" But the Internet had said the opposite, that they would fall apart like most couples in these circumstances. *Well, fuck the Internet.* Now they had something beyond his money and her looks and credentials. A normal son would not have been a project. The nannies and the tutors and the schools would raise him. But getting Shiva off the spectrum would demonstrate just how exceptional their marriage had been from the start. It would erase all doubts that Seema and Barry Cohen were meant for each other.

"You're so good, Arturo," Seema said as the kid once again reenacted the bee landing on the milky flesh of his arm and screamed, with practiced hysteria, *"OUCH! It stung me!"*

"What do we say when someone compliments you?" Luis said.

"Thaaaaaank you," the child said, rolling his eyes at the imposition. But then he took off his stupid bumblebee hat and bowed on cue, and the Filipina began herding him back to a chorus of "Sleep tight, Arturo" and from Luis *"Buenas noches, pequeño abejorro."*

"A horrible Manhattan question," the doctor said, pouring out another bottle of Priorat, a full-bodied two-hundred-dollar imposition that spoke of her husband's funky midmarket tastes. "What are you guys doing for preschool?"

Seema and Barry afforded each other a one-millisecond look, as if simultaneously downloading that single scene from a year ago, Shiva standing there, motionless, screeching, in what was deemed a "movement class" at the local prenursery, one of the seven that failed to accept him, as monstrous bright-eyed children bopped around him to their parents' delight.

"Oh, we're not even thinking of school yet!" Barry said, flicking his arm, catching the brief bright glow of his Nomos. "Who needs this crazy rat race? Let the kids be kids."

"Shiva has some delays," Seema said. She held up her hand as Luis tried to pour her more Priorat, which she had barely touched.

"I'm a doctor, and let me tell you, we *all* have delays," the Hong Konger said. They laughed at her medical opinion in stereo. "And Arturo *hates* the Flatiron Montessori."

That was the first school to have rejected Shiva, and arguably the best one in their neighborhood. His meltdown there had been so epic Seema was surprised they hadn't called the cops.

"I want him to go to Ethical Heritage for K to six," Seema said. "It's such a diverse place."

"Is that true?" the doctor asked.

"Some of the dads aren't even hedge-fund guys. *They're just doctors or lawyers.*"

Luis and his wife smiled, and Barry did a fake little laugh. Seema never let her pain color what left her mouth; her gating was perfect. This was the first time in five years of courtship and marriage that he had felt pity for his wife. "I mean—" Seema said. "It's just good to have some *economic* diversity." She pretended to take a long sip of her Priorat, but it only coated her lips. It occurred to Barry, out of nowhere, that she was the smartest person at the table and the only one who didn't work.

"Luis is writing a novel about hedge funds," the doctor said.

"Why?" Seema said.

"Well," Luis said, rotating his wineglass with the hammy flourishes of his performative toddler son, "if aliens invaded and took over the earth, wouldn't you want to know who your new overlords were?"

"Luis!" the doctor admonished. "That doesn't sound nice."

"Oh, I meant that in a harmless way," the writer said as Barry did another of his "friendliest dude on the Street" laughs to show he was in on the plutocrat bashing.

"Half of the people I know work in funds," Luis said. "We're in Manhattan, for God's sake."

"In my humble opinion," Seema said, "you should stick to your beautiful portraits of Central America. Write about the voiceless."

"But to do that," the writer declared, "you have to start at the *metropole* and then expand your way out to the peripheries. Where does power really originate?" He lifted up one hand as if to imply it originated in the floor-through apartments and giant triplex above him, in apartments like the one owned by the Cohens.

"Well, I, for one, think a hedge-fund manager would make the perfect hero," Barry said. "And I volunteer to be your muse!"

"I disagree," Seema said. "People in finance have no imagination. They have no soul."

For the third time in as many minutes, Barry smiled stupidly. *What did she say?* He actually had to reconstruct the two sentences. He reached for the empty wine bottle, shook it, put it down.

"Present company excepted, of course," said the doctor, pointing at Barry. It was clear to him, suddenly, that she was educated in an international school, and Luis probably went to a prep school in the States. Old money. Laughing at new money.

"Just put four screens in front of him," Seema said, "and that's all he cares about. No allegiances to anyone."

"I love how you guys can poke fun at each other," said the doctor, looking down at her lap.

"Yeah, we're much, *much* too formal," Luis said. Then in one of the cruelest acts of the night, he leaned in across the table to kiss his wife's bright forehead and to be rewarded with her teenage-shy smile.

"The *sambar* was excellent," said Julianna, "better than I've ever had in India," and one could read the finality of that compliment as an attempt to draw the evening to a close, but Barry couldn't leave at this point, with their own social profit-and-loss statement clearly pointing toward the latter. "I got a batch of the forty-eight-year-old Karuizawa single cask whiskey," he said, "thirty-three thousand dollars a bottle, if you can find it."

"A little gauche, Barry, to mention the price point," Seema said. After all, she was the one who insisted on bringing the homemade *sambar* instead of some statusy bottle of wine. But maybe she, too, felt the need to win back some of the night. She was, in her own way, no less competitive than he.

"I can't say no to Karuizawa," the writer said, pronouncing it perfectly, which meant the bastard knew what it was.

THE SOLO elevator ride was momentary, but Barry managed to flip through his phone and Zillow the Goodmans' apartment. "SOLD: $3,800,000. Sold on 11/23/15. Zestimate: $4,100,000." The layout showed two bedrooms, three bathrooms, and the same hangar-sized closets as theirs. It was a little less than a fifth the price of their apartment, but, still, how did they afford the place on her NYU-assistant-professor-of-medicine salary and his 1,123,340 Amazon ranking? It had to be family money. It had to be! He would get to the bottom of this.

Barry stumbled into the dimmed foyer and made straight for his whiskey cave behind the kitchen, when Novie popped out from behind some Viking implement. "Shhhhh," she hissed. "Please be quiet, Mr. Barry. Shiva, he just go to sleep. He was very hard to put down tonight."

Barry and Novie had started out on good terms, lots of smiling, almost coquettishness, on her part, but since the diagnosis she clearly began to perceive him as irrelevant at worst and a hindrance at best. She was a throaty young woman dressed perpetually in Gap sweats and tight T-shirts and those Lulu pants Seema bought her in bulk. She spent her non-Shiva time on three activities: watching Tagalog soaps on her tablet, Skyping back to Davao City where her relatives were milking her for their gambling debts, and, most offensively to Barry, praying. She maintained that Shiva was absolutely fine, that the diagnosis was nonsense; it was just a question of getting Jesus to watch out for him. But she also understood that Seema now needed her a great deal more than she needed her husband, and that this home truly belonged to Shiva, the vacant boy-king.

Barry plucked the deceptively humble-looking bottle of Karuizawa from its perch in his whiskey cave, banging it, almost smashing it, against the center island as he stomped back to the foyer. What the hell was he doing? Karuizawa was a so-called silent, or defunct, distillery, meaning only a handful of such bottles still existed in the world, many being kept as investments. Barry had earmarked this particular bottle for a special occasion, like when Shiva had to undergo his next testing at Cornell, and the doctors there would tell them the diagnosis no longer applied.

He grew out of it.

We've never seen anything like this.

Maybe ten percent of the kids beat this thing, and he's one of them.

Instead, he was about to share the Karuizawa with a man he despised.

Shiva was standing in the middle of the sunken penultimate living area, his long, reedy body gently humming with either anxiety or excitement; it was always hard to tell which. "See"—Novie sighed—"he heard you and he got exciting that Daddy was home."

"Daddy has to go," Barry said, which is what Barry said almost every time he saw Shiva. The child's eyes brimmed with what seemed like sadness and intelligence, beguiling those who met him. Shiva grabbed the watch on Barry's wrist with his clammy hand. Watches clearly excited him.

"What's that?" Barry asked, in the manner he would address a dog, the only manner he knew with children. "Watch. Say it, little rabbit! Wa-wa-wa-wa. Tch-tch-tch. Watch. Daddy's watch." But Shiva just kept pulling on the watchband. Barry ruffled his wet hair, smelling Johnson's baby shampoo and that too-sweet child sweat, a combination that always made him wonder how a child with such a magical scent could have anything wrong with him. "Say it, Shiva, and I'll let you hold the watch."

"Mr. Barry, he has to go to sleep," said Novie.

"Wa-wa-wa-wa-wa," Barry kept modeling for his son. "Watch. Daddy's watch. What a nice watch. My watch."

The nanny gently pulled him off his father's timepiece, and the child began to expel a series of screeches that Barry felt had no business coming out of a human's mouth, the sounds of a village slaughter that had taken place several centuries back in his genetic history. There was an unfairness to this. To how hard he had worked for his family. To how carefully he had waited for the right woman, the right *young* woman with *young* perfect eggs. They would have three children. Some banker guys had four from each wife, but he would just have three from one wife. There were bathrooms already built in the apartment here and in their house in the country with three sinks side by side, so that growing up all three of the children would be able to brush their teeth at the same time, occasionally splashing one another in mirth. Barry was an only child and his mother died in a car accident when he was five. He had never really wanted kids, but the image of the three of them together in this miraculous bathroom with three Duravit bowls one after the other, that was the image that made him cry when the doctor told him that after God knows how many mishaps, the in vitro had finally worked, and Seema was pregnant. Three kids, one hugging another's warm body as water flowed from three taps, the smell of young hair and cut grass on their shins; three perfect lives.

THEY HAD figured it out in Venice last September. Shiva's "delays" were weighing on them, but there was no call to action just yet, and so they decided to leave him with the nanny and spend four days on the Venetian Lagoon, the kind of romantic getaway that had seemed almost commonplace during their courtship. The city was disgusting with tourists, British girls in VODKA & DÖNER T-shirts, last-breath seniors in wheelchairs crowded onto the vaporetti as if reenacting *Death in Venice* en masse. They had a suite at the Gritti Palace overlooking the Byzantine silver dome of the Salute. Seema preferred the much more expensive Aman hotel, where George Clooney had married someone, but Barry liked the Gritti because he could sit on the deck outside, where Hemingway had once sat, and have an Aperol spritz just like the man whose prose he had tried to imitate at Princeton. Also, in the drawing room they had lots of heavyweight books on watches, including a fifty-pound tome on early vintage Omegas.

He hired a private water taxi to zip them around the canal city, and within a day both of them looked appropriately dazed and sun-fucked. For the first time in ages they had sex, mostly avoiding each other's face, treating their orgasms as separate "work products." They fucked for three jet-lagged hours straight in the middle of the night, and when Barry peeked into the bathroom and saw Seema wipe herself over the toilet, so much of him still inside her, he felt for the first time in a long time that everything might be all right.

Because he had won on the hotel, Seema got to see all the art museums she wanted. Before her parents had forced her to go to law school, Seema had been an art history major at Michigan. He urged her to collect, but other than a Miró and the obligatory Calder sitting unloved in a corner of the library, they did not own much in that asset class. Venice was supposed to rekindle her passions, and so, after a morning fuck, they went on the great Venetian Tintoretto Trail with a brief flyby of Peggy Guggenheim's collection.

Barry dreaded a visit to the Galleria dell'Accademia the most, because it wasn't a church where you could at least enjoy the grandeur and the coolness of the marble and stone. A friend of his who ran a macro fund out of Miami had boomeranged from his divorce into about a billion dollars' worth of impressionism with which to dazzle some young future wife, but after all the sex last night, Barry was entirely secure in his marriage, zooming two or three rooms ahead of Seema and then coming back to check on her glowing form in tight T-shirt and tighter jeans (having a kid had somehow improved her figure, made all the good parts fuller), parked in front of some Madonna and Child with the requisite sexy display of thoughtfulness. But as he walked toward her, he saw the tears curving down her chin. He almost backed away—what if this was a private moment? One of the few you could have when you were married, even with ten thousand square feet of property between you? No, this was something else.

"Seema?" He took her elbow.

"Look," she said. It was the Virgin and Child, one of Tiziano's.

He couldn't understand what was happening exactly. He looked. He looked closer. "What?" he said, and then he saw it. The Virgin was gazing into her Son's eyes, that obscenely mournful Italian gaze that the Venetian women on the streets still seemed to carry between bursts of cell-phone conversation. That wasn't the issue. It was the Child, looking up at his Mother. It was his eyes. His eyes were locked with his Mother's. This was what being a child was about. Seeking out your mother's gaze and mirroring it. Learning to connect now and for the rest of your life.

Barry felt a sob building from somewhere deep inside him, an unarticulated, unmanly place. At first, his grief was for himself and the mother he'd never really known, the eyes he could never remember. There was no way to pinch and expand the Polaroids of the time the way he could with an iPhone image, no way to really see her face up close and to intuit what kind of person she had been. But it was Shiva, really, who made him want to cry alongside his wife. Shiva, who at age two had still never looked either of them in the eye. Shiva who wasn't merely delayed, but in some terrible way broken.

She screamed at him that night. Screamed about their fucking hotel, because the one thing, the *one thing,* she had asked him was to stay at the Aman with its unmarked back door, its breakfast rooms splashed with ontological paintings from mythology, its fucking *privacy.* Didn't she deserve something special once in a while? Well, didn't she?

Barry recoiled. This was exactly how he pictured his banker buddies' marriages, ungrateful women screaming at stupefied men over absolutely nothing. Once, when he was still huffing his way up the VP-MD axis at Goldman, he had gone to a party at a Greenwich manse, and the architect who had designed the house was there on the veranda completely shit-faced. Barry asked him the secret of his success, and the architect had pointed at the lawns full of glimmering couples beneath them and said, "I have the easiest job in the world. Bankers. The same four houses, the same four cars, the same four wives." He took another drunken look at Barry in his loafers and Moncler sweater and said, "Here's my card." Barry decided right then: No Upper East Side, no Greenwich, no S500, no hundred-and-ten-pound white wife with the knuckly shoulders and the re-troussé nose. And here he was in Venice at the wrong hotel, with his brown wife's face contorted into pure pain like some poor Lucchese or Pisan or Florentine soldier spiked through the gut in one of those interminable Renaissance battle paintings.

They still had two days of this nightmare left, and the next morn-ing, sexless but civil, she took him through the rainy streets and ca-nals to the Audemars Piguet boutique on St. Mark's Square and bought him a twenty-eight-thousand-euro pink-gold Royal Oak for which he had absolutely no use. Her version of an apology. The gor-geous young woman whose job it was to arouse the wallet of the kind of man who wanted a watch shaped like a porthole was clearly overjoyed by the effortless sale but could not understand why the man and the woman did not celebrate their new purchase. The sales-girl had repatriated the umbrella embossed with their hotel's crest inside a tasteful umbrella stand, offered them espresso, which they duly drank, and chocolates which they nibbled, and, when Seema's black Amex had cleared, had shouted: "Congratulations!"

They left Venice a day early and, through the good work of his chief of staff, were at Weill Cornell less than a week later. He remem-bered the date, September 23. Seema, dressed as if for work in a blazer and pearls, legs crossed, wrote down everything she saw, ev-erything she observed, as if she herself were a doctor and not a lapsed attorney. She had brought daily logs of Shiva's development, his food intake, and his bowel movements since the day he was born; weight, height, and head-circumference graphs from the pediatri-cian; a page entitled "Questions," another, written in shakier script, "Options." There were two doctors and a speech therapist, and from the moment they saw Shiva, it was over. He didn't speak, of course. But he failed at everything else, too. He was given a baby doll, but instead of holding it or feeding it Play-Doh, he merely flicked its scary blue eyes open and shut, open and shut, open and shut. "I would've done the same thing," Barry said, "the eyes are the only interesting part," but Seema gave him a kohl-eyed stare, and he said nothing for the rest of the session. Shiva was given a toy car, but instead of using it "functionally," he spun its wheels again and again and issued a sly smile. Then he dropped the car without ceremony, went over to the light switch, found a screw right beneath it, and touched the screw while breathing deeply in and out. He spent the rest of the session caressing the fascinating screw.

If he were a novelist like the neo-Guatemalan and he had to write a chapter in a novel about what it was like to get the diagnosis, he would say it felt like being young again and being told for the first time that someone you loved didn't love you back. He wasn't thinking of anyone in particular, there were so many girls in his middle school that didn't respond to the awkward advances of the Pool Man's Son, as he was then known, and not until he excelled on the swim team and his shoulders filled out and he had finally mastered his friend moves did he start to find a tongue or two to entwine his own. But that's what hearing the diagnosis was like. This feeling that the future you imagined with someone would, in all actuality, never exist.

They didn't use the A-word anymore either. It was "spectrum" this and "spectrum" that. And "kids with Shiva's profile." Yes, there was a lot of "kids with Shiva's profile" talk and all the therapies that could benefit such a class of children, nearly fifty hours of behavioral, speech, and occupational (whatever that was) therapy per week. Seema and Barry were too stunned to cry, too stunned to cry for several weeks, until a printed report arrived that said, in no uncertain words, that Shiva was not just "on the spectrum" but on the "severe" end of it.

Later at home, Barry held Seema for a small eternity, while, in the corner of his room, Shiva, in perfect calmness, looked past them, out the window, at the giant clockface of the Met Life Tower, the gears of his own mind either turning rapidly, or not.

"I LOVE what I do," Barry was saying. "I think of it as an intellectual exercise." They were twenty-three thousand dollars into the Karuizawa, which Luis had deemed "a little too rummy" for his tastes, but which he continued to drink avidly, often scratching his nose in pleasure after each inhale of booze.

"So in your own way, you add value," he said.

"Exactly."

"Enough to justify your compensation."

"I find that people get hung up on the compensation part," Barry said. "Okay, sure, we earn a lot *by comparison*, but the money is there as a scorecard. We don't have the book awards, the Pulitzers, or whatnot, and we can't keep track of our *sales*"—he paused meaningfully as if to remind the writer of his Amazon numbers—"so the money tells us who's winning."

"But couldn't that wealth be better redistributed? How about after your first thirty million we give you a medal and tell you, 'You won!' And the rest goes to poor people."

"I will posit that most poor people wouldn't know what to do with substantial sums of money," Barry said, much too loudly, the liquor stirring him up. "They're very low information, and wealth can be confusing. In a sense, you have to train yourself to be wealthy." Seema gave him a look from the opposite end of the couch, where she had been talking with the doctor about child-rearing. He knew Seema would never reveal Shiva's diagnosis, just as she hadn't to her parents or to her college friends, most of whom were still working in Internet sales while dating Brooklyn losers, and he wished she had someone other than Novie to confide in. It was easy for Seema's parents to pretend that nothing was wrong. Einstein didn't start talking until he was three, and Shiva was clearly going to show Einstein a thing or two. "Indian genes, Jewish genes, how can this boy be stopped?" her father had more than once remarked.

"Why don't you cool it, Barry," Seema said.

"My wife, the Democrat," Barry said. "But of course, she's way smarter than I. She's the smartest and most beautiful woman I've ever met." He looked around the room seeking their approval of his magnanimous declaration. The women went back to their hushed conversation.

"You were saying," Luis reminded him, "that the poor wouldn't know what to do with additional funds."

"That was very inelegantly said and I take it back."

"But do *you* know what to do with your money? We're drinking two Hyundai Sonatas' worth of whiskey tonight. But the only reason this whiskey has that price tag attached is that men like you can afford it."

"And who does that hurt?" Barry said. "Who doesn't win from this situation? The Japanese distillery? The whiskey merchant? *You?*"

"I just worry that the new signorial class distorts the picture for the rest of us. You create a world where anything but the utmost in wealth is seen as a moral failing."

"But isn't it?" Barry asked, quietly so that Seema wouldn't overhear. "A moral failing? Maybe not in your Guatemala, where, as I've read in your book, there is absolutely no hope for anyone, but here in America. Half of the portfolio managers in my fund, half of them, are either immigrants or the children of immigrants. My wife's an immigrant. Your wife's an immigrant. Heck, *you're* an immigrant. Of sorts."

"But we're different kinds of immigrants. We're not the traditional arrived-by-steamer-with-three-suitcases or scampered–over–the–Rio Grande kind of immigrants. Our parents came here with college degrees."

Aha! The Zillow price was about to be explained. "So your parents were wealthy."

"Not at all. They were schoolteachers."

"Both of them?" Luis nodded. Barry looked at the Hong Kong doctor. "And—" He still couldn't remember her name.

"Her dad worked as an accountant at the Fulton Fish Market and her mom was a nurse."

"And still, you can afford all this," Barry said, sweeping his arm around the living area, which was half the size of his own and faced not the majestic clock of the Met Life Tower and the whole of the glowing Midtown skyline behind it, but rather something ill lit called Schnippers, which he didn't know what it was despite passing it every day, maybe a deli or something. Still . . . "SOLD: $3,800,000. Sold on 11/23/15. Zestimate: $4,100,000." "Your books must be doing very well," Barry said.

Luis and the doctor both laughed. "I think Seema is the only person I've met who has randomly read Luis," the doctor said. "I almost couldn't believe it!"

"It's true," Luis said. "I'm what they call a 'writer's writer.'" He took a long drag of the *rummy* Karuizawa. "This bottle cost about half of my last advance," he said, thoughtfully.

Barry was confused. "So how do you, uh, monetize your art?"

"Well, here's the thing," Luis said. "I do have some admirers in university departments, Latino studies, Jewish studies, multicultural studies. My peg fits a few holes. And so they often ask me to do a reading for the students and the community."

"And they pay you for it," Barry said.

"Yes, quite handsomely."

"How handsomely?"

"*Barry!*" he heard from Seema. "Shut up about money already. We're not on your trading floor."

"Obscenely handsomely," Luis said, his green eyes sparkling in the reduced, urbane light. "Up to twenty thousand dollars for a twenty-minute reading."

"I see," Barry said. "I see." The whiskey now tasted sour and pointless in his mouth. "So you must be very popular for that amount of money. Twenty thousand people must come to your readings."

"Ha! *Twenty* people would be a good number. I did one at Ohio State the other month, and *no one* showed up except the Jewish studies faculty and a Guatemalan janitor."

"Well, then it's socialism!" Barry said.

The doctor and the writer laughed. Seema stared Barry down. "I suppose it is," Luis said.

"And you're not even Latino!"

"Oh, God, I think it's time we leave," Seema said. "I'm really sorry about that. When Barry gets stressed out at work, he drinks."

"No, no," Luis said. "He's right to explore questions of identity.

What is a Latino exactly? Who qualifies? These are just the kinds of questions we ask at my university readings."

"Which no one attends," Barry said. "At twenty thousand dollars a pop."

"Exactly," Luis said. He looked at Barry with cheerful malice. "You do fifty of those a year, and, well, a million bucks ain't a lot in New York these days, but you're at least welcomed into the *anthills* of the one percent." Now he turned to his wife and they both smiled at each other.

And then Barry realized what had happened. He had been had. The whole thing had been a setup between the writer and the doctor. He needed material for his novel about finance. She ran into Seema in the lobby, learned whom she was married to, arranged this dinner. He needed a hedge-fund character and now he had one, screaming about poor people and socialism and demanding to know the size of his host's salary and ancestral wealth while swinging around a thirty-three-thousand-dollar bottle of whiskey. The writer had been taking mental notes the whole time.

Seema's hand was around his elbow and she was all but lifting him up while still apologizing for his behavior, to which the Guatemalan Tolstoy was laughing his pretty, tall boy's laugh, saying, *No, no, no,* he found Barry *charming, just charming,* and, per the doctor, *they should all do this again next week.* For the first time Barry took note of the living space's artwork, which was, basically, nonexistent, except for a Spanish-language vintage James Bond poster. James Bond, *el espía 007, el más extraordinario espía de la ficción.* It didn't have the uniqueness or value of Seema's Miró or the neglected Calder in their library, but it was a found object that signaled that the writer had an *identity.* It didn't matter if it was invented. He had invented it. He was the fucking writer! That's what he did.

Oh, and that IWC skillet of a watch to casually demonstrate his taste and masculinity.

And that child, safely asleep in his bed next to his bumblebee hat, his oft-praised mind full of fine-tuned *words* and *thoughts* and *dreams.*

Seema still had him by his elbow and was leading him out through the kitchen. The cabinet and consoles looked like they were etched out of a single rock and inlaid with LEDs. It was, actually, a duplicate of their kitchen. Were all the kitchens in their building the same? He was drunk. He was so perfectly and completely drunk. Did the writer even *have* anything to drink that night, or was he like the strippers at the clubs he used to go to with colleagues during his very early years at Morgan who would get you to order overpriced drinks for them and pretend to drink them, or else have a complicit bartender water them down. And then, when you were barely standing and they were perfectly sober, they'd pounce on your black card while flicking away your impotent whiskey dick.

Barry felt the sweat gathering at his temples, the flop sweat he expected on the morning after a night like this. He looked at the feminine lugs of his watch in desperation. They were at the front door, in a gray hallway of some sort. The hallway was so featureless it could have been a part of the Goodmans' apartment. The Goodmans were so featureless, they could have come with the hallway.

He felt the first flicker of it. Get out of here. Escape from Seema. Escape from Shiva. Escape from the SEC. Richmond. El Paso. Layla. The Greyhound. The open road.

Seema was still apologizing for him, when would she stop apologizing already? All he had done was question the *faux* Guatemalan Latino-ness. In his office, this would be a joke you could utter first thing in the morning, before the farm and payroll numbers came in, and nobody would take offense. But she was still apologizing like some rube, like some Michigan humanities major, like some *lawyer,* the kind that they always had at meetings, sitting in the outer circle behind the real players.

The writer was still flashing his watch at him, and the women were talking, talking, talking. He tuned in, if just for a minute, because even in his drunkenness he seemed to catch a glint of his wife's extra sadness, a preset frequency on his dial. "You know what we have to do," the Hong Kong doctor was saying, and now he was catching on to the thickness of her fobby accent, which she had hidden all along until 1:30 A.M., or whatever the Nomos Minimatik said it was, the *l*'s

and *r*'s not quite replacing each other but flirting with the possibility. "We have to get Shiva and Arturo together for a playdate."

"Fuck you," Barry said right into her fobby face. "Just fuck you."

And this time no one laughed.

They didn't know how to fight. This was the upshot of twenty marriage-
counseling sessions at the feet of a fat older Jewish woman who
looked like half of Barry's relatives from the Bronx, the Cohens'
ancestral seat before his father had struck out for Long Island with
its burgeoning collection of pools in need of cleaning.

*They held things in. They were never honest with each other. They never
engaged.* Well. Tonight they unburdened. Tonight they were honest.
Tonight they engaged.

"He's a fraud!" Barry screamed.

"You're a fraud," Seema answered. She didn't scream back. She
was better than this. She had inherited from her mother a deep,
husky fighting voice that Barry could only dream of matching with
his father's high-pitched Jewish hysteria.

"He gets twenty thousand for a reading nobody needs! Just because he's put out a shingle saying he's an intellectual! This is why
our country hates the elites."

"He gets twenty grand a reading. You lose six percent of your
clients' money a year while taking two percent for yourself. And on
what? *Valupro?* I could have told you that was a dog. You're down
eight hundred million over three years. Your lifetime P&L is negative. So which one of you is the bigger fraud? And I'm not even
going to mention, you know. The other thing."

Barry stood there. He looked over at the watch winders in the
closet, like incubators full of intensive-care children at the Lenox
Hill ward where Shiva had spent his first week on earth. The papers
and CNBC couldn't shut up about his losses on Valupro, how Barry
had been the last true believer in that obvious scam, but how the hell
did she know what his lifetime profit and loss was? How the hell did
she know about the other thing? He discussed business with her in

the broadest, most upbeat terms, the ones he reserved for his Qatari Ahmed investors, never mind the pensions and endowments. But she had been *monitoring* him all along. Evaluating. Were there already divorce attorneys in play? He had done the crazy love thing and never asked for a prenup. He thought he had married his best friend.

Their bed was raised, thronelike, over the negative space of the vast bedroom. This didn't seem like the right venue for this kind of discussion. But where else would you have it? In a hotel room in Venice? At the Gritti Palace? They fought best in tubercular lagoon cities. That's where this fight belonged, not six rooms away from Shiva.

There was something he needed to tell her.

"I want you to have an abortion."

"Ah," she said. He had half expected her to put her hand on her negligible stomach, but she didn't. "Because you can't handle another imperfect son."

"You know it's a boy," Barry said. "You know what the odds are of another boy with—" He couldn't say it either, not even in the drunken heat of the night. "The diagnosis."

Seema came up to him so close he could smell every decaying fiber of Hakka chicken on her breath, and it disgusted him. "You never loved Shiva," she hissed with that shitty sarcastic middle-class immigrant smile her grandparents had carted over with them from Tamil Nadu. "Before the fucking diagnosis. Before any of that. He was just another luxury good to you. One child to put in front of one of your three fantasy sibling sinks. Check mark, check mark, check mark. And now, how about that, an old man's sperm gives rise to a kid with problems."

"Your eggs!" he said. "Your twenty-nine-year-old eggs can't even bind with my fucking sperm! How much money did we spend on IVF? Two million? And yes, that was the clients' money, the clients' money you think is so fraudulent. And I was going to bundle for Hillary for you. That treasonous bitch. I was going to bundle money to get you a job with the attorney general when she won. So you would have something other than Shiva to live for. Fraudulent? It's your insides that are fraudulent. It's your genetics."

She didn't cry. She never cried. Only once, when they got the letter with the diagnosis stated in print. Goddamn it, what kind of
woman never cried? Barry cried every few weeks, cried about his son,
his failing business, his dead parents, the fact that he didn't really
know who he was. When he could sense the tears coming, he put on
an old Omega Speedy with the patinated brown dial and the ghosted
arabic numerals on the subdials. But she just stood there, ready for
whatever he had to give her, which apparently wasn't much.

"I see the perfect kids coming out of the Flatiron Montessori,"
Seema said, quietly. "I see boys like Arturo, singing that bumblebee
song. I don't want Shiva to be any of them. And I would never trade
him for any of them. My love for him is so clear. And the road ahead
of him is so tough. Oh, Barry. It's so tough. And the toughest part
of it all is that he doesn't have a good father. That's the toughest
part, isn't it? Forget your sperm, forget my eggs. He doesn't have a
good father. His father is not a good man. His father is not a good
anything."

Barry sat there crying, the tears dripping off his chin. But that
wouldn't last long. The anger was coming. He could feel it. Sometimes it thundered in the office when the motherfucking worthless
PMs motherfucking fucked up again, sometimes it thundered at the
Equinox as he cut across the pool as furiously as he could, him and
a bunch of other finance guys in the adjoining lanes, beating the
water as if it were their father's face. What had Seema said to the
Guatemalan? *He had no imagination. He had no soul.* He sprang up.
For the first time in their relationship, Seema backed away, as if, like
the proletarian she must have always assumed he was, the Pool Man's
Son, he would strike her.

He was out of the room. He was out of the room, into the hallway, then another hallway, then another, the bulk of his own apartment forming an unfamiliar Ottoman market around him. But he
knew where he was going. Novie's face was lit up by some Tagalog
action movie, her own way of putting herself to sleep in the cold,
sleek city of her indenture. Barry was past her as she began to stir,

and into the inner sanctum, Shiva's room, with its carefully stacked Loro Piana clothes in the closets, because "like many kids with his profile," Shiva had skin sensitive to all but the softest fibers. Barry tore past all the stuffed giraffes and giant FAO Schwarz doggies that meant nothing to Shiva but an obstacle on his way to his beloved light switch, which he could flick on and off for the duration of a day.

Before he knew what he was doing, the child was in his arms, Barry crushing him, holding him tight. "Just talk," Barry said. "Just talk, my sweet, sweet rabbit. I love you so much. Please talk. I know it's in you. I know it's in you. I'm your father. Don't you see that? Don't you see that I'm your father? Daddy's here."

The child's scream formed a funnel of its own, reaching upward into the ceilings and drilling straight into Rupert Murdoch's triplex. The room was nothing but the sound of his scream and the flapping of his maddened pigeon arms. And then they were on him. His wife and Novie, these two brown, long-nailed women, scratching at his face, punching him, slapping him.

He found his way back to his own watch safe and dumped six of his beauties into a rollerboard along with a fistful of underwear and a bottle of Veraet watch spray. He couldn't do this without the watches. He couldn't live without their insistent ticking and the predictable spin of their balance wheels, that golden whir of motion and light inside the watch that gave it the appearance of having a soul. Each timepiece told a story of physics and craftsmanship and countless hours of someone else's exacting toil. The watches would help Barry stay in control. Even as he fled from everyone he knew, he would retain control. He grabbed the passport he had gotten with Joey Goldblatt from Icarus Capital, the one made out to Bernard Conte, a name Barry pictured as a more aristocratic version of his own. He tried to open the tiny safe hidden beneath the watch winders—his safe-within-a-safe—where he kept stacks of hundreds bundled together in their standard-issue mustard bands, but was too drunk to remember the code. He put on the hated Citi vest.

Shiva's screaming continued, punctured by the sound of at least one woman crying, but not the right woman, not the one he wanted in tears, his best friend, the smartest and most beautiful woman in the world.

"ARE YOU okay, sir?" Someone seemed to be shouting at him. He opened his eyes to catch a billboard floating by.

HEY, NEW JERSEY, LLAMA A LATIN AMERICA POR 5C A
MINUTOS, SPRINT.

The cars all around them were honking into the blue-black darkness.

"Are you okay, sir?" The shouting and honking continued. There was a warm, clean-smelling presence by his side. The woman screaming wasn't screaming at him. She was screaming at the bus driver in the marines jacket, who was weaving from one lane to another erratically. "Sir, wake up, please!"

"Wake up! Wake up, sir!" Some of the other passengers picked up the cry in their kaleidoscopic accents.

The driver must have awoken, because the Greyhound straightened out, found one lane to call its own, plowed from one darkness into another.

There was a man with his head on Barry's shoulder, his legs twisted around his rollerboard, a small Mexican man. Barry gave him a kind shove. The man stirred. "Sorry, in the back it fucken stink," he said. "I think the bathroom explode. You see everybody moving up." He pointed at the filled-up front seats to justify his presence next to Barry.

"That's cool," Barry said, now fully awake. "Hey, how do you get the seat to go down?"

The man reached over him and pressed a little lever. The seat went down maybe five degrees. Barry was lonely and wanted to talk some more, to suss out some commonalities, but the man was asleep and snoring in no time, his arm warm against Barry's own. His dark hair smelled like hair gel and kept out the affront of the urine-and-bleach odor, which stung Barry's eyes. He was beginning to see that to ride the Greyhound was to be a part of someone else's life. If this were *On the Road*, and he were Neal Cassady or Allen Ginsberg or whoever, he and the little Mexican would probably end up fucking. That wasn't going to happen, but the fact that he could ride on this stinking bus with this Mexican guy was appealing and broadening. It required *imagination*. It required *a soul*.

At ten minutes to five, light was becoming a thing. People were snoring like they had entire planets up their noses. The light was getting stronger. They were somewhere near Trenton. In his four years at Princeton, Barry had never been to the violent nearby capital of New Jersey. At thirteen minutes past five, daylight was complete. How quickly the world filled with light! In his new life, he vowed never to miss the break of day again. The PA system didn't work, but it emitted a staccato ghostly sound, a sound that only grew in volume the farther south they went. Perhaps it came from the souls of former passengers who were still trapped aboard. It was an awful sound, but no one complained, and most of the passengers stayed asleep, until the bus began to swerve again and they had to beg the driver ("Sir! Sir! Are you okay? Wake up, sir!") to not drive off the road.

Around 6:00 A.M., they quit the New Jersey Turnpike and, with a flicker of bayside industry, made their way into Delaware. He was beginning to see how the states all fit into one another. Tankers were rolling into Delaware Bay, beckoned by gusts of refinery smoke. They continued on until Baltimore snuck up on them. It seemed to have no sprawl, but appeared out of nowhere like a walled Tuscan town, guarded by nothing but cell-phone towers. For a while it appeared to be a lovely greenbelt city, with billboards extolling its crab cakes and baseball team. Then the bus off-ramped onto a street filled with boarded-up houses. This was just like the HBO show Seema used to like, the one about the drug-dealing gangster types and the drunk Irish cop. He reached into his jeans pocket to fish out his phone, but realized, with a chill, that he was phoneless. He couldn't call Seema. Couldn't send her a photo of boarded-up Baltimore.

He had to get off the bus. He would take a little breather here before continuing on to Richmond. He had never been to Baltimore. The Maryland state retirement plan was an investor, but its staff always insisted on coming up to New York to yell at Barry in person.

When he stepped off the bus, the summer humidity struck him right in the pits. He looked at his Mexican companion unloading his luggage from the bus's hold and realized that the fellow was missing an eye, that he just had this hollowed-out hole with a little bit of skin flap around it.

Running away had been a smart move. He didn't know who his wife and son were. One hated him and the other seemed incapable of feeling. Which wasn't his fault, the poor rabbit. It was the Diagnosis. It was his *Profile*. But what could Barry offer them? How could he assuage his wife's hate and be a role model for his son? And what if she went ahead and had a second son with the same problems? Shouldn't he just start all over again? Starting over was what half of the country seemed to desperately want. There was a great boredom that coursed through Barry's body and, he imagined, through that of his countrymen, rich and poor, but all it took was getting on a bus and getting the hell out of town. It wasn't America that needed to be made great again, it was her listless citizens.

The whole idea of marriage now seemed insane. His fund had an initial lockup period during which investors couldn't withdraw their money no matter how much of it Barry lost, but that period was a mere *two years*. Marriage was supposed to be a lifetime. At one point Barry thought he could handle it, but what if he couldn't?

The sky above Barry was endless. There was an intense clarity to everything, as if he were surrounded by holy truth.

In the near distance across from the bus terminal, a large building that could have been the library of a state college was festooned with the words HORSESHOE CASINO and attached to it was a Holiday Inn Express. Barry could rest his tired head there, and soak off the rest of the hangover that was sure to come.

Outside the station, exhausted-looking black men were standing at a local bus stop, wearing bags across their shoulders, their caps turned backward. At least three of them were on motorized wheelchairs jerking around the broiling tarmac. Barry trailed his rollerboard past them until he found an entrance to the Holiday Inn Express amid some unwell shrubs.

The two black men behind the desk were dressed in Orioles T-shirts. "Checking in," Barry said.

"Say that again?" one of the men said.

Barry repeated himself.

"There's some kind of altercation on the third floor, room three fifteen," said the other man with deep indifference.

A short yellow-skinned black man ran into the lobby. The ridge of his nose had been broken and spurts of blood webbed his freckled face. A taller black man walked behind in languid pursuit. "You do not disrespect me!" the short man screamed back at him, his face bleeding all over his Ravens V-neck and his tight blue shorts. "You do not disrespect me! Call the police!"

The men behind the desk in the Orioles T-shirts did not seem to warm to the idea. One of them made half the motion of shrugging.

"He disrespected me!" the first man shouted.

His friend called him Sean. "Sean, calm down," he said. "Calm down, Sean."

Barry put down his heavy black Amex with its unlimited purchasing power, but he got the sense that nothing would impress the Baltimorean hotel clerks. A middle-aged white woman next to him was checking in with nothing but a hair dryer in her hand. Sean, the short, bleeding man, left the hotel lobby still screaming about being disrespected, and his larger friend followed him out, asking him, with great fortitude, to remain calm.

Barry's room on the third floor had an unbroken view of the monolithic immensity of the Horseshoe Casino and of the sliver of downtown skyscrapers beyond. In the shadows of the Horseshoe, Sean chased his assailant. Then they would stop for a while, pant heavily, and his assailant would chase him back.

Barry laughed. It was all so fucking ridiculous. His first laugh in private in as long as he could remember. Nobody cared about his black Amex and nobody cared about Sean's bleeding face and nobody cared that his son was severely autistic and nobody cared that his marriage was over and nobody cared about the Valupro fiasco and nobody cared about what would befall the woman checking in with only a hair dryer in her hand as the morning rolled into day. The immensity of the land was too big for any of these concerns.

Barry had broken free of the surly bonds of his own life.

He had been granted refuge in America.

2 *A WOMAN OF PURPOSE*

Y THE time they put Shiva down it was already 5:00 A.M., and his first therapist of the day—the occupational therapist whose job was to help Shiva "locate his own body in space"—came at eight, so what did that give her? Three hours? Without a proper Xanax-Ativan smoothie, she would never sleep. And so much for benzos, now that a second boy lay in her womb.

It was 6:00 A.M. The building had a proper marble lobby, but she couldn't face the possibility of running into Julianna or Luis, not after what had happened last night. She left through the service entrance and walked briskly to a coffee shop on Third Avenue, whose name she had forgotten. She forgot the names of places the way Barry forgot the names of women. It was the most nothing place in the city, bad omelets, bad coffee, but it reminded her of the suburban diner near her childhood home in Cleveland Heights, where her parents had settled in the seventies, almost a decade after America started welcoming Asians by the planeload.

She ate a bowl of despicable oatmeal in silence, her head thrumming in her unwashed palm. She wanted a cigarette, too. And the benzos, oh, God, the benzos. She got a text from their chef, Mariana, asking her what time she wanted her egg whites. Nothing from Barry. And if he thought *she* would send *him* a message, well, he knew better than that.

Three fortyish women in gym clothes came in and sat down with their back to Seema to have their shit-bowls of coffee before their workouts, because all the decent places with the Intelligentsia beans were still closed. Seema tried to keep track of their conversation, but their voices merged into one urgent, caffeinated din. "Modern dance at Morris for a year but it kind of sucked . . . Anytime the girls walk in there, they have tons of friends . . . Stephen liked to hunt . . . SoulCycle . . . Jackson Hole . . . We should do something else fun with Barbara . . . Kid looks just like him, but shorter and chubbier . . . Stephen's under a lot of stress . . . We had *Nutcracker* tickets . . . Barbara made fruit salad, whipped cream from scratch . . . Stephen didn't mean to . . . We went from the *Nutcracker* straight to LaGuardia . . . He thought he left his backpack in the cab, but it was at school . . . *Thoroughly* exhausted . . . And with Stephen yelling like that . . . It was like a socialist country, everyone gets on the plane at the same time . . . What a clusterfuck . . . Poor Barbara, one of her kids is autistic, and the other goes to BU."

Seema laughed loudly and, to her surprise, genuinely. The women didn't even notice. They just kept at it. A small New York mercy. She sat there for what might have been hours listening to their song of anger and surprise, which could have been subtitled "We Have No Idea Whom We Married," and which, despite all that she had let herself believe for the last four whirlwind years, was now her song as well.

SHE WENT back up through the service entrance. A morning fog hung around Madison Park, which felt like an unwelcome reflection of her own mind. Only Shiva's beloved Metropolitan Life clock tower stood tall through the miasma.

"He had trouble sleeping last night," she told Bianca, the occupational therapist, a pretty young girl from the Bronx whose care for Shiva rivaled her own. Novie rolled her eyes, but Seema shook her head to quiet the nanny. "Nightmares," she said, hopefully imbuing Shiva with the inner life the literature now unanimously said he had.

"Poor pumpkin," Bianca said, softly brushing the darkness beneath Shiva's eyes. She sat him on a ball that had tiny ribs and indentations, designed to stimulate his sense of touch, and bounced him up and down, increasing the tempo as they went. Shiva smiled and flapped his arms. Bianca smiled back. Novie smiled. And Seema smiled, too. Here was this twenty-eight-pound kid, surrounded by three lovely smiling women, bouncing in the air.

With that image as her fuel, Seema went to her office down the hall and began to figure out some next steps. Every morning was a series of next steps. There was a special swimming pool at NYU for kids "with his profile," and a sensory gym at a school nearby. Barry had hired her a personal assistant, some twelve-year-old who just popped out of Wesleyan, but Seema wanted to handle Shiva on her own, and so the assistant had been set free. She looked through the stacks of reports from the last week. The continued lack of speech was highlighted. On every single sheet was the word "Noncompliance." Shiva would not do what he was told. He could not follow basic directions, possibly could not understand such instruction. Noncompliance. *Like father, like son.* She really needed that cigarette.

What would Luis's face feel like beneath her plush palms, the warm scrub of it, that richly endowed chin? She knew Barry had failed to notice every single sideward glance Seema had cast his way, the silent smile they exchanged in the perfect forty-seven heartbeats it took Julianna to show Barry to the bathroom. The only time Barry would get jealous is when a richer man entered the room and took full libidinous stock of Seema, like his friend the Miami billionaire with the impressionist collection, as if she would ever touch that walking carbuncle of a man.

Novie knocked. "Sorry to disturb," she said, "but I just feel like I have to say."

Seema sighed. She pointed to the papers on her desk to indicate that she was slammed with work.

"Mr. Barry, he's not right," Novie said. "I think, maybe you should call somebody."

The prow of the Flatiron Building floated through the fog several hundred feet below Seema's office. How she used to love this view, possibly the best in New York, the very reason she had convinced Barry to live here and not in some aircraft hangar in Tribeca.

"This is something I can take care of on my own," Seema said.

Novie shook her head. "I don't know," she said. "All I care about is Shiva."

"And I *don't?*" This came out much too loudly. But then again, she was being given life advice by a woman who had twice declared that you could get HIV from a banana.

"Sometimes the wife don't see things because she still loves so much."

This from someone who thought their alcoholic doorman would make a perfect life partner.

"Let's put a pin in that," Seema said, leaving her nanny to look up the expression on her tablet. She walked into some minor bathroom, splashed water under her armpits, went back to the office, put Shiva's paperwork into the monogrammed satchel her mother had bought her for Li at Yale, changed her T-shirt to something from the swag bag of a Robin Hood Foundation gala, took the elevator down, and walked out of the service entrance onto Twenty-third Street.

THE HAMBURGER scent of Shake Shack had made the southeast corner of Madison Park a Brahman nightmare for Seema. Lately she had cut down on the red meat, and even the chicken. Recently she had been seeing a lot of young desi couples, and while the idea of marrying her own kind had always revolted her, in times of trouble it made an awful kind of sense. Barry's Judaism was a nothing. He supported Israel with great bouts of inarticulate noise, the way some of her relatives still held a candle for the lost Tamil cause in Sri Lanka. She had picked up more on his religion from her past Jewish boyfriends—yes, there had been several—than he had in years of being a Jew. She remembered his genuine surprise upon hearing from her the concept of *tikkun olam,* or "repairing the world." "Neat," he had said, whereas when her first boyfriend at Michigan explained it to her at a Hillel soup-kitchen event, she had found herself so moved, she couldn't figure out if she was in love with him or the immovability of his past. There had to be a Hindu equivalent to *tikkun olam,* but she had been too busy with her 4.13 average and charity work and law-school applications to figure out what it was.

She avoided the part of the park where the Filipina nannies all gathered, Tagaloging among themselves with cries of *"Loco loco!"* and engaging in an endless competition over who had raised the fattest baby. Novie had once proudly told her that the nannies compared all their households' net worths on the Internet, and that for at least a month she and Barry had come out on top. The second-worst part of that was how proud she had been of Barry. And the worst part? How proud she had been of herself.

She settled in among a gaggle of Caribbean nannies. The paperwork was soothing. The feel of her mother's folio against her bare knees calmed her. When she had told her mother about Barry, her mother had treated their engagement like it was her due. Like it was one of two acceptable choices, a white-shoe law firm partnership being the other one. Holding the leather folio, probably scored at the sad Dillard's at Cleveland's overblown Tower City Center, was almost like none of this had happened. She hadn't met Barry, had gone on to Cravath after the Eastern District, was living in Fort Greene with her friends, Netflixing away the first half of the night, snoring heavily through the second, working the daylight hours silly. She couldn't believe that Barry was considering bundling for Hillary to get her a job with the AG. "So you would have something other than Shiva to live for," he had said. Were all men separated from their children and wives by an invisible ribbon of cluelessness?

Seema reviewed the checklist for Shiva. He was ranked for everything from engagement to mobility to speech to fine motor skills to just fucking breathing and being generally alive. Next to each box, the physical, occupational, and speech therapists had written down his age of development. He was three years and one month, or thirty-seven months, but most of his metrics were scored at fourteen, ten, sometimes seven months, basically at the level of a half-year-old infant. Only his gross motor was age appropriate. Shiva ran across the apartment faster than Novie. You could close your eyes and he'd cover half the floor-sized apartment in one tormented screech.

Seema looked up from the checklist. What if Barry was right? What if the immensity of her task pleased her? What if she was like him, except, instead of four monitors blasting the Hang Seng and the Baltic Dry Index, she needed this challenge to feel like she mattered?

The classical, almost Venetian proportions of the park were dwarfed by their own tower and a similar glass pile going up next door, but this was New York, not Paris. This was the vitality of their class, and a part of her loved it. Jesus Christ. *All these thoughts.* How to stop them? Would one cigarette, something slutty and mentholated, really kill her second baby boy?

And then she saw him. Just like that. Sitting on a bench across from her, a steady stream of orbital Bugaboos and lesser Maclarens separating them. He was pretending to read a book, its cover replete with dollar signs, a downward sloping graph, a title filled with invective, something about Wall Street. He smiled at her. He was wearing shorts that exposed the Barry-like furriness of his legs and a T-shirt with the lowercase letter *m* atop a tractor. Mina Kim, her still sort of best friend in Williamsburg, would probably know what that meant. Seema should probably smile back, point at her watch—a five-dollar Timex she kept at the bottom of her vanity when she wanted to truly fuck with Barry—and run back to Shiva and his therapists, the predictable stylish sweep of her floor-through, and the Flatiron Building beneath them, where it belonged.

He was sitting next to her in an instant. His gross motor skills were apparently as good as Shiva's. And *her* fine motor skills? She shuddered and actually covered one half-naked leg with the other. *Breathe!*

"Hey, what's up?" Luis said. Of course, that's what he'd say. Why couldn't he be living in farthest Brooklyn with the rest of his social class, away from her and her ruined family? He smelled darkly of cigarettes.

"Hey," Seema said.

"Damn, it's hot," he said.

She quickly hid the pages relating to Shiva's diagnosis, then made a show of fanning herself with a sheet of blank paper.

"Hey, thanks for coming down to dinner last night. I know you guys are super busy."

"Are you kidding?" Seema said. "I can't believe you would even want to speak to me after what happened."

"You mean the 'fuck you'?" he said.

"For starters. Poor Julianna. I was going to write her a letter of apology."

"Oh, she can take it," Luis said. "She did her residency in St. Louis. She's seen it all."

"Well, it was a shitty thing to question your identity," Seema said.

"You can't blame Barry," he said. "You either get it or you don't. He's not an immigrant like us."

"I was born in Ohio," Seema said. Assuming that she was born abroad because she was Indian was a major faux pas, the kind of thing that Barry's white colleagues were habitually guilty of.

But Luis just shrugged. "Do you mind if I smoke?" he asked. He took out what looked like a Nat Sherman with a honey-scented clove tip—did they still make those?—and lit up with a filmic gesture, as if he were the Spanish James Bond on the poster above his living room couch.

"I've got to go home," Seema said. "This is really embarrassing, but I need a shower."

Luis leaned in closely. There was honey and clove on his breath along with the disgusting life-taking tobacco. There was an Uncle Nag in Bombay she and her sister adored, who briefly flirted with a film career and actually had a small role in a commercial for a skin whitener. He was handsome, but his real strength was that Nag looked like he could do or, more important, say anything. This was Luis. He owned his words.

"You smell really great to me," he said. His eyes were upon hers and hers were in flight. "Let's have lunch," he said.

"I really have to get going," she said.

"I haven't showered either," he said, quite proudly. "Come on, two huddled smelly immigrants, yearning—"

"I'm not an immigrant!"

"Sure." His large hand was upon her elbow, and they stood together. His wrists were thick and veined, and she knew what an IWC Pilot's Watch was, and how Barry wished he had the circumference to wear one.

"Let's invite Julianna," Seema said. This was a strategy she usually used with grosser men.

"Are you kidding?" Luis said. "With her schedule? I see her like once a month. I'm basically the put-upon house husband. Have you seen *Mad Men*? I'm Betty Draper."

They left the park chatting about Trump. Seema liked that Luis had to bend down at least half a foot just to talk to her. It wasn't only that he was tall, it was that his height made him a bit clumsy, and that was sweet. They continued to talk about Trump on autopilot, the way people were doing that summer. All of a sudden, Seema wanted to say something real. "When things are tough with my family," she said, "I like to watch Trump, because he just takes my mind off stuff. No matter what happens personally, there's this much greater disaster taking place."

"Very well put," Luis said. "I do a lot of private-slash-public toggling of my own. So, how do you handle shame?"

"Sorry?"

"Is there a Hindu mechanism for dealing with shame, or is it just internalized like Julianna's Confucianism?"

Seema had to think about this. And also to consider whether or not Luis was dissing his wife. They were passing trickles of a lunchtime crowd on Broadway, the street jammed with Escalades without passengers. Being with Luis reminded her of a previous version of herself, the single girl, aware of her physical and other gifts, walking across the city with a boy, trying him on for size, talking about stuff she never did with Barry. She tried to picture the word "Confucianism" coming out of her husband's mouth.

"I guess," she said, looking up to Luis's unknowable green eyes, "I'm always ashamed."

"Hold that thought," he said. "Cambodian pork sandwich or the best hot dog in New York?"

If she rejected the *best* hot dog in New York, she'd look stupid. They went to a place called the Old Town Bar on Eighteenth Street, which Luis explained in his twenty-thousand-dollar-per-reading voice was one of the grandest of New York bars, with a ceiling made of tin tiles and a fifty-five-foot mahogany-and-marble bar and the oldest, *the* oldest, dumbwaiter in New York City, and although the joint was known for its hamburger, the *Times* had once declared it the best in Manhattan, it was revered by aficionados for its crisp delicious grilled frankfurter, and, and, and—

As he talked, waving his hands in a way that her mother would describe as Jewishly, which maybe was wrong on her part, Seema had a thought:

I'm twenty-nine years old.

She was a twenty-nine-year-old with a man not that much older than she was in a bar in the afternoon. When she caught their reflection in the mirror with her arms folded against her breasts in a kind of shy twenty-something pose (when was the last time she had the *luxury* of being shy with Barry's predator friends and their wives?), and the sunlight streaming in through the high stained windows, she thought, *What if this is who I am?*

She felt so guilty over this happiness, she quickly checked her phone and found herself relieved that Barry hadn't called, which meant nine hours had elapsed since he fucked off God knows where with his watches. Her phone. Since what had happened in Sardinia, *that other thing,* as she had once overheard Barry and his chief of staff Sandy refer to it, her phone was an object of fear. It contained the video that could undo Barry's life. That might destroy their entire family. Maybe it was too late already.

He ordered a Bushmills, which Seema remembered from her truncated dating career was what men with *his* profile ordered. She ordered a seltzer, but Luis said mock rudely that that wouldn't do, so she asked the atmospheric old barmaid what was on tap and then accepted some kind of summer ale. Right, because it was summer. She had forgotten that, too, that it was her favorite season, had forgotten the New York stickiness that had first made her love the city and its people, her people, because Manhattan was not just for the winners, but the *winners* of winners.

He talked about himself for a long while. She caught bits of it, a beloved dead father, a teenage sojourn (brief but instructive) in the wrong part of Cambridge, Massachusetts, unchecked feelings of despair over never winning some prize, and a lot of passive-aggressiveness toward his perfect wife. She smiled, but he was sensitive enough to know he was losing her.

And then he said, "You're a woman of purpose."

"I don't know what that means." He told her that he watched her carefully the other night, knew that her life was not what it seemed, that she was suffering, but that something was driving her forward, that she had a purpose no one knew about.

"You're being presumptuous," she said, but not unkindly. She wasn't going to take more than a sip or two of the beer, but even that small amount was going to her head. The frankfurter, so crisply grilled, so perfectly lean and smoky, was the best thing she'd had in a long time, her Brahman genealogy be damned. She was so *present*. But what the hell was he talking about? A woman of purpose? Had he seen her with Shiva? Did he know about the diagnosis? Or was this merely a riff on her unfortunate marriage? *Her* misfortune as a part of *his* seduction?

"Relating to other people's suffering," Luis said, "that's what I do."

"When it comes to the indigenous Maya of Guatemala," she said. "Not to a rich man's wife."

"What's the fucking difference in the end?" he said. The Bushmills had clearly gone to his head and to the warm red tuft of neck atop his small-case-letter-*m*-on-top-of-a-mysterious-tractor T-shirt. They were sitting at a bar with two plates of franks and fries before them, and it was very clear to her that she was being desired.

This actually made her sad, because she knew that when the frank was gone, she would have to say to him, *I'm sorry but I have to go home*. And she would disappear up their glass skyscraper, seventeen floors above his, and then have to pray for another chance encounter, but mainly she would have to be Shiva's mom again.

And when she did eat the last bite of the hot dog and when she did tell him, he put his hand on her arm, and he said, "Can we hold hands just for a couple of minutes?"

Yes, he was so much like her uncle Nag in Bombay. He could say whatever came to mind. And he could get the desired results. And like everything else about this afternoon, his touch was perfect. Skin like dry parchment but brimming with the heat that she knew extended to the rest of the body. The three sips of beer rising up through her tired, two-months-pregnant body, she found herself rubbing his knuckles counterclockwise, and as she did so, he unspooled himself farther over his tiny barstool, a big stupid smile on his face. What she missed most about dating men was that small, disconcerting time frame when you thought that maybe you could change them.

She had a seductive voice of her own, but it had gone flat from disuse. She had a smart-ass voice, too, one she had sort of modeled on an Indian comic actress on TV, and she thought maybe she'd try to bring that one out as she said, "So this is what you do? Hold hands with married women in low-rent bars?"

And instead of denying it he said, "Yes. And this is my only pleasure."

"Not your son?" she said. "Not your wife?"

"I'm going to ask for your number now," he said. "And you can say no, and I would understand. But if you said yes, and every afternoon we could come here, or somewhere else, and just hold hands, I would be the happiest man that has ever lived."

LATER SHE tiptoed into Shiva's animal-stuffed room, even though this was against the rules. When a kid "with his profile" finally fucking went to sleep, you lined up all your gods on a shelf and prayed to each in turn. But she stood there over his crib as he clawed and jerked his way through what she assumed was a medium-sad dream. At times like these, he had exactly her father's bony, inquisitive face. Her parents. They came to the States in 1973 to attend college at the ages of eighteen and nineteen. Teenage immigrants. They adapted, lost 83 percent of their accents, and bled into the cracked soil of the Midwest. But Shiva would be a permanent immigrant. His encounters with the world would always contain the unexpected. Even his young mother's love would need subtitles.

Her phone beeped with a text message. An unfamiliar number. His number. TEST, it said.

3   *OMAR COMIN'*

I T HAD been only one day since Barry had been set loose on the country, but already he felt young and bold and ready for anything. He was finally doing his junior year abroad, the one his father wouldn't pay for. He was backpacking through his own version of Europe. That mythical thick woman with the crablike walk and many stories to tell who would bring him a plate of vinegary beans and pulled pork, she was somewhere close at hand. Any minute now, he would meet her, and she would say to him, *Hush, child. Don't be so hard on yourself. Everyone gets to start over again. This America, hon. One dream dies, you get another.*

He had left the Holiday Inn Express as soon as he awoke, walked past the immense Horseshoe Casino, which even this early in the morning was blasting Billy Joel's "You're Only Human" from its outdoor speakers, and then through a low-rise housing project where, unlike in Seema's favorite show about Baltimore, nobody was dealing drugs. What a delight it was to float through the world without a phone pinging at you with the latest news on Valupro's cratering stock price. How lovely to see a young man of drug-dealing age sitting on a stoop at seven in the morning with only a bottle of Gatorade by his side, his Ravens cap backward. "Morning," Barry had said to him, to be rewarded with a curt nod.

He was getting close to downtown. The public housing had run out, and he now found himself in a regular marginalized neighborhood. A blue storefront read THE BOOK ESCAPE. A bookstore? That could be a treat. How long had it been since Barry visited a bookstore? He had to think about it. Ten years?

The Book Escape was full of books. This shouldn't have been a surprise, but their sheer number made Barry breathless. How he had loved books in high school and in college. They were his ticket out of eastern Queens. As early as ninth grade, his body a mess of natural chemicals and desires, the Pool Man's Son would pack a knapsack full of books and take off for a stretch of Long Island Rail Road track between Little Neck, the working-class Queens neighborhood where he lived with his father, and fancy Great Neck, which, Barry didn't know yet, was the West Egg in *The Great Gatsby*. Before he went nuts over Fitzgerald at Princeton, Hemingway was his man. Pretending it was some exotic Pamplona shrub, he'd sit beneath a dogwood tree by the railroad tracks right on the borderline between New York and its richer suburbs (where the sky seemed endless and opulent), mouthing the lines of Jake Barnes and Lady Brett Ashley and Robert Cohn, who had a last name much like Barry's and who was, in his own mind, also detestable, as the Sun Also Set over Queens and the rest of the country to the west. Within Hemingway's sparse prose, he sensed an unbridled romanticism, a way for men to slyly broadcast their love. With Seema and Shiva, he had the opposite problem. He didn't know how to harvest love out of sorrow.

The books at the Book Escape were ordered by categories, but there was a freewheeling aspect to them, as if they had been walking around on their own accord, finding new homes and families for themselves. The Strand in New York offered books for sale by the yard, and Barry planned to take advantage of that service for the summer home he had almost finished up by Rhinebeck. He was building what he called his Hudson River View Library; his estate also overlooked a set of railroad tracks, reminding him of the silver whoosh of the LIRR trains of his childhood, a way for his successful self to wave to his youthful self across the back channels of time. But the Book Escape was a more personal shopping experience. He poked around the fiction section. There were lots of new writers he had never heard of, along with dusty examples of his favorites, Hemingway and Fitzgerald.

Weathered couches and ottomans were scattered around for atmosphere and comfort, and the books smelled old. He remembered Chop Suey, the bookstore in Richmond, Virginia, where Layla and he had gone to kiss in one of the back rooms. She had taken a few creative writing classes with him at Princeton, and although she was a sociology major, she read fiction like a maniac. The memory of those kisses made Barry pause and consider the watch he was wearing today, a Patek Philippe Calatrava 570. He had chosen it this morning because its white gold would feel just heavy enough for a brand-new adventure, and it would glint blindingly in the summertime urban sun. A watch blog had once described this model as "pure sex on the wrist," and he found that apt. It had been a gift from his guys at the fund, Akash Singh and his team. When the Valupro fiasco was fully under way, Barry would hide in the office bathroom and turn the watch over to console himself with the inscription on its back: TO BARRY COHEN, A LEADER OF MEN.

Barry could feel his hand under Layla's blouse caressing her back, the first real woman's back he had ever encountered, hot to the touch, fragrant, and taut, and how scared she was, like a good southerner, that somebody would discover them necking in the back of Chop Suey, friends of her family, maybe, even though her family was as progressive as it got in Richmond back then. Their first night together in Virginia, the parents out for a Clinton-Gore fundraiser, he had tried so hard to please her, but Layla had grabbed him by the forehead wedged between her legs and said, "Baby, I'm all out of juice." That became a little private joke between them all the way through graduation, when she did Teach for America and he went to Morgan, then Goldman. "I'm all out of juice," she'd write him in the long summertime letters traveling back and forth between South Dakota, where she did her teaching stint, and Queens, as they tried to hold on to the last sweet beats of their love.

"Hi," Barry said to the sole proprietor, who was a shy, tall liberal-arts type with an ancient graying corgi sleeping at his feet. "I was wondering, how many books do you stock by the writer Luis Goodman?"

The man disappeared into the comforting dust of his store to search for the quasi-Guatemalan jerk. When he had been due-diligencing Seema on Facebook five years ago as a potential wife, Barry encountered a lot of "friends" like this gawky shop owner, some of their profiles leading back to photos with Seema that could be misconstrued as romantic, lots of entwined arms, summertime taco stands, a trip to Tanglewood. She had had three serious boyfriends before him, which seemed like a lot for a twenty-four-year-old.

He had met Seema at a Bloomberg party for a cultural art thing, back when the little guy was still mayor of the city. Barry had always felt shy around Bloomberg and not just the way he felt shy around billionaires in general, his own net worth somewhere between 60 and 135 million, depending on how you were counting. Bloomberg was someone who actually *added value*, who had created his own bespoke piece of technology, the terminals that made Barry's world go round, that kept track of everything from the Thai baht to the latest Argentine default to cargo vessels full of terrified Filipinos plying their way around the pirated Horn of Africa.

The roof garden was divided into roughly two demographics: capital on one side, and cultural capital on the other. It wasn't quite as split as a Hasidic wedding, gender-wise, but it was close enough, and Barry worked up the gumption to leave some of his Wall Street bros behind and wade into the more dangerous territory of feminine culture-meisters. Seema wore a pantsuit, a nearly Clintonian one, that made it clear she had just escaped from work. So she worked! And probably in a field more serious than culture. That was titillating in and of itself. She also laughed a lot, but looked super intelligent and credentialed. Only rarely had Barry seen women combine humor with success. And Seema's creamy pantsuit contained a plush young body he could picture himself drowning in forever. Yes, three seconds into meeting her he was already dropping the F-word in his mind.

"Uhhhhhhhh," Seema said as he eye-sodomized her belly over a plate of tuna tataki hors d'oeuvres being bandied about by another hottie. The first word she had said to him wasn't even a word. "Hello?"

"Sorry," Barry said. "I do this thing where I just space out."

"While staring at my navel."

"I can't really see your navel. Because you're dressed."

"Okay, weirdo," Seema said.

Weirdo! She sounded so young. The suit made her look older than her twenty-four years. She had an actress's way of stretching out her words.

When he found out that she clerked for the Eastern District, he could already see the three beige babies they were going to have to- gether right after her small, bittersweet going-away party in judge's chambers. When she found out he had just started a hedge fund, she lit into him, rather cutely, he thought, about how hedge funds trans- mitted risk and screwed the economy. Barry couldn't get enough of her erudite outrage. Our nation's financial crisis was already three years behind us, and people were still going on about *that*. She was like a smarter version of that Indian comedian woman he liked on TV.

"Well, that's what Paul Krugman wrote," she said.

"Who's that?" he said, bending down over her, rearing up the bulk of his swimmer's shoulders.

"Seriously?" she said. "Nobel Prize winner? *New York Times* col- umnist?"

"I'm a *Wall Street Journal* kind of guy."

"You don't read the *Times*?"

"Can't stand their line on Israel."

"Well, we'll have to fix that," she said. Did she really say that? He imagined she did. The takeaway being . . . *We.*

A few minutes later they had found themselves standing next to Mayor Bloomberg and, if Barry's memory served at all correctly, some kind of old woman wearing some kind of thing. He couldn't remember her name, but Seema later told him she was the editor of *Vogue*. They were talking about This Side of Capital. "Is that a new shop?" Bloomie asked, looking up at him with his inquisitive little face.

"Started last year. We've got almost a billion AUM. But plenty of room to grow. I'd love to pick your brain someday."

Bloomberg smiled kindly as if to say, *There will be no brain-picking, my friend*. He then directed his golden gaze appreciatively at Seema. It was as if their relationship was already sanctified by America's eighth-richest man.

"Wow," she said after they had descended from the roof terrace and found themselves deep into the halal-kebab stench of Midtown. "You really just walk up and talk to people. I wish I could do that." The seriousness of her expression made Barry believe that she really did yearn after something he had besides money. They would complement each other. Their kids would have her intelligence and his bravado. Princeton plus Yale equaled Harvard? Two flutes of Four Seasons Moët later, she consented to give him her number but not to go home with him. He went back to his empty Tribeca loft and found himself too excited to even masturbate with her in mind. He emptied a bottle of thirty-year-old Balvenie, cried for a few hours about an indeterminate female image that was *not* of his dead mother, no, *no*, it was not, and slept through the incoming weekend and two conference calls with investor relations. When he woke up, he knew what he had to do.

"I'M SORRY," the shop owner said upon his return. "You said 'Luis' Goodman? L-u-i-s?"

"That's right."

"We don't have anything by him. I'll be honest, I've never heard of him."

"Hot damn," Barry sang to himself after he had left the bookstore. "Hot dammity-damn!" He found himself all but skipping down the hot asphalt toward downtown. None of Luis Goodman's novels were to be found in just the kind of smelly alternative book-store that should have stocked them! Not even *The Sympathetic Butcher,* that indigestible piece of shit. Here was a sign, if he still needed one, that *his* journey was the special one.

Barry decided to take note of things, just like a real writer would. Baltimore had a harbor thing going. He counted several dozen yachts, none of them terribly impressive. The skyline was topped by Transamerica, Bank of America, PNC, and those usual fraudsters SunTrust and BB&T. Even this small, embattled city was completely financialized. Barry wanted to get away from the familiar be-khaki'd figures, all those low-level, back-office types who ran around through the heated streets with cartons of Starbucks iced coffee, their mouths full of Bluetooth.

He made a hard left and headed west, amazed by how quickly the business sections of the city gave way to poverty. A young white guy in dirty blond dreads was begging for change right off of Martin Luther King Jr. Boulevard. The white guy had a cardboard sign next to him that just read HOMELESS. No greater story to tell. When Barry dropped a twenty-dollar bill, he mumbled "Thank you" but did not look up at his benefactor. Perhaps he also had the diagnosis, this bleached skinny white guy in his twenties. Barry had only learned to hate Trump after he had made fun of a disabled reporter at a press conference, fluttering his arms around in imitation of his affliction. Shiva did the same thing—"flapping," it was called—whenever he tried to express some great unspoken pleasure. Any-one who could make fun of one of his son's few private joys didn't deserve to live.

The neighborhood continued its decline. The street he was walk-ing on was full of single-family Federal houses, a few glowing with health, but more peeling, and some boarded up with cardboard upon which things were written in incomprehensible Baltimorese. When he was a kid, Barry's father had given him a map of Queens with large chunks of it crossed off by red Magic Marker stripes—no-go zones where "those people" lived. The vast neighborhood of Jamaica was especially to be avoided, though Jamaica Estates, where

Trump himself once resided, was not. Barry had finally made it to Jamaica proper. He was on the brink of something big.

By a curb next to some Park Slope–grade town houses fitted with iron bars around every window, he found an attractive woman in her forties in charge of her own microbusiness, a bunch of Purell hand-sanitizer bottles repurposed to serve what a handwritten sign called PIMP JUICE. Barry was intrigued. The woman had colorful braids, a playful if tired smile, and patches of pink psoriasis running down the lengths of her arms and glowing at the elbows. Her breasts were high and round. "You from the group?" the woman asked him.

"Group?" he said.

"Never mind." She smiled brightly at him and leaned toward her wares.

"What are you selling there?" He felt a bump of need between his legs.

"Pimp juice," the woman said.

"And what's in that?"

"I guess mostly coconut flavor."

She pronounced the word "mostly" with great care.

"I'll take a large."

An icy, greenish liquid was poured into a paper cup. Even her psoriasis was beautiful, a part of who she was, so imperfect and real. "Doing much business today?" Barry asked, relishing the fact that his appearance did not intrigue this woman at all, nor the fact that he still had two large scratches across his face.

"It slow," the woman said. "Everyone inside 'cause the heat. Six dollars."

The pimp juice was delicious. Perfectly cubed chunks of ice left the imprint of coconut flavor on his tongue. He reached down to his pocket to fish out his phone and call Seema and shock her with his news of the world, but, of course, the phone was gone. He had to stop the old urges to reach out to his best friend. He had to prepare himself for Layla. She had been his best friend as well, for over three years. His best friend and his most passionate lover. Sure, they were younger then, but they used to have sex twice a day.

He walked a few more decrepit blocks. A bald young man was seated on a stoop, following him with his eyes. He was wearing what could have been a real Audemars Piguet, a bigger, more golden version of the one Seema had bought him in Venice. "Afternoon," Barry said.

Moments later, he heard the scrunch of loafers behind him. He was being followed. Barry increased his speed. What if the young man wanted to own *two* watches? He looked nervously at his Patek 570 as it swung back and forth over the inner-city blacktop. It was too understated to attract the attention of most people. It was a Veblen scarce good. You had to have a certain net worth to even understand what it was.

The man was now directly behind him. "Hey, ole head!" he said. "Wassup?"

Ole head? Barry was just lightly flecked with gray. He decided to turn around and see if he could make friends. He could picture the sequence of events like he was at a sales conference. Eye contact. Handshake. Unexpected connection over something trivial. "Hey, my man!" Barry said. "Wassup with *you?*"

"What you want?"

"Just enjoying my pimp juice," Barry said, lifting up his Dixie cup and holding it awkwardly in front of him. "I can't recommend it highly enough."

"You with the group?"

"Nope. Just me. What's this group?"

"You up?"

"Up for what?"

"You buying?"

"Oh, no thank you."

"Then why you up in my shit?"

"I'm sorry?"

"If you ain't buying rock, get the fuck off my block."

Or at least that's how it sounded to Barry. Still, *rock?* Crack co-caine? On the HBO show they were slinging what they called *heron.*

"Hate to break the news to you," Barry said, "but it's a free coun-try."

The young man walked up to him in three brisk steps. Their faces were now inches apart, and Barry could smell the heat off his face, as well as an underlying layer of baby powder. The man was breathing into him aggressively. He had prominent ears set behind his bald head, and a strong vein running across his forehead. His nose sloped to form the shape of an anchor; a narrow gap had wedged itself be-tween his two front teeth. "You think you the one with the high card," the man said, "but you not."

"I don't follow."

"I'm saying you best tip on out, faggot."

"Okay," Barry said, his voice now unwillingly experimenting with a different register. "I'll just keep walking. No harm, no foul."

"Nah," the man said, his thumbs hooking the front of his belt. "This *my* block. You ain't walking my block. You turn around same way you came."

"Wait a minute," Barry started to say, but the kid reached out and slapped the pimp juice out of his hand. It sounded like a weapon being discharged. The broken street filled with green liquid and ice.

And now they were in a different space. Now the kid was asserting himself *over* Barry. Humiliating him. He could feel it rising up inside him, the anger, the 2.4 billion under management, all the work he had done to become Barry Cohen, the way he had stood up once to his own moderately violent father and punched him clear in the lip maybe a week after his Bar Mitzvah. What would Hemingway do? He'd come out of this with some *real* scars, not just some tiny, fading Filipina-nanny scars. But what if Barry lost? What if the young man was armed? A gun tucked into the back of his belt? Did people still use knives on one another? He could feel his breath, its sweetness, some hint of cherry like those old bricks of Bazooka gum his father used to buy him when he was "good."

Barry looked down at his feet, which were now quickly taking him away from the young man, back in the direction from which he came.

"Yeah, you best *hop to*," the kid shouted behind him.

The asphalt crunched beneath Barry's feet. So *this* was America. A cruel place where a man could be thrown off the street because of the color of his skin, the cut of his watch. It was disgraceful. He didn't want any part of it. Maybe it wasn't too late to turn back. He could picture it all. His office, Seema's fine body, an endless stream of macchiatos and *uni* rolls. A Manhattan life for a Manhattan man. He could rejoin the winners' circle.

He thought of the young man's eyes. Their hue was the same as Shiva's. He didn't know what it meant, but he was somehow scared of the drug dealer in the same way he was scared of Shiva's meltdowns. Both promised violence. Both were a world run amok, lawless, chaotic, not fit for someone of Barry's stature and hard-won grace.

A large van with a sign reading THE WIRE/DER ANFANG scotch-taped to the side had pulled up to the pimp-juice lady's stand and she was now surrounded by tall, mostly blond tourists with wide-angle cameras, all of them wearing black T-shirts that read, "YOU COME AT THE KING, YOU BEST NOT MISS"—OMAR LITTLE.

So this was "the group" everyone was talking about. Some of the men looked at Barry's pale countenance with unconcealed anger, as if he was disturbing their inner-city safari. An older black gentleman in sunglasses was leaning against the van, thoughtfully cleaning his mouth with a toothpick, while listening to a game on an ancient pocket radio. GROUP LEADER, his T-shirt read.

The juice lady was both making her product and putting on a show. "Pimp juice! Pimp juice! Come and *git* it. I bet this the shit Omar drink when he not robbin' dealers."

Eventually the Germans started wandering down the street with their green drinks, taking well-composed shots of urban decay, from a bleached tuft of grass to a crumpled cigarette pack littering the street. The juice lady wound down her act.

"Hey," Barry said to her, "I just had a run-in with this guy. He told me if I wasn't buying rock, I should get the fuck off his block."

The woman laughed. "Oh, that's just Javon," she said, carefully sorting her bills by denomination. The fact that she was laughing made Barry feel worse. Was the kid not dangerous?

"Javon?"

"Yeah, he's from round the block. He sell rock, but everybody they want one and one."

"What's one and one?"

"*Heron* and coke. He selling rock like it the nineties. Nobody know where that boy get his package. That's why he angry."

"So it's not me, it's him."

"Uh-huh. You pay him no mind. He just a kid. Hey, you drink that pimp juice real fast! You want another?"

Barry found himself walking back in Javon's direction, so lost in thought he nearly knocked down a German woman in denim shorts documenting a pothole. He had to solve this. If he got his ass kicked or worse, he was fine with it. If he got killed on the streets of West Baltimore, at least his obituary in the *Journal* wouldn't end with Valupro or GastroLux or the fucking SEC. He was Barry Cohen, a leader of men.

When Barry was a kid, he had been super smart. He could program his Commodore 64 to make a graphic of the USS *Enterprise* from *Star Trek* gliding from one side of the screen to the other. But he knew that if he wanted to get out of Little Neck, out of his father's tropical basement, he had to make friends. So each day, he'd stand in front of the mirror and practice ten opening lines that he could say to the other boys in homeroom, the boys who didn't know he existed or would make fun of the chlorine smell that seemed to attach itself to the Pool Man's Son.

Wow, what a rainy morning!

Did you go to the Lake Success mall over the weekend?

I fished off Kings Point with my dad, but we didn't catch anything.

And then Barry would try to think of at least ten responses the boys could give him. And then ten more responses for each of their responses. It was a bit like programming his Commodore. He could store about ten thousand combinations in his head.

Javon was back on his stoop. He was wearing a Ralph Lauren Polo shirt buttoned up at the neck just like the Guatemalan writer had worn his Brooks Brothers the other night, giving him a formal, almost clerical look. He was wearing it nonironically in the blasted heat of the afternoon. Barry's mind was buzzing with overtures. He stuck out his hand with a twenty-dollar bill.

"Oh, *hell*, no," Javon said.

"I want to buy some rock," Barry said. "But I want you to subtract the cost of the pimp juice you spilled. So you give me twenty-*six* dollars' worth of rock, and we're even."

Javon laughed. His laugh was actually bright and unexpected. Childish. *He's just a boy,* Barry thought. The realization made him ache inside. The street was empty, devoid of life, iron bars covered in flecking paint, and this kid with nothing to do, no customers, no friends, not even a home computer.

"I like your watch," Barry said. "Can I look at it?"

"No, you can*not*, faggot," the young man said. But his eyes were still smiling. He looked away down the street, shy suddenly.

The atmosphere was cooling around them. Barry pocketed his twenty. "Just that I know a lot about watches," he said. "They call people like me Watch Idiot Savants. 'WIS' for short."

Javon sighed. "Idiot be right," he said. He snorted, then locked eyes with Barry. Barry smiled, then shrugged in return. He held the kid's gaze until it became painful.

The kid took off his watch and gave it to Barry, the metal hot in his hand. "My best cuz got dropped. This his watch."

"Dropped?" Barry said.

"Dude from the Perkins Homes served him up one in the face. Some East Side shit."

Barry examined the watch. It was gold-*plated*, not gold, and already flaking at the lugs. Half of the blue tapisserie dial had turned radioactive orange. The last *u* in "Audemars Piguet" was missing, rendering the watchmaker's name as "Piget."

"Looks real to me," Barry said.

"Serious?" The young man's eyes were robust with hope and grief.

"It's a forty K watch," Barry said. "Congratulations."

"You a po-lice?"

"I'm a hedge fund."

"Say again?"

"I make bets."

"Roll bones up by Fayette?"

"Huh?"

"Dice game."

"Sort of," Barry said. He could never successfully explain what a hedge fund was, other than the betting part. "I'm sorry about your cousin. May I ask, was it drug related?"

"Drug related." Javon laughed. "Yeah. Might could be."

This is where Barry's friend moves dictated that he insert a few beats, establish a little quiet time between them. Men needed to know from one another that they could stop talking for a while and it would not prove awkward. Barry visored his eyes against the sun with his hand and looked east, trying to figure out how far they were from downtown and the harbor full of yachts. His guess was not that far.

"Hey," he said, "speaking of drug related, I heard people are more interested in one and one, not rock. I'm a businessman. I could help talk strategy. I run a multistrategy shop. My advice: You're young, you can take on more risk, go really big in your trades. Do rock *and* a little one and one. Now your competition's off-balance."

"No offense, but it don't look like you in the game."

"You'd be surprised," Barry said. "The government's always look-ing for ways to shut me down."

"You got heat on you?"

"I guess you could say that."

"Where you jail down?"

Barry thought it over. He pictured being in prison with Javon. They would have to hang out with their own race, like in that prison show Seema liked to watch, but they could be secret friends. Barry would send him signals across the prison yard. "Nowhere yet," he said.

"Then shut the fuck up." The kid chortled and Barry followed suit. A cloud passed and now the sun was bearing down hard on them, the flaked façades of the row houses aglow. Barry felt like he was in a painting. "Why the cops buggin' on you?" Javon asked.

"Business I'm in, I'm always looking for edge, same as you. Like what do I know that others don't." Barry sighed. "Sometimes you have to get close to the fire."

"I hear that."

"That's why I want to help you."

"You mean we start doin' for each other?"

"I guess?"

"I don't need no partners."

"You work alone?"

"Yeah," Javon said, "I don't need nobody on my shit all day. Like, 'What's the count? What's the count? What's the count?' I don't got a crew. No lookouts. Things slow now, but one day my name gonna ring out."

"You're an independent contractor."

"Uh-huh. Everything I make go into my pocket. You feel me?"

"I feel you," Barry said. He let that term course through him. *Feel.* In this usage, it meant to "understand," and despite the language barrier he understood Javon. Unlike the impenetrable Shiva, Javon was an undervalued stock. He was all upside at this point, a vibrant young man who wanted to be in business. And unlike Barry he didn't give a shit about his investors. He was running a family office. "Do you mind if I sit down next to you?" Barry asked.

Javon didn't say anything. Barry could almost hear the kid's mind turning, trying to find a reason to accept him, this white man from nowhere, this Watch Idiot Savant. Barry was running a different set of calculations in his mind. What could he say to make Javon understand him? What could he say to make Javon feel understood? All those childhood years spent in front of the mirror practicing his friend moves, and this was his biggest move yet.

Barry took a seat next to Javon, the stoop hot and gravelly beneath him. A summer breeze stirred up. A loose fire escape started clanging against a building. Barry imagined a photo of the two of them appearing in a foreign magazine, maybe *Der Spiegel*. *"Zwei Amerikaner,"* it would read. *Two Americans.* And that's all. Nothing about their race or class. He felt himself overcome with emotion. His father had been a racist, and Barry was the opposite of his father.

"When I was growin' up," Barry said, trying to adopt the local accent, "I didn't have my momma. She died in a car accident."

A window opened up with a bang across the street. An older woman popped out between two plants, her hair in curlers. "Javon!" she shouted. "Who you talking to?"

"No one."

The woman crossed her arms. "Don't look like no one."

"He all right."

Barry smiled at the compliment. He lived in a skyscraper where most people didn't even share floors. Here, your own mother could open a window and shout down to you.

"Hello, Mrs. Javon!" he yelled.

The woman rolled her eyes at him. "Get on up off that stoop!" she shouted to Javon. "Germans comin'! I can hear they cameras from up here!"

"I think you better bump," Javon said to Barry.

"What?"

"Germans comin'," Javon said. "They pay twenty you let them shoot a photo of you. I gotta work."

"If I come back tomorrow morning, can we talk more?" Barry asked.

"I don't think so."

"All right. Well. I got a whole bunch of watches I could show to you."

"Where you crib?"

"The Holiday Inn Express. Down by the Greyhound."

"I'll get at you when I'm at you."

There was a flash of skin near Barry's pocket, and a baggie was deposited inside. "Later, Idiot Savant," Javon said.

He got up and walked toward the tourists advancing up the block, the long lenses of their cameras pointed at him. "Yo, wassup?" Javon shouted to them, pretending as if he were pumping a shotgun in their direction. "Omar comin'! *Ich bin ein Drogendealer!* Woop woop!"

Two blocks away, Barry took out his gift, a sizable Saran-wrapped rock, as polished as Carrara marble, with the sharp yellow tinge of a newborn Parmesan. While his hedge-fund peers spent hundreds of thousands of dollars to wake up at four in the morning Uzbekistan time to bake sesame loaves with the best baker in Samarkand or have a one-on-one with a marine iguana on the Galápagos, Barry had been given a genuine piece of America three hundred miles south of Central Park West. And all he had to do was be kind.

HE PACED his small hotel room. Should he stay on in Baltimore one more night? His mind was on fire, the same way it had been at Louis Pasteur Middle School when he felt like someone was about to become his friend. That's how it started, first Joey Paramico, with the spiked leather bracelet and at least one aerosol can's worth of product in his hair, then Joey's cousin Ronnie, then the Irish twins from up the block. And now he could have a young black friend. More than a friend, really. Almost a student. No, a son.

He wanted to make Javon a force to be reckoned with. He wanted his name to "ring out." If Barry had had his father's support, he would have been a billionaire by now. He pictured the two of them working some kind of start-up. What if they launched a foundation? One that would help urban youth buy their first mechanical watch and learn to care for it? A device that recorded time, not to mention showed its scarcity, would add order and rigor to their lives, as it had added order and rigor to his. That was the problem, right? These kids' lives had no rigor. Sitting on a stoop on an empty street, trying to sell drugs that had gone out of style decades ago, no one to monitor them or set measurable goals. They didn't mean to be inherently irresponsible people, but that's what they were.

So many of his hedge-fund peers were obsessed by the scholastic records of black children, trying to shut down their public schools and turn them into charters. But Barry's Urban Watch Fund would be a better way to disrupt the system. It would turn children into stakeholders. Whatever that meant. Outfitting hundreds of children with real Rolex Oyster Perpetuals, their cheapest model, would be expensive but, as he had seen some guy say on one Baltimore billboard, "If there is no struggle, there is no progress." The kids would have to learn the histories of Hans Wilsdorf and Alfred Davis, Rolex's suave London-based founders. There would be trips to Baselworld, the industry's trade fair, and visits to the Patek Philippe Museum in Geneva. A crest would be drawn—a watch's movement surrounded by the words RIGOR and RESPONSIBILITY or however you said that in Latin. RIGORUS. RESPONSIBILITUS. And then when Barry's Urban Watch Fund scaled, he'd present Javon at the Salon International de la Haute Horlogerie, and he'd say, "I found this young man selling crack on the streets of West Baltimore, and now he's selling Breitlings at the Tourneau on Madison," and then Seema would have to take back all that shit about his lack of soul and imagination.

Barry sat down hard on his bed. He had to breathe. Sometimes excitement disoriented him. Should he go back to see Javon first thing in the morning with his watches in tow? No, first he would find Layla. He would find her in El Paso and present the story of Javon as a calling card, a way to show her that he had changed. Better yet, that Morgan and Goldman and This Side of Capital had not changed him. But this chapter wasn't over. He would be back for Javon. He realized now that he had forgotten to note the street on which Javon and the pimp-juice lady operated. No worries. He still had resources. He would hunt them down.

With the crack lodged in his pocket and his watches safely in the rollerboard, next to the passport made out in Bernard Conte's name, Barry took the elevator down to reception to check out. The man in the Orioles T-shirt was talking to a familiar-looking woman with a Pat Benatar shag and a sleek little blouse that may have been from one of those shops Seema loved downtown. This woman clearly wasn't from anywhere near here. Maybe *she'd* be impressed by his Amex black card for a change. As Barry approached, the Oriole was scrolling through a computer screen. "Cohen," the Oriole said to the woman. "Room three twelve."

The mention of his own name surprised Barry, as if he had just become famous. He looked closely at the coils of the woman's hair. The insistent jab of her finger in the Oriole's direction. The haughty posture that was somehow the opposite of Baltimore. Recognition came with a pinch of desire that immediately rearranged itself as panic. He turned and ran just as she shouted, "Wait! Barry! No!"

It was Sandy, his chief of staff.

But he was already out the door, running as fast as his middle age could carry him, the rollerboard swinging in his arm, a pulse of pain down his spine. But his breath was even and strong. He would survive this, he was the Queens All-County Swim Champ of 1989, and he was going to toast the rich wimps from Douglaston Manor and get into Princeton over and over and over again.

He ran across the highway separating the Holiday Inn from a gas station and convenience store called Royal Farms. Once inside, Barry peeked back through the automatic door, but Sandy was nowhere in sight.

Sandy. How the fuck did she know where he was staying? Well, that was easy. All his credit cards were tied into This Side of Capital. Every time he traveled on the Hound or checked in to a hotel, she would know where he was. He had to dump the cards. *My God!* He had to dump his black Amex. He needed cash. All this could have been avoided if he had just packed some cash. He had three cards, the Amex and some Visa and MC crap tied into airline-loyalty programs he never really used anymore. He stuck the cards into a cash machine one by one, but kept getting a message about a four-hundred-dollar daily cash-advance limit. *Fuck.* He got out his allotted twelve hundred dollars among the three cards, the bills fanning out like capitalist magic into his waiting hand, stuck them next to the crack rock in his pocket, then threw the cards into the trash can, the black Amex pinging against the metal rim.

· · ·

HE BOUGHT a twenty-dollar ticket, paying in cash, but he would not surrender his watches to be checked in to the hold of the bus. He hid in a stall in the bathroom where, to pass the time, he sprayed and wiped down the cases and dials of his watches with Veraet watch spray and an extra-soft pocket square he had brought with him. He lavished particular attention on the Universal Tri-Compax, a 1940s specimen that had never quite breathed right from the moment he picked it up at a Boston dealership, via two NetJets flights that cost ten times the value of the watch itself. At some point in his journey he would have to find a good watch hospital for this creaky fellow. He looked into its complicated face, the moon phase showing a perfect full moon over Baltimore tonight. Shiva, the lunar aficionado, surely wouldn't sleep tonight. "I'm sorry you have to go through this," he said to the watch.

The surrounding stalls were now filled with men at the peak of their exertions, making Barry's eyes tear. He put his watches away and went into the main hall. Richmond was boarding.

Barry snuck up to the bus, glancing in all directions for Sandy. A Greyhound man in a green vest insisted he put his watches in the luggage hold, and there was no time to argue. A giant tag with his name and destination was wrapped around the handle of the roller-board. Barry scrambled on board. Scanning the seats, he realized the bus was full. "Sir," he said to the old driver. "There are no seats left."

"Been doing this thirty years," the driver said, staring into the middle distance. "Never gets easier. No, sir." Then he sighed and threw some Chinese nationals still holding their starry red passports off the bus.

Just then, Barry spotted Sandy out the window, running between buses, her New York poise all shot, another Greyhound official shadowing her with a clipboard and an attitude. *Shit.* Even in these heightened circumstances, he was still miserably attracted to her slim, blunt form, the many times they had drinks together after work and he could all but *feel* the little hairs on her arms as he got all sloshed and slurred talking about the unfairness of his early life, the Pool Man's Son, and she would nod and press her cold hand on top of his, and it was all theoretically HR and Seema acceptable because Sandy didn't like men.

Barry scampered down the aisle to the toilet and locked himself in. Was this what the rest of his life would be? Hiding in bathrooms from Sandy? The bus's engine turned over, then started to whir. The bathroom stank of bleach, but it also stank of freedom. There wasn't even a sink, only a giant canister of Purell. Barry held on to the Purell as the bus rocked out of the station. He breathed with his mouth, but his throat was getting scorched from the bleach. Then he shut his mouth and breathed with his nose. He breathed like a man on a bus running for his life.

4 *JUST STROKE ME*

THEY HELD hands. There were so many places in New York to hold hands. Paris was for sticking your tongue in someone's mouth, but New York was for good old-fashioned Protestant hand-holding. Did she want to do more? Yes and no. Was he being respectful of the four carats on her finger? If so, good. Was he still in love with his wife? If so, bad.

They held hands at the hot-dog place. They held hands at his favorite bar on Canal. Clandestino was its name (how perfect), and its bartender was some kind of movie-handsome genius in a vest who made Manhattans out of alchemized gold. Luis used to live right above the bar and three hundred feet from the best Malaysian beef jerky in the city, but marriage had "forced" him to the Flatiron District. Another dig at his wife? Please, God, yes. They held hands while watching summer action blockbusters that he pretended to loathe. Here, in the darkness interrupted only by immoderate thermonuclear explosions, his hand formed a warm, heavy weight against the inside of her thigh. She moved her head in his direction, so that he could smell the fragrance of her hair. He breathed heavily, squeezed her hand. Oh, how wonderfully pathetic they were!

The day after Barry disappeared, she got a call from his general contractor upstate. They were putting in the Olympic-sized pool, but the size seemed to flout all local ordinances, and their neighbors hated the Kyoto-style pergola Barry had built, which robbed them of their views. "Talk to Barry," Seema said. The contractor said he had tried to reach him, but his phone kept going straight to voice mail. "Fuck the pool, then," Seema said. "Let it rot." She hung up. So Barry was going to ignore her calls. Or his phone was gone. Stolen? Taken at gunpoint? He didn't take his contractor's calls. That was worrisome. Being the Pool Man's Son, Barry had long dreamed of installing the largest noninstitutional pool in the Mid-Hudson Valley. What if he had—no, Barry couldn't and wouldn't do anything that drastic. Anger was his bag. Self-pity. Not depression.

A few days into their hand-holding relationship, they were looking at New Jersey across the Hudson, their bodies leaning in over the metal railing along the esplanade. It wasn't anywhere near high tide, but the water felt close upon them, dangerous. Neurotypical children shrieked adorably beneath a nearby water fountain. There was a hotel across in Jersey City bearing the giant letter *W*. On a sulky riverside stroller ride with Shiva a year ago, her son had made a concerted sound, the most articulate of his life, and pointed with great emphasis at the *W* across the river. For a kid with his profile to *point* to an object was considered a milestone.

Shiva seemed to like letters. He was a big fan of the Cookie Monster song "C Is for Cookie." It was part of a *Sesame Street* alphabet CD his speech therapist played, but whenever she let it segue into the next song, Elmo singing about his love of the letter *D,* Shiva let out a shriek and rammed his head into the nearest wall. They had to sit by the CD box and press the rewind button back to Cookie Monster's song again and again. And Shiva would smile with his mouth open as if he had just discovered the universe. But when Seema played the *W* song he cupped his ears, fell on the ground, and started to shake as if there was a rolling temblor beneath him. *Well,* she thought, *so much for the fucking letter* W. *Cross that one off the list.* He did seem to have a thing for *H,* and she was glad she hadn't dropped the *h* in his name and called him Siva, the Tamil way. Barry had said that having a Seema and a Siva in the house would confuse him. South Indians gave their kids long variations on the name Shiva, like

Sivaraman, Sivamurthy, or Sivarajan, but she did not want to push Barry's limits. "I'm not riding a freaking elephant," he had said prior to their wedding in Cleveland.

They were talking about how they met their spouses. Julianna and Luis met at one of his book signings at the PEN World Voices Festival. "The PEN festival!" Seema said. "That's kind of a big deal."

Luis vehemently shook his head no to indicate that yes, it was. "I guess I made a good podium impression on her," he said, "and then I seduced her with my intellect." He yawned slowly to show how he wasn't taking himself seriously.

"Was she wearing something really beautiful?" Seema asked, to her own surprise. She thought Julianna was very stylish, especially on a doctor's budget.

"I can't remember," Luis said. "All I know is we kissed that same night. At the Russian Samovar. I thought she was a big drunkie because of how much vodka she had, but she was just nervous."

"Okaaaaaay." The Indian comic actress voice; that goofy, girly, twelve-year-old voice. So he did *kiss* women.

"And how did you meet Barry?"

"Ugh." The whole thing had been a shitshow to celebrate 120 years of *Vogue*. Her friend Mina Kim had invited her and then forgot to show up. Seema didn't know anybody there, was kind of left to her own devices, and then she had to rebuke this Wall Street creep for looking at her tits. "Let me guess who that was," Luis said, squeezing her hand all the more, his eyes scanning her body at the mention of "tits."

But Seema had talked to Barry, falling into her charming standoffish-flirtatious mode. Maybe there was some of that midwestern politeness in her. Maybe, and she hated to admit it, there was something sultry about being pursued by an older rich guy. When she looked up at the sky on that roof terrace, she could almost see an airplane carrying a banner reading COSMOPOLITAN ELITES over them. Wasn't that what she was brought up for? She remembered how her mother, still a lustrous-haired beauty, but halfway into her first of several American bellies, would hover over her bed at all hours of the day and night (good luck finding the word "privacy" in Tamil), imparting all those ludicrous and painful life lessons. Freshman year in high school she had drawn Seema a chart of the social acceptability of her friends. Jews and WASPs fared at the very top, one had "money (increasing)," the other "social power (decreasing)." The Asians were separated into several tranches, with the Japanese—who had bought up so much of our country just the previous decade—leading the pack. Tamils hovered several blank spaces above Hispanics, who themselves rested on the shoulders of blacks. Her mother circled "Jews" several times and wrote "accessible," "liberal," "emotional," and "sober" next to it. Seema had called her mother nuts to her face, almost earning a rare slap, but no childhood lesson ever just disappears, especially when it's from a parent who has crossed an ocean.

She didn't tell that little tidbit to Luis, nor the fact that after the *Vogue* thing she went home and Googled Barry's net worth and found it comforting. A man that rich couldn't be stupid. Or, Seema thought now, was that the grand fallacy of twenty-first-century America? In any case she vowed to never let him forget that *Vogue* and Anna Wintour were, in some ways, the reason for their meeting. But he forgot anyway. "We met at a private Michael Bloomberg party," he'd say. "Bloomberg *loved* Seema. We were both checking her out."

THEY TOOK in the permanent collection at the new Whitney by the High Line. Luis had a lot to say about Edward Hopper, not all of it positive. It turned out that all realism was reactionary. No exceptions. She hadn't told him about her art history major at Michigan and decided to remain silent. When she Googled Luis, she found herself proud that he had a check mark on Twitter, though few followers, his pronouncements not gnomic enough for that medium.

Luis often sounded more like a professor than a writer. He adjuncted at Columbia, but they never offered him a full-time job, and he had no strategies for getting one. "I wouldn't even know which dicks to suck up there," he said, pointing in the direction of Morningside Heights. "It's all political." But he had ideas about everything. Like Palestine. And Monsanto. And *Orange Is the New Black*. (Who knew that show tacitly endorsed neoliberalism?) The *one* idea out of Barry for the last four years—other than the daily arias about horology—was his plan to launch a collection of billionaire trading cards for poor kids, with all the billionaires' financial stats, such as net worth, *Forbes* list ranking, and liquid and paper assets, on the back ("And federal charges pressed and pleaded down to measly fines," Seema had added), so that the "black kids could get inspired to do better at school." He kept saying, "Oprah would have her own card, too." His Miami billionaire friend seemed ready to throw down some funding—nobody loved poor black children more than white billionaires. At least Luis harbored no illusions about changing the world. He just wanted to write about it in his poorly selling books and tear it down for his nine hundred followers on Twitter.

SHE FOUND three hours during which Shiva was supposed to be comatose (good luck with that, Novie) and went to see her best friend, Mina Kim, in her apartment four L stops into Brooklyn. She hadn't left Manhattan in so long she felt pathetic. She was after all still in her twenties. She needed to reconnect with her pre-Shiva self. She needed to laugh.

Mina lived in an archetypical five-story walk-up, the kind Seema had given up for Barry, albeit hers had been in much poorer Crown Heights. The stench of the vestibule floored her. What was it? Just garbage, traces of a soiled human being, New York City. Goddamn it, how had she become this scummy rich person?

"What's up, wifey?" Mina said, grabbing her by the cheeks, then smacking her ass. Seema always felt better about being the child of immigrants when she hung out with Mina, her first-year roommate. The girl had no plans before, during, or after Michigan. She worked in graphic web design, which these days was simply a catchall category for anything not involving finance or escorting. Then again, her parents were so rich she didn't even have to grow up Asian.

Mina banged a six-pack of Lagunitas on the West Elm floor rug that served as her living room couch. They sat down cross-legged. "So, let's see pictures of the little muffin. I never get to see him, *damn you!*"

Seema had a whole photo gallery of Shiva not slamming his head into things which she sent out to family and friends. He was asleep in at least half of them. "Aww, he really looks like Barry, I hate to say," Mina said. "But whatevs. He's got your eyebrows. Cute." Seema hated her eyebrows. She had spent one-third of her life keeping them in check. In any case, the topic of children was now closed. They spent four beers talking about Mina's sex life. It was intense. Women receiving oral sex on a first date was now this big thing. "Guys are so locavore," Mina said. "Didn't you say Barry used to just live in your pussy?"

She couldn't believe how much she had shared with Mina. What if their mothers could hear them talking like this? Mina couldn't give a fuck about her Korean heritage, which made Seema feel better about her own lack of Tamil knowledge. She had once dragged Barry to Bombay, where most of her non-NRI relatives, handsome Uncle Nag included, lived. They mostly ate flaccid foreigner food at the Taj where they were staying, but Barry still managed to get the runs. And the way he recoiled from those little hands reaching into the carriage of their Ambassador asking for rupees, hands that might one day look like those of their own children, well, she had been embarrassed for the both of them. "Kind of how I imagined a really low-income third-world country," he had said in the Air India lounge on the way home. "*Developing* world," she corrected him.

"So listen," she said to Mina, "things with Barry are not so hot right now."

"Yes!" Mina said. "Woo-hoo!" Mina, of course, had always thought Barry was a tool, even though she had "borrowed" five hundred bucks from Seema here and there to meet her rent payments whenever her folks temporarily disowned her, which meant, in effect, borrowing from Barry.

"There's this guy," Seema said.

"Hell, yeah!" Mina tucked her legs under her and shrieked in delight. So this is what it would be like to still be a twenty-nine-year-old without a special-needs child.

"You would actually like him," Seema said. "He's a writer. Very formal. He only holds hands with me. Nothing more."

"Was he airlifted out of the nineteenth century?" Mina asked. "Steampunk is kind of dead, ya know."

Seema remembered a short story about adultery she had read in a Russian lit class back at Michigan. She couldn't recall the name of it. It didn't end well, obviously.

The beer started talking for her. It said: "I don't know, Mina. I don't know. I'm feeling something strong, something real. No, I wouldn't use the term 'love.' I wouldn't. I'm just so lost. There's so much I can't tell people."

"You can tell *me*," Mina said, offended.

"I *am* telling you. Are you listening?" Seema started to cry.

Mina's rail-thin arms were around her. "You look so beautiful when you cry," Mina said.

"Maybe I should cry for Luis," Seema said. "Maybe then he'll kiss me."

This was starting to sound like grade school. "Fuck you, girl," Mina said. "You've been married to that douchebag too long. Him kiss *you*? You have to kiss *him*." And for the next three hours on the crappy West Elm rug they strategized on how to make that happen. Seema cried some more, but she was also unbelievably happy. At least one of her secrets was out. At least she was being listened to and held in someone's arms.

IT HAPPENED on a day when lightning broke out all over the city followed by peals of super-loud thunder, scaring the shit out of Shiva *and* Novie, who thought that Jesus's Dad had finally had enough of the sinful city. They were in a cab on their way to see the play *Hamilton*, for which Luis had somehow snagged two-thousand-dollar front-row tickets. He was preparing himself for how much he was going to hate the play. He had seen an interview with its creator and was now full of anger. Seema agreed with him, although a part of her, no, most of her, wanted to be emotionally moved, to replace her fears of Trump with the love of country that Hamilton so implicitly promised.

They were stuck in traffic around the elevated road that bracketed Grand Central and the Met Life Tower, when her phone rang with an unfamiliar 917 number.

"Ms. Cohen, I'm really sorry to bother you." The voice was ingratiating and acidic: Barry's chief of staff, Sandy. Barry clearly sweated the deranged young woman, but she was a committed lesbian, a fact which had always calmed Seema. She listened to snatches of Sandy's monologue as her hand found Luis's. "Haven't seen him . . . An important meeting . . . Qatar Investment Authority . . . Baltimore . . . Greyhound . . . Redemptions coming in . . . Richmond, Virginia . . ."

Seema stopped her. "What's in Richmond?" she asked.

"I don't know, Ms. Cohen. But he asked me to buy a Greyhound ticket there."

"Don't fucking call me Ms. Cohen." There was a pause. The chief of staff was recalibrating, like a computer rebooting after a fatal error. "Sorry," Seema said. "Barry's first girlfriend in college was from Richmond. Layla." She couldn't think of the last name, but she and Barry had once laughed over its Waspishness. "Hayes. Layla Hayes. They lived in the bad part of town." Luis raised an eyebrow. "Although I think that's most of Richmond." She was not the person saying that. No, she wasn't.

"That's enough for me to start on," Sandy said. "I'll call you the moment I find something."

"Don't bother," Seema said, disconnecting. She looked out of the window. The rain was brutal, the light weak, one art deco skyscraper was weeping on the shoulder of another. *So.* Maybe Barry hadn't just run off into the night. Maybe he was—what? Marching across the country in search of Layla Hayes? *On a Greyhound?* Nice. Probably some fat southern housewife with three buttermilk children by her side. She would most certainly *not* try to look her up on Facebook. That would require her to still love Barry. And here she was, in this cab with another man.

She let go of Luis's hand. He looked at her, surprised. He tried to read her eyes. Failed. She put both of her hands on his cheeks and leaned in. How wonderful his lips tasted, how surprising his dry tongue, how sad his immediate expression, how happy just a second later when he realized what had happened. He started stuttering cutely. Julianna was in São Paulo for a quickie medical conference, and Arturo and his nanny were spending the night with friends in the Hamptons. They turned the cab right around.

His bedroom. Okay, *their* bedroom. Fortunately, no photos of Luis and Julianna together, just lots of framed snaps of Arturo being Arturo, performing in a nursery-school play in a pirate's outfit or dressed like Abraham Lincoln. What goddamn nursery school put on Presidents' Day plays for three-year-olds? Her face hurt from all the scrub-bearded kisses. His shirt was wet from the rain. "Seema," he said. "Please."

"Please, what?" she whispered.

Mina had been right about this one. He wanted to go down on her. Begged to go down on her. "Let me take a shower first, honey," she whispered. That "honey" surprised them both. But he was very aggressive about eating her out right that minute, and just the feel of her jeans and panties sliding down around her legs made everything glow at the edges of her vision, and she saw this imaginary mirror on the ceiling, which showed these two beautiful people who loved each other.

It lasted for five minutes or it lasted for an hour. It kept going and going, her legs bracketing his head and then doing these strange aerobic moves she had never done before, pumping and cycling in the air. The storm raged outside. Peals of fresh thunder broke out. She knew that seventeen floors above her, her son was afraid. But she couldn't move.

"Just stroke me," he said, when she had finished whispering his name. "I don't want you to blow me. This isn't quid pro quo." She sighed. Men didn't know what they wanted anymore. It was sad for them. Ten minutes later she was blowing him. She cringed when she felt the acid in the back of her throat, it did not taste good (when did it ever?), but she kept him inside her mouth until the last spasms subsided. When she ran into the bathroom to spit it all out, she saw herself in the mirror, her lips wet, a triangle of want at her neck. She smiled at her reflection. She was perfect. She would never be this perfect again. She locked the bathroom door, sat on the toilet, and put her hand in between her legs. She ignored his calls for her immediate return.

Finally back in bed, she slipped on her panties and bra. He crept over and cupped the fullness of her ass. "Honey," she said, "we can't do this anymore." She just wanted to say that. She just wanted to say the most painful thing in the world and see if it would break his heart. He let go of her ass, fell back on the sheets, and covered both his eyes with his hands. Was he crying? No. He was still erect.

"My son," Seema said. She was about to say more. But she didn't. "Hold me," she said instead. He did as he was told. "Wait," she said. "Put on your underwear."

They went into the living room, she in bra and panties, he in his Jockeys, and sat there on the couch, watching the rain curtain Madison Square Park. After a while, he turned on MSNBC. Trump was howling about how people were doing him wrong. He looked hurt and delighted at the same time. She buried her head in the safety of Luis's slightly gray chest hair.

The world was magnificent.

ARRY SAT on the stoop of Layla's parents' house. It had been a long ride. They had passed the National Security Agency in Maryland, then stuttered through DC's egregious, socialist traffic, which finally let out to Virginia proper, a series of low Confederate fields bracketing the highway. They passed a particularly fragrant southern skunk and entered the town of his first love.

Lightning lit up the sky. Was it pouring and thundering up in New York too? Shiva would be scared. Seema should give him one of his watches to hold for comfort. Though not one of the terribly expensive ones. The Max Bill, for example, which was accessible Bauhaus.

The last time he had seen Layla's parents was right after senior year. Layla's sister Celia, all of twenty, had gotten married to some boy just out of Davidson. He was from a rich local family, and she was dropping out on a partial scholarship at William & Mary. Both those things had driven the Hayeses nuts. They had wanted to see Barry and Layla married instead. But despite their misgivings about the rich boy and Celia giving up on her education, the wedding of their younger daughter was glorious. The Hayeses were still so *young,* him with his flamboyant ponytail, her with her horsey laugh, cutting it up on the dance floor to "You Can Call Me Al." The reception was at the Jefferson Hotel, which on a weekend had the feel of an eternal Dixie high-school prom. The groom's family was strait-laced and Jesus fearing, but everywhere you turned there were the Hayeses' people, VCU professors on their ninth bourbon screaming about Chaucer and Bill Clinton and "Don't Ask, Don't Tell," a woman with a Snoopy tattoo on the underside of her arm talking to some bearded rock guy. Actual black people.

Barry got drunk and then fought with Layla over nothing at all for most of the night, until her father took him into the white mar-ble tomb of the bathroom and told him, "Son, you ought to calm down. This isn't the night for it." Barry remembered that first sen-tence with shame. The "son" and the "ought to," both so uncharac-teristic, and that ponytail slapping against the dark blue suit of his almost father-in-law, the men behind them plastering the urinals with bourbon steam. What a fool he had been to lose her. To lose them.

A dog was barking inside the otherwise-empty house. Remember-ing the Hayeses' ancestral preference for dachshunds, Barry knew that's what it had to be, that absurdist long woof, the sound of a sausage trying to assert itself in the world. The dachshund in charge of the household during their college years had been called Jeff Dave, because he had been as savage as Jefferson Davis. But Jeff Dave warmed immediately to Barry, who had grown up in love with dogs. Barry's father, a Bronx transplant to the quasi-suburban reaches of Queens, had always wanted a large canine with which to fill the backyard of their semidetached house on Little Neck Park-way. He kept a kindly half-blind sheepdog for a few years, until she died from the melancholy of being a working-class Jewish pet. Jeff Dave treated Barry like the owner he never had, his head bent sub-missively beneath his fingers, eyes crossed with the pleasure of being petted. "See, Dad, Barry's a real country boy at heart," Layla would say, the southern twang she had kept repressed at Princeton coming on full tilt.

Her parents both taught sociology at Virginia Commonwealth. Being liberal professors who didn't hunt prey for dinner made them half southern at best, but Barry's blue-collar background was always welcome. "She's from Virginia, and your daddy actually works for a living," Layla's mom would say, "unlike some of those other Princeton brats. So you both got to look out for each other up there." "Gotta look out for each other up *thur* in Yankee-land," Layla drawled. The whole family would laugh. Sometimes it felt like it was culturally more difficult for Layla up in Princeton than it was for Barry.

The two of them were in the same senior-year creative writing class, taught by a pretty famous gay writer in his fifties, his rotor-blade honesty an object of adoration and fear among all budding Princeton writers. The final story Barry had submitted was, he thought, the best one he had ever written. In fact, he had to hide under a blanket as he was writing it, or else Layla would see him cry, that's how moved he had been by his own work. The story, which he read aloud in the last class, was about a forty-something partner at Goldman Sachs who is driving through Vermont in his S500. He's the kind of banker who's completely misunderstood by others, because he alone sees no contradiction in the need for both a vocation and an avocation. The vocation is banking, which may seem abstract but actually uses a lot of his imagination. The avocation is writing, which helps him connect to his younger self. Banking keeps him alive, but writing reminds him to love. And there's the only problem in the banker's life: he hasn't loved anyone since college, since he broke up with his girlfriend Sheila (pronounced like "Layla").

This changes during the course of the drive in Vermont when the S500 overheats and the banker walks out into a kind of "prelapsarian paradise." There's a hill covered by sheep followed by another followed by another, forming "a city of sheep." The banker scrambles under the wire fence and, as if in a trance, walks through the ranks of sheep, who part before him amiably. He confronts a sheepdog named Luna (the name of Barry's dead pet), who nearly chews his leg off, but finally succumbs to the dog-whispering advances of this gentle banking creature. And then he sees a woman by a stream. She looks as if she's painted into the landscape like some Flemish peasant, but as the banker and Luna approach, she is revealed to be

Sheila, his college ex. As much as he immediately knows who she is, she can't, for the life of her, recall his face or name. "But who are you?" she keeps asking. "Why have you come here?" Her life is so simple and beautiful that merely the intrusion of this man with both a vocation *and* an avocation, with his overheated Mercedes by the side of the road, throws her into confusion. Eventually, she begs him to sit down and be still. She takes off his Kiton Carracci cashmere/ vicuña sports coat and washes his hands and feet (Barry had just taken his first religion seminar). "I wish none of my life had ever happened," the banker says. "But it's too late."

"Yes," the Flemish shepherdess says. "It is too late."

You weren't allowed to clap for other people's stories, but Barry had, of course, secretly wished that the rule would be broken that one time, that the students, four of them men and hence his rivals, and three of them women, including Layla, would just give it the fuck up for him. *You touched me,* Layla would say, afterward. *Don't I always,* he'd kid. *This is different. This is a whole new level. You know yourself so well. You know me so well. I just wish you hadn't shared it with others right away. I just wish you'd shown me first.* Even the prof would ignore his imposed order of chastity and give him a serious Tiger hug after class. "Let's have port at my house," he'd say. "We've got a brideshead to revisit."

But no one clapped. The other three men in the class read their stories. It was male night, as it frequently is behind FitzRandolph Gate. The three boys, one of them a fellow diner at the Tiger Inn and also an erudite swimmer, read pretty much the same story for their final submission. Their heroes were all complicated bankers in the first throes of middle age, stumbling upon a lost girlfriend, re-considering their lives, wishing they had held on to their college loves. There were differences to be sure. At least one guy had plumped out for a vintage Porsche 356B instead of Barry's S500, the same scribe who had gone full Fitzgerald and actually put in a dock at the end of his story. (The action took place in Japan, and his banker worked at Nomura Securities. His shepherdess was an oyster diver.)

"So," said the professor after the last sensitive syllable had been rendered into the Ivied air. He was wearing a leather vest and his face was covered with rakish stubble. "What do we think about these stories?" He turned to the women in the class, including Layla. The women were silent. The professor was mercurial. This could go either way. But Layla's normally engaged face was blank, her gaze directed somewhere above Barry's head. "So," the professor repeated, "the narrators of the stories we've heard today want us to believe one thing: That their lives were never about money. That their faults lay in neglecting their tender young selves. Ignoring the brief fires of whatever counterculture they experienced between their lovers' imperfectly shaved legs. But the truth is this. Money defines their lives. It's the only scorecard they have by which to measure themselves against other moneymakers. And the melancholy they experience is a precious good, one that they can also afford along with their vehicles and Kiton suits, their Vermont shepherdesses and Nipponese oyster divers. Even the volatility of their emotions is a financialized asset which can be traded between them at will."

One of the women who took notes on everything the professor said had to know: "So does that make the stories *good*?" She positioned her pen for the answer.

"In a sense," the professor said. "The best fiction is the fiction of self-delusion. It contrasts the banality of our self-made fictions against the hopelessness of the world as it really is. The worst thing that we can tell you at a place like Princeton is that you can have it all." He scanned the small group around him and brushed the leathery buttons holding his vest tightly over his large body. "Well," he said. "You can't."

Barry couldn't help himself. "But which story was the best?"

The professor shrugged. "I don't know, Barry," he said. "Let's say yours." Then he sprang up, rather athletically for a man of his size, and walked out of the room. The semester had come to an end. Barry smiled at Layla, but she did not smile back.

They fought through the remains of that day and most of the night. They fought essentially for the next twenty-six postcollege weeks. "You just don't want me to do IB," he had said. "*IB*, you can't even say the words," she said. "In-vest-ment bank-ing." "And then what else should I do?" he said. "Everyone I know is doing it. You want to starve together? I don't come from money." "And I do?" "We can't break up. I've told you things I've never told anyone."

She was the first person he had told about his mother's death. Five-year-old Barry had been in the backseat of the Corolla coming back from the Douglaston Mall, where his mom had bought him a rare toy at the Toys"R"Us, a Han Solo action figure with a little gray detachable pistol (*Star Wars* had come out that year), when it smashed at full speed into a BMW that had drunkenly sailed across the median on its way into the city. Sometimes he could see his mother's forehead, the steering wheel's bloody indentation, black blood pooling over her face. Who knew how black blood could be. Sometimes he thought he remembered himself screaming for her help, trying to get out of the booster seat as the car lay crumpled by the side of the road, its cheap engine still turning, headlights pouring out over the Queens-Nassau border. Throughout the entirety of his childhood, his father never mentioned the accident, and if someone else did, he'd lift up one chlorine-bleached hand and say, the Bronx hard in his voice, "Enough."

Mommy, help me.

Mommy, help me.

But she was the one who needed his help.

That same night he had told Layla about his mother's death, he asked if they could try anal sex. She didn't want to. This was before the Internet. But they had both read the professor's books in anticipation of getting into his class senior year, and something about the ready combination of pain and intimacy excited Barry. He couldn't control his erection while reading the prof's first coming-of-age novel, especially the stuff about the notorious baths where faceless men just let you plunge into them. He wanted to do that to Layla. After telling her about his mother's death, he wanted to be close to her, and to hurt her. "I'm so sorry," he said afterward as she lay next to him, clenching and unclenching herself in pain. "In the book—"

"Shhh," she said. "We're in this together." He went to wash himself off, and when he returned she was still staring up at the ceiling, her hand on her side.

A VOLVO pulled up. Was it them? He had been meditating on the yellow-hued church across the street, across from the Hayeses' row of 1899 salmon and ocher Italianates, their porches united by rows of columns and ironwork. A large old bus was parked outside. SHARON BAPTIST CHURCH, REV. PAUL A. COLES, PASTOR, it read on one side. Jackson Ward had once been known as the Black Wall Street. The Hayeses had moved here in the eighties, at which point they had probably been the only white people in the neighborhood. Barry shook himself out of his reverie. As the Hayeses opened the doors of their twenty-year-old sedan, he slipped off his wedding ring and dropped it into the baggie with Javon's crack rock for safekeeping.

The Hayeses looked at the middle-aged man sitting on their stoop, hunched and tired looking in his Citi vest. A bank clerk who just got off work? "May we help you?" Mrs. Hayes asked. The "may" part of it. And the "we." Always together. The Hayeses smiled at their interloper.

He rose and straightened out his sweaty Vineyard Vines shirt. "Mr. Hayes, Mrs. Hayes," he said. He had never referred to them by their Christian names. Had forgotten what they were.

The husband recognized him first. They approached gingerly, perhaps confused by the fact that now all of them had grown into adults.

"Barry," the wife said, a sad statement of fact, as if they had expected him to turn up all along. She hugged him, then stood up on her tippy-toes and kissed him on the cheek, as was the custom. They were both in denims and T-shirts. His T-shirt was plastered with a cover of the *B.B. King Live in Cook County Jail* album, a favorite even back during the Barry years. Hers read THE NOTORIOUS RBG. Barry didn't know what that meant, but below the headline there was a

face of a familiar-looking old lady in thick glasses. He shook hands
with the man once slated to be his father-in-law. Unlike their five-
foot-ten daughter, the Hayeses were short people, but, much like
their collection of dachshunds, they themselves did not know it. Oh,
how her mother resembled Layla. The dimpled chin and the snub
nose and the crinkled eyes. "Hi," Barry squeaked, the present col-
lapsing before the past.

They warned him about Randy, the new doxie's name, but once
inside the house Barry immediately grabbed the furry hot dog and
slung him over his shoulder. "Now you must have known Jeff Dave
in your time," Mrs. Hayes said. "Randy's much kinder, because he's
a long-hair. He's got some spaniel in him." Randy buried his chocolate snout in Barry's cheek as he locked eyes with him, as if worried
that Barry would disappear as quickly as he had come. Barry found
a sweet spot in the white-gray tuft of hair beneath Randy's collar and
massaged it. Lacking a human face, the dachshund nonetheless
smiled.

"Well," Mr. Hayes said, "you still got it with them weenie dogs."

The house was brilliantly proportioned. There was a modest but
wide sitting room flowing into a living room of almost equal size,
bracketed by an unreformed kitchen without so much as a center
island, each room with a granite fireplace but lacking in the ostenta-
tion of new construction. The bookshelves were lined with Joan
Didion and Flannery O'Connor, a small, unexpected collection of
musicalia, essay collections on Leonard Cohen and Neil Young.
There was a framed poster of an exhibit of romantic landscape paintings in Dresden. Intellectuals had their own thing going, that was
for sure. If only Barry's Rhinebeck house could look so effortlessly
fussy, especially his Hudson River View Library. Layla's grandmother's plain, jowly face stared down on all of them from above the
mantelpiece. As a first-year at a boarding school up near Roanoke,
she had had to lie about being born on February 12, a birthday she
shared with the hated Abraham Lincoln.

"So I came on a Greyhound bus!" Barry announced. "I felt like I
needed to see the country as it really is."

"While it's still here," Mr. Hayes said. Barry assumed this was a reference to the election. Also, a pair of black motorists had just been shot by cops in Minnesota and Louisiana, and five policemen had been killed in Dallas. Barry hated gun violence, but felt it was a cost priced into living in America. There was a chance—a small but not-insignificant chance, a "three-sigma event," as the quants in the office would say—that if you lived in our country, someone would shoot you or your family. Japan had earthquakes, Australia brush fires. America had guns and people willing to use them on one another.

Randy was now burrowing into Barry's neck. "Well, if you've been traveling by bus, you must be aching for a shower, you poor thing," Mrs. Hayes said. "Would you mind staying in Layla's old room?"

He wouldn't mind in the least. He was nineteen again, being loved by two parents of the kind he never had beyond the age of five. A complete family. Ogre-free. Even their choice of dachshund had improved with age. All that was missing was their sweet daughter.

They had kept Layla's room just as it had been, almost as a memorial, as if she had never survived college. All those posters of the stuff they used to listen to, Aphex Twin, Lead Belly, Sonic Youth, Pavement. All those CDs they bought with their summer-job money down at Plan 9 Records in Carytown still stacked on a night table. Posters of the bluegrass festival they had gone to in Boone, North Carolina, Amnesty International, Smash Racism, Mandela. She had kept her childhood Rainbow Brite sheets through college, because she didn't want to be wasteful with new ones, and now Barry couldn't help himself, he bent down and sniffed them, but there was nothing of her, just the damp of an unused bed in an old house. He peeked into her younger sister Celia's room. It had been converted into an office crammed with sociology texts, the discipline both Hayeses taught, VCU mugs scattered about, and several of Layla's line drawings from high school. Layla was the beloved daughter and Celia the merely loved one. If their parents had one clear fault, it was favoritism.

He showered in a bathroom that also felt like it was 1992, a piece of Ivory soap stuck to the sink from disuse. Rivulets of Greyhound rolled off of him. He needed to buy a razor, but having stubble made him feel good, too. He wanted to look nice for Layla's parents, but the best he could come up with was his hated Citi vest.

"I hope this thing doesn't offend you," Barry said, when he had clambered down the stairs, pointing at the Citi logo.

"You work for Citibank now?" Mrs. Hayes asked. "I remember Layla said you got a job at J.P. Morgan." Her memory was unerring.

"I do customer service," Barry said. It pained him that they didn't get his joke.

They walked to a restaurant in the perfect humidity, the Hayeses in front of him, Barry following like a child twice their height. Mr. Hayes had put on an inexpensive blazer for the evening, and Mrs. Hayes's T-shirt was now draped by a string of store-bought baby pearls. All of this was terribly new for Barry. The college radicals had settled down a bit. They were dressing up for dinner.

Jackson Ward had gotten a little bit fancy, too, like one of those formerly "urban" parts of Brooklyn he had heard about but never got around to visiting. So many of the once-boarded-up buildings had been renovated. There were now Korean barbecue restaurants and French coffee places and elderly black couples dressed as if for Sunday services (what day was it anyway?) strolling along arm in arm. One church was being converted into a condominium named the Sanctuary, while another promised its parishioners "THE YEAR OF ORDER" ISAIAH 38:1. Living in Jackson Ward had been an act of rebellion back in the day, but now it had turned into a wise investment decision. Folks had draped strange flags over their iron porticoes with drawings of pineapples and the word WELCOME. The South was like that, festive but impenetrable. Still, the streets could have used more people, and he could feel a quiet desolation emanating from the Gilpin Court projects north of the highway, a feeling that the new parts of the neighborhood were just grafted onto the violence of the past.

Barry remembered how scared he would be to walk down the

street with Layla back in the nineties, when the place was still years away from Korean BBQ and slow drip. They'd spend hours drinking whiskey sours at Babes, the lesbian place down in Carytown, which was still a big deal for Richmond back then. When they got back, they would park in an alleyway behind the Hayeses' house and all but scramble inside, Barry making sure the path was clear, the ADT alarm flashing its promise of safety, the two of them tiptoeing up the stairs to have a last kiss and fondle without waking up her parents, before Barry self-exiled himself to Celia's empty room. Celia was widely considered the more beautiful daughter, but Barry praised himself for not finding her attractive. "I'm in love with your intellect," he'd say to Layla, only to be met with her patented cold stare. The wide floorboards creaked just the way they should in a century-old house, making each move all the more illicit. The Hayeses knew their daughter wasn't chaste, but despite their liberalism there were laws built into the soil of this part of the country, some of them ugly, but others that made Barry wistful for something warmer than his own life back in eastern Queens. When he thought of his patrimony, all he heard was the incessant rumble of his father's house, a complaint du jour here, a Yiddish-laced insult there, mixed in with the solipsistic mourning of his dead wife and the demand that as soon as Barry graduated from college he get a job at a "lore office."

The noisy restaurant the Hayeses had chosen looked like it had been tractor-trailered in from the part of Brooklyn where Seema's funny Asian friend (Tina?) lived. There were gilded Victorian mirrors, drawings of horses, and a giant, pointless map of Latin America. Bearded bartenders were slinging tiki drinks, and the young clientele was in full possession of their looks. They were—and it was hard to miss this after eight hours on the Greyhound—white. Every single one of them. The prices were white, too. A bit of cornbread with a pat of foie gras butter was five dollars, a hanger steak twenty-seven, a gin fizz twelve.

"Customer service for Citibank sounds like an interesting job," Mrs. Hayes said. "You must get all kinds." They had ordered a bottle of Chardonnay and three hanger steaks, although Barry felt he deserved two martinis to start. He tore through the both of them in no time, his voice getting louder and friendlier.

"I was kidding about that!" he said. "I run a hedge fund. It has an AUM of two-point-four billion. Down from three-point-nine, but still."

"That sounds very impressive, Barry," Mrs. Hayes said. Her accent was so graceful. Barry would pay good money to hear her say the word "time" (*"tahm"*) or something really regional. *Looks like the devil is beating his wife with a frying pan.* That meant it was raining and sunny at the same time. Or *It won't rain if there's enough blue sky to make a sailor suit.*

"Very impressive," her husband echoed. "So you're a billionaire."

"I wish!" Barry said. "It just means I have two-point-four billion of assets under management."

"Well, that's *still* very nice," Mrs. Hayes said. "As I recall, you were very determined to work in business."

"Finance," her husband corrected her. The fact that his career choice had been more or less responsible for his break with their daughter wasn't mentioned.

"I hear Layla's in El Paso," Barry said.

"Oh, we didn't know you two were in touch," Mrs. Hayes said. Barry tried to catch a hint of hope in her voice.

He couldn't very well confess that he had been Facebook snooping. "Some mutual pals told me," he said. "How's she doing? I was actually hoping to get out to El Paso myself."

The Hayeses looked at each other. "She's good," Mr. Hayes said. "Loves her job. And of course our grandson is just gorgeous. Wish she could bring him around some more."

Barry stopped breathing. His head turtled back into his shoulders. She had a kid. This whole trip. All he had been through. The Greyhound. She had a husband. Some middle-class doofus. A Texan life. The hanger steak was placed in front of him, but he couldn't look at it. He poured himself a massive glass of wine, watched it flow over the rim. The universe wanted him to be alone. "Easy, son," Mr. Hayes said. "Son." That's the word he had used with him the night of Celia's wedding. The more the Hayeses drank, the more proper they became, and the more out-of-control Barry seemed by comparison. What had happened to the Mr. Hayes he had actually gotten stoned with once, senior year? Just the two of them down in the basement, the women of the house running errands, as Mr. Hayes and his ponytail blasted his favorite 1930s Creole and cowboy tracks from the Works Progress Administration.

"I'm just glad she's happy," Barry said.

"Well, the divorce was no picnic," Mrs. Hayes said.

Barry returned to breathing. Divorce. That glorious word. So she was a single mother now. Could he work with that? He probably could. Learn to love her child and save her from a life of female sadness. But why didn't her sparse Facebook posts show her kid hugging llamas or scampering over floats at ethnic festivals? Wasn't that the whole point of Facebook, to demonstrate to your classmates that you were more than okay in the world?

"How about you, Barry?" said Mr. Hayes, taking a minuscule sip of wine. "Any family?"

"I'm getting divorced," Barry said. There. He had said it. Even if drunkenly. So maybe it was true. It was over. Was there any grander way to say *"I divorce thee"* than getting on a Greyhound bound for El Paso? "No children," he added.

The Facebook photos of present-day Layla had shown something remarkable, a forty-three-year-old woman who looked barely in her third decade, facing the sunset in a peasant blouse and jeans, just a hint of local turquoise around her youthful neck. Mrs. Hayes looked decades behind her God-given years, too. The whole family was investment-grade.

The Hayeses made reassuring noises about Barry's divorce and childlessness, her mother's hand stroking his, the smell of Ivory soap mingling with that of the three pieces of charred meat on the table. "Another bottle," Barry said to a passing Virginia hipster. Mrs. Hayes reflexively put her hand on her glass. Mr. Hayes made a "just a pinch" motion. "May I tell you something?" Barry said. "Back in college, Layla and I were actually thinking of getting married!" The

Hayeses looked down at the table. Was he being too loud? "Just like you guys wanted us to!"

"That was a long time ago," Mrs. Hayes said. "Maybe it's best—"

"I remember, Mr. Hayes, you told me this story, about how you skipped some important academic conference to spend a day with Layla. She was all of seven. And you asked her what she wanted to do all day. And she said, 'I want to read with Daddy!' Do you remember that? And you just spent the whole day reading together. Well, I never had a father like that!" Barry stopped for a big swig of wine.

"It's awfully kind of you to say that, Barry," Mr. Hayes said. "Awfully kind of you to remember."

"Layla said I had to ask you for her hand in marriage," Barry said to him. "She said it was the custom. She called it retrograde or reactionary or something, but she still wanted me to do it. And I suggested that I propose to the both of you. Well, she *loved* it. Sort of tradition plus feminism. She was so happy that I would ask you both."

The Hayeses did not say anything. The noise in the restaurant was becoming deafening, but Barry spoke louder still. The hipster waiter, his key chain jangling, came over and asked them about dessert. "None for me, thank you kindly," Mrs. Hayes said, and looked pleadingly into her husband's eyes. He declined as well.

"I'll have the soufflé," Barry said. "How long does that take? Twenty-five to thirty minutes? Great!" He burrowed into his uncomfortable chair. "The thing about Layla—"

"So tell us more about how this bus trip idea came to you," Mrs. Hayes said. "You just got on a bus?"

"I just got on a bus!"

"I have to say, that's very courageous," Mr. Hayes said. Any residual bebop had gone out of his voice. There was a slight sheen of perspiration on his forehead. They were all getting old.

"Mrs. Hayes, didn't you once do a longitudinal study on long-distance bus ridership?"

"University of South Carolina Press," Mrs. Hayes said. She looked at a text coming in on her phone. Was it from Layla?

Barry finished another glass of wine, and poured yet another. So many good things were happening inside him. The marriage to Seema, the heartbreak with Shiva, all that was Act 1, and whatever Fitzgerald said about second acts did not apply to him. Not that he was going to completely leave Shiva. They would still be . . . What was the word? "Associated." "Well, I'm doing something similar, except maybe more anecdotal," Barry said. "Average American folks are so welcoming! A Mexican man with one eye fell asleep on my shoulder. I've had pimp juice in Baltimore and I met a young drug dealer who has a lot of potential. I guess I saw him the same way you saw Jackson Ward back when it was a dump. Oh, and he gave me this!"

He took out his crack rock and put it on the table. He was ready to offer an explanation, but the Hayeses knew exactly what it was. "Barry!" Mrs. Hayes said. "Now you put that *away*!"

"Son, that's not appropriate," Mr. Hayes said. Again with the "son." What was Mr. Hayes trying to tell him?

"You know what that *did* to this neighborhood," Mrs. Hayes said. "You were here in the nineties. You *saw*."

Barry was being reprimanded by the people he loved. The soufflé was maybe twenty minutes away. He grabbed the rock and squeezed it back in his pocket next to his wedding ring. "Let's just get the check," Mrs. Hayes said. "Barry needs some rest."

"I'm sorry," Barry said. "I'm just. It's very emotional seeing you."

"It's okay, Barry," Mr. Hayes said.

"This whole trip, I'm trying to find my way back to the man I was with Layla. Please don't tell her I said that. Or—I don't know."

"It was so long ago, Barry," Mrs. Hayes said. "We're all such different people."

"You're exactly the same! Well, maybe the pearls. See, when you're good inside, you don't have to try to change so much. You just keep going through life. Layla's the same way."

"Layla's had some tough years," Mrs. Hayes said. Her eyes were glimmering. Barry reached out for her hand, but upset a water glass. Mr. Hayes proved very gentlemanly with his napkin.

"Is her kid normal?" Barry slurred. The Hayeses once again looked at each other. They were still so in love. How was it done? The check arrived and Barry reached for it.

"Barry, you're our guest," Mr. Hayes said. But Barry shooed him away. He wanted to show off his black Amex, but it was now living in a garbage can in Baltimore, maybe floating on some barge to a state far poorer than Maryland. He looked at the check again. It was over three hundred dollars. Seriously? In New York with his black Amex that would be nothing, but that much for a meal in the depth of Virginia? What the hell was happening to this country?

And then Barry did the math. He would have less than a thousand dollars to his name. He was approaching insolvency. Every dollar suddenly mattered. He laid out sixteen twenties and, despite the protestations of his nonparent-in-laws, polished off the acidity and vanilla of the Chardonnay. They walked out of the white restaurant and into the black neighborhood. On the way back, he fell over a minor tree branch and needed the Hayeses' assistance.

BARRY WOKE up in the night's middle darkness and he knew he was not alone. A slender figure in a negligee, her hair a moonlight halo, stood over his luggage. "Layla," Barry whispered.

"Shhhh," the figure said. "Close your eyes." He did as he was told. A comforter was drawn over him. He luxuriated under its weight. A door was shut. The silence of a small city returned.

Barry awoke again. He was thinking of a word and that word was "trombone." Randy was snoring at the foot of the bed. A woman had been leaning over his suitcase in the middle of the night. He padded over to the suitcase to find a wad of cash had been tucked in between two pairs of underwear, next to the passport made out in Bernard Conte's name. Barry counted it off. Three hundred twenty dollars. Where did that amount come from? He played the evening backward, finding mostly blank spaces in the cinematography, eventually remembering the dinner bill that he had covered with his own cash. Three hundred and twenty dollars. Mrs. Hayes had returned his money! Did they think he was lying about his hedge fund? Did they think he was broke? A broke and broken drunk traveling across the country on a bus searching for their daughter?

Barry fell back on the bed as the sun rose over Jackson Ward. People cared enough about him to return his money, him with his 2.4 billion AUM. How kind and insulting of them. The Rainbow Brite sheets no longer had Layla's animal scent, but they had made love on them back at Princeton. He could never understand who Rainbow Brite was, only that she rode on a sarcastic horse, which, itself, rode over a series of rainbows. Layla had explained this to him once when they were both high, and it was all very mind-blowing. Barry's breath was shallow and he could feel his right hand traveling down his thigh. He fell back asleep right after he finished, the steady inhalations of the dachshund at the foot of the bed reminding him how blessed he was to be here.

No one spoke of the previous night, but he was given a potent green brew from the Vitamix. The Hayeses were grading papers at home. He borrowed their Volvo and took I95 over to Carytown, the sort-of-hipster district where he and Layla used to hang out. He stopped outside of the variety store called Mongrel, which always had quite a bit of custom. On a shelf near the cash register, he saw a toy called Peter Rabbit Jack-in-the-Box. It was a jack-in-the-box, but instead of the scary clown this plush gray rabbit popped out holding a bright orange carrot. And instead of "Pop Goes the Weasel," it played "Here Comes Peter Cottontail" when you turned the crank. Cottontail. *Rabbit.* Shiva. It was the perfect toy. It was thirty-two dollars, way over his new budget, but he couldn't help himself. The rabbit popping out was still likely to frighten Shiva, but maybe if he played it gently, holding the rabbit down with one hand, so that it wouldn't just pop out but would emerge with his carrot slowly, maybe Shiva wouldn't melt down. This is what he meant about being *associated* with Shiva. He wouldn't live with him, but he would visit quarterly and constantly send him perfect gifts. *Daddy's here!* the

Filipina nanny might say on one of his visits. *And look at the toy he bring you!*

Barry got back into the Volvo. He hit the posh West End, drove around what looked like miles of Gothic Princeton houses. This is where Layla had gone to parties as a high-school kid. In college, she hadn't wanted to be a writer like Barry had, but she had a memoirist's vibe going, remembering her city and her childhood block by block, and telling Barry her own mythology with relish. He never said it, but he had also been envious of Seema's connection to her heritage when they went to Bombay. She had gone there for no more than three summer vacations when she was a teenager, but every corner elicited a memory. "They used to sell the best *chaat* over there!" "My uncle Nag lived behind the Shroff eye clinic." "Oh my God, I used to go to that study corner when it got too noisy at my aunt's." This is how you became a writer, by having a past.

Barry stood at the top of Libby Hill, storied old homes to his back, old industry and the James River at his feet. So much of the city was swaddled in green from this vantage point, it looked like one of those 1970s apocalyptic movies where the earth had reverted to its natural state and was overrun by hairy men and apes. He glanced down at his watch. He was wearing his Omega Railmaster today, a sturdy, handsome piece with PAF, or Pakistani air force, engraved on the back. It had cost him nearly what a year at Princeton used to cost when he and Layla attended.

Libby Hill is where they'd had their very last fight on his final visit to Richmond, crack vials crunching like candy beneath their sneakers, their eyes glancing back to the safety of her parents' car every few seconds. They were talking about their writing class. "You think that story made me look heroic?" she said. "I looked like an idiot. Like I threw my whole education away." "What's wrong with being a shepherdess?" he asked. "That's how you think of me? As this noble savage? Remind me, was I even wearing clothes in that story? At least a loincloth? A loin-bra? Just because I didn't grow up on the Upper East Side like Myra Brennan." This was a girl who had fancied Barry. Barry actually liked an athletic black girl from his Applied Game Theory class, a fellow econ major, but back then he did not think he could bridge the racial gap. Every time he saw a black person he pictured those no-go zones his father had drawn across a map of Queens. "No," Barry said, "I was saying that the banker hadn't forgotten his first love over all those years." "Right, but he still broke up with her." "You're the one who's breaking up with me." "Just go. Go to New York. Do what you want, Barry. You've planned everything already." "And that's so wrong, to have plans? My father never had any plans. There's a well-put-together human being." "Nothing more boring than being a reaction to your parents, Barry." He looked at her, trying to be hurt. "I know, Barry," she said. "*Parent,* not parents. Yes, I get it. I feel your mother's death every day, I swear, sometimes I feel it more than you do. And where do we go from here? Who am I supposed to be? Mother? Shepherd? Savage lover?"

He hated how well she fought with him. At first he loved having a brilliant sparring partner, but now he despised the agility of her mind. They must have driven home afterward, but the last thing he remembered of Layla Hayes was her crooked look of disgust and victory up on Libby Hill. She had taken the sweetness of his fictional shepherdess and used it as fuel for her own spite. And now it was too late to try to make it with the athletic black girl in game theory. School was over for good.

He parked the car outside her parents' house. What was he going to do next? He would take the Greyhound to El Paso. He would make a passionate case for moving back to Richmond. He would tell Layla about his encounter with Javon to seal the deal (*This kid let me hold his murdered cousin's watch*). He took out his wallet. He had roughly eight hundred dollars after today's expenditures. He tried to think of all the people he might know between Richmond and El Paso. One of his protégés had famously ditched Wall Street for Atlanta to be close to his parents. An Asian guy, Jeff Park. He had been fired from This Side of Capital after a trade had blown up spectacularly. Barry couldn't remember if he had personally fired him. It must have been the mercenary Akash Singh. He would have to ask Jeff Park for a little bridge loan, "no big" as people Jeff's age liked to say. The whole thing would be funny. And then, on to Layla.

Barry shut down the Volvo's engine. He looked at the package from Mongrel next to him, the hipster socks and Shiva's rabbit-in-the-box. Anything with the word "rabbit" on it made him smile. One of the nice things about having a child, even a malfunctioning one like Shiva, was that you were constantly surrounded by plush animals and your own lost sense of innocence. He often dreamed that that innocence could rub off on Shiva. That he could ask his father, *Daddy, why do you call me a rabbit?* And Barry would say, *Because you're sweet and cuddly and you hop around the room when you're happy.* Of course, Barry knew that none of those things was true.

As soon as he rang the Hayeses' doorbell, he could hear Randy flinging his weenie body at the door, desperate for a belly rubdown from his newfound friend. Mr. Hayes came out in a denim shirt and a collegial sports jacket, looking ever the host. "We have a visitor," he announced. "A friend of yours."

THE HAYESES had politely left them alone. Barry sat there with Randy on his lap, and on a couch opposite sat his chief of staff in full battle regalia. There was a smell of New York about the room, fresh tar on her fringe sandals, Yankee heat on her V-neck zip dress. It was weird to see Sandy without the Bloomberg monitors behind her, a bottle of La Colombe cold press in her hand. What was she doing here amid Neil Young and Joan Didion and the Dresden romantic landscape paintings?

"You spoke to Seema," Barry said. "How else would you have known where I'd be?"

"I'm sorry," Sandy said.

"What right do you have to come down here and stalk me?"

"None. I just want to make an observation." Sandy and her observations. "Nobody faults you for Valupro."

"Why not? What kind of fund are we if people don't fault me for losing a billion dollars?"

The motor in her head was running so hard he thought he could hear it. "In the grand scheme of things, what's a billion?" she said. "You made us who we are. You're a rainmaker. I left politics for you."

"That's on you," Barry said.

"Is the air conditioner on?" Sandy asked. "It's so hot in here." She picked up a nearby copy of a local magazine devoted to Richmond's top high schools and fanned herself with it. "Do you want to hear about the redemptions?"

"I don't care," Barry said. Which wasn't entirely true. There was one investor the fund hinged on. "You came here because of Ahmed," he said.

"He's flying in from Doha on Thursday," Sandy said. "He pushed up his annual visit because of you. We can't keep the Qataris in much longer. Think of all the people who count on you. Think of your family."

"What do you know about family?" Barry said. "You're not even *married*." He wanted to bring up his admiration for the institution of gay marriage very badly. He wanted to hurt her with it. After all the money he'd given in support of New York State's Marriage Equality Act.

"Seeing you and Seema actually encourages me," his chief of staff said. "Maria and I have been talking. You guys are like an example to us." Barry laughed. Sandy had met Seema once at a Robin Hood gala and, in her nervousness, had asked his wife, "So, do you *work?*" Seema wouldn't let that go for weeks. She even threatened to get a part-time legal job at Planned Parenthood.

"What has Akash been saying about me? Last time I saw him he said, and I quote, 'You're not very bright, you don't do due diligence, and you like *every*one.'"

"That was way out of line. You're a mentor to him. A father almost."

"But what if he's right? Who needs guys like me anymore? It's not about relationships. It's all about the quants and their black boxes. And how does someone like me even pitch funds that are so quantitative that *I* don't know what the fuck I'm pitching? Everything I've worked for is pointless. I should have stuck with my Commodore. I should have applied to CalTech. What is the *point* of me?"

"Akash is worried," Sandy said. "We all are. Your guys really miss you. Armen Kassabian got a Patek minute repeater at the Christie's auction. They're thinking of getting a plane and going to next year's Baselworld. They're being poached by Icarus Capital. I know you don't want that. You're a team. I've got a NetJets ready at RIC. We can be there in twenty, wheels up in twenty more."

"Sorry," Barry said. "Not interested."

"And then there's . . ."

"What?"

"You know."

"I don't know," he lied.

"The other thing."

Barry waved her away. But she wouldn't stop talking. "Herb Rabkin thinks it's coming soon. A subpoena. How will it look if they subpoena you, and you're on the lam, or whatever?"

Randy decided that this was an optimal time to rear up on his hind legs and give Barry's nose a long faithful lick. Barry and the dachshund looked at each other. Unlike Shiva, the dog lived for eye contact. Before the diagnosis, Barry would lie next to his son when he would get scared of the thunder and lightning and say, "It's okay, Shiva. Because the thunder's happening *out*side. And *in*side with Mommy and Daddy it's safe. You see the difference? Outside and inside." When Shiva was born, Barry thought he could just disappear into his wife and children. A lot of guys in finance said things like "I work hard to buy time to be with my kids." But Barry thought he could actually pull it off, make his family the center of his life. Until that fateful meeting at Weill Cornell last September, a family had seemed a reasonable way to substitute for his failure as a titan of finance.

A subpoena.

Barry set the dachshund down. How much seed he had spilled thinking about Sandy and her large-assed Latina girlfriend in the months after he had hired her. Seema had rarely gotten that much sex, at least since the diagnosis, at least from behind. He went over to his chief of staff, bent down on his knee, put one hand on her cheek, and kissed her on the lips, his tongue briefly popping in to taste the coffee and Listerine pocket strips. He leaned back to examine his handiwork. Her pale Irish eyes were darting above his head, and her mouth remained open. She breathed desperately like a fish on a dock. "See," he said. "Now you don't have to worry. Now you can just sue me. And then you'll have enough."

As he was getting up, she threw her arms around him and pulled him in toward her, her hands stroking his back wildly. He pushed her away. "For fuck's sake," he said. "Money! Money! Money! Money! It just never ends, does it?"

He ran up the stairs. Sandy was shouting his name and Randy had started to bark ferociously.

Mr. Hayes was up in his office, reading the *Oxford English Dictionary* with a loupe. "A bit of a commotion down there," he said.

"I need you to drive me to the Greyhound," Barry said. "Can we sneak out the back door?"

"What happened? Is it that New York woman? We can call the police."

Barry apologized for the trouble and asked if he could quickly use the computer to look something up. Jeff Park lived on Peachtree Street like most everyone else in Atlanta. Barry scribbled down his address and went back to Layla's old room to sling his watches into his rollerboard. He put the $320 Mrs. Hayes had returned to him under a Rainbow Brite pillow. He envisioned Sandy and Seema together, circling his money, living off his talents, his friendliness, his charm. How alike they were. How mercenary. Maybe it was better back in the day when you just married your secretary and got it over with. He took out his wedding ring from the baggie it shared with the crack rock and trashed it in the wastebasket beneath Layla's desk. He felt nothing.

. . .

THE CAR was idling outside the brutalist element of the Greyhound station. Mr. Hayes and Barry were staring ahead quietly as passengers were dropped off around them. "Well, that was quite a visit," Mr. Hayes said.

Barry was looking at his bare ring finger. "I'm going to come back," he said. "And I'm going to bring Layla back with me. You can tell her that. And that she should start looking for houses in the West End."

Mr. Hayes put his hand on Barry's shoulder. "I like you, son," he said. "I always have. You're smart. You're basically decent. You're kind when you want to be. But that's not enough for a life. That's only barely just a start."

"I'm going to bring her back," Barry repeated. "And then you can be with your grandson all day long." He had this image of Layla's kid being basically brought up by the Hayeses, leaving him and Layla to their love.

"I do have a job, you know," Mr. Hayes said. "And we're not completely alone. Celia's just up in Lexington." The whole time he had been keeping his hand on Barry's shoulder. If only this moment would go on longer.

"You'll see," Barry said. "You'll see what I can do."

THE GREYHOUND ticket to Atlanta was $50 with a transfer in Raleigh, North Carolina. He was down to about $750. He had to be very careful with that sum. He might have to go out to some expensive dinners with Jeff Park before he could broach the subject of a bridge loan. At the Greyhound café, decorated like an old-timey saloon, a Caribbean-sounding mother and her fat son were guzzling Pepsis while Barry sipped a watery cup of Gold Peak arabica that had cost just a little over a dollar. There were no monitors here, but they had CNN blasting out of overhead speakers. The Republican convention was on and it seemed that Trump's Slavic wife Melania had stolen Michelle Obama's speech. Trump was complaining about the mainstream media. Without the visuals, he sounded like a genuinely sad older man from the outer boroughs. He sounded like Barry's own dad, who had caught Trump fever from the start. "You had to marry the world's darkest Indian," his father had said after the tiny ceremony in judge's chambers. "It's not like I disagree with her right to exist," he said after Barry had unexpectedly started to cry, the weight of having been his father's son for four decades crushing him all at once. Barry was a moderate Republican, and his father was a moderate Nazi. They were a moderate family. That's how it went. And now one of them was at a Greyhound depot in Virginia and the other in a grave by the Pacific coast.

They crossed the James River, and Barry caught sight of the old Lucky Strike smokestack up on Libby Hill. Richmond was neither striking nor ugly, and that made it more real than a bubble like Charleston or Savannah or a hipster makeover like Detroit. Here in Richmond there wouldn't be this endless parade of hedge-fund and private-equity wives who had been tempted away from their high-flying careers. Here, he wouldn't mind her working. She'd be Professor Hayes-Cohen and he'd run his watch foundation for black kids out of a converted industrial space. Facebook said she had some kind of university job at the university down in El Paso. Now she would be able to teach at VCU alongside her parents.

The Greyhound passed bucolic creeks, their rocks overgrown with moss. Signs promising ROAD WORK AHEAD yielded no such results. They abandoned the iconic I-95 for some dingy thing called 85. In the town of South Hill he saw a Walmart and wondered if that was the first one he had seen in real life. It would be fun to check out and maybe buy some cheap underwear, but the bus just rolled past it to a convenience store proudly selling Hermie's Famous Fried Chicken. The passengers spilled quietly out of the bus, their children racing ahead in anticipation. Barry took in the premises, the "Trucker's Lounge" filled with the genuine artifact, white men with ankle tattoos watching Fox. The selection of chips in the store was extraordinary. In addition to an extra-large bag of Lay's dill-pickle-flavored chips, he could get a Hermie's famous thigh-and-drumstick combo and one of her famous banana puddings and a famous ice tea for about twelve dollars. But, no. He could not. His money had to last. He had to channel the parsimony of his father and his father's fathers, all those pennies and kopecks stacked from the Bronx to Belarus.

The whole bus resounded with the ecstatic crunch of fried chicken. He imagined the smell must be like a southern church on Sunday, maybe even the one in which he and Layla would get married. He wished his father would be alive for his wedding to a white woman, but Barry was also happy he was not. Oh, how he wanted that crispy chicken and the creamy banana pudding a single mom and her three boys were slurping up across the aisle. He had never known what hunger felt like. It felt like the last exhausting stages of a panic attack, right before your consciousness let out.

They crossed into North Carolina, THE NATION'S MOST MILITARY-FRIENDLY STATE, according to the welcome sign. Barry looked down at the Omega Railmaster on his wrist to try to take his mind off the hunger. This was the watch he had worn on last year's visit to Cardozo High School, his alma mater, after the Young Investors' Club had invited him to talk about a career in hedge funds.

The Investors' Club had taken a booth at a pizza joint on Springfield Boulevard, one Barry did not recall from his high-school days but bearing a familiar sticky outer-borough feel, the slices dripping with sauce and studded with oregano, the counter crowded with plastic containers of ancient red mystery juice (Hi-C? Hawaiian Punch?). Barry's old high school was now overwhelmingly Asian, black, and Latino, but the Young Investors' Club lacked the last two categories. It consisted of eight boys, one was Indian and one was probably half Jewish and half Chinese, both were a touch dorky and a touch outgoing, probably valedictorian/salutatorian material; a couple of protein-shake wrestlers who would do ROTC somewhere and then end up at a trading desk the moment they graduated; and some of the more polished dudes who would become lax bros at Colgate or Duke and saunter into his office Monday morn all full of fraternal cheer and stories about smashed Lambos and capsized Bay-liners. Even here, on the far edge of Queens, these high-school kids already resembled a mirror image of This Side of Capital.

The boys inhaled sodas and ate a Sicilian pie that Barry would graciously pay for, burning with quiet working-class smarts and tes-tosterone ambition. They mostly wanted to know how much they'd get paid. One of the two dorky boys wanted to know why the first three years of the fund had posted returns of 6, 9, and 12 percent respectively, while the current year had seen a drop of almost 20 percent with about a third of investors already heading for the exits. And was Valupro really a smart trade?

"I think your approach to the industry is counterproductive," Barry said, fingering the remains of a thick Sicilian crust. "You want to know the first rule of running a billion-dollar-plus hedge fund? Don't sweat the metrics. We're not really about the numbers. Do you know what we are? We are a *story*. Hedge funds are a *story* about how we're going to make money. They're about being smart, gain-ing access, associating with someone great. You. You are someone smart enough to make others feel smart. You are bringing your in-vestors something far more elusive than a metric. You're bringing them the story of how great you'll be together."

Two of the future lacrosse bros were nodding, but the future quants looked confused. "Take this watch, for example," Barry said. "It's an Omega Railmaster. You can find one on eBay for two grand. But the one I'm wearing? Twenty K. Why?" He took it off and pushed it into the young half-Chinese boy's face. "Because it was one of the limited watches issued to the Pakistani air force. You see it on the back? PAF. And the 'Railmaster' markings have been switched to 'Seamaster' because on the subcontinent the railmaster is the guy who collects your train tickets and the British used to run all the trains, so 'Seamaster' sounded better for air-force pilots. My wife is Indian. See, I've already told you three stories just based off this watch. And its price just went up two thousand percent while its utility did not change one penny. If you want to be a hedge-fund manager, you have to be a storyteller first and last. That's why my fund is called This Side of Capital. After the Fitzgerald novel. That's why I have a minor in creative writing from"—he paused— *"Princeton University."*

"But what about the recent wave of redemptions?" the kid asked. "Pension funds pulling out."

"What did I just say about metrics?" Barry said.

"Okay, then what about rumors that the SEC is investigating you for using MNPI on the GastroLux trade. That a Wells notice is imminent."

Barry dropped his crust. MNPI. Material nonpublic information. The world shimmered at the edges like some bad college acid trip. Who the fuck was this kid? That *look*. Nerdy, but not an outcast. How the hell did he know about Wells notices? Did his parents work in finance? Why weren't they living in Manhattan or Brooklyn? Did they think their progeny would have a better chance at the Ivies applying from a nongifted public high school?

"You sure know a lot about what's going on," Barry said. Big smile.

"My uncle works for the U.S. Attorney's Office," the kid said. He had probably gone to Ethical Heritage or one of those liberal rich schools before his parents moved him to Queens for a chance at Dartmouth.

"Well, then you know that rumors are just that. Our compliance measures are super robust."

"I heard your chief compliance officer doesn't even have a finance background. He's just a comp lit major from Middlebury."

"An excellent school. You should be lucky to go there."

"Are you worried?"

"Do I *look* worried?" But the two boys were still not satisfied and wanted to know what plans he had to turn things around. Barry claimed a pressing meeting with a made-up pension fund back in the city and got the fuck out of there.

He had done nothing wrong. Even if this went beyond the SEC, even if the Department of Justice and the FBI came down on him, they had no proof. He was not going to prison.

. . .

BARRY HAD to transfer at Raleigh. Once again he was the only white man waiting for the bus. Overhead, the CNN was showing the GOP convention in Cleveland. On the bus line, some dudes in camo shorts and hoodies and a woman in a complex red headdress were riffing off of Trump.

"That man ain't gonna win. He just having fun running."

"But if he do win, we gonna burn this shit down."

"His wife stole Michelle Obama's speech. Probably wrote it down in crayon."

"I didn't vote for Barack the second time. He hurt my feelings. He didn't do nothing for us."

"Yeah, he was just a show president."

Barry wanted to get in on that one. "He leaves behind a complex legacy, that's for sure," he said. The woman in the red headdress stared at him, but not for long.

It was going to be one of the urine buses this time, but that was okay with Barry. Someone broke out a paper container of early morning grits with hot sauce and that delicious smell filled the bus. Barry felt the hunger overwhelm him. He was growing dizzy. His teeth vibrated, his stomach knotted, his feet tingled numb. What if he asked the person with the grits for a bite? No, he was too proud to beg from a poor person.

They rolled through Charlotte, the skyline all new angles and condos with predictable names. The Vue. Barry watched an Asian woman and her grandson doing their morning condo walk. He was going to be Jeff Park's friend in Atlanta. And he was not going to prison. His whole body itched from being on the bus. If he had to describe poverty in one word, it would be "itchy." Material nonpublic information. What did that even mean? He had done nothing wrong. Yes, his fund had shorted GastroLux, a pharma with a new GERD medication in Phase II trial that was supposed to have cured the esophageal difficulties of stressed-out yuppies belching up their

Acela coffee and egg-and-sausage rolls. And, yes, he was a major shareholder in Valupro, which had almost bought GastroLux and whose management knew the drug would fail. And, yes, they had made about two hundred bucks on the trade, their last really successful trade. Their AUM had just dipped under three billion, so the two hundred million was welcome. But it had all been a great big coincidence. Everyone else had piled into that trade anyway. What proof did they have that he used his relationship with Valupro to make money off the demise of GastroLux? It was like the whole of society was positioned to make sure Barry didn't make money off *anything.* It was socialism. He didn't want Trump to win, but he was glad the Obama years were sputtering to an end. Even the black people on the bus didn't like him. And no matter what she said, Hillary seemed copacetic with high finance. Her daughter had married a hedgie. Barry scratched at himself terribly, tearing the seam of his Vineyard Vines.

They passed into South Carolina, firework stores and adult-video emporiums. The land was both rural and industrial, sunburned and tired. Unlike North Carolina's green streams, the rivers here were brown and murky, the shrubs by the side of the road looked like they had been dazed stupid by the sun. When Barry closed his eyes, he dreamed of fried chicken and banana pudding. He saw a fresh stream of Dasani water—they didn't seem to have any Fiji or Evian in Greyhound Land—trickle into his mouth.

They passed signs for Fair Play, Seneca, and Walhalla, cleared the Cherokee Foothills, and crossed over into Georgia. The acres of late-model BMWs, both shimmering on lots and glistening on the road, told them they were approaching Atlanta. They passed Jimmy Carter Boulevard. How Barry's father hated that man, because of Israel or Iran or something. A billboard advertised HAIR TRANSPLANTS AT $2 A GRAFT, another ACTORS, MODELS & TALENT FOR CHRIST along with a photo of two saved hotties, a boy and a girl, rocking out to the Lord. Every other billboard was for Delta.

An African cabdriver picked him up from the station and drove him from Downtown to Midtown and up Peachtree, Atlanta's spine. After he paid him, he had $740 to his name. Barry could barely get out of the cab. His whole body was shaking.

The concierge in Jeff's building was an Ethiopian woman who might have been the most attractive creature on some top-shelf planet in Alpha Centauri. Every part of her body belonged in a better place. She looked at Barry with concern, her eyes as big as moons over a desert. He looked down at himself. His face itched with stubble. His body itched from the bus. His Vineyard Vines shirt was torn in such a way that one collar listed to the side. On the Greyhound you could look like that if you were a white meth head, but this was a luxury building called the Vantage on Peachtree.

Barry tried to smile, but it came out as something else. He tried to raise his arms, feeling the billows of his once-crisp Vineyard Vines. The Ethiopian goddess was asking him a series of questions, but he did not know the answers offhand. He did not know whom he was visiting. He was not sure if he had come to deliver a package. And he did not know his own name.

He leaned over her desk and felt the muscles knot in his shoulders. "Water," he said. She couldn't hear him. He tried it louder, but the effort was too much. Someone or something had smacked the back of his head and he was looking up at a tall, well-lit atrium, like a megachurch in heaven.

6 *NOT ENOUGH LOVE*

HIVA THREW a stapler into his nanny's face. For someone little aware of his own body's journey through space, his aim had been impeccable. Novie needed six stitches above her left brow, and while his nanny was proud of her looks, she took comfort in knowing her Christmas bonus would be tripled and Seema would deliver an hour-long lecture on how she should keep the money and invest it in low-cost index funds instead of sending it back to the Philippines.

"Please don't leave us," Seema had begged her the next morning. "You're all I have left." The words were meant to be as melodramatic as anything Novie watched on her tablet, but even Seema herself did not expect them to sound so pathetic. She started sobbing.

The nanny didn't know what to do. Her boss never cried. "It will be okay," she said. "He'll come back." Which was the opposite of Novie's usual "You should call someone," meaning a lawyer, but who cared at that point. Maybe it would be better if Barry came home. And then what? Every time the phone rang she sighed with relief when a string of numbers appeared on the screen. The last time the agent had called, it was a blocked number. She hung up as soon as she realized he was from the Bureau. She knew what he was going to say next. The video on her iPhone. Sardinia.

"Tell Novie you're sorry," Seema told her son, not knowing exactly how that would work, but, for the first time in a while, the boy smiled brightly at both of them, or at least *past* both of them. Was he taunting them? She couldn't hate him. No, she could not. None of this was his fault. None.

Over the past few weeks, all Shiva's therapists had begun voicing concerns that he was becoming increasingly "dysregulated." Whatever progress had been achieved was being reversed. The one time last winter he had picked up his sippy cup and *drank from it on his own* was now relegated to the category of "miracles." Even his pointing had stopped. Was it because Seema was seeing Luis? Could Shiva sense this? What did he know? An increasing body of literature on the subject, some of it written by adults on the spectrum themselves, told Seema that Shiva knew and sensed quite a bit.

Seema knew she had to let go of the idea of a perfect, "normal" child. To find strength. To develop, as one book urged her, a sense of adventure and wonder. But what if she wasn't qualified to be the parent of an autistic child? What if the fact that her nanny almost lost an eye did not inspire adventure and wonder, but anger, helplessness, and shame? What if she was, in some horrible, selfish way, just not a great *person*? Maybe, if she had gone to Cravath after her clerkship like she had planned and not met Barry, she could have been a great *lawyer*, but not necessarily Sidd-fucking-hartha at the end of his fat boy journey.

But this was all just self-involved nonsense. The real news was that she was two months pregnant and she was working overtime to find extra love for the little boy inside her. And what if there wasn't enough? Plus her body was changing. After Barry stopped loving her and Shiva's problems became clear, she actually *lost* more weight, a whole range of downtown boutiques suddenly opening up to her black card. But now her belly looked like a half-empty fanny pack.

Luis noticed. They had started taking a room at the Gramercy Park Hotel, an unspectacular, overpriced room in which they would go down on each other and then use the keys to private Gramercy Park to complete some midday fondling behind the privet shrubbery. The Gramercy was his idea, even though she picked up the considerable check. It was a storied, slightly musty boutique hotel, and it felt old, almost European.

The lack of actual intercourse was scorching, in ways both good and bad. There was something to look forward to, something still left for her twenty-nine-year-old self to enjoy, and when it came to oral sex, he just cleaned her out. One day he brought up "rimming," and she had to look it up on her phone. "What kind of millennial are you?" he asked, before commencing. It tickled and wasn't much fun, and was actually kind of embarrassing. But right after, without even bothering to use the mouthwash in the old Gramercy bathroom, he reached over and cupped her stomach. "You're getting a little quinoa belly," he said.

She threw his hand off and turned away, the heat rising up to her forehead. "What?" Luis said. "It's cute! Come on, you're the last person I'd expect to have body issues."

"What the fuck does that mean?"

They fought for a bit, but it died down fast enough. He told her his wife's lack of breasts and ass always made him sad and, losing all the female solidarity Michigan and Yale had bestowed upon her, Seema let those words elbow out her own sadness.

"I want to celebrate your belly," Luis said, and he bent down and kissed the small tapered form that held Barry's second child, and that was just too much. She ran to the bathroom.

In bed, over the next few days, she tried to tell him who she was. Sometimes he listened. But only when it seemed like he needed a detail to go into some giant file labeled "Women, North American, Asian & Pacific Islander, wealthy." Perversely enough, he perked up whenever she talked about Barry, about her relationship with his money, about his relationship with money, about their relationship with money together. It was as if he pictured this giant mass of money floating on the horizon, and two ill-defined shapes were sticking out of that mass, and they were named Seema and Barry. What if, without Barry, she just wasn't interesting enough to care about? Still, she kept trying, hoping her family's immigrant roots would make her more fascinating to him.

She told him the best thing about growing up was watching Indian grandmas rock out to Jay-Z's remix of Panjabi MC at weddings, this perfect crash landing of one culture onto another. And the worst thing was that caricature of a Gujarati shopkeeper, Apu, on *The Simpsons* ("Do Apu!" Her friends would beg her to imitate his accent), who made her treble her efforts at being cool, begging her mom to buy her a crop top at the Great Northern Mall and blasting "I don't want no scrub" from her father's Dodge, the windows rolled down, when he dropped her off at school. She told him the way her father always said "Hut!" which was this British thing, perhaps, and was both loving and scolding. Oh, and "level best," as in "Just do your level best." She loved her mother just enough; she loved her father ninefold. She talked about taking all those bharata natya dance classes for girls at the temple over in Parma, and how, even though she sucked at them, the camaraderie of fellow desi girls, their out-of-control hair all tied up with fresh flowers, because one of the fathers was a florist up by Great Northern, was so nice. "We were all trying so hard to assimilate back then; I just wish Shiva would have more Tamil heritage," she said, before stopping herself.

"Can you do that dance now?" Luis said, breathing hard, his brow still glistening from that afternoon's exertions.

"Um, I'm naked," Seema said. "I don't think that would be right. It's, like, a ritual. A spiritual one." He looked so disappointed, she added, "Maybe if I put on some clothes, I can try." He showed no interest.

She asked him about his own "heritage," but he told her Cambridge, Mass, was not a heritage. What about his Guatemalan stuff? "You can read my books for that." She turned away from him. "I miss my dad." He said this whenever he knew he was being a jerk, because she put her arms around him and kissed his neck.

She decided to try something bold, getting Mina and Luis together. Wasn't that a part of being young, introducing your secret beau to your friends? Nothing would signal more to both Mina and Luis how much she wanted a new life for herself.

Luis was not receptive to the idea, especially of going all the way out to Brooklyn, which he said was just lousy with trust-funders (as opposed to what, Manhattan?) and had overrated restaurants. Fine, she would let him choose the venue for their "sit-down." He chose a place right off Tompkins Square Park, a bar that exclusively served canned Basque seafood. "Okaaaay," Mina said when told of Luis's selection.

Luis was forty minutes late. *Forty minutes.* Not that he was trying to make a point or anything. Seema found her forehead again overheating and every muscle in her face striving for composure as if she were about to take the New York State Bar all over again. She owed Novie a couple of nights of trying to put Shiva down by herself, and here she was trying to impress her best friend with her lover, or maybe the other way around.

Of course, he didn't apologize for being late. "Hey," he said to Seema and kissed her chastely on the forehead.

"We were going to order for you, but we didn't know what you wanted," Seema said with prosecutorial anger. "Canned seafood. Yum. Everything looked so good."

"Touché." Luis shrugged.

"I can already tell, you guys are hilarious together," Mina said.

Luis ordered sea cockles, razor clams, and bonito tuna out of a can. "I think this is from Galicia, not from the Basque Country," he said after his first few bites of fish. He seemed genuinely concerned.

The conversation was terrible. They talked about the election, and Luis suggested that no matter who won our country would continue to serve as "the roast beef in a global shit sandwich."

Mina's cheeks had turned a brilliant red after just one Basque beer. "You can afford not to freak out about Trump because you're a white male," she said.

"How do you know what I am?" Luis said.

"Yeah, whatever, *Luis.* I'm calling bullshit on you, cracker."

Luis laughed. They were perched on these backless barstools. Seema could feel two serious indentations building into the curves of her ass. She was constantly checking her phone for messages from Novie, but either Shiva was at his best or the Christmas bonus was going to be in the mid–six figures. Mina and Luis continued to talk at each other about identity politics, taking turns calling each other racist, their voices rising and falling, falling and rising, and Seema felt excluded, even lonely. But when they walked out of the restaurant, Mina whispered to Seema, "Now that's more like it."

"What?"

"I *lurve* him," Mina said. That probably meant "love" in Williamsburg.

"Are you kidding me? I was drafting an apology text to you in the bathroom."

"He's brilliant."

Seema kissed her friend's scarlet cheek. Later she texted Luis about Mina, and he replied, SHE'S OK, which was, from him, the highest of praise.

That night, Seema lay in the bed she used to share with her husband with a glass of the forty-thousand-dollar-a-bottle Japanese whiskey she had liberated from Barry's whiskey cave. She deserved it. Since meeting Luis, she had been very careful with where she allowed her imagination to roam, but tonight was *go* time. He would leave his wife, that was obvious. He would see Shiva as just a part of the human condition, "different, not less," as Temple Grandin, the world's most famous autistic person, had said, and Arturo, that three-year-old extrovert, would do his best to be a good brother to his challenging new sibling. She would have a child with Luis, his relatively fresh thirty-something sperm would bind with her eggs without problems. They would each have one child from previous marriages, and one together. Seema brushed her tongue against her teeth. She had to admit that even the sea cockle, or whatever the fuck it was, had tasted delicious, like sex in a San Sebastian hotel. She might start working again, but she would definitely need the best divorce lawyer to have ever graduated from one of the T14 law schools. Whatever Luis earned would not be enough, and she just couldn't picture the lifetime of suffering and worry required just to *cling* to the upper-middle class in New York City. God, what was wrong with her? Her hand found its way to the muddle of cells atop her pubic bone. Yes, and there was that.

Seema had always wanted to have a husband and a child she could hold. Family was about physical closeness. When they were kids, her younger sister, Shilpa, loved having her sister's arms around her. Seema loved to cling to her father's musky neck as they played horsey in their small University Heights cape. She spent her high-school summers in Bombay, where the proximity of others felt like instant sisterhood. Barry was always deathly claustrophobic when she tried to embrace him. The couples therapist Seema had once dragged them to, a heavyset Jewish woman in a Central Park West basement, had suggested that could be a sign of Barry's own diagnosis. He actually kept a log of the seconds each watch in his collection lost and gained every day. How was *that* not on the spectrum? As for Shiva, the only thing you could touch him with was a soft horsehair brush that was used to regulate him upon waking and before bedtime or anytime he had a meltdown. Seema desperately wanted the simple pleasure of feeling her boy in her arms. If she could, would she even need Luis? She quashed that question and finished her whiskey. *I'm sorry,* she whispered to the unfortunate creature within her.

THE NEXT day, she ran into Julianna in the lobby. Arturo was hopping all around her with a handmade turkey puppet. "Hi, Aunt Seema!" he cried. How could he possibly remember her name from just one meeting? When the Goodmans' nanny came down to pick up Arturo, he actually threw his arms around her like in the movies. His eye contact was perfect to the point of being creepy.

"Do you want to go grab lunch?" Julianna asked her. She looked stressed out, maybe from work, as her bland Theory clothes seemed to suggest. Shouldn't a doctor be wearing something more medical?

Against all common sense, they decided to eat outside at this Lebanese wrap place that sat at the intersection of Broadway and Fifth, right outside the tristate hubbub of Mario Batali's Eataly. Julianna took off her jacket and threw it over her cheap metal chair. Her body was minimalist. Was that what Luis preferred? He had claimed otherwise when they were in bed.

"I'm worried about Arturo," Julianna said.

"Are you kidding me? He's a dream child. He knows all the words to the bumblebee song." That was passive-aggressive. They had ordered Beiruti chickpea salads and water. Tourists would stop three feet away from them and break their necks looking up at the Flatiron Building, which seemed transported from a different and better time. Yellow cabs and double-decker sightseeing buses honked at one another, and the air smelled like grilled meat in summer. "He's sociable. And that's important. But he's lagging cognitively. Well, not lagging, but he's only in the top ten percent." Seema tried hard not to hate her, but it was impossible. The Beiruti chickpeas tasted inauthentic.

"You know how hard it is," Julianna said. "If he doesn't do well, forget Hunter, forget Ethical Heritage, we're talking *maybe* Bright and Happy Schoolhouse. And their HYPMS is what?"

"PMS?" Seema asked innocently.

"HYPMS. Harvard, Yale, Princeton, MIT, Stanford. The good schools can already tell you what percentage of their kindergarten class will get into one of those five. Brearley's is thirty-seven percent. Of course, that's an all-girls school. You know, I don't want to sound like one of those Manhattan moms. I just want him to have options."

Options. Was this the sliver of society, the meaningfully affluent but not rich, that she had opted out of when she married Barry? If so, hallelujah! "I went to Michigan," Seema said. "And I turned out all right." Julianna stared at her, obviously not knowing what to say. *Michigan,* her eyes suggested.

"And I went to Yale Law from there. See, it all works out."

Julianna smiled. "I know," she said. "There are many"—she searched for the word—"paths. Thanks for taking the time out to talk to me. You're very calming. We immigrant—" Unlike Luis, she stopped herself from proclaiming Seema an immigrant. "Those of us who come from certain backgrounds, well, you know it never ends, right? Parents." A large Poland Spring truck had stalled at the intersection, and cabbies were leaning out of their vehicles to yell at it.

"Do you and Luis plan on having more kids?" Seema asked, even though the wrong answer would kill her.

"Ha," Julianna said. "Like one isn't one too many in New York." Seema nodded in agreement. She could now sort of see why Luis liked her or, at least, the stressed-out version of himself that gave a shit about things like child-rearing. Seema needed to make more female friends, though maybe not her lover's wife. She had this strange feeling that she could confide in Julianna about Shiva's diagnosis, and that maybe this was a way for it to filter back to Luis. No, she had to tell him in person. She had to see his face. "Anyway," Julianna said, "I'm doing a lot of epidemiological work in Brazil, so now might not be the best time to get pregnant."

Seema chewed on the last of her fried Levantine chickpeas. Her new friend was working on Zika. She was on the front lines of a global crisis, just like Seema's younger sister, that Doctor Without a Border, although Shilpa was just doing GP stuff over in Nepal. ("Great, Nepal, you're almost back from where your grandparents started," her mom had said when she was told of Shilpa's posting.) And here was Julianna, worrying about her son's ninetieth-percentile cognitive scores while working twenty-hour days to keep the apocalypse at bay.

Seema picked up her phone. I WANT YOU INSIDE ME 2MORRO, she texted Luis.

OK was the instantaneous reply.

And then: 8AM? GRAMERCY?

"Listen," Julianna said, reaching for her own phone. "Before we get the bill, we are scheduling a playdate with our kids." She started scrolling through her calendar. "They're all girls in Arturo's class, which is cute, but he needs to play with boys too. What do they call it? Roughhousing?"

Julianna scrolled through her machine. Seema didn't know what to say, but knew she had to say something.

"Sure," she said.

. . .

WHEN SEEMA got home, she threw off her blouse and just left it in the foyer for Jamilla or the new girl to pick up. Wearing only her bra and jeans, she went to the kitchen to find Shiva sitting by the dishwasher. He kept flicking through its modes by turning a knob, DRY, ECO DRY, FAST DRY, and then minute settings, 30, 60, 90, 120. Each beep of the machine, each change of the display, thrilled him. The eye contact between him and the LCD display was unwavering, the bond between him and the dishwasher so perfect that the rest of the world need not have existed.

Novie was in her own world, too, scouring Shiva's sippy cups by hand, because she had some issues with the dishwasher when it came to her charge's tableware. She filled them with milk and water, while singing what Seema thought might be a Christian hymn, the melody so familiar and yet not. Seema loved her. Novie could have found another job, with a less-fucked-up family, for similar pay, and yet she stayed on.

Seema dawdled there, her child and nanny oblivious to her presence. She held her naked belly in both hands, that foreign mass of cells, imagining what the four of them might be like: herself, Novie, Shiva, and maybe another boy on the spectrum, another Shiva. For a moment she was filled with this new love. And then she exhaled all that melancholy warmth and resumed her day.

7   *THE LUCK OF KOKURA*

ARRY WAS trying to focus, but at what? Shapes began to material-
ize. Circles. Triangles. Three panels in outrageously bright colors.
It was that squiggly AIDS painter guy from the 1980s. A figure fell
into his head. Something he had once discussed with Seema at a gallery. One-point-eight million. Okay. He was on a bed. He was hungry, but at the same time beyond hunger. He turned his head. There
were magazines displayed on a nightstand: a Bentley mag and a
Patek Philippe mag and a *Nat Geo*. He scanned the room quickly.
The rollerboard with his watches and Shiva's rabbit toy and the passport were neatly placed at the foot of the bed. There was also a glass
coffee table topped with a bottle of Fiji water, a jar of salted almonds,
and familiar-looking bars of 70 percent cocoa Chocolat Madagascar.
Barry crawled the length of the bed to the coffee table. He began
stuffing the food into his mouth, the nuts and chocolate crunching
sweet and bitter over his tongue, pouring the water into his mouth.
He burped ferociously, his whole being coming back to life.

The lights and blinds were all Lutron and a small closet concealed
the obligatory Crestron rack for the audiovisuals, scattered among
boxes of Lanvin sneakers. He peed his heart out into a Porcelanosa.
The hand soap was by Molton Brown. He was definitely off the
Hound and back in hedgeworld. This guest room, if that's what it

was, was far better curated than the guest room Seema had put together. Jeff Park must have married well.

Barry was wearing a T-shirt with the words GEORGIA AQUARIUM across the chest and the photograph of a whale shark. Someone had changed him out of his Vineyard Vines. The Park wife again? Barry pressed the Lutron button to raise the blinds, and Atlanta appeared before him, the customary Wells Fargo and BB&T Tower, but also some old-fashioned RKO-style antennas and a deeply undistinguished 1970s edifice that scanned as Coca-Cola HQ. He could see the city still brimmed with underused space, acres of lots that called out for condos and hotels. Barry looked around for his sneakers, but they were not there. He had been in Asian households before and was familiar with their war on shoes.

A corridor of chilled marble emptied into a huge living space, and there Barry felt a burst of old pre-Greyhound hedgeworld jealousy. The living room was as palatial as the entrance to a modest New York museum. Enormous golden lights hung from the ceiling, which was at least twenty feet high—he knew the company that made them, Seema liked their work, but their ceilings back in the city were not high enough. Judging simply by the measurements of the great room, he would size the apartment at forty-five hundred square feet, minimum. This from a guy Akash Singh had fired from This Side of Capital, a guy who had to clear out his desk within an hour, a security guard hulking in the corner, watching his every move. He tried to console himself with the fact that Atlanta property, even at its gilded peak, would still cost a third of New York's. Okay, let's say forty-five hundred square feet at five hundred a foot, that would be what, just two bucks and a quarter? In New York, anything below five million didn't even qualify as luxury.

Lost as he was in his real-estate reveries, he failed to notice the sporty exhales of the property owner himself performing an impressive bout of push-ups in the middle of the light-filled space. Jeff Park still had his thick Asian hair, if not more of it, and he was clothed in some kind of black athletic gear that maybe would allow for scuba diving or travel to Mars. Eventually Jeff Park noticed his former employer casting a shadow over him. He hopped up from the floor in one youthful, thirty-something motion. "Barry," he said, "you're alive!"

Barry shook his host's hand eagerly. Full head of hair, gums that didn't recede, push-ups in the middle of the day. Jeff Park had gone to Cornell, if he remembered correctly, but had not played lacrosse. A fit striver with good, casual taste. He was to be approached just like a potential investor. Barry was ready to do a little Princeton two-step with a perfectly calibrated friend move.

"Jeff, right off the bat, thank you," he said. "You didn't have to welcome me into your home."

"I'm just glad we didn't need an ambulance," Jeff Park said. "Although I did call for a house visit from my family doctor."

"Cancel it," Barry said. "I'm feeling better than ever. Just low blood sugar is all. Hey, seriously. You're a peach of a guy. Where's your better half?"

"Still looking for that perfect girl, I'm afraid."

"And you decorated this place *yourself*?"

"Guilty as charged. Come, let me make you a corpse reviver." They walked to an area flanked by a shelf of Ciroc bottles that denoted general recreation. Jeff Park poured a glass of fizzy German mineral water. "You've got to hydrate," he ordered. "I want to see you finish this H_2O before you hit the hard stuff."

Jeff Park's corpse reviver was, as the name promised, a ridiculously potent blend of cognac, calvados, and vermouth served in a martini glass. "Jesus," Barry said as he finished his drink. Some vague memories of Downtown bars returned: Jeff Park could hold his own with the alcohol.

"So, what's up, Barry?" Jeff Park said. "Just passing through? Decided to look me up?" He had brought out a bottle of Yamazaki twenty year and was serving it straight up, quite decadent for 1:27 P.M. What the hell did Jeff Park do for a living? He had cashed out of This Side of Capital with zero.

"All of this is going to sound crazy," Barry said.

"Uh-huh."

"I'm on a journey. A journey by bus." Barry knew that he would eventually have to explain his flight from This Side of Capital to people in his bracket. He knew that news of his "meltdown" would immediately form the latest bulletin in the incestuous, bloodthirsty world from which he had sprung. But he doubted it would really surprise anyone. The people in his world could be nuts. One fund was essentially a cult with its own bible, ritual mind control, and feats of strength. A fellow at another fund, a quant billionaire-in-training, played piano at a third-rate bar while passing around a tip jar. Like your first ankle monitor bracelet or your fourth divorce, the occasional break with reality was an important part of any hedge-fund titan's biography.

"The things I've seen," Barry said, and he told Jeff a few of his adventures so far.

Jeff Park seemed interested. He poured more drinks, although he insisted Barry chase his with water. "It sounds a little bit like you're doing a version of *On the Road*," Park said. "The one-eyed Mexican guy who fell asleep on your shoulder."

"That's exactly right!" Barry shouted. "That's exactly what I thought when that happened." No wonder he had picked Jeff Park to host him, the man had literary sensibilities beyond most of his colleagues. They really did a good job of educating up at Cornell.

"I used to take the Greyhound to visit my uncle's family in Savannah," Park said. "Everyone there looked at us like we were freaks."

"Everyone looks at *me* like *I'm* a freak!"

"You kind of are a freak, Barry."

Barry took that as the highest of compliments. He was bonding with this former employee. They were going to be friends. "Are you from around here originally?"

"Yeah. I moved back down to take care of my parents."

"Your parents are, I want to say, from China?"

"Close enough."

"My wife is Indian."

"Rock."

"You ought to get married!" Barry said, completely forgetting that his own marriage was but a team of seven lawyers short of kaput, to borrow his father's favorite word. Maybe this nice Jeff Park couldn't find a woman to marry away from New York. He had given up on finding a partner just to take care of his parents. Immigrants. Barry wanted to tell him that his own mother died when he was five, but they weren't there yet. He eyed his glass of Yamazaki as Atlanta blazed cruel beyond the tinted floor-to-ceiling windows. His instinct to help Jeff Park was overwhelming. He remembered Seema's friend, the Asian woman from Brooklyn. Tina? Lena? "I threw away my cell phone," Barry said.

"Now *that's* amazing," Jeff Park said.

"Can I check something on your computer?"

A laptop was provided. The world of the Internet felt so far away from who he was at this point. Still, he brought up Seema's profile. No new posts in forever. Seema was not an avid social media person, a fact he loved about her. "Is that your wife and kid?" Jeff Park asked.

The profile photo in the corner of the screen was of Seema with her arms *almost* around Shiva, behind them the neo-Georgian shell of the six-thousand-square-foot Rhinebeck house in progress. Shiva was looking away, but in a super-intelligent way, which made the whole thing look like a portrait in normalcy, maybe precocity, and, anyway, Seema's best Bollywood smile lit up the landscape better than any sun. Her cleavage was open and ready and golden.

"What a gorgeous family you have," Jeff Park said. "When I worked for you I think you were just about to get married. That kid. Those eyes."

"Yes," Barry said, his hand frozen over the keyboard. A *Sesame Street* song started playing in his head. *C is for cookie, that's good enough for me.* "But here's what I wanted to show you," he said. He scrolled through the list of Seema's friends, looking for an Asian. He thought he hit pay dirt with one of them, but it turned out to be that horrible Hong Kong doctor, Luis's wife, Julianna Yang-Goodman, a photo of Rio's *Christ the Redeemer* statue behind her for some reason. He scrolled some more and finally found the right one.

"Now this girl is *spunky*," Barry said. "She called me a tool to my face! And I think she's pretty intellectual like you. Oh, one night, in Brooklyn, she made these great Chinese dumplings for us. I bet your folks would love her."

"Mina Kim," Jeff Park read off the screen. "Not really up my alley."

Barry was heartbroken. "But she's Chinese!"

Jeff Park stared at him. "I'm more into the southern-belle type," he finally said.

"Oh." Barry sighed.

"But thanks for looking out for me. You're like that woman from *Fiddler on the Roof.*"

Barry sort of knew what he was talking about. *Matchmaker, matchmaker, make me a match.* Jeff Park had a wide cultural reach. "Well, I'm going to make it my mission to get you married," he said. "Nice guy like you."

"I'm not averse to the ladies," Jeff Park said. "I've designed this place with them in mind."

"How so?"

Jeff Park took him on a tour, starting with a massive glass-topped dining table. "You see these lights?" he said, pointing out a trio of Sputnik-style globes hanging over the mirrored surface. "The average girl I date is five foot six, or an inch taller than the national average. I have a spreadsheet that lists the attributes of each girl I've ever dated. It's super granular. So if I'm making her dinner, and she's standing here, waiting for me, talking to me, maybe having a drink, the light from these lamps is directly level with her eyes. She can see better, and I can enjoy her glow."

Barry was impressed by Park's thoughtfulness. A spreadsheet. The rap on guys in finance was all wrong. They cared *too* much. He knew he did. If you looked at it a certain way, he had abandoned his family because he didn't have the emotional bandwidth to accommodate their special needs. He examined a frigate-sized couch. "This sofa is the perfect height for a five-foot-six woman," Jeff said. "When she sits down, the sofa waterfalls at the back of her knees." He invited

Barry to sit down. "You see, there's a gap of at least three inches between the back of your knee and the couch, because you're tall. But if you were a five-foot-six woman, you'd be completely snug."

"So you only date women of that height?" Barry asked.

"Well, there's some variance," Jeff Park said. "Maybe half a sigma. I don't want the tail wagging the dog. But, yeah, mostly."

"You're a romantic," Barry said. Jeff Park shrugged and blushed. He was not unhandsome; his face was chiseled and tanned to a dusky perfection. The black athletic gear made him look like a glossy seal in human form. Only the Rolex Sky-Dweller on his wrist did not appeal to Barry's taste.

Upstairs Park had an airy office with a full view of the awful Coca-Cola tower. Barry felt a twinge of passion at the sight of a Bloomberg up and running. Jeff Park had only one screen going, which was cute. On a glass board, he had sketched out some trades that appeared exceptionally long-term and cautious, making some kind of play around Alcoa and Dow. Just scanning the numbers on the board, Barry assumed an AUM of thirty-five million, which in the best of worlds brought in, what, a couple million a year? He probably had a net of ten to fifteen. And he could live on it. And be happy. And buy couches that waterfalled the legs of median women.

"I trade maybe two hours in the morning, and then I spend the rest of the day working on myself," Jeff Park said as they passed a formidable wall of books, most of them new and clearly not bought by the yard. "I read at least a hundred books a year, and if I'm at, let's say, seventy by November, I'll take the rest of the year off from work to catch up. I like reading books to the girls I date, Beckett plays, Chekhov stories, Shakespeare sonnets. Believe me, they need it around these parts."

"Wonderful, just wonderful," Barry said. "This is what I'm talking about. Real self-improvement. A vocation and an avocation."

"So many guys say 'I want to die at my peak net worth,' but not me."

"Clearly not."

Jeff now led him into a bathroom. They were looking at the double mirrors that functioned as TVs in the rain-shower tub. The GOP convention in Cleveland was in full blaze. Ted Cruz was saying he would not be voting for Hillary, but he wasn't going to endorse Trump either. "I used to stay at the Trump Hotel on Columbus Circle whenever I visited New York," Jeff Park said. "Never again."

"I'm a moderate Republican," Barry said. "Socially liberal."

They went downstairs for a new course of drinks. Jeff Park was making them with ruby-red vodka and Seagram's soda now. They sat at a table made from the cross section of a giant tree. Its height was also designed to seduce an average woman. Barry felt around the serrated bark of the edges. He liked his furniture slightly rustic with hints of the Arts and Crafts movement; that was supposed to be the motif of the Rhinebeck house, if he ever finished it. "Who made this table?" Barry asked. The vodka-and-soda combination was delicious.

"It's a Japanese eucalyptus," Jeff Park said. "I bought it in Kokura. It reminds me of how lucky I am."

"Kokura?"

"You never heard of 'the luck of Kokura'? August ninth, 1945. An American bomber was headed to bomb Kokura in the south of Japan. But there was too much cloud cover over the city that day. So the plane was diverted. To Nagasaki."

"Wow. Lucky for sure."

"Right. Luck. If I were born in Bangladesh to a family of ragpickers, would any of this happen?" He gestured at his forty-five hundred square feet of property. "My mother worked as a maid in Buckhead when they got here. I still remember the food stamps with the drawing of the old whiteys signing the Declaration of Independence. I memorized the words on it. 'U.S. Department of Agriculture Food Coupon.' Where else could a maid's son end up like this? That's why I'll always take care of my folks. Why I'll always live in the same town as them. I've got to honor the luck that was given me."

Barry thought of his own relationship with his parents. He had not had the opportunity to take care of his mother, of course, but he thought he had been kind enough to his father, given everything. After he had secured his first billion under management, he had bought out Malibu Pools for four million dollars, about ten times what it was worth, so that his dad could finally retire. But after that gesture, and after his father's openly racist behavior at his and Seema's wedding, he mostly avoided the old man. He went out just once to La Jolla, California, where his father was living with his girlfriend Neta, whom he had found on an online Zionist forum.

Neta was a former social worker and had two grown kids in LA. The moment she met him, she pressed Barry into her freckled décolletage and proceeded to give him a detailed tour of her beautiful garden, where she and Barry's father spent most of their time, drinking coffee and looking at their laptops. Her house was a 1940s U-shaped ranch, the ideal of a California ranch with back-to-back fireplaces, wild beehives in the pepper trees, little gardens of shiso leaf and miniature roses, two box turtles, and a rabbit named Sylvester whose very presence almost brought Barry to tears, because it reminded him of his own difficult brown-eyed rabbit at home. There were Natal plums that Neta's kids used to throw on the streets to watch them get run over, and blood-orange shrubs in the front yard, and mandarins and tangerines and green Romantica roses and pink peppercorns and magnolia trees and pretty-in-pink Indian hawthorn blossoms, and in the middle of what even the Holy Bible would have to acknowledge to be the *true* Garden of Eden sat two elderly people in their Make America Great Again caps silently scrolling through the latest outrage to their common gene pool in the dusty hills and valleys of another land.

"I'm so sorry about your son getting autism," Neta had said. "Did you give him vaccines? I'm sure that's what did it." "I told him not to get the vaccines!" his father hollered from his perch beneath a plum tree. "I sent him the link about how the Somalian Muslims were spreading it through their doctors in Minnesota." Barry was out of there in less than thirty-six hours. Five months later his father was dead of pancreatic cancer.

Maybe Jeff Park was just a better son. And maybe better sons made for better people, and that was why their mothers didn't die in car accidents, their faces caked in blood.

"But that's not luck," Barry said, returning to the theme of the conversation. "Sure, it's helpful not to be born to ragpickers, but mostly your success was a result of your own hard work. And your parents' gumption to move here."

"You don't consider yourself lucky?"

"Not for a minute," Barry said.

"You found yourself working in the right industry at the right time. No regulation. All the leverage you could eat from the banks. I'm not even going to mention the insider trading that's just part of being in the old boys' club."

"I don't *think* we're under investigation," Barry said, which was to say the FBI hadn't broken down their door yet. Jeff Park looked at him. What could he know?

"Hey, I'm not knocking what we do," Jeff said. "It takes smarts. But so much of it is luck. You execute one good trade, and people will listen to everything you say for the next five years."

"All I know is I never had any advantages," Barry said. "I wasn't even lucky enough to be born to immigrant parents."

Jeff Park laughed. "Now *that's* funny." They clinked glasses.

BARRY WAS sprawled on his guest-room bed, the room spinning around him. He had found someone to talk to. The days without Seema's chatter had taken their toll, but now he had a friend again, and a friend who wouldn't talk about Shiva's diagnosis 24/7. He took off his Georgia Aquarium whale-shark T-shirt and wondered if Jeff Park had swapped out his Vineyard Vines for it personally. The intimacy would be a little shocking, but it pleased Barry nonetheless. He was fine with his body.

The whole thing about luck made him wonder, though. Barry considered himself entirely self-made. His father hadn't collected food stamps like Jeff Park's family, but he used to get all his towels cheap from a source at an upstate prison. Every raggedy towel Barry ever knew as an adolescent had been stamped with the legend HUD-SON CORRECTIONAL FACILITY. It took three towels to dry himself after a shower. Frugality was the motto of the two Cohen men and the depressed sheepdog in their redbrick semidetached duplex on Little Neck Parkway, with the plastic chairs on the little green island of front yard and the thick security gates for the robbers that would never come. His father's business servicing Nassau County pools was seasonal, and he could never squirrel away enough for the winter. Barry's first crush must have been the blond mermaid on the Chicken of the Sea tuna cans his father bought four for a dollar at Wald-baum's.

Not that Jeff Park had had great luck in life either. Just six months into his tenure at This Side of Capital, probably a year shy of turning thirty, he had omitted a minus sign in an Excel spreadsheet and turned negative margins positive and a clear sell into a screaming buy. The trade was losing 30 million a day, and by the time he discovered the error, it was down 150 million. A simple error had cost the fund close to 10 percent of AUM. Barry hadn't been there for the actual moment, but he heard that when Jeff Park had realized what was happening, he passed out, smashing his head right into a Starbucks on his desk. He had to be taken to the hospital with light burns and a moderate concussion. The hit to his reputation was even worse, and rumors soon spread that he was selling real estate down in Florida. Beyond the actual loss of money, it was a sad story, although it cracked some people up. Akash Singh wasn't one of them. He said he had never expected such negligence from an Asian. And now Barry was lying around in Jeff Park's guest bed in his underwear.

There was a knock on the door. "Yeah," Barry shouted. "What's up?" Jeff Park wanted him to know that dinner would be at seven. "Can't wait!" Barry shouted back, and he meant it.

BARRY LOVED Richmond, but Hotlanta as they unironically called it was pretty incredible, too. They tooled around in Jeff Park's Ferrari California, simple working-class people on street corners calling out their love for the car or whistling at it as Manhattan construction workers would after a curvy woman. *"Uh-huh,"* they said thrusting their hips. The Ferrari felt a bit much, like Jeff Park hadn't gotten the "0.1 Percenter's Memo" about *experiences* not objects being the shit, but then again Barry collected watches, so who was he to talk? Over time, the ceramic brakes on Jeff Park's Ferrari had started failing from the lack of excessive speed, and the only solution, according to his dealer, was to go at least eighty miles per hour on an off-ramp and then brake like crazy. The thrust of speed and then its abrupt demise thrilled Barry. "This is like astronaut training," he said.

They were driving around hipster neighborhoods, passing acres upon acres of Craftsmen, some perched on little hills, others flush with the sidewalk, all with some kind of colorful expression of their owner's taste, an appliqué of a butterfly on the front porch or the hulk of some magnificent seventies vehicle idling by the curb in a state of tasteful neglect. Jeff Park explained that this neighborhood was called the Old Fourth Ward and that the hip-hoppy music they were listening to was called OutKast, which was a local African American group or band or something.

The restaurant they went to for dinner was outfitted with a bunch of hunting trophies along the walls, deer mostly, but also a cow and maybe an impala. "I like Hemingway," Barry said. "One of my life goals is to learn to hunt like him." There were also jars of pickled stuff—okra and string beans, it looked like. He had never seen so many stunning black people gathered together in a single restaurant. In Richmond, a place like this would be all white. He could already imagine sharing this experience with Layla.

"So I've developed a spreadsheet on the best restaurants in Atlanta, and this place is number seventeen," Jeff Park said. For someone whose career was almost done in by a spreadsheet, Jeff Park certainly kept store by them. Maybe this was his attempt at Excel redemption. "The food is great, but I had to take off points for the service," he said.

"I've been on the Greyhound for days," Barry said. "I've survived on pork rinds and off-brand coffee."

"It's like you're suffering for all of us," Jeff Park said. Barry wondered whether many Chinese people were Christians.

The food—salad garnished with buttermilk, bacon and potato, and catfish sausage with fermented lemon—practically gleamed off the tableware and tasted both southern and progressive, kind of like how Barry imagined Layla tasted right about now. He couldn't be happier. They had ordered the most expensive wine on the menu, a $136 blend of grenache and Syrah from God knows where, which both deemed acceptable if a little aggressive. Barry wanted a second bottle, but he knew he had to pay for the meal and was down to around seven hundred dollars. He was glad he had starved himself on the Hound. Every penny mattered now. He wished he still had accounts he could tap in a Wells Fargo–type bank, like normal people, but his whole life was on the black Amex, the rest funneled through This Side of Capital and some reinsurer on the Caymans. The bill came out to three hundred, or half of Barry's new net worth.

"This place is moving up two spots on my spreadsheet," Jeff said. "Although, maybe it's just the company." He smiled at Barry.

Barry could feel himself blushing. In Arab countries, you were allowed to hold a male friend's hand. He had learned that from Qatari Ahmed during a very long and confusing night of drinking at the St. Regis. "Let's put on more of that OutKast music," he said, when they got back in the Ferrari. "It's very smart."

They drove to a mall in a former industrial building called Ponce City Market, which was like Chelsea Market in New York, only it was in Atlanta. They climbed up the elevated tracks to a new park called the BeltLine, which was just like the High Line in New York, only it was also in Atlanta. As they started down the railbed, two women with thick southern accents asked Jeff Park to take a photograph of them with their phone. He said he would be "dee-*light*-ed," his own accent reverting to what it must have been before Cornell sanded off the edges. The women wore very little and were almost beautiful. One of them, a tall blonde, had a cast on her leg, which was attractive for reasons he couldn't fathom, but the other one was younger and had a goofy smile.

"Now the one with the cast, she's a classic example of the south-ern belle," Jeff Park said after the women had left them.

"That's your type!" Barry said. "Should we go back after them? You could offer them a ride in your car. They would love that."

Jeff Park shrugged. "I don't know," he said. "Probably not." The sun was setting and the humidity was unpleasant, but Barry wanted to walk deeply into the night. There were trees and grass all around them, and sometimes a clump of skyline would come into view. Barry had counted at least three skylines in Atlanta already.

"So," Jeff Park said, "a part of me has to ask. And I know this may not be your favorite topic." Barry got this idea that somehow Jeff Park had found out about Shiva and the diagnosis. He did not want to have to lie to his new friend.

"Ask away," Barry said.

"What the hell happened with Valupro?"

"Oh," Barry said. *"That."*

Valupro, RIP, had been a pharmaceutical company that Barry fell in love with many years ago; in fact, right after Jeff Park had been canned. He wasn't the only one, of course, half the hedgies he knew had gone nuts for it, but Barry's erection was more pointed than the others, and it entailed, at one point, about half of his book. Valupro had promised value—or, per its name, "valu"—but not to its cus-tomers who would see their pharmacy bills explode if they happened to be ill with some exotic but deadly disease of the tailbone or pu-dendum. No, the company promised mad *valu* to its shareholders, and the phrase "shareholder value" was Barry's favorite.

"We are a nation of shareholders," he had said more than once to Seema, trying to articulate his brand of no-nonsense but compas-sionate capitalism. Once, before the diagnosis, walking alongside Novie as she pushed Shiva's stroller down the street, he stopped both of them, pointed at some sweaty creatures emerging from the local Charles Schwab, and repeated that phrase to Shiva, who was sucking on his pacifier and didn't seem to care either way if ours was a nation of shareholders or not. Several times during his Greyhound trip, Barry had paused to consider that, although he loved his fellow passengers deeply, he could not trust them at the voting booth because they were not shareholders. They did not understand the thrill and the pain and the *obligation* of owning a part of their country.

In any case Valupro was run by a charming alcoholic nebbish named Sammy Yontif. "Wait a second, what's a nebbish?" Jeff Park asked. Barry explained that it was a Yiddish term denoting a timid, submissive man. His father had hated nebbishes even more than he hated schnooks or schnorrers.

Yontif wore triple-thick frames and not so much cargo shorts as cargo pants and cargo *shirts*, the better to hide his pouches of fat. He twitched a lot and came across as the bad-breath chemistry teacher you sort of had to love back in high school if you were at all generous with your teenage heart. "You're a smart guy," Sammy Yontif had mouth-breathed the first time he met Barry. "*You* know value." Barry hadn't been called smart since high school. He was intrigued and wanted to hear about Valupro's business model. "Here's our business model," Yontif said. "Fuck R and D. Fuck it. We're not going to cure cancer, we're not going to save the world. We're going to deliver value to investors like you."

Delivering value meant buying foreign drug companies for cheap and then using them for tax-inversion purposes. Barry loved this part. His hatred of our nation's tax regime was absolute. Why not pay taxes in Ireland instead? Or why pay taxes at all? Barry adored how Yontif cared so little about appearances, this fat fiery Rutgers-graduated nebbish in a cargo shirt who would probably have been forced to hang himself at Princeton. He and Seema and Yontif and Yontif's sumptuous Seema-grade Croatian girlfriend whiled away three days on a yacht together off of Sardinia. The nebbish and the Croat spent their time drinking caseloads of prosecco and amiably throwing up starboard. Seema, pregnant with Shiva, was not amused, and at one point demanded a helicopter evacuate her from the carnage. "This is a business of relationships," Barry kept whispering to her.

Valupro's value rocketed throughout the rest of the summer. Qatari Ahmed looked ready to give Barry a serious hummer. And then it all went to shit. Someone squealed. Most of the profits were an illusion that came from buying other companies and then using every accounting trick known to man. A roll-up straight out of the Enron manual. The media and the politicians pounced on the way Valupro had hiked up prices on some lifesaving diuretic or whatnot, and the next thing Barry knew his fiery nebbish friend had checked in to rehab with a fifteen-million-dollar severance package. Barry's chief of staff, Sandy, had done the impossible and actually got him on the phone in rehab, but all he managed to croak out was the single word "value." Barry wanted to stand by his friend, this guy who had accomplished so much with, socially speaking, so little. He held tight to his position, and a month later the stock had plunged from five hundred to fifty. Another month later, there was no stock.

"I would never trade Valupro," Jeff Park said. "There was a lot of hair on that company. In fact, to be honest, I shorted it."

"Oh," Barry said. "I thought all your trades were long-term."

"I couldn't help myself. That was low-hanging fruit. It was the opposite of value investing."

"Don't get all Warren Buffett on me," Barry said.

The men walked along in silence. They were in a deeply forested part of the BeltLine where the sounds and circumstances of city life were few, and for a second Barry felt they had left humanity entirely. "Can I offer you just one piece of advice?" Barry said. "As an older person?" He knew the Chinese revered their elders. Wasn't that why Jeff Park had moved down to this semisuburban city to be with his parents? "You can get a better watch than a Rolex Sky-Dweller. It looks like a Russian oligarch died on your wrist. That's not the image someone as smart as you wants to project."

Park laughed. "Ouch," he said. "I guess I struck a chord with Valupro. I'm sorry, man."

"You know what a Veblen good is?" Barry asked.

"Sure."

That was too bad, as Barry longed to explain it to him. Why was it so hard to mentor this slender younger man? The world was full of young Javons and Jeff Parks who were impervious to the wisdom of their elders. "All I'm saying is that you should be projecting your taste to others of your stature. Not to a southern belle in a leg cast."

"What's on *your* wrist?" Jeff asked.

"This is an F.P. Journe Octa Automatique. Journe makes nine hundred watches a year. Rolex makes close to a million."

Park held Barry's hand by the wrist and examined the watch. His hand was warm and dry, just like Seema's. "I like how the yellow-gold hour and minute dials are lost in all the negative space around them," he said. "That's very cool."

"Thanks," Barry said. He smiled. "You have very promising aesthetics."

"But the southern belles we just saw, they would know exactly what a Rolex is. But they would have no idea about your watch. They might even think you bought it at the airport. A Rolex of this size and weight merely announces the scale of my ambitions. I want to represent my value."

"But you must also own a Patek. You get their magazine."

"I got a 1518 perpetual in rose gold."

"Wow." Barry sighed. That rare watch was probably worth as much as Jeff's Hotlanta apartment. He wanted to feel good for this young man who was helping him out so much just when he needed it. Instead, he felt envious. No angry wife, no autistic child, no possible subpoena, no Wells notice on the horizon, just two good cars, a seven-figure watch, and time to read as many books as he pleased.

"I have a different takeaway from that Valupro story," Jeff Park said. They were circling back to the former industrial building that now served as a mall. "You tried to make a friend who turned out to be a bad person. And when he fell, you stood by him."

"Yeah, but that's the kind of life lesson I should have learned by high school," Barry said.

"Believe me, you're not as stunted as some of the other people I've met over the years."

"Thank you," Barry said. "I appreciate that." The Ferrari had

been parked in a special VIP zone, and now a young man ran to re-
trieve it. "Do you want to try that 1518 on for me tomorrow?" Barry
asked. "I'd love to see it in the metal."

SEVERAL HAPPY days ensued. Barry enjoyed sharing his timepieces
with Jeff Park, and his Patek 1518 in rose gold was indeed sumptuous.
The date and month were in French, and the moon phase glowed so
brightly it looked like the first drawing executed by a perfect child.
Jeff Park also kept a watch log in the form of an Excel spreadsheet,
and he and Barry spent a morning poring over each other's results.
Barry's were not good. The Pakistani air force–issued Omega Sea-
master/Railmaster had gained four seconds instead of the usual two.
The Patek 570 in white gold had gained twenty seconds a day, nearly
twice the usual. But the old Tri-Compax was the really sad story. It
had lost over three minutes a day. Maybe it needed an oil change, or
maybe it was just slowly lapsing into a coma. He could look up a
good watch guy in Atlanta on the Bloomberg, but he didn't know
how long he would be staying.

He wanted to stay just a little shy of forever. But it was a question
of money. Another meal like the three-hundred-dollar one they had
had would ruin him. He looked up some of This Side of Capital's
positions on Bloomberg. It was a massacre. How much of a dent
would this shit make in his own net worth? Dudes who were about
to belly flop often signed everything over to their wives, but he
couldn't do that if he was going to divorce his.

Jeff Park had lent him his other car, which was a Bentley something or other, informing him that the rich interior leather had cost
the lives of six cows. The whole thing smelled like a feedlot, and the
worst of it was that it had mileage of maybe nine miles to the gallon,
so that Barry had to shell out forty bucks at a Sunoco. Thank God
for cheap gas. On the other hand, wherever he parked in Atlanta, a
young black man would run out and say something complimentary
about the car before slotting it in the VIP section right out front.
Also he liked listening to the OutKast song where the lead singer

(rapper?) was apologizing to Ms. Jackson because he was for real. This was the kind of knowledge he could use on the Greyhound to spark a conversation.

He wondered what it would take to become Jeff Park's mentor again. Sandy had said that Akash Singh still considered him a mentor, "a father almost." He would sometimes take out his Patek 570 and trace the LEADER OF MEN engraving with his fingertip. Maybe some of those guys did still believe in him, despite the Valupro fiasco. He had come of age with them at Goldman, then plucked them off to form a team at Joey Goldblatt's Icarus Capital, years before he spun off to start This Side of Capital. They would eat together, go to the gym together, vacation together, and also indulge their carnal sides together.

At Icarus Joey Goldblatt used to keep a map of Manhattan with all the rub-and-tug joints clearly marked. The guys did a lot of business over at FlashDancers, and Barry was not immune to the delights of a really dirty lap dance. He was single, after all. But he dreaded the rub-and-tug joints. There was one night in particular when he found himself with his team in Oriental Touch or Seoul Cycle. The dinginess of the place shattered him. There was a decoration for some kind of Asian bird, a crane stenciled cheaply over a body of water, and a Korean Air calendar. The airline calendar was especially depressing, because it made him believe that these girls really wanted to go home to their families. He wouldn't remember the face of the woman he was assigned, she was mostly eye makeup, but he couldn't have a physical encounter with her. Instead they lay on a bunch of towels on a mattress in their underwear looking out onto an air shaft. They talked about art history, which the woman had been studying at one of Seoul's lesser universities. She made it clear that if you weren't "on the A-team" in Korea, you ended up here. She asked him which part of finance he worked in. She got a lot of guys from the European banks. She advised him to collect the works of Yayoi Kusama, a Japanese artist Joey Goldblatt was oddly enough wild about. He must have come here a lot.

The allotted sixty minutes expired chastely, the two of them lying on the towels in their underwear. It was painfully clear how much this woman didn't want to have sex with him. This just wasn't how he pictured free markets. He tried not to hear his boys climaxing next door, especially Akash Singh, who was very, very loud. The next day he gathered his team and told them he didn't think going to these kinds of places was good for them. They were going to conquer the world! One day they'd each have AUMs of over ten billion. They didn't need dirty brothels. His boys were mostly a bunch of lax bros from Duke and Cornell, with a smattering of friendly Princeton overlords-in-training and two Indians from CalTech. He was, at most, five years their senior, but that counted for a lot when you were as young as they were. The boys heeded his call, and many began to explore the world of artisanal hookers and the burgeoning new pay-for-play field of "sugar daddies."

Over the years, Barry took his capacity as a moralizer seriously, steering his boys away from paid girlfriends and into the worlds of watch collecting and moderate Republican politics. He encouraged them to date ladies from good women's colleges and acted as something of a matchmaker, even as his own bed lay cold. By the time he had formed This Side of Capital, all the boys were married, except for the incorrigible Akash Singh. On the first anniversary of his hedge fund, a week after the Qatar Investment Authority signed on and their AUM topped two billion, the boys all came together to give him the classy Patek Calatrava with the engraving he now saw before him. Until Shiva was born, it had been the proudest day of his life.

Barry hadn't had sex with Seema in three months. At night, he often dreamed of Layla. In one dream, they were in a Wells Fargo branch, and she was entirely naked. The bank had a coffee shop in the back where he and Layla were just sitting at a banquette, sipping Americanos. People passing them by with deposit stubs hardly noticed Layla's long, bare body, the hollowness above her pubic bone, the unreformed pelt below, the fine teardrop shapes of her small breasts. Her nakedness was only for Barry. She was giving herself to him. He kissed her dry mouth and cupped one warm breast, and the people just walked past them on the way to the tellers. Barry awoke in a state of horniness he had not experienced since his first nights with Seema. His mouth was coated with lust, and his hands shook.

ON THE night Trump was scheduled to speak at the convention he and Jeff Park thought of a place to go and watch it. "It would be funny to just go to Buckhead," Jeff said. "See the rich crackers. Get jiggy with the GOP."

They drove around Buckhead in the Ferrari California listening to the "I'm sorry, Ms. Jackson" song. On a busy avenue, they parked in front of the Beer Curve, where a sign prohibited hoods, baggy clothes, and PANTS BELOW THE WAIST. "Looks racist enough," Jeff Park said. Barry laughed, feeling high on the complicity. Could he imagine doing something like this a few days ago when he was still the chief desk jockey at his office?

The bar was kind of a dive and, per the prohibitions outside, entirely white. There were white men of all ages here, some dressed in pink shirts like private-equity guys, others in baseball caps and lumpy denim jeans or Dickies. Some had brought their women, who all looked like the same woman, both highlighted and nondescript. "Here's to diversity," Jeff Park said, and they clinked Miller Lites. Barry throttled his down. *I'm drinking a Miller Lite!*

The barmaid was in her twenties, and she was gorgeous in a way that suggested maybe she hadn't been fully apprised of just how gorgeous she was. She had eyes darker than the delicious Maker's Mark chocolates Barry had found in Jeff Park's fridge, and her skin was as olive as Barry's. "So who are you voting for?" Jeff Park asked her, his rose-gold Rolex Sky-Dweller lighting up a patch of bar around him.

The barmaid opened her gorgeous mouth. Barry thought he knew what her answer would be. But he was wrong. "I *despise* Hillary Clinton," she said. "I just don't trust her."

"But come on!" Jeff Park said. "Trump."

"Socially I'm a bit more liberal," she said. "But Trump's going to rebuild the economy to where it should be. The condos around here aren't being built fast enough under Obama."

Barry thought that was an odd thing to say. It wasn't like she was going to Emory or anything. She was a bartender at a lousy racist bar. Barry was as trickle-down as any guy, but what did the building of Buckhead condos have to do with her lot in life?

A filthy old homeless guy walked into the bar and said something in Spanish to the barmaid. He gave her a pair of sunglasses he had apparently found in the parking lot. "You want water or a Coke?" she asked him.

"Coke," he rasped, and then made a smoking motion with his hand. She produced a handful of cigarettes. He stood there for a good five minutes savoring his free Coke, each sip punctuated by a burp that made his eyeballs tremble, then lit up a cigarette with a wet book of matches that took another five minutes to spark.

"That was very nice of you," Jeff Park said to the barmaid.

"Eduardo comes in here all the time," she said. "He used to sweep up all the bars in Buckhead, and people took care of him. Now it's just me."

"See," Barry said to his friend, "this is the thing about America. You can never guess who's going to turn out to be a nice person."

The guys wanted to know if there was anything to eat at the bar, and the barmaid gave them a Domino's Pizza menu. "You got to try the Philly cheesesteak pizza," she said. "I could eat it every night." Jeff Park said something to the effect of wanting to eat it every night with her. They had a nice flirt going on.

Most of the young people in the bar were talking about sports and their own bygone athleticism, but then a trio of pink shirts came in from the heat and clustered around the screen with Barry and Jeff Park. "Can you believe this election?" Park asked them. He wasn't shy about talking to people at all. Did that come naturally, or had he spent his childhood practicing his *own* friend moves? A Chinese dude in the South. It must have been hard.

"Trump's going to win by a landslide," the leader of the pink shirts said. He was the kind of guy Barry had gone to college with, only Georgian. "Everyone knows Hillary's a liar. The folks up in Ohio and Pennsylvania, they sure know."

"I agree completely," Barry said. "Lower taxes and less regulation, that's my middle name. I've voted only Republican since I've been eighteen. I think Obama's been a nightmare for this country. But I'm from New York, and honestly, Trump scares me."

As soon as Barry had said the last sentence, the pink shirts turned around in unison and left the bar. They just walked right out of the place without a word. "Nice going," Jeff Park said. "You scared away the Trump Youth."

"I've never had people walk out on me," Barry said. "They say I'm the friendliest guy on the Street."

"Maybe don't announce that you're from New York and scared of Trump in one go." Jeff Park looked flirtatiously at the barmaid who slapped them with two more Miller Lites. The Domino's Philly cheesesteak pizza arrived via a gray-haired black gentleman who had difficulty breathing. Barry dug into it with the same insatiable hunger he now brought to the rest of his life. His mouth these days was mostly about salt.

Trump came on. "I humbly accept," he said. A bunch of college-age Republican boy-hipsters had gathered around Barry and Jeff Park to cheer on their nominee. They all had thick beards and were going bald. Barry was scared to say anything, lest they walk out on him, too. "I'm not voting for Hillary," one of them said to Jeff Park who was gently teasing their opinions out of them. "It has nothing to do with her being a woman, it's that she's proven she can't run the country."

"That sounds like it has *a lot* to do with her being a woman," Jeff Park said.

When Trump mentioned his support of "the great state of Israel," the most bearded of the Trump boys said, sarcastically, "Well, *that* just got you some votes," and the rest of his cohort laughed. Who were these people around him? Barry wondered. These barmaids who gave free Cokes to itinerant Mexicans but wanted to vote for a man who would make fun of his disabled Indian son?

The convention ended, and the hipster Trump supporters left to "turn it up a notch" elsewhere. Barry drank sadly. The bar was now filled with a bunch of guys in cargo shorts holding their beers at weird angles and girls in Daisy Dukes. A giant roach crawled by. This part of Buckhead was somehow at once wealthy and down-at-the-heels. The band looked like the two hairy white guys from ZZ Top. They were singing a rocked-out version of the song Barry had just heard. It was OutKast's "Ms. Jackson." "First Melania cribs Michelle Obama's speech," Jeff Park said, "now this."

Once again, Barry felt a generalized boredom around him, the boredom of a martial country without a proper war. Isn't that what Trump was promising his followers? An all-out conflict of their own choosing?

"I'm depressed," Barry admitted.

"Let's go back to my place and get some drink on," Jeff Park said.

They walked out into the night, which smelled of bad pizza and gasoline. When they got to the Ferrari, a drunk bro in a backward cap stumbled up to them. "I'll give you forty dollars for a spin around the block," he said to Jeff Park. His southern-belle girlfriend made pigeonlike noises behind him.

The guy actually took out two twenties. Jeff Park smiled sadly and shook his head. "I don't need it," he said.

"I can *see* that," the drunk bro said, gesturing at the Ferrari. They left it kind of amiably.

Barry and Jeff Park revved off toward Midtown. Jeff Park remained silent. "You okay?" Barry asked.

"That guy didn't even care about ogling my car in front of his girlfriend. I wasn't a threat to him, because I'm an Asian man."

It took a while for Barry to unpack that statement.

"In this town, you're either black or you're white," Jeff Park said.

Barry said some positive things about the inherent masculinity of Jeff Park and his automobile. He didn't get a response for a while.

"The top on this thing used to go down in fourteen seconds," Park finally said, "but now it takes eighteen. Everything's a scam."

Barry burped out some Domino's and beer and then reached over and put his hand on Jeff Park's shoulder. He wanted to add, *It's going to be okay,* but decided to let the gesture speak for itself. Jeff Park's shoulder moved unsubtly beneath his hand, the linen of his shirt slipping out of his grasp. Barry should have tried to give a friendly athletic shoulder massage, just like how his guys at the office used to do partly for laughs and partly because it felt *good,* but now it was too late. They drove the rest of the way in silence.

Back in the apartment, Barry pulled out some glasses and whiskey at the alcohol station to make them both "something to wash out that Miller Lite taste."

"You go ahead," Jeff Park said. "I think I'm going to turn in for the night."

"You sure?"

"Gentex announces premarket. My biggest position. Been long all month."

In his bed, Barry breathed hard, sniffing up the sweet alcohol of the Yamazaki in front of him. Fuck it, fuck it, *fuck it.* What had he done? But maybe it wasn't the hand-on-shoulder gesture. Maybe it was the earlier stuff about the guy in the baseball cap trying to get a spin in his Ferrari for forty bucks. Barry kept reconstructing the timeline over and over again. Ahmed had put his hand on his shoulder so many times. The Mexican man had laid his one-eyed *head* on his shoulder, and he hadn't flinched. It really didn't mean anything. It really didn't. Nothing at all. He just liked being close to his friend.

IT WAS early morning. Raining. The spires and crenellations of the Midtown buildings had taken on a gothic cast in the gloom. Barry carried his sorrow before him. "So I think it's time for me to shove off," he said.

Jeff Park was eating nuts for breakfast and sipping on a macchiato. "Okay," he said.

"Got to head to old El Paso. See an old friend. An ex-*girlfriend*."

Jeff Park smiled. "Props to your wanderlust."

Barry sat himself up on the counter. "This is going to sound embarrassing," he said. Jeff Park audibly swallowed a nut. "I'm going to need a tiny bridge loan to get me to El Paso and set me up for the first few days. I don't have access to my funds at the moment. Maybe two thousand."

"I can't do that, Barry," Jeff Park said.

That hurt Barry right away. "Why not? You've accommodated me for this long. This is just a loan."

"You're welcome to my house. Always. But I can't stake you."

"Who's talking 'stake'? Two thousand dollars. That's four percent of the cost of your Sky-Dweller. I feel like I'm getting mixed signals from you."

Jeff Park looked down at his lap. "You fired me, Barry," he said.

Ah, so there it was, finally.

"It wasn't me," Barry said. "It was Akash Singh. Everything at that place happens because of fucking Akash Singh."

"You were there. You invited me out to breakfast at the Casa Lever. And when I got there it was just you and the lawyer. What did the lawyer say? *I'm afraid we're going to have to part ways.*"

"But that's how it's done. That's just—the legal way."

"You didn't say one word."

"I wasn't allowed to say one word."

"And I thought of you as something like a mentor almost."

Barry sighed. "I'm sorry," he said. "It was nothing personal. I wanted to be a mentor."

"I know," Jeff Park said. "I fucked up. I still have dreams about that Excel sheet. I'm not making excuses. And this is nothing personal either. I like you, Barry." Their eyes locked, until Barry had to look away.

"I'm in genuine pain," Barry said. "So much of the time. Doesn't that deserve something?"

" 'Attention must be paid,' " Jeff Park said.

"What?"

"Death of a Salesman."

"Not right now," Barry said.

"I wish you had been straight with me," Jeff Park said.

"What do you mean?"

"You don't have any credit cards. You don't have a cell phone. You travel on a bus where you can pay for the tickets in cash. Is it that GastroLux trade? I mean, have you been subpoenaed? Did you get your Wells notice yet?"

"That's not why." Barry wanted to cry. "I didn't do anything wrong." He thought briefly, angrily, about that yacht off of Sardinia. The nebbish. The fucking nebbish. What did he say? It all led back to him. But even if the nebbish had said something and then Barry's fund had traded on that "material nonpublic information," where was the proof? So many funds had shorted GastroLux in size. It was the most shortable stock ever.

"I really don't care about GastroLux," Jeff Park said. "Even though your compliance department was always a joke."

"It's a witch hunt," Barry said. "They're after anyone who makes money. Anyone who has friends."

"My father used Hydroandetone. The diuretic. Frankly, he can't live without it."

"I don't follow."

"Valupro."

"Huh?"

"A month's supply went from thirty bucks to seven hundred as soon as Valupro bought the company that made the drug." Jeff Park paused, as if to let that figure register, but Barry had heard it all before. Prices went up. Shareholders profited. What part of "capitalism" didn't Jeff Park understand?

"And I've got money," Jeff said. "So I got my dad covered. But that's how I think of people like you. I always have the same visualization. I start with a row of middle-class houses like the one my dad lives in. And then I see you. You go from house to house, from family to family, and you take money from their wallets, from their purses, from under their sofa cushions, and you put it in your pockets, and when your pockets are full, you put it in a duffel bag with the logo of your fund. You don't sneak in. You don't break in. You just walk among these people as if they're invisible and you take the money they've earned. And then you go home and you buy a watch or whatever."

"Said the owner of a Patek 1518."

"I'm not blameless. But I have my limits. And I know who I am."

"See," Barry said, "that's what I'm trying to find out on this journey."

"Sure," Jeff Park said. "And then when it's over, you can tell people about it."

"I'm sorry?"

"You can tell them the story of how you once took a bus across the country. You can tell them about your 'journey.'"

THE BENTLEY entered the exciting world of Atlanta's Downtown. They passed Red Eye Bail Bonds and the Atlanta DUI Academy. A group of men had gathered outside the bus station to stare one another down with maximum malice. Several of them looked to Barry like the rapper Snoopy Doggy Dogg. "Be careful," Jeff Park said. "This bus station has a bit of a reputation."

The men outside were whooping it up about the car. "Bentley!" they shouted.

"I hope you find your southern belle," Barry said.

Jeff Park stuck out his hand and Barry shook it. "You're going to turn out better than me," Barry said. He grabbed his rollerboard and got out of the car before Jeff Park could say goodbye.

HOP, LITTLE BUNNIES

SEEMA WAS in battle mode. The whole team was gathered around her at the dining room table, their case notes out, phones shut off, bare feet on the herringbone floor. Two occupational therapists, a physical therapist, and two behavioral therapists, as well as the mega social worker who supervised them. All this was paid for by the city through its early intervention program, a fact she had mentioned to Barry several times, goading him to call it socialism. "Shit, with what *I* pay in taxes, this is the least we deserve," he'd always say, but her point was clear. The government, the city, to be exact, was providing the best care for their son.

Half of Shiva's caregivers were pregnant themselves, even though they were only in their midtwenties. Most of them hailed from uptown, Inwood, and beyond. They were sheer loveliness, the first in their families to be exposed to college and grad school, and they worked their asses off. Seema had gathered them to answer one question: how to conduct a playdate with Shiva and a child who was *not* on the spectrum. They batted around ideas. A quiet space. Plenty of his favorite Goldfish crackers, the ones without the cheddar. Lots of breaks. Playing the "C Is for Cookie" song on a loop.

Sitting at the head of the table surrounded by her team, Seema imagined what could have been. A partnership in a Midtown law office, associates flanking her on both sides, a heavy cloud of roast coffee over a table covered with briefs.

"Would it make sense to tell the other mother that Shiva's on the spectrum? To establish some ground rules?" This from Bianca, the occupational therapist who was Shiva's favorite.

Seema remained quiet, just nodding her head.

"Obviously, it's your decision," Bianca said. "Just it might be easier for Shiva. And for you." The new girl brought out the chocolate babka from a Union Square bakery that was Seema's most guilty weekly indulgence and shared it with the therapists. Bianca's pregnant belly was nearly as large as Seema's. She held Seema by her elbow. "It'll be okay," she said. "Whatever happens, it'll be a learning experience."

Seema had the Barry-like urge to give her some money in exchange for her kindness. The first thing he did right after their initial visit to Cornell last year was to call up an esteemed researcher from Yale and have him pay a house visit to Shiva in exchange for a two-hundred-thousand-dollar gift to his foundation. The Yale man spent twenty minutes with Shiva and essentially told him the same thing the Cornell woman, emphasis on the *woman* part, had said. Shiva was very much autistic. At the time, Seema thought it had been an impressive and caring gesture on Barry's part, but eventually she stopped thinking that. If only he could love his son as much as he wanted to control his own pain. She leaned over and hugged Bianca, who was licking her chocolate-babka-covered fingers. They both laughed at their hungry, pregnant selves.

THE PLAYDATE was Saturday. Luis had thankfully absented himself. Shiva was put into his favorite soft cashmere clothes that did not provoke his sensory issues. He stood there in the middle of his light-choked room as Novie and his mother fussed about him, looking like the tiny version of a pouty wealthy preppy from an eighties movie. "So beautiful," Novie said. "Such a *hand*some boy. Say 'Thank you, Mommy, for such nice clothes today.'" This was a strange Novie throwback to her native country, where children might have actually been expected to thank their parents for things.

Shiva flinched and wailed softly as his hair was softly brushed back by his mother, her palm lightly touching his warm and hard forehead. She knew not to wear perfume around her son. The air in the room was tense. Shiva's gaze was fixed entirely on the big hand of the Met Life clock tower, which would soon eclipse the smaller hand. When it did so, the two hands becoming one, the child exhaled.

Julianna brought her own nanny, who seemed like an old woman beside the vibrant Novie and the fire spirit that was Arturo. While the women shyly discussed the heat of the day and Shiva stood bewitched by the now-separating big and small hands of the giant clock, Arturo did a quick survey of the room, as if evaluating the wealth it contained. "Mommy, look!" he cried. "They have *all* the Elephant and Piggie books." His bright voice radiated toward Seema's silent son. A complete sentence. Subject, predicate, the works.

"Don't just grab things, 'Turo," Julianna said. "Ask Ms. Cohen if you could use them."

"Please call me Seema. And feel free to take anything."

"They have *Should I Share My Ice Cream?*" Arturo yelled. Shiva flinched and issued a rumbling warning from a lower depth.

"He napped very poorly today," Seema said to Julianna. "He's a bit out of sorts. Ain't that so, Mr. Grumpy?"

The Filipina nannies stood on the sidelines of the room, watching the action unfold, carefully evaluating each other.

"Why don't you read Elephant and Piggie with Shiva?" Julianna said. Her voice was authoritative but kindly. Was this her doctor's voice, even though she was probably the kind of doctor who didn't have real patients? "Shiva's your new friend," Julianna said.

"Well," Seema said. "I think at this age it's more like parallel play."

Arturo made a circle around Shiva and then finally came to a stop about a foot away from him. He looked at Shiva in a way that brought to Seema's mind the word "scrutinize." She remembered the way Luis looked at her. The three-year-old already had so many of his father's worst qualities. "Hi, Shiva," Arturo said. He waved his hand professionally. And then in a cloying, cute, raspy voice, "Do *you* want to read *Should I Share My Ice Cream?* with me?"

Shiva made another sound deep from within. Novie stepped behind her charge, alarmed. "This is so cute," Julianna said. She took out her phone and started snapping a current of photos of her son gesticulating in front of the immobile Shiva. The *Sesame Street* "C Is for Cookie" song ended and started again.

"Put on the next song!" Arturo yelled. "*D* is so delicious!"

"Shhh, maybe just speak a little softer," Seema advised the friendly child, but it was too late. The scratching noise within Shiva increased. And then, with the speed of an injured tiger, he lunged at Luis's son and pushed him directly onto his back, even as Novie leaped forward to stop him. Shiva squeezed out of her grasp and ran right into a wall that had already been dented many times with his pain. Seema felt the impact inside her. Her son was lying on the floor, then he was up again, then he was headed for the wall one more time.

ARTURO WAS crying. Shiva was looking at the world with his dark eyes, seemingly oblivious to the other child's distress, as Novie applied an ice pack to his new bruise. "I'm so sorry," Seema was saying to Julianna and Arturo. "He didn't mean that. He really didn't."

"That's true, 'Turo," Julianna said. "He's a nice boy. It was a misunderstanding." To Seema she said, "Is that a horsehair brush on the shelf? I have a nephew in Hong Kong who uses it."

Seema nodded. So that was that. Julianna *knew* what a horsehair brush was used for. And her first worry: Would she tell Luis? And her second: Was this what she wanted all along? For someone to *know*.

Julianna, now holding the brush, knelt beside Shiva. The child looked at her with either abject terror or complete hate; it was hard to tell which. She began to stroke the inside of his arms and then the back of his legs in long velvety motions. Seema was reading the Elephant and Piggie book to Arturo in her brightest voice while the nannies orbited the scene in confusion.

Julianna's bedside manner was impeccable. She knew not to hold Shiva while still letting him know she was there. "What would you like?" she asked him, following his gaze over to the Met Life clock. "Twelve-twenty," Julianna said. Shiva made a motion with his head. Was he nodding? Was he *fucking* nodding? Was that a gesture? No, it could not have been. Seema could never elicit such a thing. The brushing went on for minutes, both Julianna and Shiva settling into a kind of Buddhist hum, *Mmmmmmuhmmmmmmuh.* Seema robotically read one Elephant and Piggie book after another to Arturo. The neurotic, bespectacled Elephant bought an ice cream, but it melted before he could share it with the rambunctious Piggie. Elephant worried that Piggie had a new best friend and that he would no longer be the light of her life. Piggie bought a toy, and Elephant thought he broke it, and the two of them got mad at each other before realizing their friendship was more important than a toy. The two animals each expressed a range of emotions, which Shiva was supposed to copy, and which Arturo naturally, if not exaggeratedly, dubbed at will. Although he and Shiva were on opposite ends of a very large room, peace and calm were soon established.

"Is that a bouncy ball?" Julianna asked Shiva. His *mmmmuh* sound increased in tempo. "Would you like to bounce some?" Novie, wanting to be useful, quickly brought the ball over. Julianna picked the child up under his arms. He let her! With the same loving docility he directed toward Bianca, his favorite occupational therapist, Shiva let himself be held in the air and then deposited on top of the magical red ball. Slowly, Julianna began to bounce him and then, with a surprisingly well-tuned voice, to sing:

Hop, little bunnies, hop, hop, hop.
Hop, little bunnies, hop, hop, hop.
They're so still. Are they ill?
No! Wake up, bunnies.

Arturo upon hearing the song began to pretend he was also a rabbit, even using his fingers to replicate large rabbit teeth. He ran to his mother and Shiva. "I want to hop on the ball, too!" he shouted.

"Shhh," Julianna said. "Let's talk gently today. Take the little bunny by his arm here and let's bounce him together." Shiva flinched just a bit as Arturo's sweaty little hand touched his arm, but the bouncing motion was too pleasurable to deny. Without wanting to crowd them, Seema came up from behind and touched her son's shoulder. *Hop, little bunnies, hop, hop, hop,* they all sang as they bounced the boy, the nannies following along in their staccato accents, Arturo smiling with the same smile he had brought to their door. He was such a sweet kid. He didn't deserve Seema's jealousy. "Hop, little bunny," he whispered to Shiva. *Bunny.* Barry had always called Shiva his rabbit. She wished he could be here to see this, truly hated him for his absence for the first time since he had left.

"I want to give Shiva a hug!" Arturo said, speaking very softly.

"I think he'd rather you just stroke his arm and foot with this brush," Julianna said. She was, what, eight years older than Seema? A professional woman. A curer of Zika. What were her faults? She wanted too much for her son. Worried too much about him. Needed him to get into the HYPMS, Harvard, Yale, whatever.

Arturo was giggling and brushing Shiva. "You're such a soft little bunny," he said. Seema couldn't imagine that her child was in such close proximity to another child. She took out her phone and took a couple of pictures for the early intervention team.

When it was time to leave, Novie stayed behind to bounce Shiva some more in case he would melt down. "I want to get that bouncy ball, too," Arturo was saying. "And all the Elephant and Piggie books. And that brush!"

The part about wanting Shiva's therapeutic brush made Seema sad. But all she said was "You're welcome to come over and play with Shiva anytime."

"You have such a wonderful apartment," Julianna said. "And such a wonderful son."

Seema did not know how to respond. She shrugged. "Can you do me a favor?" she said. "Could you not tell other people? Not even Luis."

"Of course," Julianna said, although Seema immediately doubted her. What was the point of marriage if not to gossip before turning in for the night? "But let me ask you," Julianna said, "are you getting all the support you need?"

"He's getting forty hours of therapy per week."

"I don't mean that. I mean from family, friends." Seema wanted to tell her it wasn't any of her business, but that would be childish. "Because if you need help," the doctor said, "I'm just an elevator ride away."

SEEMA WAS lying in her bed, all the lights off, a hand over her eyes. She should have been happy. Shiva hadn't exactly made a "friend," even in the three-year-old sense of the word, but a boy had held his arm and helped him bounce and actually wanted to share in the sad things that he owned like that brush and that ball.

Three days ago Luis had slipped himself inside her. It was at the Gramercy, the day after her lunch with Julianna in the Beiruti place. She couldn't believe how strong he was, probably the strongest man she'd ever been with, and how he both held down her shoulders and said, over and over, that he loved her. "Can I come inside you?" he had whispered.

The answer was yes, but she begged him to keep it going for just another minute or two. She wasn't about to orgasm, she rarely came unless she was alone, but that pressure, on her shoulders, on her arms, on her belly, that could continue forever. When he pulled out, he shifted down to watch his semen flow out of her, which was odd, but Luis did a lot of odd stuff. He touched her lightly, enjoying his handiwork. "I want to have a baby with you," he said.

There was so much unexpected charm in that statement. Seema touched his prickly jawline with tenderness. "Look," she said. "I'm pregnant."

He didn't seem concerned. "Barry's, I suppose," he said.

"Well, duh."

"It's okay," Luis said. "I'll wait for my next chance in nine months. Or whenever."

She laughed. "Seriously?"

"I work fast. Latin and Jewish sperm. Instant pregnancy."

He swooped up to her and they kissed desperately, painfully. "But you would be okay with two previous children?" she asked.

"I'm fine with kids," he said. "Someone always takes care of them. Plus you're a woman of means."

"I thought you said I was 'a woman of purpose.'"

"Jesus, you don't forget anything. You're like a writer."

"I listen to everything you say. Because, you know. I love you."

His refractory period was under twenty minutes.

SEEMA OPENED Barry's watch safe. A good dozen watch winders, square cubes of dark tropical wenge wood, were humming the tune of an advanced civilization, slowly rotating the watches in a series of loops and reverse loops to keep them perpetually wound. Barry had once compared it to a prenatal unit. His prized watch was the Patek perpetual calendar in platinum, a watch Barry never wore, but which he worshipped daily. It was supposed to accurately keep the day and date and time until the year 2166. The only way it would ever falter was if it were not regularly wound or placed on a moving wrist or entombed inside a watch winder. Seema took the watch out and laid it facedown on Barry's night table. Within seventy hours or so, the watch would lose its spring energy, and the miraculous march toward 2166 would end, and there would be no near-eternity for Barry.

Seema breathed in and out, in and out, with great force, the way she had been taught by a meditation app she had abandoned a few months ago, because it had only made her more anxious. So now what? She had made a new friend and was sleeping with that new friend's husband. Her disabled child had made friends with the woman's son, also her lover's son. Her lover who wanted to have a child with her. Goddamn it. Where would it all end? And where the *fuck* was Barry? Her entire life had been made up of concrete plans, and now she was in limbo. She had done the unhealthy thing and looked up Layla Hayes on Facebook. She looked good for an old white woman, but El Paso? And no children? It was hard to believe this scrappy old scarecrow was supposed to be Barry's intellectual mate.

She took out her phone and started scrolling through the videos. There was Barry holding Shiva in the so-called Beyoncé Suite at Lenox Hill. He had one of those I-can't-believe-life-can-be-this-good smiles some of her former Jewish boyfriends sported after something incredible had happened to them, acing the GRE or having Seema go down on them for the first time. There were more videos of Barry holding Shiva, love and wonder lighting up his eyes, or burping Shiva on the little bagel-like Boppy where he had spent his nursing days. First-time mothers *sort of* knew what was coming, could feel it in their genes, but the fathers looked as delighted and scared as the first human to see the northern lights or the eternity of an ocean. The more she scrolled back through the phone's timeline, the more she knew what was coming up. Sardinia. At least a half-dozen videos of that miserable yacht trip, but only one fateful one. Well, nothing to do about that now. It was out of her hands. She had to make peace with what it portended. The end of Barry. The end of everything. Rage and fear tore at her, but also a sense of excitement. Instead, she went into Contacts and hit her mother's number.

"Mommy!" she said.

"I'm driving, Seema." Her mother's voice warbled off some sad Ohioan cell tower lost in a fake wood by the side of a near-empty highway.

"Mommy, Shiva is very sick!" Seema said.

"What? What did you say?"

"He's very sick, Mommy."

"I'm pulling to the side of the road." She could feel her mother's accent grow as her daughter's worry became her own.

"I'm off the road. Seema, what's happening to Shiva?"

"He was in a hospital." The lie felt strange, but there it was. "It was something in his lungs."

"We're flying over there," her mother said. "Right away!"

"I miss how Daddy says 'hut!'" Seema said.

"What? What are you talking about? What's in his lungs?"

Seema made herself calm down. She sat at the edge of the bed and let her body crumple into the kind of sad older body Layla Hayes surely possessed. "It was something bacterial," she said, "but now he's out of the hospital."

"He's in the hospital and now he's *out* of the hospital? What are you telling me? I don't understand you. What is wrong with you?"

"He's okay. They're going to make him okay. You don't have to come. He made his first friend." Maybe that's what she wanted to tell her mother all along. She would send all those snaps of Shiva and Arturo playing to her parents. So what if Shiva was bouncing on a ball in most of them? He was a fucking three-year-old. She could maybe edit out the horsehair brush.

Her mother was screaming so incomprehensibly now, that Seema could barely tell if some of it was in Tamil. "I want to be nearer to you and Daddy," Seema found herself saying.

"Well, of course you do," Seema's mother yelled from the side of the highway. "This is unnatural, how far away you live. We have only one grandson. And as for your sister." That line of thought would take up another three minutes, allowing Seema to regroup. "So now you want us to move to New York?" her mother was saying. "I have a life *here*." Her mother was the official All-Hindu Empress of Northeastern Ohio. There wasn't a wedding or a puja she hadn't attended in forty years. Even the Bengalis and Gujaratis deferred to her. "Or do you want to come back home? Is it over between you and Barry?"

"What?" Seema said. "Where did you get that?"

"He's just not as smart as you. So you tried marriage, but now you can get a divorce. You'll find someone else. You're good at that."

"Mommy, please."

"You have to send us *all* the doctor and hospital notes on Shiva's lung thing. And copy Shilpa. Not that she gets any damn Internet in

Nepal. Such strange daughters. Such a mess all the time. But Shiva's okay, right?"

"Oh, Mommy," Seema said, "I wish you could say a nice thing right now."

"Try to be a better daughter," her mother said.

"That's not a nice thing."

"Nice is not my specialty. Call your father if you want to hear something nice."

"Can you tell me you love me?"

"That you should know already."

"What if I don't? What if I got bonked on the head and had amnesia or something? Like in that Tamilian movie. Whatever. Something."

Seema could hear her mother start up her car again. "Is that what happened to you, Seema-*konde*? Because that would explain a lot."

"That's what happened to me."

"Then fine," she said. "Then I love you."

9   THE HORNY MENTOR

T HEY HAD driven past a sign that read WELCOME TO SWEET HOME ALABAMA in seventies cursive and, a little while later, passed through a downtown graced by art deco but unmarred by the presence of a single human being. This was Birmingham. They stopped for half an hour, and Barry got a Reese's Pieces ice-cream sandwich. His funds were low, but he didn't want to pass out from hunger again.

He was in a state of turmoil. His wife had said he had no imagination. His government wanted to slap him in cuffs. And now Jeff Park, a man he had mistaken for a friend, had accused him of taking money out of people's cushions. No one knew who he was. *No one.* Misunderstood, accused, humiliated. Back in his thirties, he had put in eighteen-hour days, hundred-twenty-hour weeks, to build his own business. And here he was on a Greyhound, wearing another man's whale-shark T-shirt, with two hundred dollars in his wallet. No matter. He would get through this. His Act 2 had begun.

New passengers boarded the bus. One of them was unlike the others. If Greyhound ever needed to advertise its services, they could use a fifteen-second roll of this young woman climbing onto the bus and reaching up to stow a Puma duffel bag. She was black and her hair was blond. She wore jeans and a dark tank top, nothing special, but all of her *shimmered* in the stuffy air, as if she was bringing youth itself onto the bus. This was the feminine ideal of fun and freedom America celebrated, only in black form. Barry thought of the double, triple, looks Seema got from strangers trying to figure out what she was, before allowing themselves to register that she was beautiful.

As soon as she boarded, people had stopped talking glumly to one another or staring hopelessly into the middle distance. Everyone was paying attention now. Everyone was asking themselves the same question: Where would she sit? There were four or five empty seats, two of them occupied by larger older gentlemen and two more adjacent to men of reproductive age. The final seat was next to Barry.

The young woman lowered herself into the seat next to him, her light blue jeans scrunching gently into the rigid Hound fabric. It wasn't so much that she smiled at Barry; it was that her smile was never ending. Who smiled on the Greyhound?

He kept trying to think of a word to describe her. A tiny band of belly ribboned between the jeans and her tank top, and he could see the imprint a pair of underwear had made right above her hip bone. Her teeth were professionally white, and every finger was a sculpture. "Trim," that was the word. Almost athletic. Barry tried to remember the black girl from game theory back in Princeton, the one he had dreamed about when his relationship with Layla was on the rocks. She had had a white name, something like Brenda or Wendy. When she raised her hand in class during the warmer months, Barry had tried to catch a glimpse of her armpit. He had desperately wanted to write a story about a banker falling in love with a black girl from the projects for his creative writing class, but Layla had been in that class, too, hence the white shepherdess.

Barry knew he had to represent his value immediately, just as Jeff Park had said. "Do you want to use my jack?" he asked.

"Thank you," she said and plugged in her phone, which was a classy late-model iPhone. "I'm always running out." Her voice was breathy and low, an ancient southern timbre overwritten by YouTube. Yes, he had found her. This was the fantasy of his whole trip. Forget the thick woman with the crablike walk. Forget the vinegary plate of beans and pulled pork. *This* was the side of the road. *This* was the woman who would understand him. He needed to talk to her. How could he become her friend?

Men whipped out their phones hard. "You're not going to believe this, fam," a man in a hoodie across the aisle said into his Galaxy, "but sitting right by me is like the baddest girl in the world."

The young woman pretended she didn't hear the compliment. Barry imagined she spent most of her life pretending not to hear compliments from men like that. She had reached over to plug her phone into Barry's jack, and a small warm part of her touched his knee. Barry's brain desperately tried to process this information. None of this was happening. "I'll make sure it doesn't fall out," he whispered.

"Thanks," she said. What was she, in her midtwenties? "Do you mind if I eat this?" She had taken out an Oscar Mayer Lunchables box.

"Of course not," he said. The Lunchables consisted of little pale disks of turkey or ham that you could scrunch up and place on a cracker, also included. "I think I had those growing up," Barry lied.

"Do you want one?"

"No, thank you," he said. "Looks good, though!"

The young woman ate the processed food with great concentration. "You got to check this girl out, fam," the man across the aisle was saying into his phone. "She's like damn. She's eating Lunchables now."

Barry ran his finger over her iPhone charger to make sure it was still plugged in. What should he say to her? It felt like this whole Greyhound trip rested on him getting it right. "So, do you attend university in Birmingham?" he asked. He hated how old he sounded.

"I got kin there," she said, chewing. She covered her mouth with one hand, her nail polish starry and purple. "I just finished school."

"And what was your area of study?" Worse and worse.

"Leisure studies. I got a bachelor's at Grambling State."

"How wonderful. And are you employed in that capacity?"

"I guess?" the young lady said in the form of a question. "I work at the Marriott in Jackson. Uhm, in the back office. Like accounts."

He was sweating, and now he needed to pee. "And how do you find that line of work?"

Barry finally understood the problem. He had never talked to a black person before college, and his industry did not employ many African Americans. His conversations with the black girl in game theory were entirely in his head or on the screen of his Macintosh Color Classic II. No wonder he had been unable to fully bond with Javon. He had to relax. He had to be the friendliest guy on the bus.

The young woman seemed to respond well to his interest in her welfare. "The problem with Jackson," she said, "is that it's real small."

"Uh-huh," Barry said. He wasn't even sure where Jackson *was*, but it was his great fortune to have a ticket bound for exactly there. He thought about the best way to mention his love of the rap band OutKast.

"I need to live in a bigger city," she said. "Dallas would be awesome."

"I've been to Dallas," Barry said, by which he meant the Grand Hyatt DFW. "I thought it was awesome, too."

"Totally," the young woman said. "There are so many people and things to do."

"Great airport. Lots of flights. It's a hub."

"I've never been on a plane," the woman said, "but I really want to go."

Barry's heart was in pieces. In her midtwenties and never been on a plane. He pictured this sweetheart on a NetJets bound for Antigua or somewhere really special. "I'm very adventurous," she said. "I want to travel the world. Yeah, I'm going to fly eventually."

"Girlfriend wants to fly, fam," the guy across the aisle was narrating for his friend.

Now it was all falling into place. He could be her mentor. He had almost mentored Jeff Park, and he had tried with Javon. Although, let's face it, Javon had been a drug dealer. But this young person had it all. She was charming and smart and spoke near-standard English. She just needed to be taken out of the back office of a Jackson Marriott and put to real use, like in marketing or investor relations. He could imagine that honeyed voice talking to the dicks down at the Louisiana State Employees' Retirement System. He would never have to deal with another redemption from the South.

"Flying's fun," Barry agreed. "But it's also kind of fun to take the bus. Kind of lovely."

"Yeah, a bus puts you into a different state of mind," she said. "It's very relaxing. You just look out the window. Last time I talked to a Mexican woman whose son was in Afghanistan. And once I talked to a professor."

"Do you want to switch places with me?" Barry asked. "So you can be near the window?" He wanted to hem her in. Keep her all to himself. "You can be closer to the outlet, too."

"You're sweet," she said. "But I can see all right from here." They were passing a Waffle House.

"I'm Barry," Barry said. He stuck out his hand.

The woman smiled. "My hand's all greasy." She reached down into her purse and took out a baby wipe, as she ingested another Lunchable. She wiped her fingers carefully, then shook Barry's hand. It felt to Barry that she shook it for at least three seconds beyond what was required. Every square inch of her was warmer than the chilled Greyhound air around them. "I'm Brooklyn," she said.

"Brooklyn her name," Fam-Man said across the aisle.

"What a cool name," Barry said. "Did your parents meet in Brooklyn?"

"Tell you the truth, none of us ever been," Brooklyn said. "But that's like the top of my list. What about you?"

"Well," Barry said. "I live in Manhattan. Right across the river."

"Wow!" Brooklyn said. Her eyes were a color he had never seen, a copper sunset over a green country field. "I never thought I'd meet anyone from New York."

Breathing was the thing now. Simple respiration. He squeezed her hand affirmatively. The air around them smelled of baby wipes. "Surely in the hospitality industry," he managed to say.

"I'm in accounting," she reminded him. "So what's Brooklyn like? Is it crazy?"

Barry thought of Seema's friend, Tina or Kina. "It's *really* crazy," Barry said. "The people, they ride these old-fashioned bicycles. And I never know what anything is. They have doughnuts made out of spaghetti."

Brooklyn sighed. "I gotta say, I never learned to ride a bike," she said.

"It's really easy," Barry said. "I could teach you in under ten minutes."

Brooklyn smiled. "Is Brooklyn like that show on HBO?"

"It's exactly like that show," he said.

"Huh," Brooklyn said. "I guess I wouldn't know what to say around girls like that."

"Those people are silly," Barry said. "They have no authenticity. That means they're not real. *You* have authenticity."

"I know what it means," Brooklyn said.

"Anyway, you would rock Brooklyn," Barry said. "Let's go sometime. There's a lot I can teach you. A lot about the world that you'd find interesting. Useful, even. You remind me of someone else I met on this trip, back in Baltimore. You remind me of myself when I was younger. You want to improve yourself. I've done a lot in my life, made hundreds of millions, but it's not enough. I have this friend, Joey Goldblatt, and I told him that if after we die our epitaph says that we ran super-successful funds, then we've failed. There's so much more to the world than money. But first you have to have lots and lots of money. Then you can do all the really good stuff. Like mentor people."

Brooklyn was thinking about it. "Well," she said. "I do want to succeed. I don't want to be unchristian about it, but I do want to come out ahead. Like, be a business leader."

The PA system screeched to life. "Tuscaloosa," the driver sighed, as if he had had his heart broken there. "Fifteen-minute stop, Tuscaloosa." Great, just as their conversation had started to flow. Just as she had basically told him she wouldn't mind working in finance. *Fuck you, Greyhound.*

Brooklyn got off in front of him, her denimed butt leading the way, and Barry had to squeeze past Fam-Man to get out first. "Easy," said Fam-Man.

They were parked at a RaceWay convenience store opposite an EasyMoney check-cashing place. Brooklyn hit the Frito-Lay aisle, stopping by each choice with an inquisitive finger on her chin. He scanned the aisles quickly for something special to get her and finally found a row of Kind bars. Strange that they would have them all the way down here. She would love one of those. He trotted through the store, but she had already left. There was a low-burning heat in his nostrils, a teenage pinch of romantic despair. He grabbed the dark chocolate with sea salt, paid quickly, and ran into the humid evening. Sure enough, Brooklyn was talking to Fam-Man, who was eating a plate of chicken while somehow smoking a cigarette at the same time. Like Brooklyn, Fam-Man also had blond hair, but it was dreaded into little stalks, and his dye job looked sloppy and contrived. *Country,* thought Barry malevolently. He could try to squeeze into their conversation, but what if more stupid words came out of his mouth? Oh, this wasn't fair. Meanwhile, the $3.69 Kind bar, a significant chunk of his present net worth, was melting steadily in the heat. He decided to climb on the bus and hope that Brooklyn would make the right choice and continue to sit by his side.

From the window, he watched Brooklyn and Fam-Man. Every once in a while she would laugh uproariously. Barry wished he could make her laugh like that, instead of talking so seriously about her work and education and prospects for self-improvement. But that's what mentors did. Fam-Man was doing funny stuff like feeding some chicken bones to an ambling dog from the check-cashing place. He loved her laugh even more than he loved the way she filled out her jeans.

The bus driver was yelling at everyone to get on the bus. Many "sirs" were exchanged. Brooklyn climbed the stairs with Fam-Man on her heels. He touched one of her bare shoulders and tried to steer her toward his side of the aisle. If Barry lost her to his rival, he thought he would just get off the bus in despair and bed down in the cheapest motel in Tuscaloosa. But Brooklyn scooted in next to him. "Real nice chatting with you," she said to Fam-Man.

Barry felt sorry for him. Fam-Man slumped into his seat and popped open his shit phone. "No, fam, she's still sitting next to that guy," he said. "Her kin from Jefferson County. Homewood. Yeah, I told her about my 4Runner."

"Hey, I got something for you!" he said. He produced the Kind bar. "This is what *everyone* eats in Brooklyn."

"Should we split it?" she asked. "Chocolate and sea salt."

"It's supposed to be very healthy and slimming," Barry said.

Brooklyn opened a bag of Nathan's hot-dog-flavored potato chips she had just bought. "Is this from Brooklyn, too?" she asked.

"No," Barry said, very sternly. "That's just not—"

"Authentic," she said. They smiled. She took a bite of the Kind bar. "Huh," she said. "It's super salty."

"But it's the good kind of salt," Barry assured her. "Probably from Hawaii or something."

"Have you been to Hawaii?"

Barry nodded his head modestly. "Just Molokai and the Big Island," he said. "And Maui, of course. Kauai. Oahu. Let me ask you, where do you picture yourself in ten, twenty years?"

"I guess as a hotel manager. Maybe at the Dallas Marriott City Center. My cousin works there. It's beautiful."

"That's it?" Barry said. He knew right away that he was belittling her dreams. "I mean I think someone like you, the potential is boundless."

Brooklyn looked at the remainder of her Kind bar. "I guess maybe in real estate," she said, very quietly.

Barry was not approaching this tactically enough. He wanted to relate to her that she was an extraordinary person, but everyone probably told her that. Coming from a guy on the Greyhound, even one who claimed to have made hundreds of millions of dollars, it didn't amount to much. Her iPhone rang. She picked it up with a smile on her face. Barry was worried. "Hey, Coach," she said. "Yeah, I'm on the bus to Jackson. Yeah, I'll call you when I get there. Nicole's spending too much time being cooped up in the house with Momma. She's gotta be in school or get a job. There's a website that'll teach her how to write a résumé. It's super simple. Or I can help her on Sunday after church. That's not what I said. You know I'm real proud of her. Yeah, Coach, put me in!" She laughed for a while. "Yeah, I love you, too," she said. She hung up and turned to Barry. "Sorry about all that noise."

"I like watching you talk," Barry said. "Who's Coach?"

"That's my dad." She laughed. "I guess it's goofy that I call him that." Barry didn't think so at all. He would give anything for Shiva to call him Coach one day. To call him anything, really.

He had settled into this peaceful mood of just admiring her. This was a real person. None of that New York "sophistication." No wonder Barry was fleeing the city. No wonder so many of the women he met in bars below Fifty-seventh Street looked at him like he was the enemy. One girl he had stared down in a bar on the Bowery had actually said to him, "I'm sorry, but I feel like you're ejaculating all over me with your eyes." Brooklyn had no biases. She wanted to be a hotel manager. She wanted to live in Dallas. She had a degree in leisure studies. She called her father Coach, and they'd laughed together, plotted her family's affairs. These were the dreams and actions of a consistent person. He was falling steadily in love.

Brooklyn yawned and put her head on his shoulder. "Gosh, I'm tired," she said. "You mind if I finish that Kind bar later?"

Barry leaned his own cheek into her hair. It smelled of apricot with an undercurrent of musk. Maybe it was her mention of church, but he remembered a brochure some Seventh-day Adventists had left at their house on Little Neck Parkway before his father and Luna the sheepdog had chased them off the property with extreme prejudice. A lion and a lamb lying side by side, their faces entwined in tenderness.

Lightning shook him out of his reverie. While they continued to snuggle in the near dark, a serious storm had begun. The highway was lit up by opposing high beams. He rubbed against her cheekbone. She let out a little laugh. Her lips tasted of salt and sugar and the dust of the road. She deflected his tongue and then reached up to whisper in his ear, "My mouth is kind of gross."

"No, it's not," he said, but she would only let him kiss her cheeks and sealed lips, his nose canvassing the rest of her face. He willed the storm to continue and the darkness to gather around them. He couldn't see her face, but he knew she was smiling. There was a motel sprawl building around them, and the density of Waffle Houses increased, which maybe meant they were approaching Jackson. "Your nose kind of looks like Jon Stewart's," Brooklyn said. "Your eyes, too. Although his hair's a lot more gray."

"Oh," Barry said. "Wow. Thank you."

"It's nice that you think about my work and all," she said. "My father always tells me to look for boys who are into my mind."

"I am *all* about that," Barry said. "Every woman I've dated has been super smart."

Brooklyn stared into his eyes. She traced his lips with her index finger. "And you know what else?" he said after she had taken her finger off his lips. "I also came from a place where people didn't value ambition. But I got out."

"You left your family?"

"It was just my dad. And it wasn't a healthy relationship."

"Guess I'm just looking for a good reason to leave, too," she said. "But I got my sister and stuff. She needs looking out for."

When they got into the station, Fam-Man ran off the bus without glancing their way. It was getting close to ten. The driver had turned on the lights. Barry and Brooklyn blinked at each other awkwardly. She used the screen of her iPhone to fix up her face a little. He had unplugged her phone cord and helped take down her Puma duffel

bag. They waited for their luggage to emerge from the hold of the
bus, his rollerboard full of watches and Shiva's rabbit toy and her other
two very large duffel bags, one a Puma, the other colored like a leopard. "So where do you recommend I spend the night?" Barry asked.

"Oh, that's easy! The Marriott. It's a five-minute walk from here."

He had been prepping this thing he was going to say to her and
he prayed it wasn't a deal breaker. "My wallet was stolen in Atlanta,"
he said. "So all I've got is cash. And I'm guessing you need a credit
card to check in to a nice place like the Marriott." He wanted to
show her that he thought well of her job. "I'm good for it, I swear."

Brooklyn reached up and kissed him on the cheek. "I'll fix you
up," she said. "Stop worrying."

Barry somehow managed to carry all three of her duffel bags and
roll his own luggage to the hotel. He wasn't doing so badly for a
forty-three-year-old, even though he hadn't exercised in forever. An
early night fog circulated around the empty corners of the old city,
feeling noirish, like those Hopper paintings Seema had forced him
to look at during a recent supposedly romantic cultural weekend for
just the two of them. Jackson made no sense, as if its urban planners
and architects had just rolled the dice over and over. Ugly office
buildings ran into old art deco jewels. Most of the population must
have retreated to the suburbs or wherever they lived when the sun
went down, but tiny pockets of habitation still thrummed here and
there, a lone nightclub, the sounds of jazz from a hotel lobby. White
seniors peeked out of a neon-lit window of a restaurant, examining
Barry and Brooklyn with curiosity bordering on concern. Just how
unusual was it for them to see a tall older Jew and a pretty black
woman walking down the street together in the night? The Mississippi flags outside the state office buildings bore the Confederate
emblem in their upper-left corners. Brooklyn's phone rang again.
"Hey, Coach, so I'm going out with some friends tonight. I might
be late or I might just stay over."

Barry couldn't believe where this was headed. He didn't even have
to make a long pitch like when he was a kid, or his first time with

Seema. But how could he reconcile the need to both touch Brooklyn and mentor her? And how much experience had she had with boys her age? Could he satisfy her?

The Marriott was an ice pick stabbed into the heart of the city. Black people in suit and tie were serving underdressed white people in the hotel's lobby. Brooklyn ran behind the front desk, where an older bespectacled lady, not unlike Layla's mother in her dress and composure, was talking into the phone. She returned with a room key and her leopard bag. "You're amazing," Barry said. "I'll settle up tomorrow."

"Ta-da!" Brooklyn said when she opened the door to their room. There was free bottled water, he made a note of that, and when he pulled open the curtains he saw the monumentally lit outline of the capitol dome, which was a huge affair for a state so small and poor. Could he live here? Could he start again? He had an erection. He put his arms around Brooklyn, felt her heat. "Baby, let's order room service before it stops at eleven," she said. He pressed her into his groin, but she pushed him away with a smile and handed him a menu off the nightstand. "Bus makes me hungry," she said. "Get the buffalo wings hot with the blue cheese and ranch dressings so we can mix and match. And the shrimp cocktail and two Lazy Magnolias." The food came right away, and it was sixty dollars. How the hell was Barry going to afford that on top of the room charge?

They sat cross-legged on one of the beds, eating quickly and silently. Brooklyn had set the TV to a show called *House Hunters.* She licked her fingers after every wing. He started kissing her again as soon as they were done. "Let me brush my teeth, honey," she said.

When she came back from the bathroom, she took off her top and exposed a very simple white cotton bra. Her skin was cut through with beginner's cellulite, especially at the stretch of her breasts. He loved all of it, even the tattoo of a rose above her right hip bone and the word BLESSED above the left. This was his last chance. He could turn back now. Leave the story untold. Open the possibility of something bigger, more beautiful. Imagine if he had become Seema's friend instead of her lover and husband. Imagine how much easier his life would be now.

But it was no use. He grabbed her hard and pressed himself against her. "Oh God," he said.

He wanted to go down on her, but she wouldn't let him. "Let's try it like this," she said. She took his hand and parked it safely in her wetness, while taking gentle hold of him. Nobody really had actual sex anymore since the Internet, but it was fine. They kissed each other a lot and he tried to let his fingers slide inside all of her. "Easy, easy," she said at times, showing him how, as if this were his first time. She tasted entirely of toothpaste, and, after they got established, the sounds she made were sweet and kind, as if Barry was responsible for all of her happiness. Barry came in long operatic arcs, but Brooklyn merely shuddered to a stop.

He was dizzy with love. He wanted to celebrate the moment some more, to share *all* of himself with Brooklyn. He walked over to his suitcase and took out the watch winders and the manual watches.

"You didn't tell me you were a watch salesman!" Brooklyn said.

Barry smiled. "No, no," he said. "I work in finance. I just love watches and I took a bunch of them on the road with me."

Brooklyn scooted over to the luggage. The fact that a stunning young woman with bare genitalia was examining his watches was probably the best thing that had ever happened to Barry. Every clock in the Swiss Alps was ringing for him. He wished he could post this photo on *WatchSavant,* his favorite watch website, but of course they had standards and practices. "I love this one," Brooklyn said, holding the glowing shape of the F.P. Journe, arguably the most attractive of Barry's watches. "Are you saving up for a Rolex?" she asked.

Barry laughed. But it still kind of hurt. He could correct her, point out that the F.P. Journe and the Patek cost at least three times the average new Rolex. He wanted her to respect him. "This watch retails for thirty thousand," he said.

"There are neighborhoods in Jackson where you can buy like a house for that much," she said. Her tone wasn't accusative. "Oh, my gosh, look at this!" She pulled out Shiva's rabbit-in-the-box and turned the crank. The happy song of Peter Cottontail filled the room. The rabbit popped out of his metal home holding the orange carrot before him. "Cute!" Brooklyn said.

Barry was confused. When she stuffed the rabbit back and turned the crank again, he felt himself getting angry. "That's not for you," he said. "It's a toy."

Brooklyn looked back at him, her copper eyes worried.

"It's just that you might break it." She dutifully put the rabbit away in his luggage between the Patek in white gold and the passport made out in Bernard Conte's name. She pulled on her panties. "I'm sorry," Barry said. "Thing is I'm divorced, but I have a son. And I was going to give that to him one day. Or send it to him."

"You must miss him, being on the road and all," Brooklyn said. Barry lay down on the bed and motioned for her to come near him. She lay down and he put her head on his chest. He stroked her crinkly blond hair and made figure eights in the luster of her left shoulder.

Barry remembered her saying she might want to work in real estate. She also said she didn't want to leave her family. What if, after This Side of Capital imploded, he would start a new fund with her as his chief of staff? Starting a fund in Mississippi would be so counterintuitive, the press alone would be incredible. He pictured a photo in the *Journal*, maybe him and Brooklyn standing outside a grand old town house beneath a magnolia, the sign reading ABSALOM IN-VESTMENTS. And they could do his Urban Watch Fund on the side.

But how was he going to mentor her after this? How would he sit down and explain how our economy worked after she had seen him naked? He wanted to look into her unblemished face, her expression always bordering on some unspoken, built-in contentment, and say: "A REIT is a real estate investment trust. It trades in property but acts more like a stock." He would make *House Hunters* look like kindergarten.

They were asleep in no time.

• • •

THE SUN blinded him awake. He was in a middle-class hotel room with a local southern girl next to him—what could be more perfect? He turned to see if he could give her a morning kiss, but she was gone.

Barry shot up in the bed. He ran into the bathroom. It was empty. He opened the door to the hallway and peeked out. She wasn't there. It struck him immediately.

His watches.

His luggage was missing from the corner of the room where he had casually placed it. *Vanished.*

His watches. The Tri-Compax he had meant to give to Shiva. The rabbit toy that was going to thrill his son. The whole thing had been a scam.

He picked up the phone, not knowing whom to call. She had talked to a woman in reception when checking him in. An older white woman. She had probably been in cahoots with Brooklyn. He would call the cops. He would sue them. He would sue the hotel. Although Brooklyn must have figured out he was on the run. No credit cards, a bunch of expensive watches. *Fuck!*

As he was about to press the button for the front desk, he saw a note on the bedside table written on a Marriott notepad. The care of the handwriting could only mean she had written it.

Dear Barry,

   That was so much fun and I feel like I've learned a lot. When I finally do get on a plane, I know I'll be thinking of you! You said you wanted to try something authentic, so if you stay in Jackson you should check out the Big Apple Inn, which is in an old neighborhood called Farish. Their pig ear sandwich is famous. The front desk will draw you a map. And thank you for the Kind bar. You are very Kind. XOXOXOXO Brooklyn. P.S. I put your suitcase in the closet and the watches in the safe. The code is 7291 which also happens to be my birthday ☺

Barry felt sick. He ran to the closet. His rollerboard was propped up on a suitcase stand. He pressed the code for the safe. He took out his watches and arranged them on the hotel desk in a row, the way he had seen Shiva arrange compact discs and toys. He saw the high beam of the Mississippi sun reflected in their acrylic and sapphire crystals and bent down to hear the clicks of their movements, inhaling and exhaling with each tick of time.

Barry read the note over. So what did it mean? Was she breaking it off? Why had she told him her birth date? Did she still want him to help her get into real estate? He read it again and again. It was a stupid thing to notice, but her punctuation was perfect, commas and all. He had portfolio managers who couldn't type a fucking e-mail.

He sniffed his hand to make sure she had been real. Then he threw on Jeff Park's Georgia Aquarium T-shirt and his jeans and ran downstairs. A woman in oversize glasses was minding the front desk. She was light skinned and freckled. "Do you know where Brooklyn is?" he asked her.

"She doesn't work weekends."

"But I need to see her. Can you give me her number?"

"We don't give out that information, sir."

Once they said "sir," the game was over. Barry grabbed a pen and pad. "Dear Brooklyn," he wrote,

I'm sorry if anything I did was displeasing last night. I did not mean to hurry you along, if that's what happened. I know you're a very smart and proper young woman and that is very attractive to me. I also know we're from very different worlds, but I feel like this is a once-in-a-lifetime connection. I don't think of you as just someone to mess around with. The messing around was really incidental. It happened because I was weak and because you are so beautiful. I want to be a mentor to you. I want to teach you about real estate investment trusts. I want to take you to the volcano atop the Big Island in Hawaii. There's so much more we can share in a nonsexualized way. There is nothing like taking a private boat from Naples and seeing the cliffs of Capri looming in the distance. But

more than anything, I just want to have the honor of helping you
succeed at whatever you want to do. Yours sincerely, Barry.
BCohen@ThisSide.com.

"Please," he said. "If you see her, tell her to e-mail me immediately. Well. I might not respond right away because I lost my phone, but—" He was sounding demented, he knew.

"Of course, *sir*," the woman said with what sounded like finality. He was panting miserably. The aquarium T-shirt stuck to his back despite the air-conditioning. "Would you like a glass of water?" she asked.

"She's just a really wonderful person," he said.

"We're all real fond of her," the woman allowed. Barry thought of asking which church she attended, but instead asked directions to the Big Apple Inn, the place she had recommended. Maybe he could have an early lunch there. A map was drawn for him and a gracious set of directions tendered.

The Farish neighborhood was just a block away from downtown. The main street looked abandoned and ruined like the parts of Havana he had once seen on a luxury tour of Cuba. Signs declared its former glory; apparently Farish had done for black life in Mississippi what Jackson Ward had done for Richmond.

The Big Apple Inn was the only business open on the street. A young girl was working the grill, and a big woman who looked like she was related was counting money. "My friend told me to get the pig-ear sandwich," Barry said. The countertops were fake, the chairs seventies orange, the walls plastic, and the extension cords were draped over the joint like kudzu. What kind of dedication would it take to stay in a place like this? "Do you know her?" he asked. "Her name's Brooklyn."

They did not. "She told me she really likes this place," Barry said.

"Medgar Evers used to have an office upstairs," the girl said. It sounded like the kind of thing she would say to a tourist. Barry knew Evers was a civil rights person; there was a CUNY college named after him. He sat down on a hard orange chair. Jews had a connection to Mississippi, but he couldn't remember what it was. The pig ear was soft and hot and gelatinous and came enclosed in a sweet little bun. It felt like he was eating someone else's pain. Brooklyn had given him a quick snapshot of who she was, or at least where she came from. She said that some houses in Jackson cost less than his watch, and this was probably one of them. Maybe her father was a small-business owner whom he could help. He never liked Obama's hatred of people in finance, but he had been slightly interested in Ben Carson's candidacy until the surgeon had mistaken "Hamas" for "hummus." He touched his own face. The scars inflicted by Seema and the nanny had healed and formed into little ridges.

Was it so wrong to want to help a younger person? He would never be able to teach Shiva a damn thing. The child had kicked him in the chest the few times he had tried to hold him, to soothe him, to instruct him about the world the way every animal was pro-grammed to teach its offspring. His own father would have broken him to pieces if he acted the way Shiva did, diagnosis or not. He pictured that happy family scene that had first led him to plunge into Seema with neither a condom nor a prenup: three half-brown chil-dren in front of a row of three Duravit sinks in the upstate house, splashing one another with mirth. But no one needed him as a father or a lover. He had scared Brooklyn away. What if Layla rejected him, too?

Outside, he passed a billboard for Big Mama's Bail Bonding. A blond-haired woman who looked like an older version of Brooklyn was holding a small child wearing a red ribbon in her hair. There was a phone number to call and the legend I'M ON MY WAY BABY. A large church hunkered down in a beat-up A-frame behind the sign. COME UNTO ME next to the rendering of a large red cross. Barry did as instructed. What if this was Brooklyn's church? What if he could hear her voice in prayer? Maybe add his own? He peeked inside. A dozen elderly black women in all their Sunday finery looked back at him in confusion, their eyes blinking behind large golden glasses. He caught sight of his own reflection in the window: a rumpled white man, unshaven, his T-shirt bearing a whale shark. Barry waved to them and walked back down the street. There were signs everywhere attesting to the area's civil rights struggle. Black cities in majority white states had a particular sadness. All those dusty freedom trails. What if our country never healed?

He left Farish for the Marriott. The same woman at the front desk was there. He would probably be at least seventy dollars short. Which watch would he leave as collateral? "Says here your room's been comped," the woman said.

"That's impossible," he said. "There was a room-service charge, too."

"All comped."

"Did Brooklyn pay for this? She shouldn't! I'm so embarrassed."

The woman shrugged. "That's all I know, sir," she said. When she saw the look on his face, she added: "I'll give her your message, I promise." He collected his rollerboard and took one last look at the room where she had touched him. Someone had come and tidied it to perfection.

ONCE YOU made a bad trade, you moved on, and Jackson had been a bad trade. Everything and everyone looked hurtful to him, even the poor people gathered to take the bus to Dallas, even the hunchbacked old man in the green vest who loaded his rollerboard into the bus. The world had dimmed around him, like he was wearing sunglasses. What had he promised her in that stupid note? Capri? The Big Island? *He* was a fucking island.

Pff, the bus said. *Pff.* The intercom came on, and the passengers were asked not to drink or curse. "On behalf of Greyhound and myself, I just want to say thank you," the driver said. She was a woman. And then they were on their way. A hawk coasted over the fields, his head slung over his shoulder as if he had forgotten to look for prey. BIENVENUE EN LOUISIANE, a sign said. The Mississippi River spread below them like a vast brown lake, even the riverboat casinos could not diminish her. They passed a field of sugarcane so green, Barry lowered his gaze. He was dreaming of Brooklyn, the weight of her breath against his collarbone as she slept.

"The body of Joshua, the body of Abraham." A loud voice woke him up. Unlike previous rides, there was a handful of white people on the bus. Some were in uniform; others were truck drivers talking about how they had stashed their rigs in one city and were now headed across the country for another job. The person speaking of the bodies of Joshua and Abraham was sitting in front of Barry. He had a scruffy little beard that ended before it could truly begin, darting blue eyes, and a buzz cut. He was talking to another young white man sitting across the aisle. Both of them were wearing denim shorts and ankle socks. "They say God is strange and sinister," the man said. "Me? I hate ignorance, any kind of ignorance. What if Jesus had believed everyone when they said he was crazy? What if Moses had? Or the Wright brothers? Do you read *Breitbart* and *InfoWars?* I'm thinking of going to school for church. Like to be a pastor. Can you get an apprenticeship there?"

"I think so," said the guy across the aisle. "I think you can apprentice with a pastor and then after a while they let you preach."

"I was having depression for a year," the would-be preacher continued. "I wanted to die. I was taking methamphetamines and then I joined the army and that's where I'm at now. I'm going to take it as far as I'm going to take it. I have a contract with God as to what I eat and what I drink. There's a difference between a slave and a servant, and I'm not a slave." Barry noticed a marine tattoo on his bicep. Weren't the army and the marines different? He had the feeling that the preacher wasn't in the military at all. "They're trying to create slaves, but I ain't a slave. They even talk to you like a slave."

"I know how that goes," said the man across the aisle. A short black man in a hoodie was seated between him and the would-be preacher. He was thoroughly asleep as the white men talked past him.

"Do you read *Breitbart* or *InfoWars?* The times are a-changing. Mike Pence is a good man. He knows that big things are coming.

That's why they nailed the Jews to the cross. That's why Muhammad was killed, because he couldn't accept Jesus Christ as permanent. He was like that his entire life. Obstinate, they call it."

Barry realized that the man was now looking at him. And also that he was a Jew. He hadn't really thought of being Jewish since he was in grade school. But he did now. The preacher had a short hunter's knife tucked into his belt, its serrated edge exposed and gleaming. "All things work for the good of the Lord. Do you believe in the Bible?"

"Yes!" the other man said.

"People can change their perspective, even the Jews."

Another storm had started, and the bus was hydroplaning. Barry was staring out the window. "We just have different perspectives on who the Messiah was," the man was saying, as much to Barry as to his friend across the aisle. A group of men in ankle socks and shorts in the seats just up the aisle were also half listening, half talking about their next long-haul jobs. "But why did God feel the need for Jesus to come again if nobody needed to change? And this is the summer of change, too. The angels are watching. He's coming again. Coming one last time. Maybe he's already here."

The rain turned to sunshine, and the cars on the highway left slick rainbows behind them. The bus had detoured onto a cinder-block campus. GRAMBLING STATE UNIVERSITY WELCOMES YOU TO TIGER LAND, a sign read. It was a black college. The campus was half empty for the summer, but attractive men and women still hurried along in the heat, the recent burst of rain spreading a tinge of happiness across the dusty quads. Some of them wore funny T-shirts: 0% IRISH, one said. Barry felt lonely for their company. And then he realized why.

Grambling State. Brooklyn had gone here. Brooklyn had been one of these students.

The two white men were watching the scene with narrowed eyes. Their associates up the aisle had gone quiet, too. One of them made a low whistling sound, like he was trying to expel something between his teeth.

"Look at that," the would-be-preacher said. "Just look at that."

"They must have their own police department," said the man across the aisle. "I'm sure they need it. And I'll bet you we're the ones staffing it. They can't police their own."

Barry felt himself starting to rise up from his seat. No, he had not worked out in a long while, but there was still force in his shoulders and his upper arms. He did not have a knife stuck in his belt, but he could still wreak havoc. You did not have an AUM of 2.4 billion without being able to turn the world upside down.

"This is fine," the would-be preacher was saying, his voice loud enough to reach the back of the bus, but suffused with the calmness of authority. "This is good. They have their own universities, and one day we'll have ours." *Ours? White universities? What did he think most campuses looked like?* Barry was still in his half-risen position. The black people on the bus were looking out the window and pretending the preacher wasn't there. They formed the majority of the passengers, but they knew better than to take action. What could Barry do? How could he avenge them? Avenge *her?* The preacher looked so clean-cut, despite the knife under his belt.

He mustn't win, Barry thought to himself. *For Shiva. For Seema. For Brooklyn. He mustn't.*

Barry sat down. He was from Manhattan. He understood the consequences of his actions. He did not need the police dragging him off the bus. In fact, he needed to hedge against any sort of conflict. It wasn't just these two men; they had at least four more associates up the aisle, a minor *Breitbart* franchise. At the Greyhound depot in Shreveport, a Gujarati man sold him a New Testament coloring book for $4.99. His stomach ached, but the pinkish hot dogs turning within some kind of hot-dog rotisserie made him ill. He got back on the bus. Somewhere Brooklyn and Coach and the rest of her family were sitting down to a full dinner, a big juicy bird on the table, collard greens, and yams. And he was on a bus full of racists with nothing to eat.

"There will be one world government," the preacher with the knife was saying. "Look up George Soros and Paul Singer, and you'll start to understand." Barry had met both of them at broker dinners. Both were Jewish like himself. He knew the preacher was looking at him directly now. One of his best friends in fifth grade had once used the expression "Jewed him down" and had apologized for it immediately. That was the extent of him being called out for the religion of his fathers. He took out his New Testament coloring book and turned to something about Matthew collecting taxes. "Sir," the preacher asked. "May I ask you, what's your heritage? I don't mean any disrespect."

What if Barry told him the truth? The preacher's stare brushed up and down Barry's swimmer's shoulders, sizing them up. He leaned into the aisle, his knife fully visible. Barry saw it all. The searing pain, the strobe lights, the police interrogating him in the county hospital after the doctors finished stitching up his face.

Sir, why do you not have a form of identification?

My wallet got stolen.

We're going to need you to come down to the station.

But I'm the victim here.

"I'm Greek," Barry heard himself saying. "Greek Orthodox." He held up his coloring book.

"Are you a workingman?" the preacher asked. Barry could feel the preacher's excitement, how much he was enjoying the situation.

"I clean pools," Barry said. "I have a small company."

"That's good," the preacher said. "It's good to have a trade. I was supposed to be a welder, but it never worked out. A man with a trade can never be a slave."

"Amen," said the man across the aisle.

"Greeks were the progenitors of the Europeans. Greeks and whites are the same people, almost. Do you know that word 'progenitor'?" He was now preaching to both of them, his eyes darting between his congregants.

"No," Barry said.

"It means they started it. Zeus. Apollo. The Morning Star. Jesus. It's all the same thing. Different folks just call him different things throughout the years. Let me tell you something right now, the whole reason I got into drugs was that I couldn't see my son."

Out the window an oversize sign read WELCOME TO TEXAS. DRIVE FRIENDLY—THE TEXAS WAY. What if they learned somehow that he was a Jewish Wall Street guy? The Internet was all around them. What if Barry asked to get off the bus right here? The thought of being in the same state as Layla calmed him, but they were still eight hundred miles apart.

"Past three years I spent fifty-one thousand on drugs. I cajoled, I thieved, I took from my loved ones, including my daddy. Do you know how much drugs cost?" Barry still had the crack rock in the pocket of his jeans. "Well, neither did I. I watched *Breaking Bad* and all, but it's even more than that. It's three hundred for an ounce of heroin. Meth don't come free either. That's how it is. It's called endorphins. Life goes into a life and then it goes into another life and eventually it changes the world." He was looking at them as if he needed a response.

"That's right," the man across the aisle said. The black man next to him had fallen asleep again, his breaths gentle and light like he was skimming the surface of something in his dreams.

"That's what I heard, too," Barry said. He tried to look back into his New Testament coloring book, but the voice continued to boom at him.

"Anyway, I got sent to jail for something I didn't do. I just grabbed her arm, told her not to walk away, and she got a bruise. I went to jail for eight days. My daddy posted bail. I was on suicide watch. This N-word threw a punch at me." Barry winced. "I started yelling so loud, *I* got scared of myself. And then I met this guy, he was just twenty-two, but it wasn't his first time in lockup, and he got me to go to church with him. He said, 'You get out of this life.' Then the woman I *allegedly* hit didn't show up in court. I don't even know where my boy is."

Barry and the preacher were looking at each other now. It seemed to Barry that the man wanted both to cry and to punch him. "I have a son, too," Barry said. "And I'm not allowed to see him either. My wife stopped loving me and I lost my child."

The preacher stuck out his hand and Barry shook it. "Well, I'm sorry to hear that, my friend," he said. "We're all brothers in this world." Something about Barry's declaration of pain took the stride out of him. He slumped back into his seat and said nothing for the rest of the ride.

Barry was agitated. The man in front of him needed anger management and an associate's degree in some trade. He and his traveling companions had so little, but they would give up some of that "little" to make sure Brooklyn had less.

The sun set in an apocalyptic pink over the Texas horizon, the redness of the star leaching into the darkening clouds. Hours passed, and they were into the night, approaching Dallas's desperately colorful skyline. At the depot he watched the preacher disappear into a beat-up Ram truck, the person in the driver's seat a grizzled man in an IRAQ WAR VETERAN cap, maybe the daddy who had bailed him out of jail. They said nothing to each other in greeting.

In the morning, Barry was happy to get back on the bus, but he was frightened, too. He was bringing someone to Layla, but who was that person? A failed businessman? A man who couldn't close the deal with Jeff Park? A cheating husband? An unconvincing lover? There was a young trans woman in front of him who couldn't afford the fare to San Francisco. She was eating an ice cream and crying. But even in her tears she knew who she was.

Texas went on for twelve hours, much of it featureless. The state had had to invent its own greatness. There were Mexican children in front of him admiring the scenery in precise detail. *"Caballos!"* they cried. *"Mira! Caballos!"*

Wind turbines, maybe a thousand of them, clustered on a distant ridge. They looked like friendly giants, and the children certainly took them as such. One of them, a girl, started singing "Old MacDonald" in a tragic monotone. A diorama of cotton, oil, and cattle rolled by. A giant balloon Elvis was hoisted atop a KIA dealership. They stopped by a Subway, and Barry bought a large Italian sub full of enticing meats. The bathroom floor was covered in dead roaches. He ate his daily bread while keeping his feet hovering over the floor tiles.

The topography around them was changing. The hills were ocher. Cows clustered around high-tension wires. The scrubland was the opposite of lush, but it was humble and honest. "Man, I love the West," a man behind Barry said. "Why live anywhere else?"

Three gorgeous Mexican women got on at a place of great abandonment called Big Spring, their arms straining with laundry packed into Children's Place bags. Barry was hoping the odd one out would sit next to him, but it didn't happen that way. The sun dropped like a rock. "This is Odessa," the bus driver said. "Watch your eyes, here come the lights." He snapped on the lights, and everyone groaned. They came up hard on Pecos and then a place called Van Horn. In the convenience store, they were playing a song Barry remembered from his youth, from the time he got his learner's permit and drove down the Cross Island Parkway in his father's pool van. *Carry a laser down the road that I must travel.* Or that's how it sounded to him. The band might have been called Mr. Mister. His father was okay with him playing pop music loud when he was driving, but he kept the radio off when he was behind the wheel himself. When you got old, the facts about your past bounced around your consciousness like heads of lettuce in a sack.

Outside, the desert wind chilled him. A new driver came to relieve the old one. "No cruise control, but she runs good," the old driver said to the new. "As soon as we leave Van Horn, we switch to mountain standard time," the new driver declared over the PA. Tomorrow he would have to change the time on his watches. That would be a treat. He hadn't thought of Shiva since yesterday.

And yet he was happy. He still had his rabbit-in-the-box. He still had the Tri-Compax, which, one day, he would gift to his son. *Watch. Say it, little rabbit! Wa-wa-wa-wa. Watch. Daddy's watch.* What if he wasn't a bad father after all? There were portfolio managers at his shop that worked such long hours, they never got to see their kids. The daughter of his head of Asia had once asked, "Daddy, where do you live?"

His Act 2 was really about to begin now. His brief romance with Brooklyn had been a mistake, but an honest, heartfelt one.

What if Layla had a perfectly curated child, devilishly funny and smart, and a perfectly curated southwestern life and was willing to share both with him? What if there was enough room in the bathroom for those three side-by-side Duravit sinks? He'd need two more kids. Layla was forty-three, and his own sperm was faulty, but there was always adoption. What if each moment at the dinner table would be one of learning and loving and mirth? What if, for once, he would let the woman he loved race ahead of him? He had spent so much time trying to mentor others, but what if he could learn from Layla instead? As a professor, she was herself a professional mentor.

A sudden sleepiness overtook him. In the headlights of passing trucks, he could see the silhouettes of mountains, but he would never know their beauty.

A COMPLETE AND TOTAL PAVAAM

N JULY 30, *FiveThirtyEight* gave Trump a 50.1 percent chance of winning the White House. Seema fell into despair and found herself crying at breakfast. Shiva started screaming and poking at his face, trying to blot out his own eyes, perhaps out of sympathy. "Mommy's okay." Novie started soothing him. "She got a bug in her eye." She caught Mariana, the chef, staring her son down from behind the kitchen island. In her country they would probably throw someone like Shiva off a cliff. Right now is when she could have used Barry at her side. He had a way of talking about the country that seemed definite and true, even if he was, in his own words, "a moderate fiscal Republican." Luis was still on some kind of meta-riff about *both* candidates being sleaze, even though he said it was costing him Twitter followers.

I NEED YOU TO BE NICE TO ME TODAY, she texted him.

OKAY, he texted back. GRAMERCY?

She tried to remind herself that she was in love, that tenderness awaited her, and that she would be a fool to let it slip by. But she needed him to know her thoughts about that 50.1 percent. She kept seeing a world in which Shiva was bullied and mocked, in which nice kids like Arturo were few and far between, a world in which even Barry's money would not protect him. If there would be any money left.

She paid for their room in cash, as always, ponying up the extra three-hundred-dollar deposit for incidentals. Paying in cash used to make her feel transgressive; today it made her feel like an adulterer. They usually went straight to the bedroom and took off their clothes, but this morning she wanted it to be different. He sat down next to her on the green velvet couch and sighed. "So," he said.

"I'm worried about the future," she said, "and I don't want you to delegitimize how I feel. You think I'm just like floating on this cloud of money and nothing can touch me. Well, you're wrong."

"What are we talking about?" he asked.

"The election."

"Oh." He was eyeing her breasts, and she didn't like it. She shifted away from him. She was beginning to appreciate Shiva's fear of others. "It does look very close now."

"I want you to appreciate how I feel before you speak," Seema said.

"You'll be fine," he said.

"That's exactly the opposite of what I need to hear."

He reached over and put his hand on her belly. She was wearing a peasant blouse, which she hated for its contrived rusticity but which fully concealed her bump. "This is what you're really worried about," he said.

"No, that's *not* what I'm really worried about. I'm worried about Donald fucking Trump becoming the motherfucking president of this cocksucking country," she said.

"But we'll be okay," he said. "You, me, Shiva, the baby."

"And Arturo?" she asked.

"Yeah," he said. "Why not?"

"And Julianna?"

"I guess."

Seema looked at him.

"She's got her work. Seriously, I'm the last thing she needs."

"But someone like me, without a job, without dreams. I'm *perfect* for you."

"Where's all this coming from?"

"Did Julianna tell you she and Arturo came over yesterday and met Shiva?"

"Yeah, Arturo said Shiva's got some kind of super hairbrush made out of horsehair. You people live quite the life."

"And what did Julianna say?"

"I don't know. They didn't release the transcript yet. Why are you being so pissy? What the fuck did I do? You want me to hate Trump, I'll hate Trump. Done."

"Did she tell you what the hairbrush is for?"

"Brushing his hair?"

Seema took his hand off her belly and turned toward him. Starlings were flying outside, headed for Gramercy Park, which they could access without the coveted keys. Even in the middle of this, a part of her wanted to have sex badly. Would he still love her? More to the point, why did she love *him*? Because he was closer to her age than her husband? Because he had soft eyes, decent breath, and easy style? Because he fucked better? Because consequences meant less to him, as if he were native born and her husband the immigrant? Because society insisted he had stature? Because he wrote about people with challenges, migrants, the Maya, the indigent? The goodness was in his work, and that meant there was a wellspring of it somewhere inside him, too. Didn't it? In the social chart her mother had drawn for her in high school, Luis would hover near the top. Although Barry would *be* the top.

"Shiva's on the spectrum," she said. "He has autism. He's autistic."

Luis blinked and put his hand on his throat. "Like Asperger's?" he said. "Because I've always felt like I've had a touch of that."

Now she wanted to hit him.

"It's not Asperger's," she said. "He's nonverbal. He's never said a word."

Luis got up from the velvet couch. She looked sadly at the large imprint he had left. "Huh," he said. "Well." He walked over to the window and tapped on the glass. He didn't exercise at all, as far as she knew, unless he was on top of her, but he always looked fit. "You know what I'm angry at you for," he said.

"I'm *sorry?*" she said. "Did you just say you're angry at me? Did you just say that right now?"

He turned around. "I'm angry that you hadn't told me."

"What?"

"I'm angry that I've never met your son." He had gone from being *Shiva* to being *your son.* "It's like you hid him from me."

"Okay," she said. She slapped her thighs, a gesture from her mother. "Let's all go to the park together. Right now. You, me, Shiva."

"Don't be like that," he said. "I'm not accusing you of anything. We're just talking."

"And full disclosure," she said, patting her stomach. "This kid, he's a boy. Statistically there's a pretty decent chance that he might be autistic, too. Just like his brother. Just like my son. *Shiva.* Whom I love."

"Okay, this is ridiculous," Luis said. "This is a witch hunt. I'm being accused of things I haven't said. I'm sorry Shiva's autistic."

"Well, I'm not," Seema said. That sounded like a lie, but maybe it wasn't. She didn't know. She tried to picture her child in this room with them, the Shiva who loved the letter *W,* the true acolyte of the Cookie Monster, the boy who could be soothed by a bouncing ball and a horsehair brush. How could anyone be sorry he wasn't some-one else?

"Is that why Barry left you?" Luis asked. "Because if he did, he's an asshole." Luis was trying to redeem himself.

"You don't know what it's like," she said.

"Are you defending him?"

"Aren't you the guy who rails against black and white? No one's a saint. It's all relative."

"Your husband's not a saint, that's for sure," Luis said. "Do you know what Valupro is?"

The air conditioner wasn't doing its job properly. Or maybe it was the heat racing through her body. "So," she said, "now that we're at it, tell me more about what you think of me and Barry."

"I didn't say 'you.'"

"I married him."

"And now you want to unmarry him. Wherever he is."

Seema looked at her sneakers at the entrance of the junior suite. How carefully she had stacked them one next to the other. What a good daughter, what a good student, what a good person. "Let me ask you," she said. "When I leave Barry and it's me and you and Arturo, and, possibly, two autistic boys, how does it work? Whose money do we use?"

"I never wanted your money!" Luis shouted. "It's blood money! Money from patients who can't afford lifesaving drugs, thanks to your husband. I wouldn't take it. And neither should you."

"What a despicable woman I am," Seema said.

"Don't feel sorry for yourself," Luis said. "You bitch about Trump, but you and Barry are half the reason we're in the mess we're in."

"An ambitious monster. Living off others. No interests of her own. Can't keep a husband, can't mother her child."

"Sounds like you're enjoying this dialogue," Luis said. "Sounds rehearsed."

His cruelty oddly appealed to her. The reckoning was here. All of her stupid little sins. "Tell me more," she said. "Tell me more how you hate me."

"I don't hate you," he said. "But I can't trust you. You lied to me."

"Ah," she said. She got up. She smoothed the pleat of her blouse. "No one likes an untrustworthy woman."

"Here comes the Hillary comparison," he said.

And after all he had said about her, it was the Hillary line that moved her. She walked up right to his face, she could smell the folds of his chin, the sweaty aroma that sometimes lived there. "Luis," she said. "Luis Goodman. A noted Guatemalan American author with his thousand followers on Twitter."

"You know what you need," Luis said. "It's very simple. You need a job. You need to do whatever those hundreds of thousands of dollars of education trained you to do. And then you wouldn't have to be up here fucking someone else's husband in the middle of the day."

But she was already walking out of the room.

She walked past the privacy of Gramercy Park. One life had just been canceled and no replacement ordered. She was tired and sleepy and unfucked, but her feet carried her into one of those perfect New York summer days, the air sultry but crisp. She thought of calling Mina, but what good would that do? Another wasted evening of talking shit about men. And she would have to tell her about Shiva's diagnosis, tell her that she and her son had been rejected in tandem by another heartless human being.

A nexus of high schoolers had clogged up an intersection. They brushed past her, shouting at one another in pairs and trios, flashy new high-tops and buoyant hair. How *confident* they sounded. This was their city and their world. Seema stood there at the intersection letting the humanity coil around her. Suddenly she longed for her father. Nearly thirty years of life and she still had only one true friend in the world. She had tried to replace him with Barry, to be her "own person," as they said, but look how well *that* had turned out. She dialed Novie and told her she would be gone for at least two days and that Shiva would be hers.

THE COUNTRY looked brown and indistinct beneath her plane. She saw wide swaths of geography but could not identify what it was. Anonymous rivers snaked and glistened. She stared at Lake Erie and thought of wind. The rinky-dink airport was touching. It was supposed to have been a United hub, but that hadn't worked out, and now a new terminal extension sat empty. The star-crossed city of her birth.

It had been four years since she'd been back to Ohio, almost the entirety of Shiva's life. The little house had aged even faster than her parents. The roof was at a loss for shingles; the waterlogged stucco was turning into an exhibit of undiscovered continents. Did Seema still have money to throw at the problem? Even if the SEC came a-knocking? After marrying Barry, she toyed with the idea of buying her parents a new house, somewhere in University Heights, because her mother would never leave her beloved Indian community, maybe a McMansion closer to the Legacy Village mall. But she disliked the idea of Barry's money vanishing her own childhood, this tiny House of Accomplishments. They had never been poor growing up; their neighborhood had had that rare idyllic midwestern middle-class vibe, two-thousand-square-foot capes blustering through the early autumn wind, two Chryslers by every curb. Standing in front of her parents' house, she thought of her own sleek apartment, and Luis and Julianna's apartment, and all the town houses her husband's friends inhabited, and realized that maybe she had never really understood money. Somewhere along the line it popped out like a jack-in-the-box, and she lacked the finesse to cram it back in.

Her mother was angry that she had not brought Shiva. "Where's our genius baby boy?" she asked even as she was hugging her daughter tight. "How could you visit without him?"

Her father's feet slapped down the stairs in the Havaianas she had brought back from a trip to Rio. He was wearing a This Side of Capital vest. "Take that off!" her mother screamed at him. "Don't you know she's finished with Barry?"

Her father looked confused, but at the same time ecstatic that his daughter had come. "Hut!" he said. "We don't know anything. Young people fight."

Seema smiled. "I came for your 'huts,' Daddy." Her father smiled and looked away, overwhelmed by his love.

"She married an *old* man!" her mother said, never letting go of a line of attack. "Always a mistake!" Her father sighed and took off the vest. When he sat down he had to elevate his leg on a footstool because of a recent knee injury. They were in their early sixties. Her mother was fearsome in her thick-bellied furor, but her father was shrinking into the skinny nineteen-year-old she had seen in black-and-white photos, smiling so tenderly, goofily, in his prized oxford shirt brought over from Bombay, even as the seventies dawned around him.

They spent a good portion of the day making *sambar* and *idlis* in the kitchen, traditional breakfast foods that Seema and her parents loved to have for dinner, her mother talking about divorce and "the future," like it was an item for purchase over at Legacy Village. While her mother was distracted by the lentils, Seema snuck away to be with her father, who was sitting in the living room humming slokas and reading the *Economist* and his science journals. She sat down across from him on the slightly too-leathery immigrant couch. "I missed you," she said. "Why didn't you tell me about your knee?"

"Your sister's the doctor," her father said. His pride in his daughters was almost hilarious to behold, like a summer hose spraying in all directions. Seema knew what he would say next. "One doctor, one lawyer. I'm covered for life."

"So you talked to Shilpa about your knee."

Her father cringed, the pink of his gums exposed. "She's so busy over there in Nepal."

"So then you're not exactly 'covered for life.'"

"It's just a simple meniscus tear. Dr. Pinchas said, 'Lay off it for a while,' and to use the footstool. He went to Case Western, almost as good as Shilpa's Vanderbilt. I looked up the rankings. They're both in the top hundred for primary care and in the top twenty-five for research." Case Western was the alma mater of both of her parents, and they were relentless boosters.

"I was actually thinking maybe I could go back to work," Seema said, quickly scanning her phone for the Mayo Clinic's page on meniscus tears, which were apparently painful and debilitating and often afflicted much younger, sportier people, then sending Shilpa an angry e-mail to check in on her family *right fucking now.*

Her father sat up, excited, his knee creaking. "Legal work?"

Seema nodded. She thought of Luis's parting words to her about her lack of employment. She couldn't believe how happy she had made her father by merely mentioning the word "work." Even if it was a lie. She thought of all the other well-credentialed hedge-fund wives explaining, in unison, why they had left their jobs: *My income was pretty good, but given Larry/Joey/Barry/Sung Min's marginal tax rate, why bother? My salary wouldn't even pay for the help.*

"Wonderful!" her father said. "Oh, there's so much you can do. You just took a little break to have your son. Do you know I still subscribe to the *National Law Journal* and the *New York Law Journal*? Just in case."

Seema thought she was going to cry. He probably understood those journals better than she could at this point. Her father looked like a delicate little slice of clam within the shell of the oversize sofa.

Her mother thundered in in her apron, the scent of ginger clinging to the thickness of her plaited hair. "Why won't you help me, Seema?" she shouted. "You're acting like a guest in your own house!"

"I'm talking to *appa*," she said.

"Plenty of time to talk to him. You should call him on the phone. He doesn't do anything, you don't do anything. You're perfect for each other. Help me with the *idlis*!"

"Amma!"

"Ushuru vaangadhey!" her mother shouted. A Tamil saying she and Shilpa had heard every day growing up. *Don't take the life out of me.*

Seema trudged into the kitchen. Her mother had consigned her to poking the holes of the stainless-steel *idli* contraption with a toothpick to get the steamed batter out. The *idlis* had cooked up perfectly soft, fluffy, and slightly sour from the fermentation. How did her mother cook so well, while Seema had difficulties getting beyond *sambar* rice 101? How did her parents live so simply in this tiny house, happily lost between Ohio and the world they were born to? They were so mismatched, and yet they made it work. In old age, their interests bent toward each other's like never before. Gardening, complaining, looking things up on the Internet. Not that Seema hadn't tried with Barry's watches, ordering all those magazines about goddamned fluted bezels and floating tourbillons, attending the industry shitshow that was Baselworld every year until Shiva's diagnosis.

"You have to send me pictures of Shiva every day," her mother was saying as she sliced up a row of shallots. "Otherwise you're stabbing me in the heart. And what was all that on the phone about him being sick? You take your son to the hospital, I'm the *first* person you call. And then I'm on the next plane."

Seema thought "on the next plane" sounded like something glamorous a person might have said back when her mother was young. This was the time to tell her that her daughter was overwhelmed and scared. But those emotions paled next to the real one, the deciding one: she was ashamed. Ashamed that she gave them an imperfect grandchild. That another might be on the way. "Don't Grieve for Us" was the title of an essay written by one autistic person, but how could you tell parents who still subscribed to the journals of a profession you no longer practiced that their grandchild might not be the big man on campus at Stanford, that, in fact, he might drink out of sippy cups and wear a diaper for the rest of his life? How could you bring to them the first real grief of their adult lives?

"The greatest blessing out of all this," her mother said, "no prenup."

"Isn't Shiva the greatest blessing out of all this?"

"Shiva's not a blessing," her mother said. "Shiva is the reason I live and breathe."

SHE TOOK a long shower in a bathroom most people in her world, even Brooklyn Mina, would find tragic. The paint was flecking from the steam. There was a family-sized bottle of "Aromatherapy Stress Relief." She would buy them a new house. Yes, that was the only way around this. She didn't have the strength anymore to deal with the maintenance of her memories. She had always been drawn to Jewish boys because their culture also seemed deeply sentimental and revered the past. Maybe that had been a mistake. She imagined a handsome WASP family where all the victories and defeats of life were simply acknowledged and checked off without an emotional acid bath. Autistic child? "Oh, dear. Well, we'll see you in the solarium for whist." Maybe that's why Barry was chasing down his Layla.

The sari she had worn in college still fit her, even with the baby bump. Well, that was pretty impressive. A small, disused shrine by the window elicited a fifth-grade memory. This little evangelical kid in class had gone on and on about church and how that's where God lives, and Seema had said, "Our God lives with us at home." And all the kids laughed at her, but then the teacher and her mother had organized a class trip to their house to visit their shrine. She made her first white friend that day, Sally Perkins with the missing back teeth. Such innocent times.

She looked up *FiveThirtyEight* on her phone. They were basically tied.

Every year for her birthday her grandparents would give her the biographies and memoirs of powerful people to encourage her, and they still lined the bookshelf of the bedroom she had shared with Shilpa. Bill Clinton, Hillary Rodham Clinton, Indira Gandhi, Edward M. Kennedy, Michael J. Fox. There was a Recognition Award from something called the Center for Talent Development. Even Seema had forgotten what that was all about.

She put on the sari for dinner. She wanted to look beautiful for them.

Downstairs, the plates were left out and some inconsequential bottle of wine her mother had picked up with Seema in mind, since neither of her parents drank. Her mother was in the basement lovingly screaming in Tamil at one of her friends. The basement was a kind of five-hundred-square-foot all-purpose desi rec center where she let her friends hold pujas, where the first Ohioan Tamil to go to MIT could meet the first Keralan to go to CalTech. An entire dance troupe from Madras, or whatever they called it now, had camped there for a month when they were still in high school, driving everyone but her mother nuts with the whine of their *tanpuras.*

Why didn't Shilpa e-mail back? Sometimes she envied her sister for becoming even more independent than she was. The girls had never been defiant toward their parents. Mom had been a nightmare, but not in the usual intergenerational immigrant sense. No whippings, no hair pulling, just steady emotional abuse of the caliber most of her Jewish friends endured. Her parents, arrived as late teen-agers, were half immigrants at best. Their accents were slight. Their love of the Cavs complete. Sheltering Tamil dance troupes in the basement must have been an act of penance for all that assimilation.

Her father limped into the room. "Don't you look lovely all dressed up," he said. "Let's go for a walk."

"No way," she said. "Not with your knee."

"It's good enough for a quick walk. I can hold your arm. We won't do a twenty-in-twenty. We'll do an eight-in-eight."

This was their favorite thing to do on Sunday evenings all through her childhood, even when she came home from Ann Arbor. The "twenty-in-twenty" meant five blocks north, five blocks west, five blocks south, five blocks east, and they were home. The idea was to walk one block in one minute, so the whole thing would be just twenty minutes of father-daughter heaven, before it was time to go home and play a frenzied game of Monopoly with Shilpa and their mom, who always cheated and always won.

It was a brilliant evening. Canada geese were rooting around in the last of the sunlight. They walked past the houses of their neighbors, all those humble capes, though none as peeling and water-logged as her parents'. Lots of Orthodox Jews were moving into the neighborhood. *"Rebbe!"* an old woman was shouting from a front porch. "Come back inside!" Their neighbor next door was a black handyman married to a Hungarian seamstress, if that was still a voca-tion, who gave her parents homemade sausages they would never eat. University Heights, as far as Seema was concerned, was as wel-coming as America got.

Her father's limp was brutal, but the weight of him against her was near perfect. She had to repress the desire to put her arms all the way around him, but if she did he would sense just how wretched her life had become. Any hug would be a cry for help.

The sun set, and a yellow moon emerged to greet them, father and daughter: she in a crisp beige sari and he, an older man in Western dress, limping along in his penny loafers. She was so much taller than he and her mother. How did genetics work like that? She touched the baby inside her. Someone had to help her through this mess, but who would it be? What if the right answer was "nobody"?

"*Appa*," she said. "I think we should both go back to work."

Her father laughed. "But I quit. You told me to quit. There are so many books I still have to read."

"No," she said. "You should go back to work. You were a great engineer. You can teach math to kids in East Cleveland. You're such a good teacher. You'd inspire them!"

"I think it's too late for that," her father said.

"But otherwise what will you do? Stay in the house with *amma*?"

Her father looked at her. His eyes seemed clouded and tired. "If things really *are* over with Barry," he said, "and I'm not your mother, so no pressure. But if your marriage is over, then maybe you could move back? It will be like the old times! We'll have more dance troupes stay in the basement. Maybe a raga ensemble. Maybe Shiva can play with them. He hasn't even been to a proper puja since he was born." He checked Seema's startled expression. "Of course, I am only kidding. No, stay where you are. You have a life."

"Let's go home," she said, draping his arm around her shoulder.

"We're halfway there," her father said, brushing off her help. "Four more blocks." A family of deer stood in the median of the road. According to her mom, neighboring Shaker Heights had a huge deer infestation. At least someone still wanted to live in greater Cleveland. The deer were all looking at her and her *appa* with curious fear, but they did not run off, as if they were proud to stand their ground. Maybe she wanted her family back, too. Or, better yet, maybe she wanted to build a family at last. Could she get services for Shiva here? Maybe the Cleveland Clinic had a program for autism. Her father was humming slokas again while shyly glancing her way. The bizarre love parents had for their children. Biological, spiritual, no explanation sufficed.

She had to tell them.

Back at the house, she let her parents eat first. No need to induce indigestion. Dinner was sacred. They sat beneath a tapestry of the goddess Lakshmi chilling atop a lotus leaf and an enlarged photo of Seema and Barry holding swaddled, purple-faced, just-born Shiva in the living room of Lenox Hill's Beyoncé Suite. Her last meal on earth would have to include her mother's *sambar,* that insane stew of okra and shallots and black-gram lentils and every spice from cinnamon to turmeric to fresh tamarind instead of the paste. Her mom actually sun-dried the chilies and soaked them in buttermilk, giving the dish a smoky spiciness Seema herself could never quite get right. She could never say no to large quantities of asafetida, a smelly taproot sap that added a complex leeklike flavor to her dishes. Cooking took hours and involved seemingly every imple-ment ever devised, from tin bowls to pressure cookers to Vita-mixes. There were two cupboards devoted solely to lentils. How did families without such food stay together? How could Whitman have claimed to contain "multitudes" without ever having a South Indian meal?

They spoke little, concentrating on dipping *dosas* and *idlis* into the *sambar.* Both the *dosas* and the *idlis* were insane, too, perfectly sour with a pinch of fenugreek in the batter for extra flavor. Occasionally, her mother would say something cutting about her and Shilpa, while her father would extol the health benefits of Indian cooking, the way he would do with his white friends from work. "Did you know cin-namon prevents ulcers, and turmeric is capable of controlling Alzhei-mer's disease? Proven facts." His gentle nationalism.

"I have something to tell you," Seema said, after the last of the *dosas* was crunched away.

"Here we go," her mother said. "What did he do now? Probably has a mistress or is stealing from his investors. A complete and total *pavaam,*" meaning, roughly, "sad sack."

"It's about Shiva."

Her father looked up at her. He had the same ears as in that photo from the 1970s. Those ears that stuck out like they belonged to a different, more innocent grade of human. Those soft, elongated ears. And the depth of his liquid eyes. And the crack of his knee. And the pressure of his tightened lips. And Seema realized.

Her father already knew.

E LOVED Layla from the minute she opened the door. The moment he saw what she looked like now, he knew he had done the right thing. It was, for the first time in forever, a moment of victory. His P&L statements had finally turned green.

After the cab dropped him off in front of her house, a spacious ranch in what looked to be an affluent suburb, he dawdled in front of the garden beds with their yellowing desert plants overshadowed by a tall antique lamppost, gathering the courage to ring her bell.

This was it! This was Act 2! He had first seen Layla in the basement of the Tiger Inn, September 18, 1991. Every other girl there was dressed to impress, but she was wearing an oversize sweatshirt that read VCU. Later he learned that T-shirt had been a hand-me-up from her sister. Layla just did not give a fuck.

She was with a bespectacled friend who probably belonged to Terrace or one of the artsy clubs. The way Layla stuck out from the fratty beer-pong social scene around her, she might as well have been wearing glasses, too, perched low over her nose. He didn't know if she was surly or sophisticated, but he felt her loneliness. Nothing was worse than being lonely at Princeton. She didn't really know how to flirt, or maybe didn't feel the need to, which shocked Barry all the more (around sophomore year, he had begun to think of himself as attractive). Later her friend, a Jewish girl from Brooklyn, got so drunk she threw up right in front of the Ivy, the one eating club that had rejected him and which Fitzgerald himself had called "breathlessly aristocratic." Barry held up her head, and Layla moved her hair out of the way as she hurled. "Our first social protest," Layla had called her friend's purge on the lawn of the hallowed club. Barry had been looking for something different his entire freshman year, had even tried to start a book club at the Tiger Inn to bring some culture to his lacrosse, wrestling, and swimming bros, and now he had found it within the form of a dark, mysterious southern girl.

Barry breathed in the cool fragrant desert air. He brushed his hair back and pulled up his pants. He rang the doorbell, once, twice, three times, and waited.

Layla opened the door.

She was a *cool woman*. That was perhaps the best way to describe her. Cool in the way that Tina or Lina from Brooklyn could only aspire to be. Everything she wore was timeless, dusty denims and cowboy boots, simple tees bearing the name of some local business or attraction. She didn't drive a truck, but she didn't have to. And her face, her portrait-ready Virginian face, had been wonderfully preserved in the desert heat, though there was a tiny tinge of sadness around the eyes of blue. She had changed, and yet she hadn't; her hair looked a touch more brittle but remained naturally dark. Her snub nose looked like Elizabeth Taylor's. This was the kind of woman's face he would see on rare occasions at hedge-fund parties, whenever he'd meet a fund manager who hadn't remarried for some reason. The wise, older face, full of stories that actually made the woman sound smart, instead of merely flirtatious. The kind of face that would hold out for plastic surgery until the very last minute. And she was almost *too* skinny, her jeans constantly running down to reveal a heartwarming overflow of butt.

The first thing she said to him was "I do not want a crack rock in my house."

She had been warned. The Hayeses obviously did not think much of his state of mind. "Of course not," he said. "Rock gone." But he snuck out in the middle of the night and buried it by the pool. The crack was a connection to a journey he had been proud to undertake and wanted to celebrate forever. Layla next recommended that he stay at the Camino Real downtown, and Barry had to explain his pennilessness. As expected, she still harbored ill will toward his profession and our nation's financial sector. The fact that Barry was now destitute proved a mark in his favor. "I have three dollars and fifteen cents to my name," he said. He had never been more proud to declare his net worth. All that time at Princeton she had wanted him to remain poor, and now, in a sense, he was. She was wearing a T-shirt bearing the name of the Chihuahuas, the local minor-league team. Everything here had a bilingual story.

"Barry," she said. "I don't want you to think of this as the start of anything. I'm exhausted. I really am. It's been a tough couple of years. You can crash the night, or let's say two nights, but that's it. You've got to figure stuff out and I can't help you. I'm not even your friend anymore." He was sitting on a grandiose ottoman opposite her. The furniture was this oversize Stickley stuff. The house used to belong to a Jewish cardiologist, and there were mezuzahs everywhere, which was perfect given the all-Jewish cast of Layla's romantic life. She was raising a kid on her own after her ex-husband absconded to DC to join the pundit class after publishing a successful volume on Alexis de Tocqueville. She sent her nerdy nine-year-old son, Jonah, to Hebrew school because she did not want him to miss out on half of his heritage. The Holocaust, *all* holocausts, formed one of her areas of study.

"This is just a start," he said. "This is just hello." He leaned in. He was unshowered and smelled like the Hound. He wanted her to feel it, the depth of his folkloric travel. "At heart," Barry said, "I'm a salesman. And right now you don't want what I have to offer. I get that. But believe me, I'm going to make a damn persuasive case for myself. I've been thinking about it all through the ride down here. I've been meditating and plotting. The things I've seen. There was a one-eyed Mexican—"

"You were always this nostalgic person," she said, "even in college. And I kinda loved you for it. But this is something else."

"My life's taken a strange turn recently," Barry said. "Complicated stuff."

"And you think my life turned out perfectly?"

"See, we're meant for each other!" Barry said, and slapped his hands together. "I'm getting divorced, too!" *Shh*, she said. *My kid.* She tucked in her legs the same way she used to back in Princeton. Indian-style, they might have called it back then.

"Do you really want to make a life here?" she asked.

"Yes!"

"Why?"

He began to negotiate. "Because it's real."

"You just got here an hour ago."

"But I've been on the road learning about America."

"That sounds privileged."

"I just want to change."

"Nobody changes."

"You're too good to ever change."

"Shut up, Barry."

Eventually he was relegated to the little basement bedroom. There were two twin beds barely big enough to accommodate him, and each night he chose a different one to curl up in. It was a little like owning more than one watch. Now he'd just have to make her fall in love with him again. He hoped it would be neither too hard nor too easy, but something they could tell the grandkids about one day.

THE HOUSE nestled up against the Franklin Mountains. Their road was called Thunderbird, and you could actually see the shape of a red thunderbird etched into one of the hills. The house was surrounded by pink mansions with wrought-iron safety gates. According to Layla, the violence had sent in waves of rich folks from the neighboring Mexican city of Ciudad Juárez, including, at one point, that town's police chief. Deer came down from the mountains into the arroyo by Layla's house, and red-tailed hawks swooped overhead. At night, bobcats walked down the street like they owned the place. The rooms were low ceilinged and cluttered with the detritus of a failed marriage. It was *huge,* five bedrooms built in anticipation of a Modern Orthodox family, and in any normal metro it would cost two million dollars, whereas in El Paso a single-income full professor could afford it plus the full-time housekeeper/nanny who came courtesy of some southern Mexican state. Layla still kept their wedding photos and photos of all of them as a family so that Jonah would have some measure of stability, even though it likely hurt the shit out of her to see her husband's chiseled face.

Two days had passed, and she didn't kick him out. And then two more. And then a week. They said El Paso was built out of mud and dirt, and sometimes, like after a flash storm, it did look like it had just come out of a third grader's kiln, but the mountains were beautiful and strange, and the dry desert heat agreed with him. He couldn't get enough. He was reborn. He didn't e-mail. He was off Bloomberg. He didn't stay up for the Asian markets. Layla got him an old flip phone, and he texted on it like it was the turn of the century. He drove a 1999 Toyota Avalon, front-wheel drive, no Sirius.

Each morning was a blessing. Each morning he roared into his new reality. *This!* This is the life he should have lived all along, until Princeton had pushed him into the cult of Goldman, the sect of Sachs. He had to change.

Layla still didn't let him share her bedroom, but his little room down in the finished basement was just perfect. Plus there was a fully stocked bar just down the hall; Layla was, he had to remember, a WASP by nature, even if she had married—and then divorced— a Jew. There was even a case of fifteen-year-old Balvenie if he wanted to plaster himself through the night. Being a full prof at the University of Texas at El Paso meant living like a managing director at Barclays. Barry had always wondered why people who were just upper-middle class in New York chose to stay there, given that they could live like minor dictators in the rest of the country. "You're negative arbing yourself," he used to say.

In the morning Layla took Jonah to his Hebrew school and then she would drive on to UTEP. Barry would get into the Avalon, slip in one of the old CDs moldering in the glove box—the Smashing Pumpkins!—and swerve and brake and honk through the neat urban desertscape. El Pasoans didn't really recognize lanes.

He went to El Rincon for breakfast, a scene no matter which day of the week. The parking lot was full of Escalades and Range Rovers with Chihuahua plates, Mexican businessmen with their bilingual children, big dudes with tattoos and Hublot watches. Or maybe some real *"Chuco Town"*–looking guys would show up wearing humorous English-language T-shirts like STUPIDITY IS NOT A CRIME, YOU'RE FREE TO GO.

The beans were always ethereal at El Rincon, but the chilies fluctuated by the batch. "Today *muy caliente* the green sauce," the large waitress would say, and Barry would order a plate of chilaquiles smothered in that.

Seema couldn't shut up about how great South Indian cuisine was, well, fuck it. He was going to get a story of his own, a Mexican American story, which would dwarf hers with its significance. He only wished he had taken a Spanish class back at Princeton, instead of taking French after reading *Tender Is the Night*. The coffee at El Rincon sucked, but he drank cup after cup, looking at the Mexicans conducting business or taking good care of their *abuelitas*. Yes, he was picking up the language already. He stared at the giant hand-painted mural of an Aztec god carrying a princess with hot, thick thighs and flowery ankle bracelets up a mountaintop. Or he'd just meditate on the view of the minor mountains rilled with switchbacks out the window, a gorgeous two-assed woman getting out of a Durango in the parking lot.

He liked doing chores for Layla. He had all this energy and no place to put it. He went to Sprouts Farmers Market. The *really big news* around EPT (as he was starting to call El Paso, Texas) was that a Whole Foods was finally coming to town, but he loved Sprouts, which had long been the closest thing. He thought the bargains were crazy. You could buy two bottles of pretty good prosecco for $15.99. He got a whole thing of fresh potted herbs and a case of Diablo French soda and some nice deli meats. He made clumsy but heartfelt turkey sandwiches and brought them down to Layla at UTEP, so they could eat together in the campus's Chihuahuan Desert Gardens. She seemed to really like that gesture, even though everything was paid for with her money. She had given him a bridge loan of a thousand dollars.

The drive up to UTEP really excited him. He would pass through a fairly upscale segment of the American Southwest, all those new cold-brew joints and vernacular tail-to-snout restaurants, then all of a sudden this other entity would appear on the passenger's side. The other entity was called Mexico or, to be more specific, Ciudad Juárez, previously the locus of that country's narco wars. And the way it came up was as this incredible blur of run-down cinder-block shacks painted in bright primary colors. Colonias, the neighborhoods were called, and one butted up directly to the UTEP campus. Barry loved the juxtaposition. He wanted to go across the border to Juárez, but he was roundly dissuaded from doing so by many of the people he met. A lot of the violence had abated as of late, but El Chapo, the Sinaloa cartel's kingpin, was being held right across the border for possible extradition, and a wavelet of killings had returned, with one man being gunned down right over the international bridge. But it was the danger that excited Barry most of all. Hemingway had gone to Juárez, to a place called the Kentucky Club, back when it hadn't been as dangerous to visit. Imagine if Barry went there now, into the heart of the danger, with Layla and his twenty words of Spanish in tow.

The UTEP campus was designed to mimic a series of giant Bhutanese temples, and the working-class campus had an Eastern sense of grandeur. Barry wondered what it was like to be one of the poor folks in the colonias who woke up daily to be confounded by these massive Buddhist monoliths towering above them. The few times he had picked Layla up at night, especially when the desert chill really set in and all notions of summertime disappeared, Barry noticed an acrid, burnt-plastic smell drifting off from the hodgepodge of houses across the border. "They're burning tires to stay warm," Layla had explained to him in the same no-nonsense social-justice voice he remembered from Princeton. Barry was mesmerized. The smell crawled up from one of the most desperate parts of North America to an attractive regional center of learning. Like most El Pasoans, the students at UTEP were heavily Latino and, in fact, 10 percent of them commuted from Juárez, though likely from neighborhoods far more salubrious than the colonia across the border. Barry was here, but he might as well have been *there*. He burned with the excitement of having been born on the right side of the fence, of having been *lucky*. He wished Jeff Park, that amateur scholar of luck, could see this place.

DURING THOSE weeks Barry had also developed an unexpected soft spot for scrawny, friendless Jonah, schlepping around math books two grade levels beyond his own like some future quant. The little guy needed a father.

One afternoon Jonah was crouching over a dead lizard in the backyard while Barry sat by the pool watching nature play itself out, rainbows appearing at will, lending their color to the monochrome humps of the Franklins. The boy did not know how to swim, a situation Barry was going to remedy for sure, and Jonah's stick legs in his dry swim shorts made him look somehow much younger than his nine years. He was entirely white, even though he lived in a land dominated by the sun.

"Bury him in the arroyo, otherwise we'll have a million ants," Layla said. She was dressed in khaki shorts with a tight black swimsuit that made Barry aware of the contours of her small breasts and the new heaviness of her bottom. He remembered the dream he had had back at Jeff Park's, the dream in which he and Layla were having coffee naked in a Wells Fargo. He longed to shoo the boy away, strip down her shorts, move aside the crotch of her one-piece, and taste her.

Jonah had flipped the dead lizard over and was now carefully pressing his stomach. "He was just alive, honey, so you have to treat him with respect," Layla said. "He's not a toy."

"I'm examining him," the boy said gravely.

"Well, he's not a research subject either. Bury him in the arroyo."

Jonah looked up with his father's dark hooded eyes. Just like the quants at his office, the kid had a ferocious concentration. Anytime it was broken, he would blink up a storm as if he were new to this world. He spent most of his time doing God-only-knew-what in his room. "What's that bird, Mom?" Jonah asked, pointing to an angry-looking specimen in the bushes.

"That's a grackle."

Grackle. Arroyo. Just alive. The Southwest was full of lovely language like that. The fact that Layla was raising a kid in a moral way stirred something in Barry. His father had fucked up that task so completely after Barry's mother died. Bury a pool lizard with dignity? He'd probably have tried to make a wallet out of it. Layla wasn't all alone like his dad had been; she had help from the Mexican woman maybe seven hours a day, but still. The Mexican woman was easygoing and made killer chilaquiles of her own. She and Barry rapped briefly about buses. She knew something on the subject, as she took a thirteen-hour bus into the heart of Mexico once every month. One day he came home and found Jonah and the Mexican woman playing on a slide Layla had put up by the pool, yelling and squealing as if both of them were young. It was such an outrageously American scene he wished he owned an iPhone with which to take a video. They had once put Shiva at the top of a slide in Central Park, and he had started crying desperately, and an old Israeli woman waiting in line with her grandchild admonished him to be braver. Barry had slashed his donations to the Technion in Haifa by 80 percent that day.

"Hey, buddy," Barry said to Jonah. "You want me to teach you how to swim?"

"Barry was a swim champ back in college," Layla said.

"Only in high school," Barry corrected her magnanimously. "Queens All-County Swim Champion 1989. So how about it, big guy?" He immediately felt bad about calling the undersized boy "big guy."

"I've got to do cartography in my room," the boy said.

"Well, why don't I join you?" Barry said. *Cartography?* The kid looked at his mother with despair, but Layla thought it was a great idea.

"I call my room the Mapparium," Jonah said. True to the name, the entire room was covered in maps of the world, along with some posters of the world's high-speed trains, the TGV, Germany's Inter-city Express, Japan's high-speed Shinkansen. At first Barry had mistaken the maps for actual vintage ones from the twenties or thirties, but when he got closer he realized they had not been professionally made but rather drawn by a careful hand in a combination of graphite and watercolor wash, the place-names rendered in an old-fashioned art deco font kind of like the one on his Tri-Compax. An incomplete map of the mid-Atlantic states and New England took up a single wall.

"Did you draw this?" Barry asked.

"Ma-hum," the kid said, without any pride in his voice. Jonah had two stock phrases. "Ma-hum" meant "yes," and "Did you know?" meant he was about to tell you something you didn't really want to know. The boy picked up a brush and began to apply himself to the upper reaches of Massachusetts.

"May I ask why?"

"This is the Acela route," the kid said, as if the answer were obvious.

"Okay. But why are you drawing it?"

"I just like it," Jonah said.

"What do you like about it?"

"Last year, my dad took me on the Acela from Washington to Boston. He gave a lecture at Boston College. We sat together the whole way. We bought hot dogs even though they were five ninety-nine each."

Barry looked around. The room was spotless. The toys, which mostly consisted of high-speed train models, were squarely lined up next to one another on gleaming shelves, just as Barry's watches were downstairs. The blinds were drawn against the El Paso sun. Everything felt ordered and familiar. *Exact.* Barry hadn't realized that he had been smiling for several minutes now. What was making him so happy? In his father's tropical basement, his prized possession had been a Commodore 64 computer, which he could program day and night. But there was something else, wasn't there? Something having to do with maps?

Jonah made an error around Medford and was smudging it away with a wet thumb, lost in concentration. Barry decided to try a new tack. He would approach this kid as if he were a potential investor. He would seek out a commonality. "I like trains," Barry said.

Jonah turned around. For the first time, he regarded Barry as something other than a strange, useless presence at the breakfast table. "I took the Shanghai-Beijing train two years ago," Barry said.

"The Jinghu High Speed Railway?" Jonah asked. His eyes were wide and alive. The whole room smelled like Shiva's. Wasn't nine too old to still have that too-sweet boy's smell? "That's the fastest scheduled train in the world," Jonah said.

"I sat in this pod," Barry said. "It was surreal. Like *2001: A Space Odyssey.*"

"Did you know that 'Acela' stands for 'acceleration and excellence'?" Jonah asked.

"No truth in advertising, I suppose," Barry said. He regretted it right away, given Jonah's obvious love for the rail service, and hoped his sarcasm had gone over the kid's head.

"Did you know the Acela can reach a top speed of one hundred fifty miles per hour," Jonah said, "but only in three small portions of Rhode Island and Massachusetts, which I've outlined in red here."

Barry leaned into the map. The detail was striking. It wasn't just the deco font, the whole map had an early twentieth-century flavor, as if Jonah had apprenticed with a master cartographer. In its variations and gradations and charming, almost naïve use of color, the map gleamed with emotion. What some people didn't understand was that the cleanliness of a room, the care for inanimate objects like watches, could also express a love of the world. A giant yellow star was planted by Chevy Chase, Maryland, likely where his absconded father now made his home. This map was the little boy's inner life.

And then Barry remembered his own thing with maps. How could he have forgotten for all these years? "When I was your age I had a map of Long Island," Barry said, "and I would look at it every day."

"You did?" Jonah said. "Really?" There was a kind of tremor to his hands when he was excited. He moved his thumb along the rest of his fingers as if counting them or making sure they were still there.

"Yeah. I was obsessed with this one town on Long Island called Lake Success." Barry squinted, trying to make out the town, somewhere between Great Neck, Long Island, and his own Queens neighborhood, but maybe it was too small for the boy to have drawn in.

"Why Lake Success?" Jonah asked. The two of them were close enough to be touching elbows.

"I don't know," Barry said. "I just really liked the name. I wanted to be successful. I was living with my father. My mother had—gone."

"They got divorced?"

"Something like that."

"And you couldn't visit her twice a year?"

"She had gone to a different country. The point was, I didn't get along with my dad. He wasn't as nice as your mom. So I wanted to move somewhere, and Lake Success had this shopping center and all the houses had these awesome backyards you could put a pool in. My dad cleaned pools, but we didn't have one. And I kept that map under my bed all the time. It was an Exxon map from the gas station."

The memory was so unbidden, it moved Barry to sit down fast on the kid's slim bed. "I imagined I had a whole set of friends there," Barry said. "Relatives, too. Really nice ones like on TV."

"I don't like friends," Jonah said.

"Everyone likes friends," Barry said. "You just have to know how to make them."

"Well, I don't," Jonah said. He looked at his map, as if he wanted to go back to working on it. "I don't have any shared interests with my peers."

Barry laughed. The boy was obviously quoting Layla. Or a school psychiatrist. "I didn't either," he said. "You know what's right above Lake Success? Great Neck and Port Washington. One day when you're in high school you'll read a book called *The Great Gatsby*. There are these towns in the book called East Egg and West Egg, and that's them."

"I'm going to look up Lake Success," Jonah said. "I've used up all my computer time for the week, but next week for sure."

"Whitey Ford grew up there," Barry said. "He was a baseball player."

"Is it okay if I go back to my cartography, Mr. Barry?" Jonah asked. "You can watch me do it."

"Sure," Barry said. "But can I tell you just one more thing?"

"Mu-hum," the kid said.

"That book *The Great Gatsby* is about a man who wanted to improve himself. And when I was your age I wanted to improve myself, too. So each day I'd practice my 'friend moves.' Like, what are ten things kids in school can ask me, and what are ten things I can say back? It's like drawing a map or knowing all the train systems in the world. Except instead of facts, you have to memorize what they call small talk. People who aren't smart like us, they *love* small talk. 'Did you hear about this?' 'Oh, what about that?' 'So-and-so got hurt in gym class.' 'That's cool.' So I worked my friend moves real hard, and then by the time I graduated from college, I was the friendliest guy in my profession. And it made me hundreds of millions of dollars."

Jonah was thinking this through. "You made money by being friendly?"

Barry looked at the little boy. His heart was beating fast in the silence of the darkened room. If only he had had a friend like Jonah when he was nine. If only someone had told his younger self that he would grow up okay, that his father was wrong, that he wasn't a schnorrer or a shegetz or a gonif.

Layla opened the door. "So," she said, "you've become acquainted with the Mapparium."

"Barry likes trains and maps, too!" Jonah shouted.

"I thought Barry would be more partial to expensive cars," Layla said. But she also gave Barry the first real smile of the last week.

"Nope," he said. "Don't care for them at all. Train man, always have been. Choo-choo, as we say in the industry."

"Did you practice your aleph-bets?" Layla asked her son.

"Please, Mom," the kid said. "Just twenty more minutes of cartography with Barry."

"You know your father will ask you how you're doing in your Hebrew classes."

Barry let the conversation flow over him. They were standing there in a clean, well-ordered room, just as his had always been on Little Neck Parkway. A gifted son, a father-in-training, a mother who was still alive.

THE NEXT night Barry really didn't want to go to the basement to sleep by himself. He had in fact tried to teach Jonah to swim earlier that day, but when he put his hand on the boy's warm belly and tried to gently dip him into the water, as if performing an impromptu baptism, the boy's screams were as piercing as Shiva's. "Okay," Barry found himself saying in the same voice he used with his son back home. "Not now. I get it. Not now. We'll try later."

He climbed the stairs and peeked into Layla's bedroom. She was at her desk furiously typing something on her laptop. It looked like

Twitter. He saw a lot of small green frogs and what seemed like a swastika on the screen. It was probably something for her class. She looked so serious and sad, and when he touched her shoulder, her body jerked straight up. "Sorry," he said.

"It's okay, Bar," she said. Bar is what she used to call him in college, especially before sex. She touched his hand and smiled. But her hand was shaking and her skin glistened with sweat, even in the air-conditioned room.

"What is it?" he asked.

"Nothing. Work."

"I want to go to one of your classes one day," he said. "It's so awesome that you became a prof. You said you would and you did."

A new post came up on the Twitter. What kind of work was she doing? Holocaust studies? She snapped the laptop shut, got up, and kissed him. Her body was tense, but that's how he remembered it. She was a tense girl. Both of their lips were so cracked and dry it struck him immediately that their last kiss happened twenty-one years ago when everything about them was young. The pessimism of the world around them abated for a minute, and Barry realized what was about to happen.

It was funny how their generation didn't bother with the preliminaries. They quickly found each other's sour places. Then she bent over and he raged for a bit. He moaned into her dark, brittle hair and she moaned into the pillow. When it was over, both of them looked at the ceiling for an eternity.

"I want to keep being just a little emotionally detached, if you don't mind," she finally said.

"Not me," Barry said. "I'm done with that."

"Is that right?" They were nose to nose now. He looked at her mother's eyes inside her father's face. She was what every middle-aged man absent a midlife crisis would want. He could be that man.

"I have this image, but it's very special," Barry said. "If I tell it to you, do you promise not to laugh?"

"I can try."

"Well, I picture you, me, and Jonah and maybe two other kids. I don't know. Adopted kids. A boy and a girl. Maybe Mexican kids from Juárez. And so we're this family. And I build this large bathroom with three sinks next to each other. And these very high-end bowls. And the kids all wash their faces together before going to bed."

"Why do they need three bowls?" Layla asked. "Why can't they all just take turns?"

"Well, the idea is they don't have to. Because this is a large enough bathroom where they can all wash their faces together. Brush their teeth. And have fun, splash each other. Kids' stuff."

"It sounds like it's a way for you to show off your wealth," Layla said. She saw the hurt on his face. "But, yeah, it would be great for Jonah to have siblings. It would take him out of his shell and his restricted interests."

"Okay, so no on the three-bowl bathroom, but maybe yes on adoption?"

"Let me ask you something," Layla said. "When do you talk to your boy? In the mornings? I never hear you on the phone with him."

"He's just three."

"Three-year-olds talk. They talk *a lot*. Doesn't he miss his daddy?"

"I'm not like your ex-husband, if that's what you mean," Barry said. "It's different with us."

"How?"

"Do you mind if I keep that little bit to myself for now?"

"Maybe."

"Oh, and by the way, you're beautiful."

"Okay, Barry," she said.

"It was really hard for us to get pregnant," Barry said.

"I said okay."

Her hand rummaged through his chest hair. He remembered being in Bangkok on business when he and Seema were first trying to get pregnant and all the fertility stuff at NYU was falling through. He was sweating around town between meetings and came across a temple with this gigantic golden phallus, a bow wrapped around its shaft as if it were a present. The phallus was supposed to be a fertility god or something. And these young women who had trouble getting pregnant were praying to it very intently, just bowing and prostrating themselves before this big golden dick. Then these European tourist girls walked in and they started taking a photo of themselves in front of the phallus with a selfie stick. And they were all laughing in Nordic and being smug, like the whole thing was hilarious. And Barry just ran over and knocked the camera off their stick.

Barry told Layla the story. She was not impressed. "Why did you do it?" she asked.

"Because I was angry."

"Angry why? Because the tourists were hurting the feelings of the women who were infertile or because you couldn't get the desired result from your own wife?"

Barry shrugged. "I just wanted to share something with you," he said.

"You go around and you do things and you don't know why you do them," she said. "And that's the story of your gender writ large."

She picked up her phone and started scrolling through a site called *FiveThirtyEight*. What the hell had happened? How did love-making and talk of family building turn into *this*. "Listen," Barry said. "I'm sorry if that offended you. I know I have to learn to be more sensitive."

Layla laughed, but not very nicely. "So you swap your wife and kid for me and Jonah," she said. "And then what's next on Barry's incredible journey of self-discovery? How do we know this is it? How do I know I'm not just the shepherdess in your story? What does the banker say to her at the end? 'I wish none of my life had ever happened. But it's too late.'"

Barry couldn't believe that she had remembered the last lines of his story twenty-two years later. He had really hurt her. But it also meant that she hadn't forgotten him.

"Anyway, if Trump wins, we're moving to British Columbia," she said. "I have a lead on a job there."

"Where you go, I will follow," Barry said. "But he won't win."

"And what about you?" she asked. "Think you'll ever hold down a job again?"

Barry had no idea what he would do. After meeting Jonah, his Urban Watch Fund was starting to turn into a map-drawing program for shy suburban kids. "I'm going to repay that bridge loan for starters," he said.

"That's a yes?"

"I don't know," Barry said. "Right now I just want to hang out with Jonah and have sex with you twice a day. What did you always say back in school? 'I'm all out of juice!'"

She put down her phone and put her head on his chest and kissed his chin with a college girl's innocence. "One of us is making a mistake," she said.

BARRY STARTED swimming again. He had brought with him a sexy new Tudor Heritage Black Bay watch, just thirty-six millimeters across, which was completely waterproof. He loved to take showers with the watch on, just his naked flesh and the timepiece. At night, he swam beneath the moonlit Franklin Mountains, and in the morning to the chirp of the grackles in the cottonwoods. One ridiculously hot day in the middle of August, with Layla napping in the house, as she did with increasing regularity, he saw Jonah sitting shyly at the edge of the pool and was inspired to impress him. He cannonballed into the pool and started doing the butterfly so fast he nearly smashed his head into the gunite.

"Wow, you're fast," the boy said.

"I bet you'll be even faster," Barry said. "Come on, we'll give it another try. If it doesn't work, it doesn't work. Zero pressure."

"Ma-hum." The boy took off his T-shirt. He had taut but tiny biceps just like his mother. His swimming trunks looked like a pair of old man's shorts that billowed around him when he reticently got into the water.

"Okay," Barry said. "We're going to do it just like last time. I'm going to hold your belly gently and then tip you into the water. And

I'm not going to let go. I'm never letting go. The chance of your drowning is less than zero."

"That's mathematically impossible," the kid said. But he let Barry put his hand on his belly and tip him over until he was horizontal. "Please," the boy said. "I'm scared."

"I got you," Barry said. "Relax. Relax all your muscles. You're just going to float. It's easy." Barry's own father had not bothered with any of these preliminaries. He had driven seven-year-old Barry to one of his customer's pools and then thrown him into the deep end. But the end result was good, no? Swim champ, Princeton, Goldman. His whole life had begun with being thrown into that pool.

He held the boy by his warm scared belly and told him to keep his arms out straight. He would start with the breaststroke. There was a feeling of safety to that stroke. The regular breathing, the descent and the ascent, using one half of your body to propel yourself and then letting the other half take over. He would not let Jonah quit. The boy wanted so much to please a father. Finally, Barry let go of his belly and Jonah propelled himself in quick froglike bursts across the length of the pool. "Holy shit!" Barry shouted.

The boy was smiling in a way he had never seen a Hayes smile. Normally their pale lips looked like they might crack from the strain. Barry swam and put his arms around him and squeezed. "Ouch," the boy said, "let go!" But he was happy.

When Layla finally woke up from her afternoon nap and came out, Jonah yelled, "I swam across the whole pool!"

"Seriously?" Layla said. She looked at Barry with warm sleepy eyes, the setting sun haloing her hair. "Oh, my God, I've got to get my video camera. Do you think you can do it again?"

"Ma-hum!"

"Next I'm going to teach him how to make friends," Barry said.

The Mexican woman left flautas for dinner. Layla let Jonah sit in his wet shorts to celebrate his achievement. There was nothing more tragic yet moving than a skinny boy's body shivering beneath the fluorescent kitchen lights. "I had trouble making friends, too," Barry said, "but I had some techniques I've been sharing with Jonah. I ran a lot of scripts in my mind. You know, sometimes it helps to make friends with someone everyone else makes fun of. Like a poor kid. Think of him as a 'practice friend.' So who's the most disadvantaged kid in Hebrew school?"

"Are you kidding?" Layla said. "I don't think there are any."

"Maybe somebody's father or mother died and they're sad."

"Jesus, Barry."

"Just think on it. And then we'll have that kid over to the house and I'll teach Jonah my friend moves."

"Hey, let's swim more tonight!" Jonah said. "Maybe you can time me with one of your watches?"

Layla had to teach an evening class. "Can I come with you?" Barry asked her.

The boy looked down at his flauta.

"Don't worry," Barry said. "I'm not going anywhere."

ON THE way to her class, Layla told Barry she thought that the students at UTEP were better and smarter than their classmates had been at Princeton. She felt they would live more fulfilling lives. "These kids who show up at the Ivies, they're already destroyed," she said. "For them college is just this four-year interval to hammer in the notion that they tower over the rest of humanity. A working mother in my class feels more passion about learning than we ever did."

Barry disagreed. Princeton was the best thing that could have happened to him. He told her he could never have scaled the heights of finance without Princeton. He probably could never have married someone as young and pretty and credentialed as Seema, though he kept that part to himself.

When they arrived, the large, slightly down-at-the-heels lecture hall was filled to capacity. Barry figured there were at least a hundred kids in the room. There were lots of pink JanSport bags and unironic Nike caps. Barry made his way to the back of the amphitheater-shaped room so that he could look down at Layla doing her thing.

She wore a clingy floral blouse with a sober white blazer. He thought that maybe she had dressed up for him. She was unspeakably hot to him right now.

Layla's Holocaust class was intense and super interdisciplinary. She threw everything she could at the subject, from statistical modeling to a short film to a philosopher named Adorno. She was a mentor now, and her students loved and obeyed her. They raised their hands shyly, their voices shaky at times, their academic English still tentative and unsure. She cut students off by pointing her index finger at them and saying, "Nicely put. Anyone else?" Or if she really wanted to get tough: "I can't say I agree."

The students went on these long Chicano arcs about their trans-border lives. The woman next to him, in her early thirties by the looks of her, had an uncle, a repair-shop owner in Juárez, who was kidnapped by a cartel gang for not paying a *cuota,* and they took out his nails one by one until family members in El Paso paid up. "It takes that girl two hours to get to class across the border," Layla told him afterward. "Many of these kids have lost people." Layla always circled back to the 1930s and 1940s, but she let the students have some rope when it came to their own lives. Corruption, moral and otherwise, formed a ready subject. A shop owner paying a *cuota,* a Nazi-era Jew being divested of her property, a Cambodian having his glasses knocked off his face by a Pol Pot thug. Slides came and went. Cattle cars. The Rwandan killing fields. Guatemala. One showed a cartoon of a big-lipped frog smiling as a gang of men in hoods raped a heavily bespectacled woman, shouting for mercy. "This is what happens to race traitors on November 9," the caption read, followed by "#MAGA." The class gasped audibly. Barry was shocked. Apart from the cruel and crude imagery, this was the same frog he had seen on Layla's laptop. Had she been getting messages like this, too?

"Who knows who this is?" Layla asked, pointing at the frog.

Maybe two dozen hands went up. "And who's regularly on Twitter?" About the same number of hands went up.

"It's Pepe the Frog," one of several Mexican emo girls in the class explained. "He's a white-supremacist symbol."

"And what does 'MAGA' stand for?" Layla asked.

"Make America Great Again."

They launched into a discussion of social media. It was draining. He noticed that there was a profound difference between the freshman and the more senior students in the class, who were quite eloquent. At Princeton, the students were ready from day one, but many of the incoming UTEP kids seemed unprepared for college. Layla took nothing for granted and explained every term. " 'Aesthetics' is a complicated way to talk about beauty," she said at one point, and then went right back to MAGA and Pepe the Frog. Barry wished she would get off the topic of social media and show another film on the Adorno guy, say something authoritative about the six million dead.

No matter what topic Layla seemed to focus on, Barry could see that the kids remained distracted by the Nazi rape cartoon, which still dominated the overhead projection. One of the first-year kids, a white boy with a buzz cut, kept trying to defend freedom of speech. He had a lot of pop culture at his disposal. "My uncle always says there are more Lieutenant Dans than Forrest Gumps," he kept repeating. Barry hadn't a clue what that meant. "Maybe it's some rich teenager having a goof in his parents' basement," he said of the frog cartoon. Barry could feel Layla's anger rising, but he was getting angry, too. He had read about these new pro-Trump fascist memes as they called them even back in New York before he left, but now the ugliness was right in front of him and these kids. What was the point of that? Surely this stuff would pass once Hillary was elected and everything went back to normal. He felt it was unseemly for Layla to show her students something that affected her personally. How could you equate the Holocaust with a crudely drawn frog?

The kid with the buzz cut was persistent, and Layla eventually had to cut him off.

"Well, I think you're just wrong," she finally said. The class gasped.

Evidently, Layla never rebutted a student this way. "Okay, I *respectfully* think you're wrong," she added. "And please let's not mention Forrest Gump for the rest of the semester." This was supposed to be a joke, and her more loyal adherents tittered. "Where was I?" Layla said.

"Professor Hayes," a Latina girl sitting next to Barry said, "could you take down that picture, please?" *Yes,* Barry thought.

"Does it bother you?" Layla asked. Her pallid face was flushed.

"It does," the girl said.

"But we just had a slide from the liberation of the Sobibór death camp," Layla said. "The stacked corpses. That was up for at least twenty minutes. That didn't bother you?" The girl was momentarily confused. "It's okay," Layla said. "I'm not trying to put you on the spot. I know this class can be very difficult on an emotional level. What about this particular cartoon bothers you?" The girl was silent. Barry followed the second hand of his Tudor. At least something in this world still made sense. "The Pepe the Frog rape scene is sickening and vile, but it's a drawing," Layla said. "The photographs we saw were actual human beings. There were one-point-five million children murdered by the Nazis. You didn't mishear me."

"Yeah, but that stuff, it happen to people I know," the girl said, pointing at the frog slide.

"So it can happen to you," Layla said. "That's what you're saying."

"Maybe," the girl said. "I don't know."

Barry hoped Layla would show mercy, but he knew, from their three years of rhetorical combat at Princeton, that she could not. "I'll turn it off," Layla said, "but before I do, I wanted to show you one last thing." She scrolled up, past the frog drawing to show that it had been tweeted at the handle @Layla_E_Hayes. The class gasped again. "This cartoon was drawn with me in mind."

Barry wanted to punch someone, preferably a Nazi, but really anyone would do. Why didn't she tell *him?* Why didn't she share this burden with him? She didn't take him seriously. She never had. All that bullshit about Princeton not being the best was really just cover for *him* not being the best. It was like she had lied to him all along.

"But you don't wear glasses," the girl said.

"Yes, but traditionally the enemies of the people wear glasses. Cue Pol Pot. By the way, this nice fellow, CommanderGoyToy is his handle, went to the trouble to find out that I had been married to a Jewish man and was thus a 'race traitor.' He also found out that I had a child, and some of his followers got in touch with him. I had to erase him from social media entirely."

"I still wouldn't ban this GoyToy from Twitter," Forrest Gump said. " 'I disapprove of what you say, but I will defend to the death your right to say it.' That was Thomas Jefferson."

"No," Layla said, "it was a woman named Evelyn Beatrice Hall."

Barry stewed in hurt and shock and anger for most of the car ride. He rolled down his window and desperately inhaled the cool evening air. Across the border, the chimneys of the maquiladora plants were releasing bursts of steam against a frenzied urban background, like in the opening sequence of *Blade Runner.* El Paso was the future. Or maybe it was Juárez.

"What?" she finally said as they were approaching the trendy Mesa neighborhood. They passed a hipster coffee place made out of a bunch of shipping containers, which Layla frequented for their ancient-grains bowl.

"Nothing."

"It's okay to be emotionally raw. That's what the class is about."

"Why the fuck didn't you *tell* me?" That came out louder than he wanted it. "I'm teaching Jonah how to swim and make friends, we're talking about adopting Mexican kids together, but I'm still a stranger in your house. I could have done something."

"Really? What?"

"I have a friend whose fund owns a lot of Twitter. He can do stuff to make those people go away. He's what's called an activist investor."

"I know what that is."

"I didn't mean to—"

"I read up on stuff. You think I don't know about Valupro?"

Barry suddenly felt both numb and nauseated. "Oh," he said. "Oh?"

The nausea passed, but he still couldn't locate his fingers or his feet. He breathed in and out slowly. "Here comes the morality police, I guess," he said.

"Did I say anything? I'll be me and you be you. Just like back in college."

"Fine."

"What? Am I missing something?"

"There's just so much complexity in a trade like Valupro."

"Oh, God."

"So you hate me now?"

"Are we still in the same car? Do I let you play with my kid? Am I *fucking* you every night?" Barry flinched, as if hit. She was an angrier person than Seema, always had been. How did he conveniently manage to forget that fact all these years?

"I really don't think you should look at Twitter anymore," Barry said, trying to sound diplomatic and maybe a little hurt.

"Because I can't handle it?" Layla said. "It's such a *manly* medium."

"No, just, maybe give it a rest a little bit. For your mental health." She did not respond. Every time he looked over at her, he saw that hot blazer and the cool nape of her neck. He hated to admit it, but her anger and forcefulness aroused him. He wanted to kiss her. He had to find a way to calm her down.

"Look, I thought you were amazing as a teacher," he said, once they were lying in bed. "You didn't mention Trump by name once, but that's what the class was about."

She was checking her phone. Barry now recognized the scrolling-down-Twitter motion of her right thumb. Probably more of that Nazi shit. "Thanks," she said. "But that doesn't make me feel any better."

Barry sighed. "I can't win," he said.

"It's all about winning."

"Can we talk about the fact that I taught Jonah how to swim today?"

She started crying. "I'm a terrible mother," she said. "I put my child in harm's way."

He couldn't keep up with her moods. "These people are psychopaths," he said. "Did you call the police?"

"They're watching us," Layla said. "Every hour of every day."

Barry sat up in the bed. *"Who?"* She wouldn't answer.

"And today I fucked up in class. I spoke down to them. They're not fully getting this. And it's so important that they get this."

"You can't be held responsible for how this country votes."

"We're all responsible."

"Especially me, right? Mr. Valupro. Taking away lifesaving medicines from dying kids."

"Is that what you think you did?"

"Oh, fuck this, Layla. Why can't we ever change?"

She turned her back on him. They lay silently for a while, as they used to up in his room at the Tiger Inn. Suddenly she reached back and took his hand, guided it to her stomach and the mound of wiry pubic hair below. "I'm sorry," Barry said. "I love you so much." She shushed him.

He found the base of her spine and softly massaged the vertebrae with his thumb. He kissed her neck, which still tasted young. He wanted to tell her how much she aroused him in class, at least before she put up that damn frog. This smart, powerful teacher in a white linen blazer covering her bare arms.

When she turned around, her eyes were so wide, he thought she was going to yell at him. But that's not what happened at all. Within seconds she was on top of him, pounding him into her bed, and then, just as abruptly, she was done. Never once did she look at him or offer him any affection. He was turned on like always, but her behavior felt like payback. Though, for what? Their college years? The shepherdess story? Goldman? Valupro? The whole fucking country circa 2016?

They went out to the pool later, the pool where he had taught her boy how to swim, and tried to search out the thunderbird etched into the Franklins in the dusk.

Something was howling in the arroyo, and something else was screeching. He wondered if he and Layla were getting closer or growing apart. "Let's go to Juárez," she said. "I know it's important to you. You and your Hemingway and Fitzgerald. You were such a modernist loser in college. I'll put together some people. We'll do a day trip."

"I really do love you," he said. "You and Jonah."

She looked at him miserably. They leaned in for a kiss, then she got out her phone. He could hear her thumb scrolling in the darkness.

THEY HAD made plans to go to Mexico in a week. Before then, Jonah had a playdate with a boy named Menachem whose father had just been fired from the Wells Fargo downtown. Barry made sure Jonah got a haircut, something close and military that made him a bit more manly. Then they spent the whole weekend practicing his friend moves. "Do you want to be like me?" Barry said. "Lots of friends, conversing with everyone I meet?"

"Ma-hum."

"Don't say 'Ma-hum,' just say 'Yeah,' but like you don't really mean it. And never start a sentence with 'Do you know?' Always wait for your friend to tell you what he likes instead, and then say, 'That's pretty cool,' even if it's not at all. And no map or train talk. I know, I know. Listen, I'd love to just run up to people and say, 'Hey, is that an Omega Speedmaster pre-moon with alpha hands?' But first you have to know if they have the same passion as you. And most people don't have very strong passions. Not like we do."

To Barry's chagrin, Menachem did not seem overly concerned about his father's firing from Wells Fargo. He was about half a foot taller than Jonah, curly haired, and funny and fierce. He spotted the basketball hoop over the garage and quickly demanded that they shoot hoops at once. "Did you know that I got hurt playing basketball once?" Jonah said. "I had to go to the ER." Barry sighed and got out a basketball. He and Menachem did some layups while Jonah mostly watched. Things went better at the pool. Menachem's family apparently didn't have one, so the kid happily plunged in, shorts and T-shirt and all.

"No diving!" Barry sang.

"Let's race!" Menachem shouted. He began pounding across the pool freestyle and beat Jonah decisively, but that seemed all right with Jonah. "You swim really cool," he said, which wasn't the best line, but seemed to make Menachem happy. Barry was pleased that Jonah exhibited so much fairness and courtesy. The kid would be just right for Princeton someday. Layla came out with cucumber sandwiches, a Waspy touch, but assured Menachem they were glatt kosher. The boys gobbled them down so fast it made Barry heartsick. Two hungry boys. This was his dream. *These two* should have been his children.

AFTER LUNCH, the boys repaired to the Mapparium and closed the door behind them. An hour later, consumed with anxiety over Jonah's social skills, Barry knocked. "Hey, fellas . . ." The two boys were hunched over Jonah's computer and breathing heavily.

"We're on a map site!" Menachem shouted. All of Jonah's trains were scattered on the ground, the first time Barry had seen them in such disarray. He leaned over their shoulders and studied the screen. Jonah had posted his Acela map in progress along with the innocent headline "This is my first posted map. Can you tell me how I can improve it?"

The replies were insanely granular. There were hundreds if not thousands of fellow enthusiasts who knew Amtrak's Northeast Corridor by heart and had many useful suggestions. One message, however, was from CommanderGoyToy: "Did you know your mother is a race traitor and your a halfbreed spawn?" Barry was outraged. Jonah was a nine-year-old kid! But Jonah said he was used to it. Menachem also shrugged. "He can't even spell," Jonah noted.

Leaving the boys to their computer adventures, Barry wandered over to the wall-sized Acela map. There, he realized Jonah had erased parts of Long Island to make room for LAKE SUCCESS, which was identified in large capital letters and a yellow star as big as his father's Chevy Chase. Even more touching was the amateur execution on parts of the cartography. Jonah had clearly let Menachem color in some of New Jersey. He had been flexible enough to allow Menachem to share his interests. Maybe Menachem could be a friend! "Just thirty minutes of computer time left," Barry said, the enforcer of Jonah's weekly limit.

"A little longer, pleeeeeeeease," the boys said in tandem.

When Menachem left, Jonah instantly fell asleep, too tired to put his trains back on the shelves. Barry did it for him, remembering carefully where each of them went, the Shinkansen next to the ICE, the Acela next to the TGV because they were both designed by Alstom, the French multinational. Barry recalled that feeling of being deadly tired after social interactions with Joey Paramico or the Irish twins, too sleepy to let his mind run away with the usual numbers and patterns. He used to do the multiplication table to put himself to sleep, or write programs for his Commodore 64 in his head. After he had taught himself to be friendly, everything else became harder. He had to let go of his nerdy passions. He couldn't do both at once. By his forties, watches were the only thing he had left.

THE STREET signs read EL PASO STREET and SIXTH AVENUE, and then the country came to an end. The border looked like a giant shed surrounded by barbed wire. Oversize Texan and American flags greeted the Mexicans crossing over. Yellow Transborde buses with Chihuahua plates were disgorging extended families. The new arrivals were soon milling around in a well-regulated shopping frenzy. Minutes ago they were in Juárez, and now they were buying Payless Shoes in Texas. Rumors had it that some of the unfortunates in the drug wars across the border had had their lower halves dipped in acid while doctors kept them conscious. Barry did not know why, but a part of him longed to walk toward that border shed and then to accept whatever would happen to him on the other side in the worst of the colonias, no matter how violent his end. To surrender himself to fate. To never strive for anything again. To finally burn that map of Long Island with Lake Success circled in red marker that he had kept stowed under his bed up until college. It bothered him that even though things with Layla and Jonah were good and he loved Chuco Town so much, he would be willing to hand himself over to the rude justice of a poor country. Seema had said he had no imagination, but sometimes it felt like *all* he had was imagination.

"Hey," Layla said, poking him in the ribs. "Snap out of it, Hemingway boy. We're almost there." They were in someone's ancient Nissan van, the car filled with the loud voices of Layla's colleagues from UTEP. They were all brilliant and convivial and 100 percent funny, just like New York Jews, which more than half of them were. They had a competition as to who drove the shittiest car. Barry suggested "his" Avalon, but he wasn't even close.

There was a Filipina woman named Gina, who was super cute and a professor of microbiology. Barry had heard of her. She was apparently Layla's best friend. Her fiancé, Jimmy, was the dean of the engineering school. There was this other guy, Judah, who taught in the Jewish studies program and, incredibly enough, shared Barry's love of watches. He wore a very under-the-radar vintage Longines with a coveted 13ZN movement, the dial patinated beyond legibility, real Watch Idiot Savant stuff. He had brought two guys from the Jewish studies program faculty with him, both small dudes dressed in overly hot sweaters, whose names Barry kept forgetting. This Judah was as tall as Barry and had some of the same swagger Barry used to have when he was at Princeton, only his came more naturally. He called Barry "a real New York *macher*," Yiddish for a guy who gets things done, which totally charmed Barry. His father had used that term with great awe. This guy had friend moves up the ass.

On the ride downtown, Barry had locked on to one of the crowd's academically correct acronyms, "POCs," or people of color. "What's the ROI on your POC students?" he asked. He thought this might be useful info if he ever revisited his Urban Watch Fund.

They all broke up laughing. "*What?* You can't use the term 'POC,'" Gina the Filipina said. "You have to *be* a POC." Barry mentioned that his ex-wife was a POC and his son's Filipina nanny, too. The Filipina professor asked how much the nanny earned, and when he told her she just looked at her fiancé, Jimmy the Dean, openmouthed. "That's *three* times what she makes," the dean said.

"You got a job for me?" Gina asked. "I can teach your kid microbiology. Maybe he'll get into Hunter."

Before heading over to Juárez, they steeled themselves with a round of drinks in a cheap hole-in-the-wall in the art deco part of downtown, the kind of place where a homeless man wearing a green LEGALIZE GAY T-shirt might walk in with a watermelon under his arm to meet his similarly situated friends. At first, Layla's friends seemed to be scanning Barry carefully, which he liked, because it meant they were protective of her after the divorce. But eventually Barry seemed to do just fine by them. They liked that Barry had no "gating," that he said almost anything that came to mind, but his mistakes were made out of ignorance not meanness. He didn't tell them that he was a "moderate fiscal Republican," but almost felt like he could.

"Did you know Barry's into maps and trains, too?" Layla said.

"Whoa, Jonah's got a friend for life!" Gina said. They all toasted to Barry like he was the best thing that had ever happened to the kid. When Layla had gone to the bathroom, Jewish Studies Judah leaned into him and said, "That's very important for Jonah to have a role model. That would take a whole load off Layla's shoulders." Barry felt the glow of Judah's support. He really did want to be a *macher* in his eyes.

"I taught him how to swim," Barry said. "And make friends."

"He's a sweet kid," the dean said, "but he's very alone."

"*You're* very alone," Gina said. They drank to lonely weirdos, which likely each of them had been as a child, Barry included.

Their trip hadn't even begun, but already he didn't want the day to end.

HE THOUGHT they would cross down the Paso del Norte Bridge, the one running off of El Paso Street, but they couldn't find parking and ended up on the Stanton Street Bridge a few blocks east. Around them lay a jumble of railroad tracks, oil refineries, desert. The wind blew dust into his hair. The men jabbered away about how scary and fun this was going to be, how badly they needed an adventure. Some were wondering whether or not they should have taken out traveler's insurance. They walked up the bridge to a sign that read LIMITE INTERNACIONAL EUA-MEXICO. Barry looked down to see the Rio Grande, trapped like an animal in a concrete trough.

At the end of the bridge was a sign that read MEXICO in chili-red letters. Barry noticed some Mexican government vehicles, tiny orange Volkswagens bearing the legend "Grupos Beta" arranged in a lot below. "What are those?" Barry asked Layla.

"They give medical aid to migrants trying to sneak across the border," she said. "Mostly Salvadorans and Guatemalans." Barry thought of the faux Guatemalan Luis Goodman ensconced in his 4.1-million-dollar Zestimate apartment on Madison Park while he, Barry Cohen, was crossing into this inferno. An image of the one-eyed Mexican man who had rested his head on Barry's shoulder on the bus to Baltimore came to mind. Gina and Layla were wearing T-shirts and shorts and looked sun drenched and beautiful. Barry was proud of the company he kept. His life couldn't be better. He leaned in and pecked Layla on the cheek.

No one checked their papers and, just like that, they were in Mexico. There were pavements and parking lots and mini-parks to be sure, but everything looked cracked and swollen to Barry. Signs called the city HEROICA CIUDAD JUÁREZ, perhaps in reference to the recent drug war and the toll it had taken. The group whipped out their phones and tried to figure out where Avenida Benito Juárez, the main drag, was located. Barry pointed out a street vendor selling grilled corn. He was wearing a brim straw cowboy hat and had a scar across one cheek. The man took a very long look at the crew, Barry in his Georgia Aquarium whale-shark T-shirt, and behind him Jimmy the Dean talking hermeneutics loudly with Layla, while Judah, dressed in a sharp blazer as if for a faculty meeting, sang an old Jewish Bund anthem with his colleagues, who looked like freshly shorn sheep in their cardigans.

"Gringos, be careful," the corn man said.

Gina stepped forward and asked him directions in surprisingly fluent Spanish. The man waved west, his eyes still traveling over the American posse. "Gringos, be careful," he repeated.

The warning just made the men of the group bolder. "Let's win this one for the shtetl," Judah said to his crew.

Gina reminded them of the recent killings in Juárez, five men shot in a barbershop, one just over the Santa Fe Bridge, and so on. But Barry, for one, felt invincible. "Safety in numbers," he said. "I used to make bets for a living. Let's do this!"

They crossed over to the Avenida Benito Juárez. The street that, according to Judah, had once catered to generations of drunken, horny Americans was all but empty. The few people strolling past looked at them with wonder and concern. A pack of stray dogs ran by, brushing against their legs as if desperately seeking warmth. A freight train fresh out of El Paso rumbled parallel to the avenue. Other noise came from the plentiful *farmacias,* which had set up large speakers along the *avenida* and were blasting bad global dance music. The music echoed off the façades of the silent bars and dental clinics. The pharmacies were offering free packs of Viagra if you bought pain medicine without a prescription. Gina and the dean went in to buy some oxycodone for their impending marriage, and they came out with cartons of free Viagra for everyone.

"There it is!" Barry shouted. "The Kentucky Club! Where Hemingway went." The establishment was slotted into a nondescript one-story building with the words WORLD FAMOUS and SINCE 1921 in English. Barry wished the signage had been in Spanish. They went inside, and he pointed out the trough around the bar. "Did you know that, in the old days, men would just relieve themselves from their stools?" he asked.

"You're sounding more and more like Jonah," Gina said. *"Did you know . . . ?"*

The gang laughed, and even Layla seemed cool with it. "Jonah's kind of a role model for me," Barry said proudly. "Maybe we can find him a Mexican train set."

Everyone ordered drinks. The bar was dark and green lit and festively somber in a post-drug-war kind of way. Well-dressed young locals sat around the bar talking shop and drinking slowly; the prices weren't cheap. Barry ate two heaping plates of shrimp *al ajillo,* feeling his breath go from bad to worse, but not caring. They were all drunk on smoky tequilas. "This is really great!" Barry shouted. "Except for those flat-screen TVs. Hemingway was here! This place should be a shrine."

"Okay, honey," Layla said to him. "Calm down."

"Honey?" Gina said. "I've never heard Layla call *anyone* that."

"I'm very lucky," Barry said. There was a collective *Awww.* This was just the permission Barry needed to start talking loudly about how he had taken a Greyhound across the country to find Layla. He stressed the parts about running out of money and not having enough food, trying to burnish his credentials as a down-and-out romantic. "My dream is that one day Layla and Jonah and I can finish the trip as a family. We can take a bus to San Diego and visit my dad's grave. He really liked Layla."

"He kept calling me *Lay-lur,*" Layla said. "And then he told me I was too pale but had great Sabra hair."

"Here's to eugenics, Jewish-style!" Judah shouted.

"L'chaim!" his colleagues slurred. They splash-cheered with their drinks. Was there anything more convivial in the world than a Jewish studies department? Why couldn't *they* teach the Holocaust class instead of Layla?

Two hours later, after they had talked through a hundred scholarly topics including the decline of Japan's Liberal Democratic Party ("I lost a hundred million dollars in yen trades last year," Barry confided to his new friends), they finally exited the bar hooting and hollering. Barry and the profs continued down the *avenida,* each step taking them farther away from the border and their terrific lives. A crisp-looking grandpa in a white fedora walked past Layla and whispered in passing, *"Oye, señorita, un joven?"*

"Holy shit, he just tried to sell you a little boy!" Gina said.

"Does the *joven* come with female Viagra?" Judah said.

Layla was not amused. "That was pretty messed up," she said. "We can't forget there's another human being at the end of that transaction." The men looked slightly abashed.

The *farmacia* music continued to blare at them from up the street, but the *avenida* was getting gloomier. A row of Polícia Municipal trucks surrounded by cops with semiautomatic rifles took up half a block. They began shouting at a young man in a Texas Spurs T-shirt and torn sweatpants who was making his way toward them, eyes darting around, muttering something rapidly under his breath. "Let's go in here," Gina said, pushing Barry and their friends into a bar called Don Beto. It did not have the same high-end clientele as the Kentucky Club; there were white plastic chairs and tables, an abandoned-looking drum set, and lots of canoodling old-timers drinking big mugs of Sol beer.

"You think they're going to shoot?" Judah asked, straining his ears in the direction of the street.

"Now *that* would be something to see," Barry agreed.

"Do you know how corrupt the Polícia Municipal is?" Layla asked. "During the wars between the Sinaloa and Juárez cartels, they had to send in the federal police to clean them up."

Barry was proud of how much she knew. "Maybe if there's a shoot-out we can testify about police brutality or something," he said.

Layla rolled her eyes at him. "Oh, my God," she said, then, looking over his shoulder, "That's Jose! That's my gardener, Jose Luis."

"Wait a second," Gina said. "He's talking to *my* gardener."

"Are you kidding me?" the dean said. "How much *yanqui* privilege are we going to have to check this evening?"

This incredible coincidence soon led to the two gringas waving at the gardeners, who were equally shocked to see them. Having little choice, Jose Luis and his friend walked sullenly over to the table. Both wore back braces and were on the older side, walrus mustached and callused all over, as if they worked with their foreheads as well as their hands. "Hola, Jose!" Layla shouted. She put on her best Hayes smile, then spoke rapidly in broken Spanish to the two men.

Jose Luis bent over and said, "Be careful in Juárez, señora."

"Stay on this street," said the other gardener. "Don' go away from this street. Actually, even on this street, be careful."

"Come drink with us!" Layla said. *"¡Siéntate! ¡Siéntate! Por favor."*

"I don't know about this," Jimmy the Dean said, and Gina also looked unsure, but Layla coerced their workmen into sitting with them. She loudly ordered new pitchers of Sol beer from the barmaid.

"Now you are in my country," Layla's gardener tried to tell her. "So I pay." But of course she wouldn't let him. The gardener sighed and looked down at his feet.

"I think that's not cool for him," Gina whispered. "In his culture—"

"He's got five kids," Layla whispered back. Once the gardeners were among them there was absolutely nothing to talk about in any language. They sat there on opposite ends of the table looking at each other. Someone turned up the music, a mournful corrido, and a man and a woman, both in cowboy boots, got up to dance as if this were their last moment on earth. "You guys aren't even trying," Layla hissed at her UTEP friends.

"I don't really speak Spanish," Barry said, and others voiced similar sentiments. Gina, who did speak Spanish, tried to talk, ostensibly about El Chapo and the Sinaloa cartel, but that didn't go very far. Barry felt bad for Layla. The painful silence of the gardeners continued. He noted the soil on their fingertips as they hoisted their American-bought beers. They took out their phones and he imagined they were desperately texting back to their loved ones about their kidnapping at the hands of their employers. Layla took a cue from them and angrily whipped out her own phone and started scrolling through Twitter. "Honey, don't do that right now," Gina said. "The roaming charges alone."

"Look at what these fuckers are saying."

"Not that GoyToy again?"

"Yes, that GoyToy again."

"You're drunk. Maybe you should take next semester off."

"Work is all that keeps my mind off it."

"Maybe you shouldn't be teaching a class on the Holocaust until the election is over, huh?"

Layla slammed her hands on the cheap plastic table. Startled, the gardeners looked up from their phones. "This election will *never* be over!" Layla shouted. "Can't you see that?"

She stood and walked out of the bar. "What the fuck?" at least three people said.

"Outside very dangerous," said Jose Luis.

"I got this," Barry said. He jumped out of his seat and was out the door, into the florid sunlight, onto the alien street. Layla was there, running, *running,* in the opposite direction from the border. The Policía Municipal trucks were nowhere to be seen. "Layla!" Barry shouted. But she didn't look back. He ran after her down the remaining desolate blocks of the *avenida,* toward a large square. There was a Scotiabank here that he found oddly reassuring, and a big red sculpture of three small cap letters JRZ, presumably a civic-pride thing. Layla hung a left and ran through a book market full of college students that looked to Barry like slightly shabbier versions of her UTEP students. "Layla!" he shouted again. The college students stared at him. He was a gringo blur sprinting through their world.

Layla ran to a small urban park and disappeared within. Barry made his way through the old sombrero- and baseball-cap-clad men and the rows of tired seniors gathered around a lonely fountain. Mariachi music played, and loud voices were singing an insipid song he intuited was a political message. Layla rounded the Franciscan hulk of an enormous cathedral fronting the park. Barry kept up but soon found himself on an empty side street, breathing heavily, his shoulders heaving in the Chihuahuan Desert heat. He was surrounded by mauled-looking cars and crumbling buildings. The developing world, as Seema called it. But unlike in Thailand or India or Baltimore or the countless other poor places he had visited, Barry was scared.

"Layla!" he shouted. "Layla, come on already!"

Some of the pitiful houses had small unkempt gardens beyond their wrought-iron gates. Barry did not know the names of the desert plants, could not admire their fortitude. Why didn't Layla's gardener follow him? Why didn't the others? They had left him alone in the mission of fetching his girlfriend, past and present, from the bowels of a city where people had their nails pulled out one by one while their families gathered the *cuota* across the border. This was a street of death. He could feel it. If only the Polícia Municipal could come roaring around the block in their pickups. If only he could offer them money in return for his life.

Barry rounded a corner to see the poverty of the previous block replicated. A yellow maquila bus full of young women passed by. It looked like a used American school bus. Women who worked at the maquiladora factories were kidnapped and murdered during the 1990s. He had heard this from a girl in Layla's class. Is this what he had come for? Not to trace Hemingway's steps, but to walk his last?

"Hey," he shouted after the bus. "Stop! *Arrêtez!*" The bus roared ahead, spewing black fume from a clattering exhaust pipe.

No. It wasn't true. Barry did not want to die. He wanted to go home. But to which home? There was a truly scary-looking *ginecológica cirugía*, all of its windows barred with rusted metal. Women did not fare well in these parts. A shot rang out and Barry crouched down to his knees in front of the gynecologist's office. Maybe it was a car backfiring. A big car. Maybe the maquila bus. "Someone!" Barry shouted. "Someone please! Hello? *Aidez-moi!*" The crumbling façades absorbed his voice. Not one window opened. If this place wasn't death, maybe it was a different kind of eternity: an eternity frozen in fear.

The world spun around Barry, and his ankles wobbled beneath

him. "Look at your watch," he commanded himself. "Look at it." He was wearing the Universal Tri-Compax today. He brought his face up close to the slowly gliding second hand. He followed the hand around the subdial. Time was still passing. The watch spoke the same language as Barry. It told him that the world was still moving relentlessly on its melancholy axis.

The Tri-Compax was the watch meant for Shiva. It had a gorgeous creamy dial that had survived from the late 1940s, unbelievable leaf-shaped hands, and thick, golden lapidated lugs. And the moon on the moon phase had patinated to a coarse cheddar yellow, like this archetypal idea of the moon that children seem to be born with. Barry had never seen a watch, or anything else, age so gracefully, as if rejecting the very idea of mortality. He had shown the watch to Shiva, and Shiva had looked at the moon phase and then looked outside with his restless circled eyes. It had been daytime, but his son knew that the object on his watch represented the object he saw out his window at night. The watch was proof that Shiva had complex thoughts. He had taken it to a watchmaker at the PX on Fort Bliss. It might cost him a thousand dollars or more to repair, which he did not have right now, but the Tri-Compax had to survive.

Which also meant *Barry* had to survive. He stood up to the unseen menace of the street. His whole body was now shaking as if from hunger. He did not know which direction was the right one. Maybe they were all wrong. He walked down the block. Then another block. Then another.

He rounded some corner and found himself looking at a Pollo Feliz, which smelled heavenly of grease. According to a festive sign, two *pollos* cost 159 pesos *todos los días*. A cartoon chicken was giving Barry the thumbs-up. It was open. There were people inside, and they looked no different from the people on the other side of the border. A family. Three kids, just like in Barry's fantasies. Behind the chicken he spotted the familiar crests of the Franklin Mountains. So there was home. There was America. There was Jonah and his maps. There was Lake Success. It was so close. A woman was sitting on an old chair next to a bunch of shit she was selling off the sidewalk, a frilly black blouse like the kind you could find at the Casa Blanca store on the last block of El Paso, here hanging off a mannequin missing half a leg. There were many scary baby dolls that looked like they were reaching out to be burped and some kind of American packaged thing called Flavor Boost. There was a baby crib and women's shoes, but not in pairs.

"*Donde* the bridge?" Barry asked her. "*Où se trouve le pont? Donde* America?" The woman waved him in the direction of his nation. A few blocks later he had come back upon the cathedral, its surrounding benches decorated with drawings of Pope Francis, a dove at his side. Next came the Avenida Benito Juárez with its dental clinics and dick pills. The group was waiting for him outside the pub, and there, too, was Layla, who briefly nodded his way.

"What the fuck was that?" he screamed at her. "We could have been killed!"

"Yeah, it's really *dangerous* in Mexico," Layla said.

"Your gardener told us to stay off the streets. Do you know where I've been?"

"Where were you?"

But he couldn't quite describe it. It had just been an empty street. "I could have been killed," he shouted. She laughed, loudly and openly. Her friends quickly formed two groups and took them apart, Gina and the dean whispering to Layla, Judah and the Jewish studies people trying to calm Barry down.

"This is not right," he said to Judah. He was hyperventilating. "What's wrong with her? Why did she run away like that? It's like she wanted me to get hurt."

"She's under a lot of pressure. The election. The online stuff."

"And I'm not under pressure? My business is failing. My kid—" Once again, he stopped himself. Once again, he had to restrain himself from the truth. "I taught her boy how to make friends," he said. "I did that for her."

Barry couldn't wait to get out of Mexico. The Puente Internacional Paso del Norte was filled with darkened cars and, Barry imagined, patient passengers trying to see their relatives or get to an evening class at UTEP. The bridge was covered by a vast metal cage as if it were a prison. The Rio Grande was all but invisible below, a shallow grave of a river. Ahead, the El Paso skyline was bathed in moonlight, the Wells Fargo tower taking on gold against the darkened waves of the Franklins.

When Barry's turn came, he smiled moderately and handed over the false passport to the border agent. What if the passport didn't work? Joey Greenblatt said it was the best forgery in the world. They had gone to a basement in Brighton Beach, had been photographed meticulously by some Slav who kept addressing him as "Meeester Guy." The whole idea of a getaway passport was supposed to be funny, a lark, although Joey had already been through three ankle monitors and now talked often of his off-the-grid retreat in Belize. "Welcome home, Mr. Conte," the immigration agent said.

As they walked into America, Layla grabbed his arm. "Why did he call you 'Mr. Conte'? What the hell was that?"

"Keep your voice down. I have a few legal names. It's business."

She looked at him with her impenetrable eyes. Barry felt like he was back in college. Every single one of their hundred or so fights began with that look. "Got it," she said.

"No, really. It's complicated."

"I said I got it."

They took a cab home. When he passed El Rincon he wanted to stop by and bask in its familiarity, maybe get a cup of vile coffee, but they drove on.

Jonah was asleep, and Layla passed the Mexican lady without a word, even though she wanted to know how they had enjoyed her country. Why had he taken that passport with him? *Why?* It was for an emergency, in case he had to get out of the country, shack up in Belize with Joey Greenblatt and the rest of the "ankle monitor gang." He was not going to prison.

She was on the bed, her thumb scrolling down on her phone. *Good,* he thought. Let her disappear into Nazi Twitter Land. But she put the phone down and looked at him. "Barry," she said.

"The whole passport thing was a lark," he said.

"It's not about that."

"Let's go to sleep, okay? Pick this up tomorrow. It's been a tough day."

"Do you know what a burden it is to be the object of someone's fantasy?"

"What?"

"How hard it is every day to be *that* person. You wake up, you think, Oh, here's this man who says he loves me, but he doesn't really. He's just stitching together a version of me in his head. Coloring in the details. Adding nuance and plot. Every morning the same thought: Who am I supposed to be today? His lost college sweetheart? His partner in foreign adventure? His personal assistant professor? The mother to his future adopted children?"

"My friend Joey got me the passport. He's a libertarian. We were just testing the system."

"You want to hear something really weird?" Her voice was quiet. He knew that was not a good sign. He wanted to hear her sarcastic tone. He wanted her to dismember him with her intelligence. "Remember that story you wrote about me at Princeton? The Vermont shepherdess?"

"Am I going to be persecuted by seven pages of fiction my entire fucking life?"

"No. Lately I've been thinking maybe it wasn't such a bad story. Maybe you had it right all along. Maybe that's exactly who I am. Maybe I *am* the shepherdess. Maybe I get to be by myself, doing my thing. Maybe I get to be away from you."

Barry started to speak, but the words died in his mouth. "I know," she said. "You've got a lot to run away from. Your business dealings, your ex-wife. Your boy." She sighed. "Oh, that poor boy. Whatever he must have done to break your heart, I can't even imagine. But how can a child break a man's heart?"

"It's—"

"Complicated. Or maybe it isn't. Maybe you're just a coward. And this isn't the time for cowards. Not right now."

"You can insult me all you want," Barry said. "But I love you. I love Jonah."

She propped herself up on her pillow and looked at him with a tired, dim-eyed sadness. "I do believe you love Jonah," she said. "Oh, God, how it kills me to pry you two apart."

"You don't have to pry anyone apart. I'm sorry, but this is *bullshit!* You're not a shepherdess. You're a good teacher. A good woman. A good mother."

"I'm not sure about any of those things."

"Well, let me *make* you sure. Let me prove it to you. Let me prove it to Jonah, for fuck's sake!"

"I'm sorry, Barry. I can't. However hard you try, it just won't work. That boy is mine."

She turned away and curled up into herself. He watched her shoulders shake and heard the muffled sound of her crying. "Layla," he said. He sat down and put his hand on her shoulder, but she shrugged him off. "Please," he whispered. "Please, don't do this. I'm so close this time. I'm so close."

He felt like he was back on that side street in Juárez. He didn't know where to go. He looked at the laptop on his bedside table, picked it up, and headed to the bathroom.

He sat down on the toilet and opened up his e-mail for the first time in months. There were eight hundred messages. He scanned them quickly. Zero of them were from Seema, but one was from Armen Kassabian addressed to all their investors. He clicked on it. "As you are all too aware . . . ," it began. "Losses of this magnitude . . ." "Outflows . . ." "Volatility . . ." "Unwinding our book . . ." "Change in management . . ." He scrolled through the e-mail subject headings.

SINGAPORE CENTRAL PROVIDENT FUND FULL REDEMPTION
BRUNEI INVESTMENT AGENCY REDEMPTION
MARYLAND STATE RETIREMENT AND PENSION SYSTEM FULL
REDEMPTION

AUSTRALIAN NATIONAL SUPERANNUATION SCHEME
   REDEMPTION
LOUISIANA SHERIFFS PENSION AND RELIEF FUND FULL
   REDEMPTION
KANSAS CITY PUBLIC SCHOOLS RETIREMENT SYSTEMS
   REDEMPTION
STICHTING PENSIOENFONDS ZORG EN WELZJIN REDEMPTION
FUND FOR MUTUAL ASSISTANCE OF THE EMPLOYEES OF
   IONIKI BANK AND OTHER BANKS REDEMPTION
QATAR INVESTMENT AUTHORITY FULL REDEMPTION

Well, so much for This Side of Capital. Everyone from Brunei to Baton Rouge wanted out. Another was an e-mail from his general counsel. Barry was being sued by his chief of staff for sexual harassment. The process server couldn't locate him. "Good for Sandy," Barry whispered. The final set of e-mails was also from his general counsel. "Subpoena of All Phone and Electronic Records," one said.

He put the laptop down on the cold tile floor. He threw water on his face. Here's what Layla hadn't told him. That she knew he was a fraud.

She knew he was a fraud, and she wasn't the only one. It was Javon and Mr. and Mrs. Hayes and Jeff Park and Brooklyn and everyone else he had met on the road. And now the government was formally after him. The only person who respected him in this world was the little mapmaker down the hall.

Where could he go? What was left?

He got a flashlight out of the utility closet and the boy's plastic toy shovel. He walked over to the pool, knelt down on one knee, and dug up the crack rock.

THERE WAS a bus leaving for Phoenix the moment he got to the station. He bolted up the stairs and placed his rollerboard on the empty seat beside him. He was back. This is where he belonged.

He had to see the country through to its end. He had to see his dead father one last time. He had to make it to San Diego, to the roar of the Pacific. And after California, what then? He looked at the dying Tri-Compax on his wrist. Maybe after the Pacific rang in his ears, his mission would finally be over.

The sun rose wearily over the United States and Mexico. The passengers groaned from their breakfasts, but Barry was still hungry. A baby wailed behind him. "Yo, bro, eat the Cheetos," a man was saying. "You already dirty enough. I gotta clean you!"

Texas ran out and they entered the Land of Enchantment. The mud and industry disappeared to be replaced by the more symmetrical rows of pecan groves and the row of mountains beyond. "Next month will be four years since your mom and I have been living together," the guy behind him said to his child. "Hold on, Holmes, hold on," the man said. "Let me wrap that up." Barry had never had to change a diaper, but now he wished he had. "Yeah, I smell it, that's *primo* rank," the father said in a loving tone. "Hey, don't *look at me* while you do it! You a dirty, dirty, dirty boy."

Freight trains formed ant trails between mountain peaks, rusted Union Pacific engines, and crisp blue Hanjin containers from Korea. Barry had seen something like this before, on the cover of a science-fiction magazine in his youth. Stocky growths that could have been junior cacti began to appear against the mountainscape. They stopped at a McDonald's in New Mexico, and Barry bought a Hatch-green-chile double burger, which he paid for with Layla's ATM card.

The bus was rolling again. Now they were just outside of Lordsburg, New Mexico, and the wallet in Barry's pocket was cutting into his flank. He took it out and put it into his rollerboard.

The mountains were covered in green velvet. And behind the mountains were more mountains, some burnt ocher, some mottled brown. And in front of the mountains, rocks formed decaying castles and the skylines of third-tier cities. Arizona welcomed them as the "Grand Canyon State." The beauty around the Greyhound continued undiminished. It dawned on Barry that our country was so much more than the people who inhabited it. The mountains would wait patiently no matter who or what.

Barry drifted into a luscious, heavenly, continental sleep. Sometimes his eyes would pop open and he would see endless fake-hacienda suburbs. He thought the bus driver may have announced their arrival in Tucson, because for a while the bus was still. He could almost hear himself snoring. He was having a dream about Brooklyn, the weight of her perfect lips, the touch of her silky palm around him. They were on a NetJets to Anguilla, en route to the Four Seasons, where he had once taken Seema. *Wow,* Brooklyn was saying, *so this is what it's like to fly.* His hand was on her be-denimed knee, and he was promising to take her everywhere around the world.

The bus was moving again. He tried to get back to the Anguilla dream with Brooklyn, the erection still straining his jeans. *This is what they call an infinity pool,* he was telling her. But now, half awake, he couldn't remember what she looked like. Her image faded. She was just this black stranger he had loved once. He felt uncomfortable about his thoughts. What if he had *really* tried to get to know Brooklyn instead of finger-fucking her a few hours after they had met? What if he had confessed his crimes, real and hypothetical, to Layla from the get-go? Was he a coward like she had said? What was happening to him? Was he dreaming or not? Something was missing.

The bus was bouncing into a station. "Phoenix," the bus driver announced. Barry stretched and yawned. It was time to get off the bus and see about the next ticket west. Barry looked at the empty seat next to him. Wasn't there someone by his side? He had dreamed of Brooklyn, but she wasn't on the bus, was she? He knew there had been someone there. No. Not someone. Some *thing.* His rollerboard.

His rollerboard with the watches.

His rollerboard with the watches was gone.

"Excuse me!" Barry said in a shaky voice. "Excuse me!"

Bleary-eyed black, brown, and white faces turned around to look at him. Everyone was moving in slow motion off the bus. "Excuse me!" Barry shouted. "My bag is missing!"

There was a buzz of attention from the other passengers. "My bag is gone!" Barry shouted at them. He was squeezing his way now toward the exit and toward the bus driver, who was the authority figure and who maybe could help. Barry was shouting the word "Sir!" and then he was shouting a bunch of other words, and then he was falling down the stairs of the bus, and then he was on his knees, his hands on the tarmac, his lungs broadcasting the news of his terrible loss. And then there was silence and darkness.

HE WAS sitting by a gigantic bus tire that smelled like the heat of the road. There were Greyhound employees in their green mesh vests gathered around him, and some of the more proactive passengers were talking, and his hand was holding a wet cloth to his forehead. A middle-aged black woman who reminded him of someone he had known, a housekeeper, maybe, was speaking loudly. "This man, his son *autistic,* and he say something about he lost his watch."

Barry looked up at the people who were trying to help him. He felt like he should thank somebody, all of them maybe. How did she know Shiva was autistic? He tried to remember what he had said or, rather, shouted, but his mind was a maze with the entrances blocked.

"My son also autistic," a Mexican woman rasped down to him.

"Thank you," Barry said. The kindness and concern were coming at him in waves. His son was autistic. Everyone knew now. And so what? So *fucking* what? The secret inside him had not made him a good man. "My watches," Barry said. "They were one of a kind. I was saving them for my son."

A Greyhound employee bent down on one knee. "Sir," he said. "Can you think of anyone who could have taken your bag?"

"He should go to police," the Mexican woman said.

"Yeah, like that's gonna help," said the black woman.

"Sometime," the Mexican woman said.

The police. In a different life, he would turn to them right away. But then he remembered the crack rock in his pocket and the fact that he had bought the bus ticket with Layla's ATM card, which was now, technically, stolen. Layla, the woman who knew about his fake passport, which, come to think of it, was also in the rollerboard. He couldn't go to the police. What could he do? "I love my son," he said. The tears were streaming now, the early afternoon Phoenix heat building around him.

"Sir," the Greyhound man said.

"It's okay." He felt the black woman's elbow in the crook of his own. "You had a shock, honey," she said. "But you okay. You okay."

Barry was crying beautifully. He felt nothing but grace with the catharsis of a snotty exhale. The woman took him by his arm into the hangarlike Greyhound station. The passengers let them pass as if he were Jesus. At the back of the station they had something called Cactus Café and Gifts. An obese woman named Flores worked the counter. "This man, his luggage stolen," Barry's new friend said. "He don't have a dime."

"Aw, don't cry, honey," Flores said. She offered him a tissue.

"I'm sorry," Barry said.

"Sorry for what?" Flores said. "Nothing your fault." Nothing was his fault. Seema, Shiva, Brooklyn, Layla. None of it. He pictured living in a small suburban house with Flores and many of her family. The Luck of Kokura. Did her family have it? He should never have bet on Valupro. Somehow, his whole life had unraveled after that trade. His spirit had been judged and found wanting. The balance of good that Barry had always thought he had accrued, as a partial orphan, as the son of a troubled man, as a dutiful student and worker, had been tapped out. "What kind of food you like?" Flores asked. "I won't charge you." Barry got the breakfast platter. Eggs, hash browns, sausage, biscuit, and coffee. He took all the Splenda packets he could and two things of creamer.

The black woman reached into her purse. "I gotta go, honey," she said.

"You don't have to give me anything," Barry said, but he took the five dollars she offered. "Let me write down your name, I'll send you the money back."

The woman kissed him on the cheek. "I'll pray for your son, too," she said.

"What's wrong with your son?" Flores asked, as his late breakfast sizzled on the grill.

"He's autistic," Barry said. "We found out last September." He had stopped crying.

"Here's your delicious breakfast," Flores said.

He sat down with his food and felt the urge to say a prayer over it. And then he saw the dull glow on his wrist, the blued hands that had stopped hours ago.

The Tri-Compax.

The watch he would give to Shiva. It was still on his wrist. No one had taken it. His beautiful watches were gone, but the Tri-Compax remained. "Rabbit," he said out loud. He took in the landscape of the lackluster bus station, this place and time, all these mothers, all these children, all these solitary men hacking their way through the underbrush of a country that didn't want them or need them. The Tri-Compax was silent, it had stopped for good during the bus ride. The watch was no longer registering his passage through the universe, but he had it to give to his son.

AFTER HE had eaten the Greyhound breakfast, he had to go to the station's bathroom for a very long time, and when he came out he was hungry again. An older white man, his teeth likely rotting from meth, was eating the remains of his hash browns and biscuit. "I'm sorry," the man said. "I thought you were finished."

Barry told him to go ahead. There were bananas for sale and a bread pudding that was not out of date. Barry needed money to purchase all those things and a ticket to San Diego. He needed investors. A broken-down Frito-Lay cardboard box lay behind Flores's counter space. He asked her if he could have it and the Magic Marker hanging out of her shirt pocket, next to the familiar Greyhound pin reading YES, I CAN.

Barry sat down at the table opposite the meth man eating his biscuit. He remembered all the homeless men he had seen in the last two months of travel and the signs they had attesting to the state of their lives. He began to write on the back of the cardboard in his neatest letters:

THEY STOLE ALL MY MONEY.

I HAVE AN AUTISTIC SON.

PRAYING FOR A MIRACLE.

ANY LITTLE BIT HELPS!

☺ GOD BLESS YOU ☺

He asked Flores for an empty plastic cup. He brushed his hair down a little so that he wouldn't look crazy. He tried on several expressions. Basically, he needed to look penitent, but not sad, which was how he felt. He needed to show that he was one of the fallen, but that he was not ashamed of his station. He set himself down beside the front entrance of the station, next to a sign for Greyhound's very own lattice chips: CRISPY AND DELICIOUS, GRAB A BAG FOR THE ROAD. Immediately a man with a green vest marked SECURITY appeared.

"Sir," he said.

"My son's autistic," Barry said.

"You the one who got robbed?" Barry nodded. The man was young and looked like a nerdy ASU postdoc in his wire-frames. "Yeah, you can't solicit in the station," he said. "I'm sorry about what happened, but maybe you can try up the road?"

Barry walked outside with his sign, where the dry heat burned his calves and his neck. One highway ran into another, and beyond there was the endless archipelago of the Phoenix airport.

He stuck out his sign with one hand and held his plastic cup out with the other. His bald spot burned red.

Rigs passed by. Pontiacs, too. He had no idea Pontiacs still existed. People watched him wearily while they waited for the lights to change. SUVs never gave, but he got three dollars out of a Mitsubishi. A biracial woman in a Taurus gave him two dollars. Her husband was in the back feeding a soda to a small child. Freddy's Landscaping kicked in a buck. The folks were rough and leathery, working folks. One middle-aged-verging-on-old woman in a Pontiac volunteered that her son was also autistic. "Every last nickel we spend on his therapies," she said.

"I know how that goes," Barry said. "God bless you for stopping." They looked at each other kindly. Barry saw his own reflection in her sunglasses, a tired, old man in a red El Paso Chihuahuas T-shirt. A day's worth of stubble had come in gray. Right now he was all his dad, except for the flicker of human interest in his tired eyes. After six hours in the sun, he had twenty-four dollars, slightly more than half of a ticket to San Diego. He had never worked harder in his life. He needed a Dasani badly.

He went back into the station. The coolness both relieved the burns on his body and brought attention to his pain. Setting a budget of four dollars, he bought a pudding parfait and a bottle of water and sat down at a table. There could be nothing more delicious in the world than the Greyhound pudding parfait.

Standing by the coffee counter, a big muscular guy in a mesh shirt was talking to an old woman in mirrored Oakleys. They were both supplementing their coffees with plenty of free creams. "I left Kentucky on Monday," the man said. "Headed up to Vegas."

The muscleman's hair was blond and cropped, and his tired face could have been anywhere from twenty to forty years of age. One of his enormous biceps bore a tattoo of the Bentley logo, a circled B with wings. If Barry remembered correctly from Jeff Park's Bentley, the B was supposed to be white against a black background, but this aspiring young man had colored it bloodred. "I've never been to Kentucky," the woman said. "Is it nice?"

"Not really," Bentley said. "But the people are nice."

"I'm going to Dallas," the woman said. "I've got ten dollars on my debit card." Her mirrored Oakleys must be fake, Barry thought.

"Well, you have a good time whatever you're doing," she said. "I'm sure it's *none* of my business."

"I'm just going home," Bentley said, confused by the menace in the old woman's voice.

Barry went to the bathroom to wash up. He looked at himself in the mirror. His olive skin was nothing of the sort. He was a real redneck now. He took off his shirt and splashed water under his armpits. Bentley came in and nodded to him. "Where you headed?" he asked. His voice was also full of muscle.

"San Diego," Barry said, "but I'm short of funds." He reached into his pockets to check to make sure all his money was there, and the crack rock loosened itself and fell out onto the floor. Barry scrambled after it.

"That what I think it is?" Bentley asked.

"I got it as a goof in Baltimore."

"No worries. I'm cool."

Barry threw some water on his face.

"Looks like you caught some sun there," Bentley said.

"I've been begging for money out by Sky Harbor Circle," Barry said. He was half naked in a Greyhound bathroom talking about begging, but he was not ashamed. The truth was powerful. His Tri-Compax was all cream and gold in the mirror.

"I'd love to help you out," Bentley said. "Maybe you can help me out. I still got seven hours until I get to Vegas, if you know what I mean."

"I'm sorry?" Barry said.

"What you got in your pocket." Barry still wasn't following. "How much you want for it?"

"Oh," Barry said. "I've been trying to save it. You know, for a special occasion."

"No offense, but you don't look like a guy who's going to have many special occasions," Bentley said. "I'll give you twenty bucks for it. Way more than it's worth. My bus to Vegas not leaving for a *long* while. I'll let you have a hit, too."

Barry thought the rock, which was substantial, was probably

worth way more than twenty dollars, but twenty would be enough for the rest of his bus ticket and a banana. They walked outside into the mild coronary of a late Phoenix day, past an employees' lot for National and Alamo and over to a chain-link fence behind which squatted a dozen FedEx tractor trailers. Stunted-looking trees blocked them from the gaze of the wide highway beyond. The road was almost entirely free of traffic; it was difficult to imagine which two parts of Phoenix it served to connect. "Here is good," Bentley said. They settled in by the chain-link fence. "Put this on or you'll cook to death," Bentley said. He took a sun cape hat out of a duffel bag and gave it to Barry.

"Mind if I have the twenty dollars now?" Barry asked. Bentley laughed. He didn't mind at all. He took a tiny screwdriver out of his bag and smashed the Parmesan-looking rock into manageable pieces. Barry was sad to see it destroyed. Bentley's hands were covered in burn marks and cuts that refused to fully heal. He took out a Pyrex pipe, scrunched a screen into it with his thumb, and then banged a little ball of crack inside. He lit it up with a cheap Bic lighter, turning the pipe in his fingers, letting the rock soften. He was so practiced, organized, just this nice American kid on the road. The crack smelled like the burning tires coming in from the colonias of Juárez, along with the tang of something sweet like marshmallow. Finally, Bentley put the pipe to his lips and inhaled deeply. Mist filled the glass. He passed the pipe to Barry, who was leaning uncomfortably against the chain-link fence in his outrageous sun hat.

"Just one hit," Barry said. The pipe burned his fingers. "Ouch!" he cried. Bentley laughed again. He took out some lip balm from his duffel bag and passed it to Barry.

"Put it on your lips," Bentley said. "This stuff really dries you out." His eyes were the blue of an Anguilla infinity pool. The muscles inside his mesh shirt were dancing. Barry inhaled and coughed. "You want to keep turning the pipe over like that with your fingers," Bentley said. "Keep sucking on it."

The crack tasted like a hospital room, and suddenly Barry was back in the hospital as Shiva was being born, the horrors of Seema's screams, the doctor, kind but steely, shouting at her to push harder ("Get mad, Seema, get mad!"), some young woman's anthem playing on the little Tivoli boombox Seema had bought to inspire herself, and then the gasps and squeals of the little alien that popped out from between her legs. The scene replayed itself before Barry, but this time instead of being scared and sneaking off to the bathroom for shots of ten-thousand-dollars-a-mouthful Japanese single malt, he stood there fully witnessing the outlandish pleasure of a mother knowing that her child is alive.

Barry's mind and body thrummed with energy. He wanted to tell Bentley everything about his life, but momentarily the power of speech was gone. A Southwest plane, one of many, was angling its way down to the Phoenix Sky Harbor all silver and light, but instead of the roar of its jets, Barry heard the rumble of a Long Island Rail Road train making its way in from the city, the day coming to an end, the low thunder of his father talking to himself while cracking open cans of tuna in the kitchen, the absence of his mother, the loneliness of a keen mind in a tiny bedroom, a solitary SUNY-Binghamton poster depicting a bunch of Long Island kids hanging off one another's shoulders in a burst of springtime warmth. Barry finally found his voice. "I'm from Queens," he said to Bentley. "What about you?"

Bentley was talking, but Barry understood only some of what he was saying, as if it were in another language, but the import was that Bentley was missing not just one of his parents but both, and his grandmother, whom he loved and who loved him back, died over a very long period of time, her departure from the world punctuated by the loss of one limb after another. She had been in Kentucky, while the remainders of his life were scattered around Nevada and the poor inland parts of California. It was hard to understand how all those far-flung states were tied together, or in which one Bentley had originated. With each word he said, he jerked his chest forward as if he were in ecstasy, or in pain.

"I'm not voting for Trump," Barry said.

"I'm not voting for anyone," Bentley said. He offered Barry a re-up, and he couldn't say no. The pipe was hot and oily, singeing the tips of his fingers. Barry felt another wave of energy. The gentle whir of memory being erased. If he smoked all the way through the night, would he emerge reborn?

Barry removed his sun hat and tried to fix the dried clumps of his hair. The sun was setting, and now he was babbling on about his eating club back at school, how hard it had been for his dad to come up with the fees. "So you went to college and all?" Bentley asked. Barry didn't want to confirm that he went to Princeton, didn't want to open up a gulf between them, but the jittery energy felt like pride, and he told him the truth. "Yeah, right, Princeton," Bentley said. "I'm going to have to call bullshit on you, pal."

Barry laughed. How *could* he have gone to Princeton? The whole thing was a case of mistaken identity. That and Goldman Sachs and This Side of Capital. Only his love for the women along the way and Jonah and his son was true. "I used to feel bad," he said, "because I made my mother drive out to the mall to get me a Han Solo action figure and then she got killed in a car accident. But I don't feel bad anymore. After today, I'm not going to feel bad. Because wherever she is, she's forgiven me. If only I could see her eyes again. She had beautiful eyes. Do you think I have beautiful eyes?"

"I do," Bentley said.

Barry wanted to take off his clothes and show off his swimmer's shoulders. They were both white American men enjoying their country in an *On the Road* kind of way. "A one-eyed Mexican man fell asleep on my shoulder!" he shouted. Bentley used what looked like a piece of umbrella wire to poke inside the pipe and get out more juicy morsels of crack. They wanted to celebrate each South-west jet that was landing over them, but they had no idea how, and when the engine of one of the FedEx trucks suddenly kicked in behind the chain-link fence, they could neither of them give a damn. The temperature dropped a bit, and when the sun disappeared entirely and the white desert moon began to float up diagonally like in a movie, Bentley unbuckled his pants. "We're out of rock," he said. "Do you want to suck me off?"

"Okay," Barry said.

"Just put on some lip balm first."

In the encroaching darkness, he was more or less formless, and Barry was guided mostly by his musk. What he had in his mouth was so soft and human. It was sweaty and rank and tasted like pee, but he wanted it as far back in his mouth as he could stand. Barry's mind was still reeling from the contradictions of *that,* when he felt Bentley's hand on his head, pushing him up and down. That's right. That's how it was supposed to go. That's how Seema did it twice a year, his birthday and the first night of Hanukkah. His nose scrunched into the Brillo-like wires of Bentley's unshowered pubis, and that proved a little too much. He gagged, his teeth scraping against the barely erect shaft.

"Man, you really don't know what you're doing," Bentley said, pushing him away. Barry sat back against the chain-link fence. He felt ashamed but also elated. Bentley pulled himself up and began to stroke himself, and Barry was inspired to do the same. For the first time in his life, he couldn't think of anything to fantasize about, just the steady jerking motion, the Tri-Compax moon above, an occasional high-beamed Hyundai floating by. Eventually Bentley started to snore, his head sliding into the musculature of his neck. All the energy had drained out of Barry, and the only thing that was real was the taste of another human being in his mouth. "Hey, wake up," he whispered to Bentley. "You'll miss your bus to Vegas. Wake up." But Bentley would not.

"No use of alcohol or illegal drugs on this bus," the driver was saying. Barry felt a flash of paranoia. "If you try to buy alcohol, that will terminate your trip. If your meal is tuna or sardines, don't open it until you're in an outside area." The bald black driver was handsome like the star of a good TV show on a minor cable channel. Barry knew that he was going to miss the Hound. He saw the Phoenix skyline disappear behind them. Saguaro cacti appeared like one-armed men amid the scrubland. He wondered if in some way he had failed to fully connect with Bentley, despite the blow job. He could have mentioned Jeff Park and *his* Bentley, and maybe, in the midst of his high, he had. The taste of sex still burned on his lips. His fingers were singed and covered with crack dust. Mountains reared up like the outlines of Tuscan cities.

They crossed the Colorado River into California. "Woo-hoo!" some people shouted, happy to have Arizona at their back. At some point in the middle of the Mojave, an overweight mentally handicapped man in his sixties got on the bus, and nobody wanted to sit next to him, but Barry welcomed him. A woman in the back of the bus started clapping and gospel singing "Happy Birthday" to her child. Imagine celebrating a birthday in the back of a Greyhound. Barry started weeping hot tears that smelled like crack. The fat man put his hand on his bald spot and rubbed it back and forth. "I'm sucking up your brain energy," he said, kindly.

"I'm just crying because I'm going to see my daddy's grave," Barry said, very loudly.

This caught people's attention. People started telling him he'd be all right, but they also started talking loudly about their own lives. A hot Mexican girl with purple hair and a skateboard was telling some massive white guys from an army base about growing up on the streets at age five. "You're strong," one of the white guys was saying. "You'll be all right. My dad was an alcoholic. Not all the time. It wasn't all bad."

Barry's seatmate started talking loudly, too. He had grown up in Louisiana. His momma used to hit him for stealing apples. His name was Kenneth Long. The atmosphere in the bus changed, and now the people on the bus were happy to have Kenneth along, and he was one of them just like Barry was one of them. "You're all right, Kenneth," the Mexican goth girl said.

"I came all the way from Manhattan!" Barry cried.

"When you're living on the streets, there are a lot of rats," the Mexican girl said. Others had experiences with rats and with mommas who hit and with daddies who drank. The whole bus was a confessional now, and sometimes when they said something wrong, the bus driver would yell over the loudspeaker "Language!" but that wouldn't stop them, not for a minute. People talked about where they had gone to prison the way people on the Acela talked about where they had gone to law school. They started writing down one another's e-mails, and Barry found that he was unable to use the pen he was given. Had the crack scrambled his brain? "Just tell me what it is and I'll write it down," Kenneth Long said.

They stopped at a sandwich place, and Barry cried that he didn't have any money, and a bespectacled Mexican girl with a bare midriff bought him a *carne asada torta* and a tamarind Jarritos soda. The earth around the sandwich place was dry and cracked. The sky was ribboned pink. Desert sky. California sky. The sun set behind an unnamed gas station. The fat man next to him kept farting for the rest of the ride, but he was forgiven. He had motion sickness, too, and many pairs of hands helped him get to the bathroom in time to throw up. "Shut the fuck up!" a mother was screaming at her little girl. "I told you six times." The child started crying. "Don't do me like that!" But all the aggrieved and abused passengers around Barry would not let that stand, and they began screaming at the woman, screaming as if they could turn their own lives back, stand up to their fathers and their mothers, make them bleed. Black voices, white voices, Latino voices. The whole bus was screaming at the woman, and the bus driver kept saying "Language" over and over on the intercom.

San Diego approached in the dusk. They passed a PAYDAY LOANS sign lit up red and green like an advertisement for a Christmas that would never come, and Barry had that Californian feeling that the ocean was right ahead of him, that any moment it would present itself with blue-dark infinity. And it was. And it did.

EEMA AND her father and Shiva were following a hilly, woodsy path through the Ramble in Central Park, which completely winded Seema, but which Shiva and his grandfather conquered daily since her parents moved into her apartment three weeks ago, almost immediately after she had told them about the diagnosis. Shiva had to travel to this peaceful place through the regular world of noise and, possibly for him, terror, but his grandfather was determined and processed the outside world for him, explaining a sudden onslaught of ambulances or the sensory impossibility of Park Avenue at rush hour. Who knew what Shiva understood (what did *any* three-year-old understand?), but as soon as her dad pointed to something and talked about it in his step-by-step former-engineer way, the boy calmed down. Out here, in the wilds of the Ramble, without the presence of constricting walls and man-made lights and high-pitched noises, her son was an athlete. He knew the maze of the Ramble by heart, its arches and stairs and meandering pathways. He threw himself at rock faces, making his ascent by hanging on to gnarled roots and the dry leaves of city plants, every leap perfect, every foothold well placed. "Everesting," his grandfather called it.

"Watch out," a hippieish white woman was shouting at a black girl of about seven who was following close behind a young blind Asian boy using a cane. They were heading along a rugged path toward Shiva's favorite gazebo. "Stop before that ridge! Rachel!" Seema imagined the kids were brother and sister, adopted by the hippieish white parents. Each parent had coarse, early gray hair and a T-shirt that spoke of small Catskill communities. Seema wondered what it was like to raise two children on a regular income—a thought that would have never occurred to her before she married her husband—but here they were, the four of them, in Central Park, shouting to one another like it was nothing, like they were that mythical happy family with the three-sinked bathroom Barry had told her about on their second date.

"Momma, how far to the gazebo?" the girl shouted back.

Every few feet, she would take her brother by the hand and correct his course as he clacked ahead with his cane. "Rachel, watch the drop-offs."

"I got it, Mom!"

"What about the rocks?" the boy shouted.

"We already passed the rocks, Sander. On the way back, we'll let you feel them all over."

"Dad, I don't think Shiva is going to want to share the gazebo," Seema said. "He's not used to other people in there." The two kids scrambled inside, shouting to each other. Their father took off his giant, cheap canvas bag, and both parents started loudly taking out sandwiches and thermoses.

As soon as Shiva saw the occupants of the gazebo he stopped in place, shut his eyes, covered his ears, and fell to the ground. The child began to kick the dirt and spin on his back like an overturned insect. "It's okay," her father said, waving her away with one hand as he crouched down and began to rub his grandson's ankles with the other.

Seema bent down to clean the dirt off Shiva's velvety Loro Piana trousers, even as she scanned the reaction of the other family, but she felt superfluous. She didn't know why she had foisted herself upon this daily ritual of her father and her son. But what was the other option? Staying at home and listening to her mother rant about how lonely she was in New York, plucked from her community (she had twice the Facebook friends of both her daughters combined), while manically researching every brilliant autist who had ever existed, from Nikola Tesla (probably) to Albert Einstein (possibly) to Wolfgang Amadeus (a reach). The rest of her time was spent figuring out whom to blame for "this": negligent Seema, nonresponding Shilpa, the universe, or the man whose genetics were surely responsible for her grandson's difficulties—Barry. "Is New York a no-fault state when it comes to divorce?" she would hiss at Seema first thing in the morning. "Well, it shouldn't be. Because it's all his fault. You need to get a lawyer, a real one."

Her father picked Shiva up and spun him through the air, making him giggle, brown eyes ablaze. "Daddy," Seema said, "your knee."

He never really listened to her when he was with Shiva. Maybe that's one reason she had been reticent to have a child, the idea that her father would love someone more than he loved her. Damn it, she had to grow up. "Let's go home," Seema said. "It's not like we can kick those guys out of the gazebo." Her son could scale a twenty-foot rock face, but having to share a gazebo with another family brought on a full meltdown.

"I have some strategies." Her father put Shiva down. He was wearing khakis and an oxford shirt despite the early September heat, as if he were about to interview for a bookkeeping job at some small industrial concern. "First we sing a song." He crouched down to Shiva's level and began to sing "C Is for Cookie." Shiva immediately unclasped his ears, although his eyes were still shut. Four verses in, his grandfather said, "And now, we'll do the shimmy-shimmy." Shiva opened his eyes. His grandfather shimmered his own fingers in front of his face. Shiva immediately followed suit. The two of them sat there, allowing the summer light to filter through their flickering fingers, both in rapt concentration and delight.

"Dad," Seema said.

"I know," her father said.

"You're reinforcing stereotyped behaviors."

"Shhh," her father said. "Look at him."

"Okay, but some of his therapists will object. I'm just saying. We put a lot of time and thought into this. And he's the one who has to live in the world. It's fine at home, but how does it look to others?"

Her father picked up Shiva, the child docile and happy in his arms. "I never told you how much of myself I had to give up when I came to this country," her father said to her.

"That's different," Seema said. "Being Indian is not a disability."

"I'm glad you were born in 1987 so that you can say that."

Slowly, wearily, he carried the child to the gazebo where the parents of the other family were chewing on sandwiches. Everyone smiled at everyone else. The blind boy was drawing his name, SANDER, in the dirt. His sister was ribbing him about his *s* looking "stupid," but, at the same time, she was holding him by the elbow. The parents didn't have to mind the boy, because his sister did. The mother was wearing a Phoenicia Volunteer Fire Department T-shirt many sizes too big. The girl was wearing yellow clogs. Everything was brilliantly imperfect, like a scene out of a modern storybook.

"Both my kids threw a lot of tantrums when they were his age," the mother said, nodding at Shiva.

"Well, he's autistic," Seema said. This was the new thing she was working out. Just saying it out loud to strangers. Announcing who he was. Asserting it.

"Oh, sorry," the mother said.

"You're not supposed to say you're sorry," the father said.

"I mean I'm sorry that I—" She laughed nervously. "Can I offer you a sandwich?" They definitely weren't from the city if they were offering strangers food.

A few days earlier Shiva had had a meltdown in Whole Foods, and Seema had explained his condition to the cashier, and her mother had yelled at her afterward for "telling the whole world," but the cashier had just shrugged. This was New York, and everybody had *something.* Everybody. Each time Seema saw a gaggle of teenagers sitting cross-legged, absorbed in their devices, tuned out of one another's physicality, she wondered if the world to come would be slightly more hospitable to Shiva's condition. If only she could get him to speak. That had become the sole mission of her life.

Both Shiva and his grandfather were now actively flicking their fingers in front of the boy's eyes, creating their own kingdom of light. From afar, they probably looked like two magicians up to no good. "I love his outfit," the mother of the other kids tried again. She had been taking in Shiva's clothes. "Why's he all dressed up?"

"He's got sensory issues," Seema said. "This is one of the few outfits he doesn't find scratchy."

"Brenda!" the husband said. "Will you please leave this poor woman alone."

"It's okay," Seema said. She tried a laugh. A part of her wanted to do the disability tango with Brenda, ask her something stupid about her blind son in return. The daughter was now dragging the boy off to confront an especially loud orange-breasted bird behind the gazebo. The way she pulled his arm, and the way he let himself be pulled after her, felt so natural, like a diagram of the rest of their lives. They would grow into whatever people they were going to be, but these early memories would always be a part of their relationship, one person drawing a mental map for the other. If only Shiva had had a sibling who could do the same for him. But her womb was empty now.

She had done it a week before her parents arrived. The office in which the procedure was done was right around the corner from Lenox Hill, where Shiva had been born and then stashed in the Beyoncé Suite, a meal of filet mignon wheeled in upon her recovery, and Barry's chief of staff having bombarded the room with allergy-inducing flowers and over-the-top chocolates. She had been considering an abortion even before Barry left. But the moment she was in the stirrups, Seema thought, What if? What if the child inside her wasn't autistic? What if it was a boy with Barry's athleticism or her father's charm? A kid you didn't have to spend your whole lifetime guiding and looking out for and "coordinating." What if this was the last time she would ever be pregnant? What if all the other men she would ever meet in this goddamn city would all be a form of either Barry or Luis? She had the means to take care of another child. The abortion wasn't a sin, exactly, Seema didn't think in those terms, but what if it was, as her father would gently tell her when she dithered about taking the LSAT at the end of junior year or failed to get in all her intern applications early, a "missed opportunity"?

No, she didn't want to take the chance. Her body would be a cell-producing factory for just a few minutes longer, and then it would be free of the Cohen gene pool forever. She didn't want to say it out loud, but in her mind "this," as her mother called autism, *was* Barry's fault. Barry with his old sperm. Barry the keeper of the Watch Log. Which, yes, the therapists would say, was unproductive thinking on her part, blah, blah, blah.

Shiva and Arturo were having more playdates now, some in the Goodmans' smaller apartment. Other than her father, whom Seema referred to as "the Big Regulator," Arturo was the only other person who could calm Shiva, and hence she called him "the Little Regulator," although not to his face, of course. Some people just had it when it came to Shiva, and others, like her mother, did not. Arturo read the Piggie and Elephant books out loud and with great affect while Shiva bounced on his ball, each getting what the other needed: a loyal audience and a nonjudgmental friend. On the second playdate, Luis showed up from his "writing room," a refurbished utility closet recently Zillowed in as a "0.5 bedroom" to complain about all the noise, and then he saw Seema. "Are you sure this is such a good idea?" he whispered to her in the hallway.

"I think it's a great idea," she said. She gave him a little pout from the first iteration of their relationship, the Indian comic actress on TV. "What? We can't be friends, Louie?" Everything was an act in this town, even falling out of love was a performance. And it surprised her, how quickly she could fall out of love, how little of Barry's contrived, practiced romanticism had ever rubbed off on her.

The girl and the boy had stopped stalking the bird behind the gazebo and now, slightly bored, came to investigate Shiva and his grandfather, who were still shimmying their fingers, filtering in shafts of Central Park light. "What are you doing?" the girl asked Seema's father, very loudly. "They're like moving their hands in front of their faces," she explained to her brother.

"Why?" the boy asked.

"I think they want to be left alone," their mother said.

"That's not for you to say!" her husband interceded. But she was right. The proximity of the two children was not helpful. Other than Arturo, Shiva's peers provoked the worst in him, because, unlike adults, kids could be completely unpredictable, could dart and scream and push and hug unexpectedly, destroying his sense of balance and control.

"We should probably go anyway," Seema said as Shiva closed his eyes and began to shake.

"You know what this boy likes?" Seema's father said. "The letter *W*. He used to only like the letter *C* because 'C is for cookie,' but now he's in love with *W*, which stands for 'wow!' among other things. So let's do this." He spread out his thumbs and fingers in a kind of Vulcan "live long and prosper" salute to form two *W*s with his hands. The girl followed suit and helped her brother do the same. As soon as he heard *W*, Shiva's eyes snapped open. And then Seema's father gently made *W*s out of Shiva's fingers and slowly touched them to those of the children. "Double-u, double-u, double-u, double-u, *double-u!*" her father sang. And that's how it went, the girl and her father lightly smacking *W*s with her son and the girl's brother, comparing the size of their fingers either by sight or by touch.

"Has he ever pointed to anything?" her father asked Seema on the day of his arrival. Yes, one thing: the W Hotel across the Hudson in New Jersey. As soon as her father heard that, he went to work. Now they would only get into cabs if there was a *W* on the license plate, and they would chart their way through Manhattan by following an endless series of signs with *W*s, Walgreens being the ultimate beacon by which Shiva could navigate, although the McDonald's arches also appeared to be an upside-down *W* as far as the young speller was concerned. Seema was torn. In some ways, her dad was normalizing the condition. Yes, everything in New York was an act, but if everything was an act shouldn't Shiva have to learn the lines?

And yet, and yet. After her father had made a giant *W* on the refrigerator out of masking tape, Shiva would march up and point to it every time he wanted something to eat. "He's pointing! He's point-ing!" Novie had shouted. This was his first truly useful gesture—he had always been scared to death of the fridge's roar, its tumble of ice cubes—but soon he was marching up to it and pointing at the foods he loved; well, the *one* food, watermelon (which, yes, started with a *w*). And as they walked back through the Ramble toward Central Park West and spotted some lucky passing cab with a *W* on its license plate, she felt the spirit of the boy, with his hand in his grandfather's, his stiff but fast walk carrying him across the minor hills built into the concrete city. For the first time since the meeting at Weill Cor-nell last September, she allowed herself to visualize him as a teen-ager, tall and handsome if more detached and, of course, silent than his peers, and then as an awkward but viable adult sitting in front of a computer, the screen covered with whatever he needed, a string of *W*s perhaps. What if there was a future after all?

It used to be she would ask herself: Who is my son? What's in his head? Well, now she knew. *W* was in his head. And the love of his grandfather. And the love of Novie. And scalable twenty-foot rock faces in the Ramble. And playdates with Arturo. She was certain that when he closed his eyes at night, for however short a time, he dreamed of all of these things. And she wondered: Did he dream of his father?

Back in their apartment, her mother was signing off Skype with Shilpa, her other daughter's protestations that there was no "autism epidemic" like some quasi-medical hucksters were claiming, just bet-ter ways to diagnose it, were going nowhere. *Of course there was an epidemic,* according to Seema's mother. An epidemic of old Barrys stalking beautiful young Seemas. She could see Shilpa's wide nose framing the center of her mother's laptop, behind her a spare, humid Kathmandu apartment, the opposite of her own. Having received no satisfaction from one daughter, her mother would now launch into an aria with the other. Perhaps today's would be on the theme of how needlessly expensive Seema's lifestyle was, how pointless it was to have hired a cook that didn't know an *urad dal* from her ass while Seema did not have a real job herself, the waste of having three double-sided fireplaces that were never put to use, and the profligacy of having Novie full-time while her parents were here, as if Novie hadn't rightfully been the child's second mother for the last three years. "You!" Seema had shouted at her mother. "You wanted this money! It was you! The chart! Remember the chart?" "What chart?" "The one that had all the races plotted out, Jews and WASPs on top, us on the bottom. Well, here we are. Welcome to the top. Isn't it lovely?" "I don't know what you're talking about." "Seriously?" "It never happened." That was one of the incredible things, too: her mother's complete deniability. She was made for these times.

"Imagine what it's like for her," one of Shiva's therapists had said to Seema. "Remember what your grieving period was like? And your mother is someone from a pretherapeutic society."

"She came here when she was eighteen."

"Just give her time."

But how much time? Each day was an obstacle course. Everything her father did for Shiva was counterbalanced with the pain her mother brought upon her, screaming about Shiva's care or "the absconded one," as she called Barry. Seema's dream for Shiva was that each morning he would greet her, if not with the words "Good morning," then at least with a flap of the wrist that signified a "Hi," followed by the approximation of a hug. Why couldn't she expect the same of her mother?

"Seema," her mother called out. She had made a point of wearing her most ridiculous, non–New York clothes, a baggy OSU sweatshirt and pink sweats. "I think the toilet in the guest bathroom won't flush."

"You *think*, or it actually won't flush?"

"Don't be short with me. If I treated guests the way you do, I'd be all alone."

"I'll go to Walgreens to get a plunger."

"I would have thought you'd have someone to fix it."

"Waste not, want not."

"Can we come with you?" her father asked. "Somebody around here likes Walgreens." But the thought of her son staring at the giant white-on-red *W* in cursive for minutes on end, his fingers a-flicking, was just not how she wanted the day to proceed. Imagine if she went all by herself to that bar where she and Luis had had a hot dog? Or checked in to the Park Hyatt for a spa treatment? Or took a NetJets to El Paso, walked up some shitty suburban block, and slapped Barry across his surely sunburned idiot face? *Unproductive thinking!* she sang to herself. *Blah, blah, blah!* Their elevator was so fast it didn't even register Luis and Julianna's apartment. But the existence of Arturo calmed her down, too. If she had to see the world as being either in service to her son or not, then that's how she would see the world. She should put up the Internet ad right away: "Not-yet-divorced wife of missing husband seeks man to be peripheral to her disabled son. Must be at least five foot ten."

Out amid the postwork hubbub of Twenty-third Street, she could at least acknowledge that it was a perfect September day, a 9/11 day, as Mina called them. She breathed in the surprising coolness, as if the boiling planet itself were reminiscing of better times.

There was a hand on her shoulder. At first she thought it was a hand that had been there before, maybe even belonged to Luis or some past intimate, but no. The hand belonged to a man in an ill-fitting black suit, a pallbearer from the outer boroughs, his sleek aviator glasses somehow belying a general sweatiness. "Mrs. Cohen," the man said. "My name is Anthony Perelli, I'm with the FBI."

She moved so quickly the hand remained floating in the air, un-sure of itself, a large pink thing beset by a ruby-colored class ring. "I'm sorry, ma'am, I didn't mean to blindside you." The mention of blindness brought up the boy from earlier, the thought that maybe, if the universe would just tilt a certain way, she could be his mother in Phoenicia, packing simple lunches.

She was visibly shaking now, as dysregulated as Shiva had ever been. All her animal instincts for flight were kicking in, yet somehow she had to produce a human voice. "I'm sorry," she said. "I—"

"You've been ignoring my calls."

"You will have to speak with me through my attorney. That's all I have to say." She turned around and headed back for her building, past a granite outcropping of Credit Suisse and then the duo of Schnippers, whatever that was, and Charles Schwab ("own your to-morrow") and Shiva's beloved Met Life Tower clock, but the agent continued behind her, a floating paunchy form.

"Mrs. Cohen," he said. "Do you know your husband's where-abouts?"

"Attorney," she said.

"Mrs. Cohen," the man was saying into her back. "If we could just sit down for one quick coffee, or just on a bench in the park. Mrs. Cohen!" He had run up alongside her. Based only on his ac-cent, she pictured a dense ethnic New Jersey life, a hike through Fordham, maybe a second-tier law degree, the kind of man they bred for just a little taste of power, but nothing too corrupting. The Bureau guys she had known in her former life were sleek and smart. They didn't even bother to send their best after her.

"I really have the feeling that we're not adversaries," the agent said. "That our interests coincide."

"Attorney," she said. "I'll just keep repeating it."

He took out his phone. "Are you familiar with this video?" He pressed PLAY. Yes, she was familiar with the video. She knew it by heart. She kept walking. The agent padded after her, trying to keep the phone in her face. There it was. The painful blue of the Mediter-ranean, far beyond the ocher dwellings of Cagliari and a stretch of mountains that blended in with the sky so well you had to squint to know where one ended and the other began. To the left side of the screen, a boisterous, drunken conversation had broken out between two shirtless men, one of whom was Barry, that boyish, goofy, prepro-grammed, backslapping, Tiger Inn, let's-be-friends, one-of-the-guys bullshit Barry. Or maybe it was the desperately struggling, scared-of-getting-it-wrong, always-on-the-lookout-for-hurt Barry. Or maybe they were one and the same. Barry was talking to a fat man on the yacht's foredeck, both of them with flutes of prosecco welded into the confluence of their stomachs and chests, and then Seema's iPhone panned away to the slowly approaching Sardinian capital. The strum of excited conversation, the sounds of boys trying to be men, nothing to see here, except that every couple of seconds one of the men would hungrily utter the word "GastroLux!" as if expelling gas, and the other would repeat it.

"You sent this video to us," the agent was saying. "Isn't that true?" That's how they talked. A declarative statement followed by "Isn't that true?" or "Isn't that correct?" Seema was now waiting for the light to change. Ugly commuter buses heaved their way up Madison. She wanted the world to change along with the light, maybe come to a spectacular end. She wanted light everywhere and then soft white heat. Barry was always talking about how his generation feared the bomb. At this moment she would welcome it. The agent kept manufacturing words like some Aspergerian automaton. "We can't ascertain who else was on that boat other than Samuel Yontif, or 'the Nebbish,' as we've heard him described on several wiretaps, his companion Slavenka Babic, the crew, your husband, and yourself. Isn't that true?"

"That sounds like a lot of people," Seema said. "Are you sure you got the right yacht?" Which was the wrong approach. The only word she needed right now was "attorney."

"We traced the e-mail with the attached video to a cybercafé in Davao City. Your nanny, Novie Bontuyan, left for Davao City, through Dubai, then Manila, three days before the video was sent to us. Is that correct?"

So there it was. Why had she been so sloppy? She might as well have sent the damn video herself. Some fucking cover-up. The traffic light finally changed in Seema's favor. "Attorney!" she screamed and made a dash for it.

"Mrs. Cohen! Why did you have your nanny send us the video? Mrs. Cohen!" She reached the other side of the street and aimed herself squarely at her building's service entrance. "Mrs. Cohen! This isn't my purview, but it brings up your nanny's legal status."

She was about to swipe her card to the service entrance, but she turned around instead. "Please," she said. "Leave her out of this."

"I want to. I just need you to tell me why you sent us this video. You're an officer of the court."

"Please," Seema repeated. "My son is autistic."

"I'm sorry," the agent said.

"Don't be *fucking* sorry!" she screamed. "I'm so sick of you people. That's his nanny. He loves her. She loves him. Leave us alone!"

"I'm not here to penalize anyone," the agent said. "Her legal status is not my jurisdiction. I think you did something brave and honest. And we want to bring it to completion."

Seema thought of her son, how beneath all the screaming and fussing, all he wanted was a world of order and logic, a world where everything was completed, a world of beginnings and ends. "Attorney," she said. It was more like a whisper. And then she ran inside.

THE DIAGNOSIS

EVERAL WEEKS later, Barry sat in a drab, sparse government conference room downtown. The fluorescent lights and the drop ceiling were bearing down on him, filling him with nausea. Right out
of Princeton, he had once tried to take the GMAT in a room with a
similar lighting scheme and ended up running out midtest to vomit
in the bathroom. In the end, he hadn't needed a business degree; his
charm and his luck had carried him along. And now his life was coming to an end in a sad government space.

Gone the beauty of La Jolla, the Indian hawthorn blossoms of
Neta's back garden, the crying of the seals in the morning light.
Gone his father's unremarkable grave in the Home of Peace Ceme-
tery in the middle of San Diego, the inscription on the tombstone
bearing the legend MAURICE COHEN, BELOVED HUSBAND OF
RIVKA. His son's name did not even receive a mention. "He wanted
it simple," Neta had said with a shrug.

The SEC guys were not as schlumpy as he had imagined. They
were all wearing decent suits. Maybe they had worked for law firms
before switching sides. Somewhere behind them, in the outer ring of
cheap black chairs, he pictured his sun-glazed father in the fresh
pastel shirts he had adopted in La Jolla just before he died, looking
neither pleased nor angered, just nodding along at all of the charges
rendered against his son. *That's right. He had promise. He could pro-*

gram the Commodore thing. Queens All-County Swim Champ. Prince-
ton. But he never should have taken that job at Goldman. He should have
worked in a lore office.

"Mr. Cohen, is it true that in 2013 your fund was losing money—"

"Based on the Fifth Amendment . . . ," Barry began.

The SEC guy spit out some more data about This Side of Capital's
shitty performance. The upshot was that Barry's fund had been
doing so poorly he had used material nonpublic information on the
GastroLux trade to try to save it.

"Based on the Fifth Amendment . . . ," Barry began once more.
His lawyer tugged on his monogrammed cuffs. Pleading the Fifth
was not the smoothest move, but what choice did they have?

"Is it true that your chief compliance officer had no relevant experience in the financial industry? That his sole educational credential
was a bachelor's in Russian studies from Middlebury College? That
you met him at a party thrown by your friend Joseph Moses Goldblatt at the FlashDancers Gentlemen's Club?"

"Based on the Fifth Amendment . . ."

It dragged on. Different questions, the same answer. He wished
he still had his Patek 570 in white gold to look at for comfort. TO
BARRY COHEN, A LEADER OF MEN. Finally, the videotape was produced. *Seema's videotape.* Sammy Yontif on the foredeck, Sardinia in
the distance, a slam dunk for the government in the conference
room.

He remembered his first feelings upon seeing the video in his
lawyer's office. The complete clarity of the morning's first espresso,
followed by the same devastation he had had upon hearing of Shiva's
diagnosis, the shock of being told for the first time that someone you
loved didn't love you back. Which was exactly what Seema was telling him through the release of the videotape. But immediately after
clarity and loss came the feeling of social self-preservation. Barry had
been ratted out by his own wife.

The tape was clear proof that Barry had discussed GastroLux with
Sammy Yontif, who knew the company's GERD medication was
about to tank, and that the discussion likely influenced Barry's very

profitable short of the stock. What would his friends think of what Seema had done? They would probably close ranks around him. Everyone had been through at least two divorces; they knew that hedge-fund wives were capable of anything. Well, except for maybe this. After all, Seema stood to lose money, too. So why had she done it? She had sent the video to the authorities even before Barry had fled across the country. Did she hate him from the get-go? Then why get married? Why have a baby? Why smile across the breakfast table as they argued so charmingly about Paul Krugman's latest assault on free markets?

Barry felt his lawyer's elbow. A question must have been posed. "Based on the Fifth Amendment . . ." The testimony had been going on for over three hours, and Barry was exhausted and dysregulated, and somehow his mind had landed on a memory of one of his early days with Seema.

Six months after they had started dating, she had thrown a surprise birthday party for him. They hadn't even moved in together or bought the place on Madison Park; he was still living in the unreformed, furnitureless Tribeca loft Seema had dubbed "the aircraft hangar." Upon returning home from work at a late hour, he found all of his friends—his business associates, a couple of bros from his Tiger Inn days at Princeton, their sparkling wives, probably a hundred people in total—yelling "Surprise!" just like in the movies.

Barry had an immediate panic attack. He hated surprises and actually spent five minutes in the bathroom, recalibrating his friend moves for this new development, running new lines and scripts. But as time passed and he acclimated to the party, he felt gratitude. No one had ever thrown him a surprise birthday party before. Layla would have scoffed at the very idea, its unnecessary subterfuge and waste. But Seema had done this for him. She could not afford to hire waitstaff on her public salary, so she had single-handedly transported two hundred Taiwanese bao from a place in the East Village and then matched the little vegetarian and pork buns with tubs of chicken tikka and slightly soggy paratha from a joint on Lexington. She had spent hours if not days planning this with no help whatsoever, even while working an eighty-hour-a-week job. All of the attendees seemed to understand the effort involved and looked at Barry with a newfound respect. Sure, he had a lot of friends, but Seema's obvious commitment crossed the line into the unexpected. Barry was loved. There were still little dabs of residual love between some of the couples in the "aircraft hangar," but most of it was in the service of duty and dynastic wealth. "You gotta marry this girl," Akash Singh was yelling into his ear. "Remember when you told the whole team we had to stop seeing skanks and get married? You gotta do this right!"

In the conference room, Barry had the sudden feeling that everyone was looking at him. He noticed his fingers were fidgeting just the way Jonah's did, thumb lightly touching his other four digits in quick succession, back and forth, back and forth.

HE MET with Seema two weeks after the testimony. He had been staying at the Mandarin, trying to soak up every bit of Central Park's greenery out his window in case he had to spend the next ten years in prison. Maybe he should have fled to Belize on his fake passport. They were going to get him. How could they not? Princeton, Goldman, hedge fund. What jury in at least four of the five boroughs wouldn't convict? One insider-trading conviction involving the pharmaceutical industry had led to a nine-year prison sentence for some lowly portfolio manager. Barry ran the whole fund.

But to his surprise, nay, his *shock*, the SEC settled for 4.5 million dollars and the Justice Department decided not to bring any criminal charges.

He didn't even have the wherewithal to laugh when they told him. He wanted to hug everyone at Paul, Weiss. Four and a half bucks was nothing, even if This Side of Capital was close to done, with lawsuits from investors still on the horizon. And the SEC hadn't banned him from associating with anyone at his fund, not even for a year or two. *He didn't even have to admit any wrongdoing;* he had only had to plunk down the cash. What had saved him? His reputation? The fact that he looked like an especially miserable basset hound in that government conference room? The fact that his law-yers stressed, over and over, that he was raising a "special-needs child"? He was not going to prison. *He was not going to fucking prison!* Barry Cohen was free. He went back to his room at the Man-darin and collapsed onto a daybed. They couldn't touch him. He was a respected member of society, and anyone who thought otherwise didn't understand how this country worked. That very same night, drunk off room service, he sent Seema an e-mail with the heading: "Let's talk."

THEY MET in Central Park's Sheep Meadow. Barry had remembered a scene set in the meadow from the movie *Wall Street,* which he had watched over and over as a kid, begging his father to take him to the movie theater because the film had an R rating. "A good lesson on what can happen when you don't obey the *lore* properly," his father had said after the Charlie Sheen character was arrested. This was back when his dad was still a Democrat. In the movie, the two main characters met in the Sheep Meadow in the waning daylight. Then they got into a tussle. Michael Douglas hit Charlie Sheen and drew blood. Barry remembered watching, breathless, every time the punch was delivered.

Barry stood in the middle of the empty field, eyeing the new pencil-shaped ninety-story residential towers that had gone up around Billionaires' Row to help Russians and Malaysians launder their money. Mist was rising off the meadow from a recent sun shower.

Seema made her way across the grass. A new Burberry trench coat was cinched tight around her waist. Clearly she had lost weight. Barry immediately recognized that their second child was no longer with her and suddenly, unexpectedly, he felt a profound sense of loss.

She was beautiful. A small beautiful woman, all of her bundled so efficiently into her pale raincoat. The shock of her glowing skin, the patina of her dark brown eyes, the mist rolling beneath her feet, the end of the long hot season. They were in a movie and she was its star.

They surveyed each other in silence. "Hey, Barry," she said finally. "How are you?"

"Did you get the rabbit-in-the-box?" he asked.

"Yup," she said. "Thanks." Her voice was husky, as if she'd been drinking the previous night. Could she be as nervous about this as he was?

"The rabbit pops out of the box too fast," she said. "It scares him." Her voice shook a little. He was sure now: she *was* nervous around him. He wanted to say a hundred million things to her, but didn't know where to begin.

"You have to hold the lid and let the rabbit pop out slowly," he said, finally. "I'm sorry. I shouldn't be giving you parenting advice."

"The rabbit is cute," Seema said. "Shiva likes his orange carrot. If you want to get him something next time, maybe get a toy with the letter *W*."

There was more silence. The wind blew little pinpricks of moisture into their faces. "If our therapist was here," Barry said, "she'd ask, 'Where does this land?'"

"Where *does* it land?" Seema asked.

"Why did you do it? The video."

Seema shrugged. "I don't know," she said. "It was the one time in my life I did something without thinking it through. People like me, people like you, all we think about is consequences. Practically from the day we're born. And look at our fucking lives."

"That four-point-five million could have gone toward Shiva's care. It could have been much worse. I could have gone to prison."

"I had a feeling you'd get a slap on the wrist," she said.

"You're an expert on securities law now?"

"I'm an expert on how this world treats Barry Cohen."

"He could have had a daddy in prison."

"How often do you see him when you're not in prison?"

Barry sat down on the wet grass. "Point taken," he said.

"You'll get grass stains," she said of his expensive trousers. He had dressed in his best for her.

Barry warmed to the gentle, almost motherly reminder about the grass stains. "Do you remember," he said, looking up at her, "when you threw that surprise party back on Franklin Street? It was the kindest thing anyone had ever done for me. You must have loved something about me back then. You must have thought I had an *imagination*. A sense of humor. Something."

She sat down next to him, draping her sharp naked knees with her raincoat in a way that made him long for her. Everything she did had an echo somewhere back in their past five years together. "My therapist said I shouldn't get pulled into this kind of conversation with you," she said. "But yes, I loved things about you back then."

"Like what?"

"I loved that you wanted to be alone," she said. "You were always social, but you just wanted to be by yourself, or maybe with your watches. I thought maybe you wanted to retreat to a quiet world with me. Because I'm kind of a loner, too."

Barry liked where this was going. *She was a loner, too.* He had never articulated that thought, but it was true. She had, what, maybe one good friend? The rest were more by way of Facebook and Instagram. They were talking so quietly, so peacefully. It was hard to believe that one of them had almost sent the other up the river.

"I took a bus across the country and I met someone," Barry said. The way she looked at him, her eyes narrowed, told him she still cared. "A boy," he explained.

"Oh?"

"A nine-year-old. He reminded me of me so much. He's into trains and maps. Have I ever told you about Lake Success?"

"My parents moved in with us," Seema said.

"That's okay."

"My mother hates you."

"Do you hate me?"

"I do," she said. Suddenly she reached up to touch his red, over-shaven cheek, as if trying to understand the depth of his stupidity and his sincerity. "But that's just one part of it," she said, drawing her hand back. "I mean there's more I feel for you. And, anyway, you must hate me, too."

Barry contemplated the warmth of her brief touch. "I hate what you did," he said. "Why didn't you tell me? Why did you have to go to the feds?"

"I wanted you to acknowledge something. Someone."

"You?"

"Someone else."

"We were in counseling."

"That's just a form of breaking up."

· "And you didn't want us to break up."

"I wanted you to be a father to Shiva."

"I think I can do that now. I think maybe this trip has made me into a father."

Seema laughed. "Man takes a bus across the country and discovers he's a father. You're such a fucking weirdo." That reminded him of one of the first things she had ever said to him at that Bloomberg party, when she had caught him checking her out. *Okay, weirdo.*

"You know what's crazy?" Barry said. "I'm kind of having fun right now."

"Well, you shouldn't," she said. "We have to figure out a way to split things up." She saw the look on his face. "No, Barry, it wasn't always about your money. You people are so sensitive about that stuff."

"You people?"

"You have an imagination, Barry. I'm sorry I said that."

"Why don't you have a drink with me?"

"Terrible idea." The way she had said that, free of rancor or disgust, the way her glistening knees kept popping out from under her raincoat, the way they were sitting on the wet grass next to each other, their bodies almost touching—Barry was awash in hope. He wasn't going to jail. And now he was going to get his family back.

"Just one drink," he said. "We'll go up to the Center Bar in Columbus Circle. Wasn't that one of our haunts?"

"Haunts? We had 'haunts'?"

"Just one drink. I know you're capable of stopping at one."

She laughed. He thought he saw a red-wine stain on one of her front teeth. Was she a little soused already?

Up in the Center Bar, they drank three Blood and Tears each to eulogize the end of summer, their mouths awash in citrus and spice. In the square below, Chris Columbus stood on his plinth at eye level, gazing down at the hedge-fund offices to the south as if, in addition to a quicker passage to India, he was also seeking alpha. They laughed and tried not to look at each other for too long, but they were getting smashed. He talked about his trip, omitting Layla; she talked about her time in New York, omitting Luis. As the sun set on Columbus, as more overtly romantic territory approached, she claimed she had to take Shiva to occupational therapy, which he knew was a lie this time of day. She gave him a goodbye peck on the cheek. It was November 16, 1987, all over again, the first time he had ever been kissed. Rosalie Lupo at the eight-fifteen showing of *Three Men and a Baby* at the Douglaston Mall, his father angrily waiting up on the porch along with Luna the sheepdog, maybe wondering what it would be like if his son left him for good.

THEY STARTED "dating." He knew it was provisional, and the proviso was that he had to be a father to Shiva. For a little while they took it slow, just some strong and bitter 7:00 A.M. macchiatos among the media and start-up crowd at 71 Irving, Barry being the oldest guy in the coffeehouse by far, or strolls along the autumn swells of the Hudson River, or a hot dog at this new place Seema had discovered called the Old Town Bar, which was both gloomy and romantic. He checked out of the Mandarin and in to the Gramercy Hotel to be close to her, but he nonetheless had to keep avoiding her mother, which added a kind of sexual frisson to the whole thing. *They were sneaking around.* Except that Seema did not let him have sex with her. Again, he had the feeling that she wanted him to first prove he could be a father to Shiva. On the other hand, she never brought Shiva around. "I want to see my son," he had said once, passionately, even though a part of him was too scared to reconnect with the boy, to witness all of his frailties. *Soon,* she had promised him. And then another goodbye peck on the cheek. At least she let him hold her hands. Sitting at that Old Town place with their hands intertwined, empty beer glasses in front of them, they were as happy as they had been for years. Barry talked in streams about the non-sexual parts of his Greyhound trip, she talked about galleries and restaurants and politics, making sure she didn't just go on about Shiva's many therapies or the indignities of living with her mother for the whole evening. Sometimes he caught her looking at herself in the full-length mirror behind the bar, her face dreamy and young.

In October, the Republican candidate for president was overheard on an old videotape saying that he liked to grab the genitals of attractive women. The common wisdom was that this had to be the end of his candidacy. Seema and Barry went out to their favorite Italian restaurant, which also happened to be at the Gramercy, and ordered a suckling pig in celebration and three bottles of Barolo. They felt brave enough to sit at a table by the window, even though Barry had once seen Seema's mother running by Gramercy Park in her sweats, screaming something into her phone.

"Grab my pussy," Seema whispered as he was paying the bill, and they both cracked up, but there was something dangerous and sexy about it, too, and her eyes were liquid and needy, so he decided to do as she asked, and moved his hand under the table, but she stopped him at the last moment. "Please," he said. "Just come up to my room for a minute. We don't have to have sex. Just let me go down on you." Seema looked thoughtful, like she was considering it, but she still held his hand in check beneath the table. "I really want to see Shiva," Barry whispered, pressing his case, although what he really wanted to see was her ass high up in the air, but, in the end, all she let him do was kiss her on the lips for a good ten seconds (he counted). After all of his sexual adventures that summer, Barry could find nothing more sultry than kissing his wife on the lips.

Finally, she arranged for him to see his son. They met in Gramercy Park, to which Barry had keys, since he was staying at the hotel. Barry was holding a giant silver balloon with the letter *W* prominently displayed on both sides. His son looked exactly as he had left him, his expression vacant, otherworldly, uncomprehending. *Rabbit,* Barry started projecting into his mind as the child ran toward him. *I love you, my little rabbit. Come to me.* But Shiva was not focused on his father at all; rather his eyes were tracking the giant *W* floating above him. "Here you go," Barry said, bending down to his level. "Daddy's back. Daddy's back and he got you a *W*." Shiva grabbed the string of the balloon, but it floated away from him in the autumn wind and he began to give chase through the tiny park. Barry had not expected a hug, but the fact that Shiva did not even register him after a three-month-long absence was difficult to take.

"Look at how well he runs now," Seema said as they followed the boy around the manicured shrubbery, dynastic oaks, and oversize birdhouses of the private park. "Yes, that is something," Barry said, concealing his hurt. She laced her fingers with his and looked up to him with a smile. They were, suddenly, a unit. The summer had been hard, but after Trump's pussy grabbing, *FiveThirtyEight* showed the odds were vastly in Hillary's favor. It was all going to work out for the country and for the Cohens. Barry ran ahead and fetched the balloon for Shiva. His son smiled at the *W* and traced the letter with his finger. Barry imagined that the smile was meant for him as well.

The next week he was invited to visit his own apartment. He wore his best suit for the occasion, the windowpane with the double-vented back in case he started to sweat from nerves, and spent half an hour getting his hair to drape over a slight but expanding bald spot. He was sick of staying at the hotel and wanted to reclaim his home. He knew what he had to do. He was going to teach the little rabbit how to swim.

He bought Seema's father the most expensive version of Talisker he could find, the thirty-year-old limited run. He went to Kalustyan's on Lexington where he bought a gift basket of Indian-like spices for Seema's mom. Entering his own apartment was strange. The lights were dimmed in the usual way, per Shiva's sensitivities, but something new hung in the air, the closeness of three generations, the sharp tang of Seema's mother's cooking. He understood that Mariana, their chef, had been fired.

Seema's father hugged him and seemed overjoyed by the present of whiskey. His mother wordlessly lifted up the basket of Indian-styled spices as if it were better to weigh it than actually deploy in her cooking. Seema's dad wore his old This Side of Capital vest; the mom had put on a sweater from the last millennium. "Hello, Mr. Barry," Novie said, without looking him in the eye. "I'm going to get Shiva for you now." The "Mr." part was new and depressing. He was no more than a visiting dignitary.

His mother-in-law sat on a little stool in front of the fireplace, staring down at a patch of herringbone floor pattern as if she herself had the diagnosis. The hatred she felt for him was comical. Barry had never hated another person as much as she hated him. He probably couldn't even muster that much dislike. His whole life had been about making friends.

"You know something?" Barry said to Seema's mother. "The lavender spices I got you are meant to promote relaxation."

Seema's mother lifted her head and stared directly over Barry's left shoulder. He was convinced an innocent vase in her line of sight was ready to shatter.

"So we hear you've been on quite a journey!" Seema's father said.

"Just needed to meet with some pension funds in person," Barry said. Seema's mother snorted at the lie. He couldn't quite gauge Seema's expression. It was cloudy at best. "But I'm back now. Back for good. I missed my family. Family is everything."

As if on cue, Novie walked Shiva into the living room. The boy ran to his grandfather immediately and they locked their fingers into a *W*. Barry was both amazed by how the boy related to Seema's father and saddened that he could not produce the same result. "You know what," he announced to everyone, but mostly to Seema's mom. "I'm going to teach Shiva how to swim! I've read on the Internet that swimming can really help children with his profile." Shiva and the grandfather had now separated their *W*s and were filtering light through their fingers. "Oh," Barry said. "I didn't know we were allowed to do that sort of thing. Isn't that called something? Reinforcing stereotypical behavior?"

"Shiva," Novie said, "why don't you come play with your daddy?"

"Yes, I can make a *W* with my fingers, too!" Barry said.

But the boy did not want to leave his grandfather's side. "Look, Shiva," Barry said. "Look what I brought with me!" And he took off the Tri-Compax he was wearing. "Watch! Daddy's watch. Wa-wa-wa-wa-watch."

Shiva finally walked over to his father. He still had the sweet maple-syrup smell of childhood, if not more of it. Brown hair draped the length of his large forehead. His teeth were perfectly white and straight. *A fucking stunner of a kid.* The diagnosis just wasn't fair. "Wa-wa-wa-wa-watch," Barry kept saying. "And guess what? 'Watch' starts with *W*!"

The child took the watch and shook it, as if trying to get the second hand to move, and then started to cry. "It's broken," Barry said. "But Daddy will fix it. Daddy will take it to a shop." But Shiva continued to weep inconsolably. He dropped the watch and ran past Novie into one of the cavernous hallways, as if seeking a further absence of light and sound and Barry. "Well," Barry said. "Looks like I have a lot to learn from Grandpa."

"I would be happy to share my findings," Seema's father said, in his usual overly formal way. Meanwhile, Seema's gaze shifted from her father to her husband and back. When she smiled, her chin wrinkled in a way that wasn't particularly pretty but was hopelessly real, like a portal into a future older self. She was smiling at him now as she led him out of the apartment. "I know that wasn't easy with my mom," she said, "but you did well." So now they were aligned against her mother. Barry couldn't think of a better development. At the door, she let him squeeze her tight denim-clad bottom as she kissed him, and the more he squeezed the more he felt deflated and in love. *My life is starting again,* Barry thought. *Not going to prison. Reborn. Reborn.*

. . .

ON ELECTION Day, Joey Goldblatt of Icarus Capital Management threw a party at his Fifteen Central Park West duplex. There were two bars at opposite corners of the five-thousand-square-foot spread, one serving the Nasty Woman, a lemon-vodka concoction, and the other the Bad Hombre, a tequila-based drink. "I don't like that both drinks are named after things Trump said," Seema was yelling loudly over the din of the partygoers and the voices of the cable news announcers blasting from the speakers. "It's like the only things that matter in this election are what he says."

"He won't matter ever again once they call Florida!" Barry yelled, and they both kissed hard. Hillary's victory felt like it might seal the deal not just for their country but for their relationship as well. He was banking on getting laid with his wife tonight.

"Take it to a hotel room, horndogs!" Joey Greenblatt shouted.

"That's my plan!" Barry shouted back. Joey's latest divorce had just been finalized, and he was in a particularly good mood. He kept telling people how he had voted for Gary Johnson, because he found both Hillary and Trump detestable, even though he liked how the latter would "simplify the tax plan."

Later in the evening Barry watched Seema talking with the other hedge-fund wives. They must have heard the rumors that she ratted him out, but her good humor and bravado suggested the marriage was totally secure. He even heard her mention that she was thinking of getting a job at a law firm, which was news to him. He liked the idea that she was there for Shiva, but he would support her going back to work, too, if she wanted. If Hillary could do it, why couldn't she? They were living in a new world. Most of the young wives at the party were their husbands' second or third, and Barry was proud that he had waited until he was almost forty to get married and would now have just one wife for the rest of his life.

He ran into a former investor in This Side of Capital, one who was not involved in any legal action against him, and, with a hand to his heart, talked about his trip across America on the Greyhound and how that trip had "chastened" him. The investor was a drunk young Chinese guy, a Jeff Park type, and he responded well to Barry's new narrative, even though at the end of the conversation Barry had to promise him fifty grand toward a new organization trying to get more Asian Americans elected to higher office.

He went around the room talking about his Greyhound trip and being chastened and pledging money to different causes, and with each person he spoke to he felt his pitch was being perfected. "A one-eyed Mexican fell asleep on my shoulder and the bus nearly swerved into a ditch."

"No fucking way!"

"And this *gorgeous* black girl in Mississippi, well, let's just say I had to stop her before things got out of hand. But she was very sweet. I felt chastened."

"You're insane, you know that? Hey, congrats on beating the feds!"

"Yeah, we thought you might have to join Joey's ankle bracelet club!"

"You guys are too much," Barry said, toasting with his Bad Hombre. By the eighth person, he had this flash of starting a new multi-strategy fund. Maybe he would call it Last Tycoon Capital or something like that. Funny if it were another Fitzgerald title.

As the first results started coming in, he found Seema being hit on by a tall emerging-markets guy wearing a shiny new Rolex GMT in white gold and not-so-gently pried her away. The guy actually moaned some as he watched Seema depart, and that made Barry hot. They were standing by a window; the park was this dark mysterious space beneath them surrounded by the lights of the world's first- or second-most-important city, depending on what you thought of Brexit's impact on London. The historic nature of the moment proved overwhelming. "You know something," Barry said to his wife, "I love going out with you, but I miss Shiva, even when I don't see him for a single day." Barry sort of believed his own words. They kissed. A tiny pocket of drool had gathered in one of the corners of Seema's mouth. He minded that a little. "I love the idea of you working," he said. "When we started dating, I loved seeing you in a suit."

"You're getting a bit drunkie," Seema said. *Drunkie.* That was something her friend Tina or Lina from Brooklyn liked to say. They should have invited her, but she was probably at a hipster thing in Brooklyn. They kissed, sloppily.

"I don't want to be away from Shiva too much," she said. "Every minute matters."

"You're such a good mother." Barry was truly drunk now. "I know you don't like me to talk about it, but I saw so much bad parenting on my Greyhound trip."

"Yeah, shut up about the bus, Barry. And keep kissing me, please."

It happened quickly. The energy in the room began to flag. It was mostly feminine energy. About half of the male attendees were secret Trump supporters—many hoping for tax breaks—but the women were all on the same page. People were gathering around the monitors tuned to CNN and MSNBC. The nation's southernmost state was being mentioned with an increasing sense of urgency. "Florida." "Florida?" "Florida!"

"No, it's okay if we lose Florida!" Barry shouted. "It's the firewall we have to look at. Pennsylvania! Michigan!" He had done his homework, but so had everyone else. The bartender couldn't make Nasty Women fast enough, as if that could help things. Seema smiled, but he noticed that she was breathing heavily. Her fight-or-flight response was not ideal. He kept rubbing her hand and kissing her cheek. He wasn't sure which of them he was trying to comfort.

Closer to 10:00 P.M. the *New York Times* needle began to swing from "Likely" Clinton to "Leaning" Clinton to "Tossup" to "Likely" Trump to "Very likely Trump." The markets were starting to tank. "Thank God we've got a lot of shorts, a lot of hedges!" Joey Greenblatt shouted into his face. Barry wished he still had a fund to worry about—This Side of Capital was nearly dissolved—at least that would take his mind off of what was happening, give him a set of actions to consider for the next morning. He thought of Trump mocking a disabled man, those fake twitches. No, this could not be happening.

He had always wanted to spit in the faces of liberals who kept calling everyone they disagreed with a "fascist," even liberals like his wife. But now?

"I want to go home," Seema said, miraculously sober. She squeezed his hand hard to show that she meant it. Others seemed to have the same idea. A mass stampede was under way. Joey Greenblatt and his nineteen-year-old-looking new girlfriend were trying to stanch the flow at the elevators, but people needed something familiar at this point, their families, their servants, their homes. Barry had always loved taking a cab through Central Park at night; it felt like driving through a darkened canyon with occasional glimpses of Midtown's towers, the glowing civilization just out of reach. But tonight the skyline looked hollow and empty, the dark apartments free of their Russian and Saudi masters.

"Why don't you come and stay over tonight?" he said.

"I don't think so," she said. "I think I want to be alone."

"Right now is when you *don't* want to be alone. We need to get through this together."

They went back and forth; he found himself begging for her to stay with him, throwing himself at her as if he were a horny sad-sack teenage suitor. She claimed that she had to take Shiva to some therapy first thing in the morning.

"You're treating me like this is my fault," Barry said. "How is this my fault?"

"It's not all about you," she said. "I promise."

He tried to sleep, but there were ambulance sirens and the *thwump thwump* of helicopters, as if there was a national emergency happening right outside his window. Barry had had his suite outfitted with roses and chocolates; it was corny, but he wanted her to know that he wouldn't take their lovemaking for granted. The room was hot, but Barry curled in on himself as if a new ice age were beginning. He didn't want to check the results on his phone. HEY, he texted Seema, SORRY IF I CAME ON TOO STRONG. She didn't text back.

The next day they knew it was true. Donald J. Trump, the deeply troubled New York businessman, would be their president. Barry didn't want to stay cooped up in his suite with the cable news going all day. He decided to walk the streets of the city, hoping that Seema would soon respond to his text. It was an appropriately rainy and gloomy day, and a group called the Auburn Seminary was handing out sunflowers to mournful New Yorkers in Washington Square Park. Barry imagined this was what Paris might have felt like after the Germans had slithered into the city. NYU students were singing and crying together. Barry noticed a smug asshole was wearing a BERNIE COULD HAVE WON T-shirt. A small group of smiling cops appeared impervious to the desolation around them.

The Wednesday farmers market at Union Square was shrouded in fog. Some rumbling of protest was building, and he could hear the drawl of helicopters up above. Young people were carrying ragtag signs reading LOVE TRUMPS HATE, FREE HUGS, POC AND LGBTQPOC LIVES MATTER. Barry remembered the UTEP Filipina laughing at him for using the term "POC." He felt both with the protestors and apart from them. He remembered the cattle cars on the overhead projector of Layla's Holocaust class. He started texting Seema obsessively.

WE'LL GET THROUGH THIS.
WE HAVE THE MEANS AND WE HAVE EACH OTHER.
SHIVA'S GOING TO BE OKAY. HE'LL KNOW A
    BETTER WORLD.
WHAT DID I DO WRONG?
WHY ARE YOU TAKING IT OUT ON ME?
YOU'RE LIKE YOUR MOTHER SOMETIMES.
MEAN AND COLD FOR NO REASON.
DOMINEERING AND WITHDRAWN.
I'M SORRY, I DIDN'T MEAN THAT.
REALLY, I JUST GOT EMOTIONAL. I MISS YOU.
LAST NIGHT I WANTED TO MAKE LOVE TO YOU SO
    BADLY.

I DON'T KNOW HOW TO MAKE THE HEART
    SYMBOL, BUT HEART HEART HEART HEART
    HEART HEART.
HELLO?

He sat on a Union Square Park bench next to some high-school kids wearing all black and eating burritos. They reeked of hormones, onions, and pot. They were white and Asian and a little alternative, maybe goth. All of them had buds in their ears and were both present and not, which seemed like a good place to be on November 9, 2016. Barry imagined them growing older together like siblings, being there for one another. Who would do the same for Shiva? Would Barry?

These kids would already be in college by the time Trump left office. *If* he left office. No matter what they did or whom they loved or who they became, Donald Trump would dominate at least a part of their lives. He would try to drag them down to his level. That's what he did. Barry's phone pinged. He whipped it out of his pocket too quickly and dropped it on the concrete. The high-school kids looked at him and laughed, but good-naturedly, because they were sweet multicultural kids who probably played whatever version of Dungeons & Dragons they had on the market these days. The text was from Seema.

COME TO THE GYM @ 5. BRING YOUR SWIM
    TRUNKS.

BARRY'S GYM took up a nondescript double-wide town house and had a fifty-meter lap pool in the basement which was pretty much private. You could reserve a swim lesson for children, but tonight he did not see an instructor. Barry knew what he had to do. He had to represent his value to his wife. He had to teach Shiva how to swim.

No one could fill out a bathing suit like Seema. She wasn't the

skinny type the junior traders in his office used to crow about, showing off photos in which they counted their girlfriends' ribs or pointed
out something called the thigh gap. Seema had small rolls of fat
under her arms and the equivalent around her ass, and her thighs
touched, but her turquoise one-piece sang of youthful warmth, the
deep dark thread of her cleavage was honest and real, and he could
see the outlines of her large nipples. If they could only be alone together in the pool, some pool, any body of water.

But they were not alone. In addition to the Latino lifeguard nodding off into the middle distance (how dare he ignore Seema's
beauty?), she had brought Shiva, who stared at the pool's steady
ripples of water with wonder verging on terror, his usual mode. His
son wore a goofy-looking swimsuit studded with pink crab shells,
beneath which peeked out a swim diaper. Seema held him slightly in
front of her because you couldn't really hug him without conse-
quence, or at least you had to work your way toward a hug with the
aid of a horsehair brush and untold amounts of patience. But Barry
could see that the child liked the water in some fundamental way, his
little brown legs stroking the surface, delighting in the feeling of
relative weightlessness, a place where the cruelties of the sensory
world were lessened. "I'm going to start calling you the Aqua Rabbit," Barry said, coming closer to the boy, until the three of them
stood next to one another, as if posing for an awkward family portrait.

Seema dipped her son into the pool and then pulled him out very
quickly. She did it again and again, until his initial shudders built up
to a happy squeal. The motion was regulating him. This was going
to be a joyous occasion that Seema would never forget. "Shiva Rabbit," he announced, "right now I'm going to teach you a little bit
about swimming. Daddy was a swimmer in high school and in college and maybe one day you can be, too. So just watch this." He
dove into the water and crisply made his way to the other end of the
pool in about ten seconds, flipped over, and made his way back to his
family. He hoped Seema was minding his form, the graceful kicks
that generated only a modicum of splash, the torque of his shoul-

ders, the crisp half turn of his neck when he took a quick breath. But when he surfaced he realized no one had been looking at him. Seema was still dipping Shiva into the water, each dip followed by a screech of delight on the boy's part.

"Okay," Barry said. "Daddy's turn."

He reached over to pick up his son. "Easy," Seema said.

"I know what I'm doing," Barry said. "I just taught another boy how to swim."

"He's not another boy," she said. Which was true. As soon as Barry's hands were placed under Shiva's armpits, the boy began to kick backward and flap his arms forward like some maddened dolphin. Barry quickly turned to look at the lifeguard, to see if he had registered that his son was different. Seema slipped her hands under Shiva's arms and he calmed down a little.

"Okay," Barry said. "Let's just do what we were doing. Up and down, up and down, but now Mommy and Daddy will *both* hold you." They resumed the old rhythm, lifting the child out of the water and then letting him splash back into it, Barry loving the feel of Seema's hands on his own, until equilibrium was restored, the child looking up at the ceiling with a smile on his face.

Barry was adding zero value to the proceedings. This family felt as lonely as the one he had known in Queens after his mother died. No one wanted or needed him, not the beautiful woman with the cantaloupe weight of her bosoms dipping into the water, not the voiceless child in the ridiculous crab swimsuit and diaper. "Okay," Barry said to Seema, "you can let go now."

"Are you sure?"

"*Yes!*" He had spoken loudly enough to stir the lifeguard out of his reveries. "Yes," Barry repeated softly as Seema surrendered the child to his grip. "See, this is fun. Fun with Daddy. Daddy the swimmer." He started to sing: "We'll have fun, fun, fun, until someone takes something away-yay." He continued to dip Shiva in and out of the water, Baptist-style, noticing that the child was actually quite tall and heavy for an almost-four-year-old. Barry's shoulders were starting to cramp some; how did Seema and Novie take care of this big boy all day long? With every dip he realized just how apart he was from the whole specialized universe that had been built around Shiva Cohen. The room smelled of salt water, clean and pure, and, if he leaned toward Seema, some of her honeyed essence. It was time to set things right.

"Okay, Shiva," he said. "Rome wasn't built in a day. You're not going to be Mark Spitz in an hour, but I want to communicate to you the basics of swimming. That's all we're going to do today. No pressure. So I'm just going to slide my hands down to your belly and gently tip you over to about three-hundred-thirty degrees."

"I just want to point out," Seema said, "that he doesn't understand you. I'm not sure *I* understand you."

"Just going to hold him in a slightly different way, and then tip him slightly into the water," Barry said. "What's the big deal?"

He moved one hand out from under Shiva's armpit and put it on his hip. He moved his other hand to Shiva's warm belly. The child made a small sound based on some form of the letter *E*, but not one Barry had heard before. *Eeeeee*, he exhaled.

"Don't worry, sweetie," Seema said. "Daddy's got you." She moved closer and began to brush his arm with the smoothness of her palm. Barry continued to tip the child over, one degree at a time, trying to position him as he would a swimmer, head first, arms ready to paddle, feet ready to kick. *Eeeeeee*. In addition to the sound, the child's inner mechanics began to thrum like some overheated car part. "Maybe let's pull him up," Seema said. "Maybe that's enough for now."

"This is how you learn," Barry heard his father talking through his mouth and past his lips. "Just a tiny bit more. You got to take risks." As Shiva's head approached the water, his legs began to kick out in desperation. "That's right," Barry said, "that's exactly how you kick."

And Shiva did kick, his haunches churning through the water, as the rest of him squirmed out of Barry's grasp, the letter *Eeeeeee* hanging in the air like some forgotten mystery vowel, the child flying out of Barry's arms and into the unforgiving tile edge of the pool marked by the marble legend 5 FEET DEEP.

The unnatural hollow sound of Shiva's head smashing against the tile rang through both Seema and Barry, but only one of them moved. Barry stood there, his arms still outstretched as if they contained a Shiva within them as Seema grabbed their child and the lifeguard ran toward them, leaped into the air, pushed Barry aside. The vowel sound was gone. Only Seema was screaming. His son lay immobile in her arms, his usual twitches and inconsistencies now a distant, welcome memory.

THEIR LAST meeting was in Stuyvesant Square two days later. Shiva was being held for observation at Beth Israel, the nearest hospital. Barry had tried to make noise about moving him to a better hospital, throwing more money at the problem, but the problem turned out to be less consequential than they had thought. Shiva had been lucky enough to avoid a concussion. The main difficulty was the new hospital surroundings, the fact that he had to undergo frightening tests and deal with new people. Seema asked in her calmest voice that Barry should leave the hospital tasks to her and her father and Novie.

Her eyes were tinged with black, which they often were, but now they were deep set and exhausted. "Whatever you're about to say, I think you should rest up and give it some time," Barry said. A procession of Filipina nurses from Beth Israel, each of them looking every bit as fatigued as his wife, trooped out of the hospital and through the park.

But she wouldn't wait. She said horrible things, but she said them gently. She didn't speak of Shiva, not really. She said, in essence, that she didn't like *what* Barry was. Not *who*, but what. We lived in a country that rewarded its worst people. We lived in a society where the villains were favored to win. There was a direct line between Barry getting off with a slap on the wrist and Trump's victory. Maybe, in her own way, she had tried to tip the scales when she sent the Sardinia video to the government. But what had that accomplished? The system was wrecked. She felt it on election night. How could people who *didn't* live in a Central Park West penthouse believe in *anything* anymore? Why would they even bother voting for Hillary?

He couldn't believe her line of argument, or how personal this had become. *Seema* was the Democrat. At one point, he was going to bundle for Hillary to get a job for her. How could Donald Trump cost him his marriage?

She looked at him sadly. There was no mistaking that look. The tired law-school eyes. *Won't you please leave us alone,* the look said.

"I know this isn't about Trump winning," Barry said. "I know this is about what happened in the pool. I've apologized a million times, and I'll apologize a million more. Here's the thing. Here's the take-away. I'm more like Shiva than you think. Yes, I gave him his awful genes, and I'm sorry for that. But I'm just like him in so many ways. I don't want to talk to people either most of the time. I make myself do it. I practice."

"He can't talk," Seema said.

"Because he doesn't want to," Barry said. "Because he's like me."

"No, Barry," Seema said. "He can't talk because he can't coordinate his fine motor movements to produce what we recognize as speech. That's why he can't talk. Not because he *doesn't want to.* Don't you see the difference?" She looked at his bewildered face. "Oh, honey," she said, "can't you see what's around you? You're not Shiva. You don't have his excuses. You're a man who makes tons of money while the world goes to shit around you. You make money *because* the world goes to shit around you. In the end, that's who you are. And if you want to change, change. But if you can't, please stop taking away whatever chance I still have of being truly loved by someone. My father, for starters. And my son."

THE DIVORCE was brutal. She knew every asset by heart. Her lawyers chopped him up while his were playing defense. "Never marry a lawyer if you're going to get a divorce," Joey Goldblatt had cautioned him ages ago, and he was right. The settlement was pretty monstrous. After the divorce and after all the lawsuits against This

Side of Capital, Barry came away with about thirty million, roughly the price of Joey Greenblatt's Central Park West apartment. He knew he had to regroup, but he was so stunned by the loss of his family and the majority of his fortune that he spent months doing nothing but watching his country disintegrate and the markets rise on his laptop.

He needed a place to live, and the Gramercy was too close to the heartbreak Seema had caused him. Joey Greenblatt invited him into the Troubadours Society, which rented him a small but high-end apartment directly above the club. The idea behind the Troubadours was that you could stay in Midtown, close to your fund, and the rest of the world would come to you from Brooklyn or Berlin or wherever. Those artists and chefs and writers and thinkers were the Troubadours, and their presence led to lots of very carefully curated cultural events, which was sort of like having a hedge-fund wife at your disposal. This is where Joey Goldblatt had met his girlfriend after his own brutal divorce, and where he hoped Barry would find someone to cauterize his heart as well.

Which is exactly what happened on his first week there.

Her name was Lyuba and she was of "Israeli and Russian heritage," which was a little bit confusing. In any case, she had grown up in Miami, spoke unaccented English, and had hair that felt to the touch either like the Platonic ideal of Brillo or like a perfect version of a Jewfro (although sometimes she intimated she wasn't really Jewish), beneath which sat an angelic well-cheekboned face which Barry consistently failed to identify as Slavic.

He found her on a stool at the bar after a lecture by some imposing Oxford professor who had told them that Western civilization was "essentially over." Usually super-tanned women in red dresses hit on him at the bar, but this time around it was slim pickings, and so he focused on the edgy-looking girl with the sheep hair. She was fighting with a man at least four times her age, with a high dry forehead but a surprisingly wet nose. When the geezer skulked off, Lyuba looked at Barry with bored bedroom eyes and soon they were sitting on cracked leather chairs in the boozy "library." "I don't need him," Lyuba declared of the older gent she had been with. "I come from real estate."

"He's too old for you anyway," Barry said.

"You don't have to worry, I like older men," the young Floridian said. "You want to touch my hair? You've been staring at it like forever."

One of the interesting things Barry learned about Lyuba, after he took her up to his little one-bedroom on the floor above, was that she liked to "freebase" cocaine, which meant putting it on a piece of foil, lighting it up from below, and then drawing the smoke through a Pyrex pipe, like the kind Bentley had used back in Phoenix. "I don't do sex on the first date," she said primly while sitting cross-legged on the weird mohair couch in his living room. "You can go down on me or I can suck you off."

Barry was excited but a little sad. Was this the kind of woman he would have to date now? The kind who liked Barry because he made money while the world went to shit around him, to paraphrase Seema? And then there were the practicalities. The last time he had tried to perform oral sex while using a coca-leaf-based narcotic had not worked out well for anyone. But what if he couldn't get it up while she pleasured him? Which was worse?

After a few minutes of work, they managed to figure it out. Despite the fine, sheepy hair Lyuba wore on top, she was entirely bald down under and sported a bunch of tattoos in Russian and Hebrew. Maybe she was one of those "alt" persons or something. Whatever the case, she tasted young and wonderful. Barry was kind of excited about her political leanings. He felt like he had been brutalized by Seema and her politics, and Lyuba was a form of revenge.

They had a date the next week when one of the Troubadours, David Chase, the creator of the *Sopranos,* came to give a talk to a full house. It was unclear if Lyuba was a member of the club or not, but her presence seemed welcome by the male attendees. Barry was super excited to get her upstairs, even though it was Shaved White Truffle Night down at the club, but he was about to learn something interesting. Lyuba was a Trump supporter. Not so much the social stuff, but definitely the simplified tax plan. "It's because I'm from real estate," she said.

And now Barry felt the full weight of his abandonment. He saw Shiva only once every two or three months, even though he supposedly had joint custody, which his lawyers had fought for, even if he didn't particularly want it. What were you supposed to say? That you *didn't* want joint custody? There was no way he could take care of Shiva by himself, so he just met him at his sensory gym with Novie, and then he'd swing him around some kind of autistic swing while trying to maintain eye contact. "Astronaut training," they called it. Barry wanted to tell his son that he was lonely, but he had no idea how to communicate that to any person, let alone a nonverbal one. In the end Barry had no idea *who* his son was, except that he had his mother's eyes, and Barry could not bear to look into them.

Lyuba and Barry dated on and off for the next month. She even took him to Brooklyn once, although she seemed as disoriented by the borough as he was. He was half hoping they would run into Seema's best friend, Tina, out there, so he could show off his edgy new girlfriend. Not that it mattered to him much at this point, but equities were doing great after Trump's win. "The markets are basically a middle-aged white man," Barry liked to explain to people outside the industry. In any case, by the start of the next summer Lyuba dumped Barry. She had gone back to the geezer. Maybe Barry wasn't staking her enough, maybe she had found out he was only worth thirty million, maybe she had only been using him to bait the old gentleman back under better terms. It turned out that the old guy also came from real estate.

The house up by Rhinebeck was nearly done, and so he moved up there for the solitude and the Hudson views, the rumble of the Amtrak along the riverbank his greatest nightly comfort.

SEEMA WAS doing no better. All her friends were saying the election results had made them feel like someone close to them had died. She found herself waking up in the middle of the night worried about the fate of the Paris accord. But every time she saw her Instagram feed, all the globalized lives her so-called friends were living, the weekend jaunts to the Caribbean, the full-month fuck-offs to Marrakesh or Rangoon, she felt guilty in front of all the people who would never know the fruits of the global order. She tried to visualize the hatred of the Trump voting class for herself and people like herself, all those brown and yellow faces on Instagram peeking out of the coolest café in the newest city at the latest hour, once-hard-won lives now spent in merriment and ease. But was it really their fault that they were coming up while white Trumpists were coming down? She remembered the story Barry had told of being on the Greyhound, the white supremacists railing against the Jewish bankers of the world. It was terrible, of course, but all the people she knew, Jews, Indians, Koreans, everyone was feeding at the trough, none more so than her ex-husband, while many of the people who hated them had nothing. So who was right?

With her country dying, she found herself wanting to be a little less American and a little more Indian, to search for her roots the way her mother had her whole life. She needed to nail down who she was. Barry wasn't the only one who could pursue that privilege. She tried to learn Sanskrit for the millionth time, attempted to memorize her father's favorite slokas, and took a car service out to Flushing once a week to feast on *upma* at the Ganesh Temple Canteen. One day, she went to a lecture at the Asia Society on Indo-Saracenic and Mughal-Gothic architecture. The lecturer was an assistant professor at Columbia named Zameer Jarwar who had roots in Bombay and had just published a well-received book about that city. He was a short but kind of cute big-eared fellow (he must have been called a "half ticket" in Bombay slang when he was growing up, Seema thought) who knew how to hold a crowd. The lecture was really about Bombay's main train station, once known as the Victoria Terminus, and how the station reflected postcolonization, the rise of Maharashtrian nationalism, the decline of the Congress Party, really the whole history of India's premier city. Seema thought she had learned more about Bombay in forty minutes of hearing this small man speak than in all the time she had spent there as a young woman.

Afterward, Zameer was mobbed by very fashionably dressed Pakistani women and some Indian Muslims. She had deduced from his name that he was, of course, not Hindu, and a crazy part of her was almost sad over that fact, in case she ever had to introduce him to her parents. Her parents? *What the hell was she thinking?* Maybe she should just run out of the room and return to the routines of her life, the caring for Shiva, the drinks with Mina, the fights with her mother. She waded through the perfume of the young professor's middle-aged admirers and noticed that he was tracking her progress through the room with his entertainer's eyes, even as the crowd was thinning in favor of the suspect Subcontinent-themed desserts the organizers had put out. "Hi, I'm Seema," she said.

"Hiya," he said. That's probably how he started every student conference, with an informal "Hiya." He was wearing Rag & Bone jeans and an A.P.C. shirt like an advertisement for his social class. He was only an inch or two taller than she was, but he hummed with energy and intelligence. She had this weird thought from the very beginning: Please, God, don't let him come from a wealthy family. What was that even about? It's like she wanted him to have come by whatever money he had honestly.

She envisioned the professor living in a small one-bedroom apartment, Columbia academic housing, indecipherable framed stuff on the wall, maybe a vintage Indian family-planning poster warning women not to get pregnant all the time, "Mother Must Have Complete Recovery Between Two Children." Mercifully he wasn't wearing a ring. Mercifully she was as beautiful as ever.

And then Seema began talking to Zameer Jarwar. Not in the manner of the comic Indian actress that her white friends told her she resembled, because he would see right through that, but in a more natural voice. She talked about the station. About how every trip to India since she was a little kid involved endless trips from South Bombay to Shivaji Park via Victoria Terminus. She had a mental map of every *vada pav* dealer near the station, the formation of the trains, the ladies' cars, the cars for invalids marked, against all good taste, with a crab for cancer, how her uncle Nag had made her jump off with him as the train was grinding into the station, per the usual custom, and she had skinned her knee something ridiculous. And being the consummate talker, Zameer matched her stories one by one, until they had both gone through a long litany of every uncle in greater Bombay, and they were all alone in the large lecture room, the older admirers long having waved a sad goodbye to their hero who was being monopolized by the talkative Tamil girl.

They complained about the inauthenticity of Curry Hill but still ended up there, at a Pakistani place full of cabdrivers and small-time merchants. "Would it offend you if I ordered quail?" he asked. They were able to summarize their backgrounds in fifteen minutes, merely talking about the diets with which they grew up. She ate meat sometimes. He drank all the time, but didn't eat pork. Not that he was religious. Not that *she* was religious. Okay, so no one was religious. It was amazing. Zameer understood more about her background by the end of the night than Barry had understood in five years. So this is what her few Indian friends meant when they talked about the pleasures of being with their own kind. Although, obviously, they were from different religions. But they were from the same place. They were from Victoria Terminus.

He asked her uptown that night. Before they left the overlit deliciously greasy Pakistani place and after she agreed to go up with him, she said, "Big piece of intel right here. I have an autistic boy."

"Well," he said, "I know enough not to say 'Sorry to hear that' or 'Sometimes I feel like I'm a little autistic myself.' But, honestly, it's not a big deal. And I like kids. I'm number one uncle to like a thousand of them."

Yes, he lived in Columbia housing, which actually proved pretty amazing, ceilings every bit as high as her apartment's, although the cab ride felt long enough to have taken them to Westchester, and shortly after their arrival she was kissing his big ears in the magisterial bed, and neither of them had a condom, but they had to do it anyway.

She was shocked when three months later it was her father who objected on religious grounds to their announcement of marriage, although probably he was representing her mother as well. "I'm worried about the gulf in your backgrounds," he had said, looking down at his new orthopedic shoes. She asked him why no such issue had come up when she had married Barry. When he couldn't find a proper answer, she instructed him to never bring up her future husband's religion again.

And he never did.

THE BIRD DADDY

ARRY'S NEW fund took off right away, and he was thrilled and vindicated. It had been three years since This Side of Capital had dissolved, and a lot of people were willing to stake Last Tycoon Capital, especially after he got a nice write-up in Bloomberg. Barry knew that people knew that he had learned from his mistakes. His investors hadn't cared about the Sardinian yacht and Sammy Yontif and all that shit. After all, they had made money off his insider trading. They just wanted better returns and Barry was poised to deliver them. And so he leased a new space, this time in Midtown, and hired a lot of Princeton wrestling guys who could snap the unicorn off their competitors. They were almost a complete replica of his crowd back in the Tiger Inn days. They buddied around and did all kinds of crazy things, buying every dip, surviving macro events, at one point building a short position in Dell. Once again, Barry found himself in the role of leader and moralizer. He tried to start another book club, this one entirely devoted to nonfiction, and constantly pointed out the lessons he had learned while traveling across country by bus, especially the hidden dignity of lower- and middle-class people, the Javons and Brooklyns and Jose the Gardeners of the world.

Eventually he and his new buddies found themselves heavily over-leveraged in cryptocurrency, and Last Tycoon Capital fell apart, but this time Barry kept the lawsuits to a minimum and came out with an additional forty million, bringing his total net worth just north of seventy-five with appreciation.

Barry knew he was good at making and losing money and getting paid for both handsomely. Yet this knowledge made him a little sad. He didn't want to be the villain of Seema's last words to him. He wanted to be respected and loved by his peers, but was running a fund the only way to get that approbation? Should he cash out and start a charity? And yet hedge funds were the only thing he knew that could consistently generate bottomless wealth for him. Not to mention take care of Seema's fantastical alimony. So after a little while, he decided to start yet another fund. It was not too hard to find backers. The consensus was that this time he had *really* learned his lessons. Balance Wheel Capital was a reference to the spinning part of a watch movement, roughly the analogue to a clock's pendulum. It was supposed to indicate forward momentum and also the fact that this fund was fundamentally *balanced*, hedged to the nth degree, and stocked almost entirely with quants in Dockers pants. It was time to stop being the "friendliest guy on the Street" and embrace his Jonah-like inner nerd. Even his old frenemy Akash Singh joined the board. Balance Wheel failed about two years in, but not before Barry came away with another thirty million, bringing his total to one hundred. No one in his industry had ever told him, "You should quit while you're ahead," but Barry decided to impose that advice on himself. He was going to take it easy, maybe try out those charities he had always dreamed of starting.

He now had a hundred million dollars. This was neither a little nor a lot in his world. Few people would stop making money upon reaching a hundred mil, unless they were fundamentally unambitious like Jeff Park. Barry was living in his house up in Rhinebeck and not seeing anyone romantically. International start-ups were a big thing now, so he began traveling around the world trying to help out in Rwanda and Myanmar, places where he thought the locals were especially entrepreneurial. But traveling to poor countries was even more exhausting than he had remembered. All he did was sit in conference rooms, chat with midlevel functionaries at the Ministry of Finance, and then travel out to the hinterland in a Nissan truck to see the peasants. He lived this way for about nine months.

One day he landed at JFK, bone weary, and spent a day at the terminal, standing there with a cup of coffee, looking at the new destinations as they popped up on the screen. As night fell, a security guard walked up to him and asked him if everything was okay. "I think I'm having a stroke," Barry said, very slowly. An ambulance was summoned, and he was taken to a sweaty public hospital in Jamaica, Queens, but it was nothing. It was really nothing. He was just okay. He would always be just okay.

The nonstroke was an epiphany. He decided that whatever he was doing with his life wasn't enough. He had to tell his own story to the world somehow. He had to reconnect to the literary person he was back at Princeton. Layla had been a dead end. Having a family hadn't panned out. None of his few remaining friends wanted to be in any kind of book club. And he would never make the mistake of trying to be in a relationship again. So what was left? The writing. The inspiration. What if he wrote a memoir about his Greyhound experience?

There was a scenic trail called Poets' Walk about ten minutes north of his estate, where Barry sat in a little gazebo by the Amtrak railbed, watching the trains swoosh by as he reread *The Sun Also Rises* over and over and over, just as he had as a teen in Queens. Simple sentences were key. A character might feel "lousy" or whatnot, but you as the author would never really delve into the complexity of feeling. Instead you let the actions speak for themselves. Barry wrote:

A broad-shouldered man walked into the Port Authority. He was drunk and rich and he strode through the main hall like he owned it. The nanny of his autistic kid had just hit him and he was bleeding from the brow.

He looked that over. Pretty good, but he took out "autistic." Then he took out "nanny" and "kid." He stared at the computer screen trying to figure out a way to tell the story without mentioning the abandonment of a child with a severe disability. Just forward motion all the way. The One-Eyed Mexican. Javon and the Crack Rock. The Passion of the Hayes Family. Jeff Park and the Luck of Kokura. The Black Girl Who Loved Me. Tales from the Mapparium.

After a few weeks, Barry abandoned the project. Now he understood why he hated Luis Goodman and other writers so much. He was a damaged person, but not damaged enough to make a life out of it.

But he had to do something. Time was passing. He missed the quiet of Jonah's room in El Paso. He needed to rediscover a peaceful hobby that would consume all of his time. Writing was a nice attempt in that direction, but one morning, sitting at a local diner, he noticed a hot Bard student wearing an iconic Cartier Tank Arrondie from the seventies on her slim, tanned wrist. Three bites of shredded hash browns later, he found himself typing "Tank Arrondie prices" into his phone's search engine. Watches. He had not thought of them obsessively since his luggage was stolen off the Greyhound. The watches he had left were prosaic and obvious. He clearly needed more.

Barry began to go to auctions. That was the only way to get the best stuff. He had a car service drive him down to the city, where he darted in and out of Christie's, afraid of running into any investor he had burned in his former life, quite a few of whom had been watch geeks. He had not aged well. He had long given up on swimming in his pool, and although he was not fat by any means, his jowls were loose, his tone slack, and he looked like he was renting space within his own body. The hair had grayed but had not become distinguished, rather had faded to something dirty and worn like a piece of nougat left out in the rain. Only when he took up the bidding paddle at Christie's did he become a formidable presence.

His favorite auctioneer at Christie's was half Swiss, half Italian, and fully dapper. Barry could hear the European's voice in his sleep, needling, cajoling, declaiming, pressuring, encouraging, hamming, navigating the waterways of international wealth with the finesse of a Venetian gondolier. "Still holding at one hundred and forty thousand. Make no mistake. It's selling, ladies and gentlemen. Sir, fair warning. It's selling above you. Make no mistake. I have a hundred fifty thousand. Hong Kong, come back to me. A hundred sixty thousand from the Czech Republic. Thank you, Czech Republic, for your passions. Asia, are we interested in this Patek? Last chance. The gavel is up. Come back to us, Florida. Are we all done? Make no mistake. Sorry, Denmark, you have to be quicker. *Sold* to the gentleman in the room."

And Barry was frequently that "gentleman in the room," the one who sighed every time he lifted his paddle, as if some terrible force of nature was *imploring* him to hand his money over to the auction house, as if the universe was robbing him of control, a feeling of euphoria and dread he couldn't live without.

His collection grew, as did his reputation. Upstate, the room he had intended to become his Hudson River View Library instead became the Watcharium. It was a thousand-foot spread fit for a ballroom done up in folksy cedar. Barry had taken out all the furniture and arranged for glass cases to be installed, behind which his new collection could be displayed for an audience of one. The room was hushed; only the cleaning lady was allowed to disturb its peace. This she did at precisely 3:00 P.M. and precisely for one hour. Barry spent the rest of the day soaking up the silence of the Watcharium while talking to an imaginary Jonah. "So. You're wondering what this is? Well, let me tell you. It's a Patek 2438 in yellow gold. What makes it so unusual? It's waterproof! A waterproof midcentury perpetual calendar. Did you know that? *Did you know?*" That had been Jonah's favorite phrase. "And this? Oh, you'll love this, Jonah. It's a 3448 in white gold. Here. Hold it. Careful. Oh, look at those thick, beefy lugs. Never been polished. And that creamy dial. Ah."

He had tried to follow Jonah on the map forums, but the boy had apparently lost interest in cartography a few years after Barry's visit, which disappointed him. Further Internet searches showed that Jonah attended UTEP, which either meant his mother was broke or that she was sticking to her ideal of sending her son to a local, public college. Barry was sure that Jonah could have made it to Princeton.

In any case, when the lights of the Watcharium were dimmed, when he sat there hunched over a piece with his loupe, humming softly into his beard, as nearly five hundred watches ticked in tandem, Barry could convince himself that his secret son was beside him, sharing, learning, ticking his way through their own little world. Barry's greatest pleasure was lining up all of his perpetual calendar watches at midnight as a new month approached and watching their day, date, and month apertures all register the change with a swift universal click. He would feel a surge of excitement as the movements coiled and tensed for the switch, and then after that satisfying click, he would relax, turn to his phantom son, and say: *All done now, Jonah, another month dispensed with, and here we are still, alive.*

In the ten years since his Greyhound trip, he had spent over 60 million dollars on watches, mostly Pateks, and bled away the majority of his net worth. Despite not being a fan of the Rolex brand, he had bought the famed Bao Dai Rolex, once the property of the last emperor of Vietnam, for 7.2 million dollars, which was one of the most expensive watches ever sold. After his winning bid, Barry threw up in the Christie's bathroom, right into the Kohler fixture which reminded him of something else, another bathroom in Phoenix, Arizona, a bus station, a journey, a careless night, a tiny burst of happiness, all of it so long ago.

Barry took off his loupe. He had been sitting at his desk in the Watcharium allowing the weak sunlight of an upstate spring to trickle onto his desk. There was a problem with the Bao Dai. The problem with the 7.2-million-dollar Rolex was that it was one of the ugliest watches he had ever seen. It was made of shiny, intemperate yellow gold, *Floridian* gold, if you had to call it something. It was studded with four ridiculous diamond indexes. The last emperor of Vietnam was, by many accounts, a silly man, an "amoral opportunist," to quote one publication, who had squandered part of his nation's patrimony on things like this pointless watch. Barry had blown 7.2 million dollars during his trading career, had blown many multiples of it, but that was never his money. *This* was his money. And, if you thought about it, his son's money, too.

His son. There would be occasional updates from Seema, meant not just for him, but for the vast reach of Shiva's extended family from University Heights, Ohio, to Chennai, Tamil Nadu. More often than not, Barry would trash the e-mails, but sometimes he would take a reluctant peek at the photos of a young man who looked surprisingly "normal," who seemed no different from any other gawky youth about to stumble out of adolescence. A tall boy who—no, he could not glance at him for more than a second. And, he surmised, his son could still not speak. He likely went to a special school where few spoke. So what could transpire between them?

Three weeks after the purchase of the Bao Dai, he got a call to appear on *The Consummate Collector,* a webcast in which the gentle young host in vintage professorial garb brilliantly discussed your watches in front of about half-a-million unique visitors. Most watch nerds he knew spent their entire lives waiting for that call. The *Consummate Collector* people wanted to see his entire collection, but the big draw was the awful Rolex. Barry couldn't sleep for a month. He rehearsed his lines, his friend moves, he delved deep into the minutiae of watch knowledge, keeping imaginary Jonah constantly at his side. As the day drew near, there were more practical concerns. He didn't know what to wear. A lot of the dudes on the show, in particular the rich Silicon Valley collectors, wore T-shirts and jeans, and he thought of getting something a little more Brooklyn to make himself look younger. But in the end he just strapped himself into the Kiton vicuña stuff, figuring they were going to mention he had worked in finance anyway. But just as the film crew and the terrifically bearded young host were driving up to Rhinebeck, Barry felt sick. At first he thought he might be having a *real* stroke this time, but then he realized what it was.

If he went on *The Consummate Collector*, that would be the final step of his life. His last achievement. If you were a Watch Idiot Savant, where could you go from there? *The Consummate Collector* was the end of the line. His story would be told, watched by the half-a-million unique viewers, followed up by two hundred snarky comments—*7.2 million for that crap? No wonder our country is in the state it's in. Didn't that guy have three funds that blew up?*—and soon there would be nothing left of Barry's collection but a string of poisoned footnotes. Barry picked up his phone. The Bao Dai glowed its awful yellow glow. The world was spinning in place. He dialed the producer's number and told him he had to cancel because he was having a stroke. *Oh, my,* the producer said. "Nah, I'll be okay," Barry said and hung up.

And six months later Barry put his entire collection up for sale at Christie's. As he was scouring the built-in drawers of the Watcharium's displays for stray timepieces, he ran into an unexpected one. The Universal Tri-Compax, the one he had journeyed across America with ten years ago. It had been stored ingloriously in a Ziploc sandwich bag. The watch was broken, but as he sat there at his desk looking at it, he realized exactly what time it was. It had been nearly ten years since that trip across the country. Shiva had been three when he got on the Greyhound to Baltimore. Ten plus three.

His son was about to become a man.

SHIVA DECIDED he wanted to have a Bar Mitzvah. He had not grown up particularly Jewish, but maybe it was just the influence of living in New York where it seemed like *everyone* had a Bar or Bat Mitzvah. In any case, he insisted on it, and Seema and Zameer obliged him. Somehow Joey Goldblatt had gotten wind of this through the Hamptons summer grapevine and he duly reported it to Barry. And so Barry rang Seema. His first call to her in almost a decade.

He spoke with a shaky voice and kind of blathered on about stuff that she didn't understand. Auctions. Emperors. A "Universal watch," whatever that meant. Finally, she got the upshot. Barry knew about the Bar Mitzvah and he wanted in. He wanted to do this for his son. To quote him, this was going to be *"the most insane Bar Mitzvah ever!"* They'd do the service at Temple Emanu-El for as long as Shiva could stand the noise of the davening (if they even bothered to pray at an agnostic place like Emanu-El), and then all the autistic kiddos from Shiva's school would get carriage rides around Central Park (because autistic people and horses went well together, according to Temple Grandin and the spectrum-friendly events planner Barry had hired), and then the party would end at the Mandarin Oriental, where there would be special spaces set up for the kids who couldn't handle an excess of noise and other stimuli. When he told his plan to Seema over the phone, there was a long silence. "I don't mean to overstep my boundaries," he said. "Especially with your husband."

"No," Seema said, "it's actually—" She stopped. She wanted to tell Barry that the Shiva he imagined was nothing like the Shiva who actually existed. But maybe it was better for Barry to see for himself. "It's actually a great idea."

"Well, I can still afford it," Barry said. "That's a joke."

"I know it is," she said. "I can't believe you did all that research on spaces for autistic kids."

"Gotta make up for thirteen years of shitty parenting," Barry said. "Or nonparenting to be exact."

"Thank you, Barry. Shiva is going to love this. I mean, holy shit!"

As soon as he hung up, the physical part of Barry returned. He wanted to shave his beard. He wanted to swim three miles in an hour. He wanted to walk up to Seema in the middle of the Sheep Meadow and sweep her off her feet. He knew, of course, that the last part couldn't happen, but it was energizing to dream about something other than watches.

Shiva's sister was named Sally. Seema and Zameer had both come up with lists of names for their child-to-be, but the Tamil and Indian Muslim names did not generally overlap, except for a few like Ayesha

(Hindu) and Aisha (Muslim), and so they decided to just go for something neutral and American. Sally Perkins was the first white friend Seema had ever had back in Ohio, and she had always been in love with that clean, native, two-syllable name. Sally had Zameer's small stature and darting showman's eyes, and even though she was five years Shiva's junior, she took care of him and guided and protected him. Seema worried that having a brother with needs would take away some of Sally's own childhood, but Sally and Shiva were impossible to pry apart, each taking turns being the other's appendage, Sally modeling social behavior, Shiva taking her into his realm of numbers and letters and ticking clocks and all the other ritualized stuff that kept his world in order. He loved her more demonstrably than he loved his parents. When Sally was two and Shiva seven, he had taken her by the hand to his bouncy ball and hummed the "Hop, little bunnies, hop, hop, hop" song, even enunciating a few of the words, particularly the "hop, hop, hop." Seema, who watched them with astonishment, thought, Fuck, I'm lucky.

Sally was the one who brought Shiva up to the bimah. Shiva could say a few words, though it took a lot out of him, so he mostly used a new tablet computer with a speech program to communicate. Instead of intoning the actual Hebrew words, he hummed the haftarah beautifully; music, the piano in particular, was one of his gifts. He followed the notes on his device, expelling this strange but true melody into the thick, reformed air of the synagogue, and Seema's parents wept while Shiva's autistic classmates squirmed and stimmed.

Barry was so nervous to see his son, he managed to be late for the service. He ran into the temple so fast that at first he didn't notice the large bejeweled crowd, the collective sense of awe, nor the fact that he and the boy up at the bimah so resembled each other: the prominent bridges of their noses, their upturned, slightly feminine hips. Shiva was nearly his father's height already, with room to outgrow him. He was wearing pretty much the same suit Barry was, a dark number with lots of ventilation, lots of butter-to-the-touch vicuña for both of their sensitivities. Shiva looked at his dad, smiled, looked away. Right away Barry could feel the boy's gentleness, the gentleness of growing up with kinder parents. So there they were, him and Seema and Zameer and Novie and Sally and Shiva's grandparents standing around him at the pulpit, three Hindus, a Jew, a Muslim, a Catholic, and the two lovely children which all of them but Barry had raised. What a New York scene this was, he thought, with unexpected pride. This was the country now. Archipelagos of normalcy amid a dry, angry heat.

The Internet had only good things to say about Seema's husband, and Barry supposed that Zameer was a better father to Shiva than he ever could be, but he was not jealous. He guessed, correctly, that the money Seema had pried away from him provided the best care and education for his son but had also kept his ex-wife shackled to a life not entirely her own. Sometimes he looked her up online, hoping she was "of counsel" at some nonprofit, but other than a brief stint at a prison reform project, his ex-wife's CV remained bare. Barry felt sorry for wounding her and burdening her, but he was happy that she had a presence in her life more stable than his own. Maybe that was as close to love as he would ever get.

After the humming of the haftarah, Shiva delivered the traditional Bar Mitzvah sermon, or rather it came through the William Shatner–like voice of his device, while Shiva synced his lips to the words. Barry had always assumed his son had thoughts and feelings, but that they would always be abstract responses to stimuli, a hurt little creature trying to make sense of an inexplicable world. *A rabbit,* as he used to call him. But once Shiva began to "speak" there was no mistaking him for anything but a deeply intelligent, if lucky and privileged, thirteen-year-old boy growing up in Manhattan.

Once Barry got over the initial shock of his son's fluent computerized voice, he assumed Shiva's remarks would touch on the topic of trying to overcome his adversity. But Shiva never mentioned autism directly. He spoke of how much he loved his family. His sister was his best friend, and maybe that was "lame," but he knew a lot of people who didn't have best friends at all. (Everyone tried to quietly turn around and see the reaction of his autistic classmates.) His mother pushed him so hard that he used to get angry and throw fits, but where would he be without her? Certainly not up at this bimah, certainly not thinking about college in five years. *College!* Barry thought. Really? Could it be? He made a mental note to send a big chunk of cash to Princeton right away. And Novie had shared that burden with her. She was his family more than anyone could know. "I'm sorry I hit you when I was little," the computerized William Shatner voice rang across the sanctuary, and Novie cried. He talked about Zameer trying to teach him to be funny and not take everything literally and how they had both nearly drowned on a father-and-son kayak trip up the Hudson. His comic timing was great and people laughed as if this was one of the best self-deprecating Bar Mitzvah sermons ever given, which it was. *He's enjoying himself,* Barry thought. *My son is enjoying becoming a man.*

Barry knew he did not deserve mention among the list of Shiva's greats, but his son had saved him for last. "A lot of people can't remember being three, but I can," he said. "And back then, in my mind, I used to think of my father as the Bird Daddy because he had to fly away for work all the time. And every time he flew away I got angry and acted out. And every time he came back, I wanted to hug him, but I couldn't because of how I am. And when I was a little older, Arturo and I used to chase pigeons around Madison Park, and I always thought one of them was my daddy but in pigeon form." They all turned to Arturo sitting between his parents, looking thirteen and lightly mustached and terminally embarrassed by his friend. "And today the Bird Daddy flew back. And he's given me the best day of my life."

Barry spent the rest of the day feeling both destroyed and ecstatic. He knew Shiva's words had meant to be loving, to fill in a gap in their relationship, but he could not process his own abandonment of his son. But the words were there, and, if he let them, they could reverberate inside Barry for as long as he lived.

As PREDICTED, Shiva and his classmates were wild for the carriage rides across Central Park. The perfume-free spectrum-friendly rooms at the Mandarin filled up with his friends who wore color-coded badges that specified green if they wanted to interact with others, yellow if they just wanted to be with their friends, or red if they needed to be left alone entirely. Shiva, with his sister by his side, had set his to green all the time, even as Zameer came up to him at regular intervals to say, "Hey, Shiv, if you need a break, just tell me."

In the noisy room where all the neurotypicals had gathered, Barry overheard a girl Shiva's age saying to her friend, "My health ed teacher says that when you're stressed out you just want to have sex. I guess that's why we do it, like, *all the time*." And he wanted to go back to the rooms filled with his son's quiet, shy, hand-flipping, virginal friends, not because their world was better or more innocent, but because he no longer knew what to do in this one.

He shook everyone's hand, allowed Seema's still-vigorous-if-stooped father to thank him for the incredible party, got reintroduced to the formerly outlandish Tina or Lina from Brooklyn and her husband, a managing director at Goldman, and tried not to wilt beneath the half-mast glare of his ex-mother-in-law, who, gesturing to the views of Central Park in front of them, told him, "At least one thing in your life you did right." And then Seema found him and put her arms around his waist. She had aged some but not much, the same smooth skin, the same three dimples, the same hazy eyes. He began to cry. "I didn't know I was the Bird Daddy," he whispered into her ear. "All this time he knew everything. *You* knew. I was the only one who didn't know. And you made this beautiful kid. Without me."

"Are you kidding?" Seema said. "He is *so* you. Friendliest fucking autistic kid on the street. A total ham. A total half-Jewish ham. You saw him up there today."

"Were you serious about college? Should I call Princeton? What's he into?"

"Computers and music."

"Computers! Just like me when I was his age!"

"I visited Oberlin."

"That the music school?"

"It's right by my parents. And we found out that there's already a kid there who's on the spectrum and nonverbal. And literally everyone on campus is a weirdo. Although some are obviously faking. I think it would be good for him to know the Midwest. Okay, you have to stop crying, Barry." They turned away from everyone, toward the view of Central Park, the same view they had enjoyed on one of their last days as a couple, the election party of 2016.

"So do you think he'll just welcome me back into his life?" Barry asked.

"What am I, his spokesperson?"

"You're so mean," he said, smiling through his tears. "I'm so glad you haven't changed."

"Is there some new meanie in your life?" she asked.

"No, I'm done."

"Really?"

"Not meant for love."

She rubbed his cheek. He could smell lotion and tuna tartare canapés on her fingers. "Well, I'm sorry to hear that."

"Don't be. You know what I just realized? I didn't bring Shiva a gift."

"This party cost, what, half a million?"

"No, I mean a real gift. Something he can keep. I have an idea! Oh, God, it's a good one." He threw his arms around her. He could see their son walking toward them, smiling without making eye contact, probably excited by the thought that his parents could still share physical warmth.

"Okay, dear," she said. "Just please don't start crying again. You'll confuse him."

But he couldn't help himself. Shiva's color-coded badge was still green. If he wanted his son's company, Barry could have it.

IT WAS a little past midnight. The autistic kids were exhausted, and Barry did not want to be stuck among the neurotypicals. The Town Car sped up the Taconic, Barry in the back. But he couldn't sleep either. Not at all. His fingers were practicing their moves, the careful moves he would need for the rest of the night. The Armageddon of the city gave way to the sulfur glow of the suburbs, then surrendered to the full country night.

Finally, he switched on the light in the former Watcharium where he retrieved the Universal Tri-Compax from the Ziploc bag and placed it on his desk. He snapped on the fluorescent desk lamp, then rolled the finger cots onto his fingers like condoms and pried open the back of the watch with a cheese knife.

A city was before him. A city of silver and gold gears and wheels. Only this particular city had been frozen in time. The balance wheel was not spinning. The Tri-Compax needed to be disassembled, cleaned, and oiled and at least one of the jewels replaced. A monstrous task given the complexity of this particular watch, with its chronograph stopwatch, its day, date, and month and moon-phase display. To think that in 1948 a device of this complexity and elegance could be designed without the help of a single computer and then assembled not by robots in a giant Asian factory but by real Swiss men and women with real Swiss problems.

And then Barry was visited by a new series of thoughts.

Things could be fixed.

Barry could fix them.

Barry could fix his son's watch.

He made *espresso lungo* from a space-age machine in one of the kitchens. This was going to take the whole night. Or longer. Before he got rid of his watch collection, he had hired the best watchmaker in the city to give him lessons in watch repair. Leo was a fifty-something Athenian intellectual who had tried to convince Barry that the Greek gods were better, or at least more curious and interesting, than the main Judeo-Christian one, whom he saw as a collector of sorts, never happy with his last acquisition, always too busy to maintain the pieces he already owned. Leo had taught him quite a bit, but Barry had been too scared to try his hand at one of his half-a-million-dollar watches.

He took a deep breath and began to work. Gaining confidence as he went along, Barry began to take apart the city inside the Tri-Compax. He took out the balance cock and dismantled the chronograph. He separated the base movement into two. There was dirt everywhere that he rubbed off with Rodico putty, handling each part with the care he had lavished upon Shiva when he was a newborn, back when he was worried that even burping him too hard might cause internal damage. The watch had been around for over sixty years, was almost a coeval of his dead father. The dirt made the gear train stick to the jewels, one of which needed to be replaced anyway. As Barry exhaled softly, he thought of all the people throughout time who were like him, like Jonah, like Shiva, lost in their Mappariums and Watchariums, stuck in front of their Commodore 64s, enjoying the soft grind of their own competence and curiosity. A terrible joy overtook him, and his hands began to shake. He put his tweezers down.

A few weeks before Shiva's Bar Mitzvah he had driven out to the Hamptons to visit Joey Greenblatt, the last remaining contact from his hedge-fund days, who was out on a work-release program after his latest misunderstanding with the government. Speeding down the Long Island Expressway, Barry spotted a sign for Lake Success and swerved his SUV across two lanes to get to the exit.

So there it was. The object of his childhood dreams. There was the Lake Success Center with a Casual Male XL, a Red Mango, and a Victoria's Secret. The strip mall looked dingy, its weird southwestern motif dated, the parking lot full of tired Honda CR-Vs. Only the new Shake Shack crammed full of Korean families gave any hint of the twenty-first century. He drove past the enormous Long Island Jewish Medical Center, which reminded him of his deceased father, and then around the quiet residential streets checking out Zillow on his cell phone. The houses were nice, but hardly the imperial domains of his early desires. Lots of basketball hoops and soccer nets, hydrangeas and hanging plants. But maybe this was what he always wanted. Just shades of middle-class garden-variety happiness and boredom, the stuff of half-forgotten American dreams. He pulled up before a split-level listed for just under 1.7 million dollars, the price of a small apartment in Manhattan. The modest house had a new roof and siding and a gunite pool in the back, along with a stack of patio chairs. There were children playing on the lawn, avoiding an erratic sprinkler, not his mythical triple-Duravit-sink children, but two, a boy and a girl, just like Shiva and the cute sister he had spotted in Seema's e-mails, except neither of them appeared to be on the spectrum. Barry was mesmerized by the children, by the way they couldn't get enough of their simple games—chasing and tackling each other while screaming some strange private phrase ("Goober town?")—until an elderly Jewish-looking neighbor in jogging sweats knocked on the passenger window. He shook away his reverie, smiled at her, started his engine, and left Lake Success behind.

All the pieces of the Tri-Compax were now in plastic containers, waiting to be reassembled in the exact order they had been before he took them apart. There were easily several hundred of them. At first he was scared he would get it wrong, but then he rose to the challenge. This would be a test of his recall and his capacity to mind small, delicate things, some of them hardly thicker than a human hair. He worked for another three hours. When all the parts were sparkling clean and oiled, he began the task of trying to make the watch whole. Watchmakers were often advised to sit in front of a window with views of nature, as well as to play musical instruments and ride on horseback. Lacking either of the latter, Barry stared out the window at regular intervals.

The Amtrak on his side and the freight train across the river no longer made their soothing honks because the banks had been flooded the last few years, just as the rising water had shut down New York's subways, but barges still made their way down to the city, and sometimes Barry would look up from his work and see those immensities right under his nose, the captain of the tugboat visible on his bridge, almost within shouting distance. That was the beauty of the Hudson. It was a working river. And now Barry was a workingman. Back when he was a trader he loved tracking the world's oil tankers on his Bloomberg using the BMAP function, but now he was seeing the real thing in real time, his sleepless eyes trailing the monumental vessel, his pink finger cots covered with oil.

Barry put the crown wheel back under the train bridge, his fingers trembling and his sleepless eyes dry from the strain of his all-night work party. At exactly 6:00 A.M., two elderly people, both in white tees and jeans, began driving their John Deere tractors in the light of the rising sun. They had headphones on and seemed like they were enjoying their solitary duties. These were the neighbors who hated him for his Kyoto-style pool pergola, which had blocked their Hudson views. Maybe it was time to give this place up, knock down the pergola, and move back to the city. Maybe it was time to get as much of Shiva as he could before his son went off to college.

The Tri-Compax's movement had been reassembled. It was time to insert the balance cock into place, to see if the balance wheel would spin back and forth, giving life to the movement, reawakening the forgotten city. Barry held his breath. He gently inserted the balance cock into its proper slot. As soon as it found its place the wheel began to spin, back and forth, back and forth, at a ridiculously fast clip, as if guided by an impatient soul. The second hand started in its subdial. Then the minutes began to accrue, as soon would the hours, the days, the months, the waxing crescent, the waxing gibbous, the full moon.

Barry sat back and looked at his work. He had built something with his own hands. He had made a beautiful thing whole again. He was responsible for this. And he had not done it with feelings or ideas. He had given life with his fingers and his memory.

He would have the case back engraved TO SHIVA COHEN, FROM THE BIRD DADDY.

And so the great shadow lifted. And the sun rose over the estuary known as the Hudson with its flooded banks and the endangered estates perched low upon them.

And the Bird Daddy watched over all of it, satisfied with the remains of the world, before he, too, picked himself up, washed the oil and dirt off his steady hands, closed up his light-filled mausoleum, and flew home for good.

JUNE 6–DECEMBER 21, 2016
New York–Baltimore–Richmond–Atlanta–Jackson–
El Paso–Ciudad Juárez–Phoenix–La Jolla–New York

ACKNOWLEDGMENTS

THERE ARE so many people to thank for their time and work on *Lake Success* that I feel like writing a companion volume dedicated to the efforts of these kind individuals. I'll start with Susan Kamil, my editor, who spent countless hours on the phone with me eliminating commas, encircling clauses, and basically making sure that I had performed my daily CPR and breathed life into the many maddening characters in this book. Clio Seraphim was another great editor, not to mention winner of the "most awesome name in publishing" award. Other folks at the House of Random were terrific, including Gina Centrello, Avideh Bashirrad, Denise Cronin, Barbara Fillon, Ruth Liebmann, and Leigh Marchant. And huge thanks to Nicole Counts.

Denise Shannon has been my agent for sixteen years, an eternity in publishing. She's as good as it gets agent-wise and has kept me in clothes, food, shelter, and now watches with sage advice and a minimum of fuss.

I owe a tremendous debt to my longtime readers, as well as members of the journalistic, legal, horological, culinary, and financial communities (some of the latter have wisely asked me not to list their names, but their contributions are appreciated). A partial list would include Ezra Cappell, Mary Childs, Doug Choi, Neil Chriss, Ben Clymer, Tishani Doshi, Joshua Ferris, Jack Forster, Rebecca

Godfrey, David Grand, Cathy Park Hong, Binnie Kirshenbaum, Paul La Farge, Matt Levine, Suketu Mehta, Carlo Pizzati, Shilpa Prasad, Prateek Sarkar, Jonathan Shapiro, Anjali Vasudevan, Dario Villani, and Eric Wind.

Lastly, my thanks to Greyhound for existing and for spiriting me from one coast of our troubled land to the other with a strange, almost melancholy competence.

ABOUT THE AUTHOR

GARY SHTEYNGART is the author of the novels *Super Sad True Love Story*, which won the Bollinger Everyman Wodehouse Prize and was selected as one of the best books of the year by over forty news journals and magazines around the world; *Absurdistan*, which was chosen as one of the ten best books of the year by *The New York Times Book Review* and *Time* magazine; and *The Russian Debutante's Handbook*, which won the Stephen Crane Award for First Fiction and the National Jewish Book Award for Fiction. His memoir, *Little Failure*, was a top-ten *New York Times* best-seller; was named one of the best books of 2014 by more than forty-five publications, including *The New Yorker* and *The New York Times Book Review;* and was a finalist for a National Book Critics Circle award. He was chosen as one of *The New Yorker*'s top twenty writers under forty as well as one of *Granta*'s best young American novelists. His fiction and essays have appeared in *The New Yorker, The New York Times Magazine, Granta, Esquire, GQ, Travel + Leisure,* and many other publications. His work has been published in thirty countries.

garyshteyngart.com
Facebook.com/Shteyngart
Twitter: @Shteyngart
Instagram: @Shteyngart

Gary Shteyngart is available for select readings and lectures. To inquire about a possible appearance, please contact the Penguin Random House Speakers Bureau at speakers@penguinrandom house.com or visit www.prhspeakers.com.

ABOUT THE TYPE

This book was set in Galliard, a typeface designed in 1978 by Matthew Carter (b. 1937) for the Mergenthaler Linotype Company. Galliard is based on the sixteenth-century typefaces of Robert Granjon (1513–89).